"Three of the most talented pens in inspirational fiction combine in a compilation destined to stand out in a crowded festive marketplace. With resplendent sensory detail and rich history, not to mention a keen cinematic flair, each novella is bolstered by hallmarks of faith and charity and underscored with a winning artistic sensibility. Characters flawed, familiar, and achingly human invite us to slip back to a time that, while far from simpler, was abundant in romance and resiliency. Best paired with sprigs of holly, a roaring hearth, and a gaslit night, *Joy to the World* is a perfectly framed portrait of Regency-era Christmastime, and I look forward to entering its pages again and again—at any time of the year."

RACHEL MCMILLAN, author of *The London Restoration*

A
REGENCY CHRISTMAS
COLLECTION

Joy to the World

CAROLYN MILLER

AMANDA BARRATT

ERICA VETSCH

KREGEL
PUBLICATIONS

Published by Kregel Publications, a division of Kregel Inc., 2450 Oak Industrial Dr. NE, Grand Rapids, MI 49505.

**Library of Congress Cataloging-in-Publication Data**
Names: Miller, Carolyn, 1974– Heaven and nature sing. | Barratt, Amanda, 1996– Far as the curse is found. | Vetsch, Erica. Wonders of his love.
Title: Joy to the world : a regency Christmas collection / Carolyn Miller, Amanda Barratt, Erica Vetsch.
Description: Grand Rapids, MI : Kregel Publications, 2020.
Identifiers: LCCN 2020025853 (print) | LCCN 2020025854 (ebook)
Subjects: LCSH: Christmas stories, American. | Romance fiction, American.
Classification: LCC PS648.C45 J69 2020  (print) | LCC PS648.C45  (ebook) | DDC 813/.08508334—dc23
LC record available at https://lccn.loc.gov/2020025853
LC ebook record available at https://lccn.loc.gov/2020025854

ISBN 978-0-8254-4669-6, print
ISBN 978-0-8254-7719-5, epub

Printed in the United States of America
20 21 22 23 24 25 26 27 28 29 / 5 4 3 2 1

# HEAVEN
# AND
# NATURE SING

—•✕•—

CAROLYN MILLER

# CHAPTER 1

*December 1813*

THE MUTED GOLD-and-rose-flowered wallpaper of the drawing room seemed to dip and sway as Lady Grantley's words crept past Edith Mansfield's disbelieving ears.

"I beg your pardon?" Edith's mother raised her chin and sent Edith a look to suggest their hostess could not truly be serious.

*Heavenly Father, please let her not be serious*, Edith prayed.

"Who did you say was coming?" Mama demanded.

Lady Grantley—Edith's godmother, widow of a baronet whose death disappointed nobody, and long considered one of Wycombe's most hospitable ladies—waved an airy hand. "Why, George, of course. He is my godson after all. I was sure you knew that, Catherine."

"To be sure I did not," Edith's mother replied, thawing not one whit. "And if we had known he had returned from abroad and would be here, we most certainly—"

"Mama," Edith cautioned in a low voice.

Lady Grantley glanced between them. "Surely you're not concerned about that silly matter of last year. It was such a long time ago."

But not quite long enough. Edith pushed aside the guilty sting thoughts of *him* always provoked and concentrated on appeasing her hostess's suspicions. "It was a long time ago," she agreed in a mild tone, of which she was both surprised by and proud. "You may rest

9

assured there will be nothing to give alarm as far as I am concerned."
*Heavenly Father, please let there be nothing that causes concern.*

"I'm sure there won't be," Lady Grantley said agreeably.

Too agreeably? Edith eyed her with suspicion.

"Now, our other guests might be less well known to you."

Therein began a lengthy summary of various guests, ladies, lords, mostly young, mostly accompanied by parents or chaperones whose role it was to oversee suitable matches. Nearly all of whom were people Edith had met at a ball or country-house party much like this one. Nearly all of whom had barely spoken to her after she'd parted ways with the district's most eligible catch, George Bannerman.

George Bannerman. Her heart grew tight again.

"Now, Edith, you will be in the Blue Room. It has a lovely view to the Chilterns. I know December can be a dreary time of year, but that view is always rather pretty."

"Thank you." Surprise layered across her other concerns. Such a room was certainly not what she'd expected, given her lowly status compared to the other young ladies and associated companions their hostess had just mentioned. "I appreciate your thoughtfulness very much."

Lady Grantley patted Edith's arm. "I'm sure your mama won't mind me saying this, but I quite consider you to be like a second daughter to me. And now that my own darling Maria has moved to the wilds of Ayrshire, well, it does me good to see young people in the place again. Especially if they possess such pretty manners as yourself."

"You are so kind," Edith said, touched.

"Oh, nonsense. Christmas is a special time of year and worth spending with people one likes, if at all possible, do you not agree? Though I feel it only fair to warn you that I may require something of your assistance in helping with certain matters, if you don't mind, Edith my dear."

"Of course, ma'am."

A noise from without made their hostess glance at the window. "Ah, someone else has arrived."

*Let it not be George.*

Fortunately, her mother seemed to read Edith's unspoken thoughts. "We shall go upstairs now and let you attend to your other guests." Mama gave Lady Grantley a smile. "Thank you, Margaret. It is truly kind of you to have us stay again."

"Well, I could not let my oldest friend and my dearest goddaughter suffer Christmas all alone. I'm so *very* glad you agreed to come."

That made one of them. Edith pushed down the uncharitable thought, managed to murmur something of her pleasure, even though it seemed much of her anticipation at such a treat had turned to ashes. She followed her mother up the mahogany staircase—said to rival Hartwell Abbey's as one of the finest in England—past the tapestries of Arcadian delights, of music and feasts with convivial friends.

She had been looking forward to visiting Grantley House, to being away where they need not count the cost of candles and cheese, to remembering their former life, even though it might prove challenging to know there would be others with whom she'd need to practice her rusty social skills. But now to know *he* would be here . . . How ever would she manage?

A few minutes later, having been taken to their adjoining rooms and approving them (and the views of snow-dusted hills) as very fine, they dismissed the maids and perched on the small blue settee beside the freshly lit fireplace in Mama's room.

"Well, my dear"—Mama patted Edith's hand—"how do you feel?"

"I am sure we shall enjoy ourselves," Edith said, smoothing her gray skirts, avoiding the real question. "It will be good to spend time away from home, and Lady Grantley seems determined to ensure we find pleasure in the season."

"Margaret is thoughtful, that is true. But no, I meant about the other."

"The other?" Edith deliberately misunderstood her.

Her mother's brown eyes, so like Edith's own, studied her shrewdly. "You know who I mean. I assure you I had no idea George would be here. If I had, then I would have declined Margaret's hospitality, no matter how kindly she phrased things."

"It is of no matter, Mama. Truly."

Edith looked away from her mother's too-discerning, too-compassionate gaze. She could not afford to let the all-too-easy tears have sway yet again. "I will be civil, and I'm sure he will be also. He is nothing if not a gentleman."

She swallowed. George had been nothing but courteous at that last, most horrid meeting. Still, she could not forget his pale face, the stricken eyes, even as he'd murmured something of his completely misunderstanding the matter, and apologized, and said he would not trouble her anymore.

Edith had no fault to find with him. He had proved gentlemanly through it all. It had been a matter of her pain, her pride, and something she'd promised Grandmama to never speak of again. But oh, how she wanted to explain, to beg forgiveness, to dare believe for a second chance, though she knew her actions deserved none.

"So"—she pasted on smiled brightness to divert her mother's thoughts—"do you think Lady Grantley indulges in all the usual Christmas traditions? I did not see an abundance of greenery decorating the halls." Nor had she spotted any mistletoe or kissing balls. Thank goodness. Her insides churned. For if he was to kiss young ladies as such traditions dictated—

"I know Margaret is generally well disposed to doing whatever she thinks will give her guests pleasure. Judging from her talk earlier, it seems she has all manner of pleasant things planned, including the Christmas Eve ball." She eyed Edith's dull ensemble. "I am so pleased we decided to forgo redecorating the drawing room in order to procure a new ball gown for you. It's time you wore colors again, and I'm sure you will look quite lovely."

Edith hoped so. *Especially* now she knew he was going to be here. She had no desire to look like the dowd she so often knew she was. And the looking glass had confirmed the dressmaker's opinion that the deep green brought out the ruddy tints in her brown hair. She had looked, and indeed felt, rather pretty for once.

"Perhaps we should return downstairs," she suggested.

"And face the other guests?" Mama sighed. "I suppose it has been long enough. But you are quite sure?"

"Quite."

"Then let us descend. It seems we'll both need to possess the Mansfield spine, I fear."

The Mansfield spine that refused to admit to weakness, that pride refused to bend, an inheritance from her father and grandmother that had hidden more than one scandal. "Yes."

She drew up her courage, lifted her chin, and prepared to meet the dragons in the drawing room.

A few minutes later, the Mansfield spine was in full evidence as she nodded and exchanged courteous greetings with the other guests here at Grantley House for the Christmas season. Acquaintances such as Lady Anne Pennicooke, Miss Amelia Mowbray, and Miss Emma Hammerson were all in attendance, as were accompanying parents and chaperones. There was an assortment of young gentlemen, many of whom Edith vaguely recognized and was able to make appropriate greetings that suggested she had not entirely forgotten them after a year's absence from the social scene. But why would she remember them, when all her attention had been absorbed by the gentleman she had not yet seen?

Her smile grew tight, her pulse beating rapidly in her veins. Soon he would be here. Soon she would have to greet him, to pretend her wound did not exist, to smile and laugh and say—

"Good afternoon, Miss Mansfield."

That voice! Her heart whirled wildly. *Heavenly Father, give me strength.* She closed her eyes for a lengthy moment, internally braced, and then turned to meet the green-gold gaze. "Good afternoon, Mr. Bannerman."

Something flashed within his eyes, then he held out his hand, which she automatically accepted. A warm clasp, a slight pressure, then he released her fingers, leaving her skin, her heart, tingling.

She nodded, summoned a stiff smile, and bade her feet to slowly move to where the other young ladies stood near the fireplace that centered the room's far wall. Not too fast, to invite speculation as to why she hadn't lingered, but neither too slow, to suggest she wanted further conversation.

There! The worst was done, and she hadn't died. Her smile might feel artificial—and it seemed from the widened eyes of the young ladies with whom she stood that she would need to keep it pinned in place awhile longer—but she hadn't died. *She* hadn't died. Sorrow panged again, twined with regret. She plucked at the lilac ribbon edging her gown, pinning her emotions under a layer of civility and consideration for her hostess. It wasn't Lady Grantley's fault that Edith still had not mastered these recalcitrant feelings.

She stepped closer to where Lady Anne was speaking, tried to focus on the here and now.

". . . and Mama says I am to be presented next season! I am certainly looking forward to seeing the princesses."

When no response from the other ladies was forthcoming, and Lady Anne's countenance drooped, Edith murmured, "I am sure that will be quite thrilling. Have you selected your gown yet, Lady Anne?"

Lady Anne gave her a look that could only be considered grateful and began to discuss in elaborate detail the intricacies of her gown: the pearl beading, the embroidery, the lace and chiffon. Eventually she wound to a stop and tilted her head. "You haven't made your presentation, have you, Miss Mansfield?"

"No."

"I suppose you could not after . . ." Lady Anne's words faltered, and she gave Edith a quick, anxious look, then turned to Miss Mowbray, whose frequent glances at her fingernails and lack of conversation thus far seemed to denote boredom. "Do you enjoy London, Miss Mowbray?"

"Yes."

With no returned inquiry, and nothing more said, the moment filled with renewed awkwardness.

Oh dear. Poor Lady Grantley's house party was not starting well. Edith shifted slightly to the fourth member of their circle and motioned to her pink gown. "That color looks very well on you, Miss Hammerson."

"Oh!" She blushed to the exact rosy shade. "Thank you, Miss Mansfield."

"Oh, Edith, please."

"And you must call me Emma. It is extremely kind—"

"I do not like pink," Miss Mowbray announced. "Mama says it does not suit me."

After a moment's uncomfortable silence, Edith managed to murmur, "Certain colors do not suit all complexions, it is true." She turned to offer the rapidly reddening Emma an encouraging smile. "So when one finds the perfect shade, then it's important to ensure one wears it as much as possible."

"Th-thank you. You are so—"

"Always wear the same color and be dressed to bore? I think not."

Edith bit back the words she wished to say, hitched up her lips, and offered Miss Hammerson a sympathetic smile as Miss Mowbray continued to give her opinion as to gowns and colors and balls before the conversation moved on to the matches and attachments of recent months.

"Have you heard about Lord Hawkesbury?" Lady Anne asked. At the various murmurs of denial, she continued with eagerness. "Oh, he is simply the most handsome man! I saw him but a month ago in London. He fought in the Peninsular with Wellesley and is said to have saved many men. Oh, I *do* love a courageous man."

"And is he single?" Miss Mowbray asked, a speculative gleam in her eye.

Lady Anne's brow furrowed. "Well, there have been rumors about him and a certain Miss Ellison—a mere reverend's daughter, would you believe—who is certainly no great beauty, but she does possess a very fine singing voice. I heard her sing whilst I was in London."

"So she bewitched him with her voice? If only all men were so easily persuadable," Miss Mowbray said with a glance at Edith that suggested the exact opposite.

Edith managed to retain her smile and hoped she did not look completely ungracious as she turned to Miss Hammerson. But before Edith could speak, Lady Anne said, "You have quite a fine singing voice too, don't you, Miss Mansfield?"

"I enjoy singing," Edith said cautiously.

"I remember hearing you sing last year at Aunt Margaret's musical evening."

"Lady Grantley is your aunt?"

"Well, not really." Lady Anne tugged up her glove, smoothing its soft luster. "She's my godmother really, but Mama and she are such good friends, she always insisted on being called Aunt."

Good heavens. How many godchildren did Lady Grantley have?

"I seem to recall that you have sung with Mr. Bannerman, have you not?" Lady Anne persisted.

Edith's chest grew tight. "Yes."

Some of her happiest memories, before life took a twisted turn for the worse.

Emma offered a timid smile. "I do hope you will grace us with your singing again while we are here."

She could not imagine Mama would allow for anything less. "If opportunity allows, and Lady Grantley agrees, then I am willing."

"I do enjoy listening to good voices," Emma said. "I think it is truly one of life's great pleasures."

Edith smiled, a cord of affection winding through her heart. Miss Emma Hammerson truly was a sweet soul.

"And Mr. Bannerman?"

Her pulse quickened.

"Do you think he might be persuaded to sing?" Miss Mowbray continued. "Or do you think he will prefer to perform solo this year?"

Edith stiffened. "I am sure I could not say."

"Well, I hope he won't mind performing duets with others. I do like to sing with good-looking young gentlemen."

That was hardly a surprise. Conscious of the conjecture in Miss Mowbray's eyes, Edith forcibly relaxed her shoulders and willed her smile to appear genuine, her voice to be gentle. "I am sure he will enjoy singing with you, Miss Mowbray. I cannot imagine a prettier partner than you."

"Oh, you are too kind," Miss Mowbray fluttered.

"I speak only the truth," Edith said.

And it was true. Miss Mowbray owned a golden sort of soft prettiness that Edith had always admired, perfect and dainty like a Dresden figurine. She had never understood why George had once expressed admiration for—

Enough! It was done. It was past. There was no point in regret, even if at times she wondered at the wisdom in so meekly following Grandmama's advice. And if her punishment for her mistake was to see him fall into the arms of another, then it was only what she deserved. God might be merciful, but even His mercies must have a limit. And after the past few years, she was sure she had used up more than her fair share of His grace and goodness. She was content. Mostly. It would be selfish to ask for anything more.

Her gaze lifted, veering to where Mr. Bannerman stood with the other young gentlemen, laughing as if he had no care in the world. As if he had no thought of her, as if she was not part of his world.

Which was true. She wasn't. And after this house party at his godmother's, she would likely never see him again.

A savage sting of tears made her catch her breath, blink hard, and turn away.

And she had no one to blame except herself.

# CHAPTER 2

GEORGE BANNERMAN FELT the weight of her gaze shift away. He'd always been conscious of her presence, had a special sense of when she was near. The knowledge that she would be here had filled him with hope; her cool greeting after over a year apart had turned his hopes to dust. It was obvious she did not entertain feelings for him anymore.

"So what do you think?"

"Think about what?" George asked.

"Distracted by the pretty ladies, are we, Bannerman?"

Only one. "Of course," he agreed, to a round of laughter. Of course not. How could he be distracted by mere satellites to the sun?

"I think Miss Mowbray has her eye on you," Mr. Barnard Drake said.

"For my money, I suspect Miss Hammerson is keen." Lord Aylmer Sculthorpe nudged George's shoulder. "Come to think of it, weren't you and Miss Mansfield once an item? Whatever happened to you two?"

"A parting of the ways." More, George would not, could not, say. Who wanted to admit to rejection?

"Then she is available?"

His fingers clenched. He forced them to relax. "As far as I know. I really couldn't say."

"Hmm. Well, that is something to consider. A little flirtation could make this party far more agreeable, don't you agree?"

"I believe the general Christmas festivities will prove more than sufficiently entertaining." He studied the other man. "I know my godmother has gone to rather long lengths to ensure her guests will find their time here amusing."

At the mention of their hostess, Lord Sculthorpe reddened, the gentle reproof leading the younger man to glance away.

"I do hope there will be fun with mistletoe and the like."

*But not with Miss Mansfield.* George consciously unclenched his fingers again. If he couldn't kiss her, he'd sooner be hung than see anyone else given the privilege. He'd have to speak with his godmother. There had to be some benefits for being her godson, after all.

But later, when he'd finally cornered her in the library and managed to wheedle the truth, it was to learn she most certainly did plan to indulge in all the Christmas festivities, and if her dearest friend's only son thought he could charm her into abandoning such plans, he had best think again.

"I know you suffered a disappointment," she said, sympathy lining her voice. "But all the more reason for you to take the time to look again. Surely your recent travels have shown you that there is a whole world of young ladies out there, George, and you need not consider yourself tied to the apron strings of one."

He eyed her narrowly. A whole world of young ladies, and Aunt Margaret had just so happened to invite the one woman he'd been unable to forget.

"George? Why do you look at me with such a frown? Do you consider yourself beholden to a particular lady?"

He ground out a chuckle. "Naturally I do not consider myself obliged to anyone, except, it would seem, my godmother."

"I am very pleased to hear that." She gave a smile of satisfaction. "I know this past year has been trying, but I truly think the Christmas season is the time when one should make amends where one can. It is not good to let estrangement carry on."

"Of course not," he muttered, refraining from pointing out that any estrangement was certainly not of *his* doing.

This was met with raised brows, so he suppressed a sigh, going so

19

far to try to restore himself into her good graces that he offered to assist with whatever muscle of the decorating was deemed necessary, including directing the retrieval of the yule log.

"Truly? That would be good. Mr. Caddy is a dear but getting on in years. Perhaps we can arrange an excursion tomorrow, if you think the young people would enjoy that."

"I'm sure they will."

"Oh, dear boy, I knew I could rely on you." His godmother smiled, affection in her eyes. "You are such a comfort to this old woman."

"Old? How dare you speak of my godmother in such a way," he responded gallantly. "I forbid you to say such things again."

She uttered a wheezy chuckle and patted his arm.

It seemed he would just need to grit his teeth and trust God to help see all such strained relationships finally restored.

❖

"And I was hoping that tonight I might prevail upon some of the talented musicians amongst you to entertain us. Amelia, might you consider?"

"Oh, I'd be delighted," a petite blonde almost purred.

He swallowed a smile. Miss Mowbray did not seem the sort to shy away from opportunities to display. He kept his gaze levelled at the front, to not turn, to not attempt to gauge the expression of Miss Mansfield. Not that he'd be any good at guessing her thoughts anyway—she'd proved too good at hiding her true feelings.

He pushed aside the sting of memory, forced his attention to the pianoforte, to the performance from the young lady who appeared undaunted by notes at which more talented young ladies might hesitate. The song concluded, he clapped as an automaton, and was unsurprised when Miss Mowbray quickly acquiesced to a second piece. This was swiftly followed by an encore, after which his godmother rose to her feet and led everyone in a somewhat forceful round of applause.

"Thank you, Amelia. That was splendid. Now, I wonder if I might persuade Miss Hammerson to share her talent. I believe you have something of a gift for the harp, my dear?"

"Oh! Of course, ma'am. I'd be delighted."

This was said in such an opposite tone to the previous young lady that George had to smooth away a smile. If he were a betting man, he'd wager she was not delighted at all. Amid a hum of quiet conversation, the harp was wheeled forward and hastily tuned, then Miss Hammerson began.

Her nerves were on full display, resulting in a hesitant performance whose conclusion doubtless resulted in as much relief for the poor performer as her listeners. He smiled sympathetically at her, which made her blush, and gave him pause. It would not do to give rise to expectations from other young ladies—he had no wish to give anyone the wrong idea.

"Thank you, Miss Hammerson. That was very pretty." His godmother looked around the room, met his eye. He shook his head slightly, and she quickly pouted and moved on. "Ah, Lady Anne. Might I ask—"

"You must excuse me, Lady Grantley, for I am not at all musical, although I admire talent as much as the next person." Lady Anne turned to Edith, seated beside her. "Perhaps you might prevail upon Miss Mansfield."

"Oh, but—"

"Excellent notion," his godmother agreed, talking over the top of her guest. "Miss Mansfield? Would you grace us with your talent?"

"Of course. I'd be delighted."

This was said in such a low voice he strained to hear the words. But there was no mistaking the irony. Delighted, she was not.

She moved to the pianoforte, and without searching for music, seated herself at the stool, lifted her hands, and began to play.

At once the perfection of her notes and tone filled the room, filling his heart with ease. Her performance held a quality those previously had not held: a poignant strain that blended with a precise confidence to demonstrate the talent she possessed. A confidence she seemed to no longer possess in other areas, if the bowed head and lowered eyes of the earlier introductions and during tonight's partridge dinner proved any indication.

What had stolen the assurance he remembered? Dare he believe it had something to do with him? But no. Such was vain foolishness. He forced his thoughts away. She'd made her choice. It was pointless wasting yet more time contemplating on what might have been. He joined the applause at the end and strove for his features an indifference he did not feel as she performed her second piece, a sonata by Haydn, and then rose, curtsied, and after politely declining an encore, resumed her seat amongst the audience.

"George?"

He started, swiveling to face his godmother's amused expression. "Yes?"

"Can I persuade you to perform for us tonight?"

"You should know I never wish to disappoint a lady." He moved to the front, resisting the desire to see if his words had any effect on the young lady in question. He only hoped she would not think he was making a general proclamation to the room about whose fault the estrangement had been. Heaven help him if he did.

He sat and immediately began his piece, Mozart's Piano Sonata no. 16. Would she remember that it had been this piece of music that had first drawn them together? Would she remember their shared times of laughter as they had tried to work the composition into a performance for two?

A performance for more than two, really. Everyone here was observing him, watching her, wondering about the cause of their parting. Just as he still did.

Frustration spurted, startling him with its intensity, so that he almost missed a note. He refocused, but his thoughts soon resumed their familiar trail. *God, forgive me, but . . .*

Would he get a proper explanation this time? Something that didn't shock him into gentlemanly civility whilst hiding a tidal wave of disbelief and despair? Something that actually allowed the wounded corners of his heart to heal rather than fester in silence until such moments of disappointment took him by savage surprise?

What a fool he was. Had he ever really thought he could be over her?

For she *should* be his and he hers regardless of whatever she had said. Fresh determination for a chance to speak surged. He gritted his teeth. *Lord, give me wisdom.*

The piece moved to a slower, reflective tempo, then the familiar refrain finished with a flourish. George stood, politely declining his godmother's request for more, and after espying Miss Mansfield's lowered head, refused to glance in her direction a moment longer. She remained unaffected.

"Thank you," his godmother said. "I do look forward to hearing more from you in the future. Perhaps you might even be persuaded to perform a duet?"

He lifted a shoulder. "Perhaps." Given the right partner, he'd perform like a shot. Unfortunately, the right partner had determined to see him as anything but.

The evening continued with poetry recitations and more insipid conversations he only wanted to escape.

Because the only conversation he wanted was with the woman who now regarded him as nothing, the woman who had moved on, the woman who had spurned his proposal just over one year ago.

# CHAPTER 3

THE SECOND DAY saw the commencement of the Christmas festivities. Edith's godmother had commandeered her guests after breakfast and informed them of the joys awaiting their pleasure. Seeing as the weather was fine, she was expecting them to participate in such activities as collecting the evergreens, culminating in the retrieval of a yule log her groundskeeper had sourced several weeks ago.

"For I do think it important to keep to the traditions," she said.

"Does this mean there shall be mistletoe?" Miss Mowbray asked eagerly.

"Mistletoe, kissing balls, wreaths, of course."

Of course.

"Oh, how wonderful!" Miss Mowbray shot Mr. Bannerman a look that suggested just which particular gentleman she wished might pluck creamy berries as a token for a stolen kiss.

Edith's heart experienced a strange twisting. Not that she should mind. It wasn't as if she should care whom he sought to favor.

Lady Grantley clapped to regain the attention of the excited guests. "Now, I have asked dear George to assist Mr. Caddy in retrieving the yule log. I know you will all enjoy a walk in our woods. We may not have had much snow yet, but it should still be quite pretty." She turned to the parents and chaperones. "Perhaps some of you might prefer to spend the time nearer the fire. I have the latest periodicals and novels, including something new by A Lady."

Edith glanced at her mother, who seemed as enthused as their hostess. Didn't she see what Lady Grantley was trying to do? Edith did not mind her machinations, but she had no wish to purposely be in Mr. Bannerman's company. Hadn't he made himself plain last night with his comment about never wishing to disappoint a lady? Her heart had writhed—still continued to writhe—at his words, spoken with such *insouciance*. She did not want to think him ungentlemanly, but how else was she—and everyone else—supposed to take his words, to take his actions? It was tantamount to saying he was not responsible for their parting.

And how could he perform *that* song, of all songs? It was not the action of a gentleman to play their song in front of everyone, to play like it meant nothing to him. Anger stirred anew. Didn't he remember all the times their arms had brushed as they performed side by side? Didn't he remember his breath catching when she had held his hand—well, positioned her hand over his—to demonstrate the notes? Didn't he recall the times when they had not practiced at all and had instead spent time whispering hopes, sharing dreams, exchanging hearts?

"Miss Mansfield." Lady Grantley's voice jerked Edith back to her present surrounds. "I trust you will participate?"

"Of course, ma'am."

"I seem to remember you have a particular talent for dressing the holly and evergreens. I do hope you will help us."

Perhaps an opportunity existed to forgo the afternoon's outing to collect the yule log and thus avoid more time with him. "I wonder, Lady Grantley, if I might please be excused in order to speak to your housekeeper about ribbons and the like. It would be helpful to know what has already been prepared to ensure we do not get carried away."

"Oh, I'm quite happy for you to get carried away, my dear."

Lady Grantley spoke with such an intent look that Edith could only blush and lower her gaze. No, she had absolutely no intention of getting carried away in that regard again. Heaven forbid Mr. Bannerman had heard, and understood, his godmother's covert meaning.

"Now," their hostess continued, as if she'd not said anything amiss,

"I shall need to instruct Miss Mansfield about these arrangements." She summoned a servant to find Mrs. Browning, the housekeeper, and go to the library. "Ah, George, might I prevail upon a few minutes of your time too, dear?"

Edith's breath suspended. She willed her countenance to impassivity, focusing on her hostess as Lady Grantley guided them both to the library, a long room papered in crimson and lined with books and deep settees. Edith silently obeyed her godmother's gesture to be seated.

"My dears, I do hope you don't mind me asking for your help in these ways. I know there are some here who might believe they possess particular talents but whose skills tend to demonstrate rather the opposite."

"I am happy to oblige you," Edith felt it necessary to say.

"Are you?" Lady Grantley asked suddenly. "Are you really? For nothing would give me greater joy than to see the two of—"

"Dearest Aunt Margaret," Mr. Bannerman interrupted, "was there something in particular you wished for me to do? I would not have Miss Mansfield feel obliged to do anything she does not wish."

This last was said in such a tone Edith could scarcely misinterpret the meaning. He was still angry with her for her decision. Very well, then. Ignoring the pain in her soul, she gathered her courage and said forcefully, "I am happy to help Lady Grantley. It is no imposition to me."

"Wonderful. I always knew you to have the most obliging nature." A rap at the open door and Lady Grantley gestured someone inside. "Ah, now here is Mrs. Browning. Miss Mansfield, perhaps the two of you can discuss ribbons and such things in here. George, may I have a word?"

"Of course. Your servant, Miss Mansfield." He bowed, offering Edith a look she could not decipher, and followed his godmother to the door.

Releasing Edith from the tension of his presence and forcing her to refocus on the housekeeper, who awaited her patiently. *Heavenly Father, help me to concentrate.*

She summoned up a smile. "Now, Mrs. Browning, about those ribbons . . ."

———— ✦✕✦ ————

"Aunt Margaret, I really must insist—"

"On what, my dear? It seems most apparent that you cannot manage things by yourself and therefore must have such affairs managed for you."

"I do *not* require managing," he muttered.

"I cannot agree. Here you are, on your second day in the company of the woman you told me you wished to marry, and you've barely said a word to her. That is not the action of a man who wishes to be reunited."

"Who says I wish to be reunited?"

"You did. Last Christmas, this past January, in February—in fact, every time I've seen you this year, you have expressed regret at how things ended."

He'd said that? He willed his teeth not to grind.

"I am sorry if you do not like my interference, but I am not sorry to interfere. Such a badly managed business as it was."

"It was not my desire to end things," he admitted stiffly.

"Well, I cannot understand how such a sweet and sensible girl as Edith Mansfield thought it right to let you get away. But perhaps it was simply a matter of bad timing, with her father so ill at the time."

"The thought had crossed my mind," he admitted. Edith had grown more and more distraught at her father's illness, something that seemed to have been premonition of his death not two weeks after their final interview, a death he had yearned to comfort her through. But no. She had refused his letters, returning them unopened—he'd realized later, wryly, as any proper young lady should.

"Surely she must have known you would not give up so easily," his godmother continued, drawing him from the mire of regrets. "I have known you to persist long after others faltered. Why, who was the person who saved your father's estate by stubbornly refusing to sell the fields and insisting on trying new crops? Who was the person who determined to help his scapegrace cousin find a new life in America when all others had washed their hands of him?"

He glanced away, flattening his lips. He might have saved his father's estate, but look how well that second action had turned out.

"So why, dear boy, did you so easily relinquish Miss Mansfield?"

"Because she would not have me." He lifted his gaze and studied his godmother steadily. "She made her choice extremely plain. I know not why the reason. I wish to heaven that I did." Her words still echoed: "A change of heart." How could that be after all they'd shared? How could a person simply change their mind without giving thought to the effects on the other? He would never, could never, understand.

His godmother sighed and clasped his arm. "You are in my prayers, dear boy. I know this has been a trying time for you, what with your cousin's disappearance and your search for him this past half year and all. But please, for my sake and yours, tell me you will use this time to somehow tell her how you really feel."

He glanced away from the earnest eyes. "I cannot make that promise."

"Please? Dear boy, I cannot bear to see you unhappy."

"It is not of your making and therefore should not be of your concern."

She sighed again. "I'm afraid that anything to do with dear Emmeline's boy is of my concern, especially now that she is not here to promote your happiness herself."

His heartstrings drew tight. "Mother liked Edith very much."

"Of course she did. What sane woman would not admire someone so sweet and good? Emmeline was a good judge of character, which is why she and I were such good friends for so many years."

A chuckle pushed past his pain.

"And what sane man would not admire Edith's intelligence and those fine eyes?" Her smile grew sly. "You, my dear George, I have long counted as one of the more discerning young gentlemen of my acquaintance."

His chuckle swelled into a laugh. He bent and kissed her cheek. "You, my dear Aunt Margaret, are the most incorrigible lady of my acquaintance."

She gave a trill of laughter. "That's enough out of you, young man. Now, are you going to speak to dear Edith or not?"

He drew a deep breath, feeling as if he teetered on a precipice. "I will."

Why did that proclamation make him sound like a young boy in leading strings?

But still, he knew she was right, and that this time together was opportunity for healing the past. And perhaps, a little whisper dared breathe, there might even be room to consider the future.

# CHAPTER 4

EDITH FINISHED TWISTING the red satin ribbon to approximate another small bow, then sat back to examine her handiwork. No, the ribbons were not precisely symmetrical, but perhaps once the greenery was incorporated into the wreath it would not be so noticeable. In fact, with a little tweaking, she just might be able to—

"Oh, Miss Mansfield, you are still in here."

Edith glanced at the round figure of the housekeeper at the library door. "I'm afraid I got a little distracted."

"Are you not joining the others in the collection of the yule log?"

"I hadn't planned to," she admitted.

"Oh. Well, Lady Grantley would like to know whether you wish to join the chaperones in the drawing room. Apparently they are playing whist."

Whist? Had her life descended to such depths she was now expected to find pleasure in whist? Edith glanced back at Mrs. Browning, hoping her expression hadn't given away her feelings. "Thank you, but I think I will read upstairs."

"Very well, miss."

Edith stared at the frivolous concoction of ribbons, the gaiety something she did not feel. Surely hiding in here was not what she should do. Her lips tweaked with wryness. Although hiding in her bedchamber was hardly different. But at least if she could avoid—

No! This was juvenile. As was any trace of former emotions she might feel. She was nearly six-and-twenty, for goodness' sake. One should certainly be able to carry on without letting the world suspect she still wore the willow for someone. Which she most certainly *didn't*.

She laid aside her materials. Lady Grantley had said Edith might continue tomorrow, if she liked, that this room would be undisturbed. She moved to the door and peered out as voices came from farther along the hall. If she hurried, she might just be able to avoid—

"Ah, Miss Mansfield. We had wondered where you had got to." A somewhat portly young man with fair hair and cherubic features—Mr. Drake?—smiled and gestured her to join the others in the hall. "We are going with Bannerman to fetch the yule log."

She could think of nothing to say but "Are you?"

"Oh yes, should be jolly fun. But I'd rug up rather more warmly than that, if you don't mind me saying so. There's something of a nip in the air."

"I thought I might read instead."

"Read instead? Come now, Miss Mansfield. Surely you know the purpose of such country parties is for people to spend time getting to know one another. And I must confess that there is no one else I'd prefer to get to know here than you."

Movement beyond his shoulder revealed that others awaited. "This flattery is too much, sir," she said in as low a voice as she could.

"Flattery? Nonsense. I simply speak the truth."

"Miss Mansfield?" Lady Anne said. "You best hurry and fetch your warmest pelisse and bonnet. I think it will be quite chilly out."

"I . . ." She stopped, the faces watching her with such interest making refusal impossible. "I will just be a moment."

She was halfway up the stairs when she nearly collided with someone, a sandalwood-scented someone who grasped her upper arms as she nearly toppled backward down the steps.

"Miss Mansfield. Are you all right?"

"Thank you, sir." She sounded breathless. "I am quite well."

He released her. "Miss Mansfield, Edith . . ." His eyes caught hers, causing a funny fluttering sensation in her chest. "I was hoping you might spare me a moment of your—"

"Mr. Bannerman!" Miss Mowbray called from below. "Are you quite finished with Miss Mansfield?"

"No."

The word was uttered so quietly she almost missed it, but she could not miss the look of entreaty in his eye, a look that made her want to hurry to the hills and hide her humiliation. Guilt panged. He deserved an explanation, but not here, not now, not today.

"Please excuse me." She brushed past him, past the tantalizing drift of spices, and hurried to her bedchamber, closing the door with a resounding thud. Oh, why hadn't Mama insisted they leave as soon as Lady Grantley had mentioned he would be here? Why could she not suppress these feelings where he was concerned? That look in his eyes . . .

"Heavenly Father, please help me," she pleaded, moving to the window, leaning her forehead against the cool glass. The rapid pace of her pulse gradually quietened as she stared at the distant hills, their proportions strangely distorted through the bubbles in the glass.

A knock came at the door. "Miss Mansfield? Edith?" a female voice called.

She turned. "Yes?"

The door opened, and Miss Hammerson entered, flush-faced and apologetic. "Forgive me for intruding, but I was hoping you would be joining us for the walk this afternoon."

Edith glanced at the book, which beckoned invitingly, then back at Emma, her features melded in appeal. "Of course." She shrugged into her dark-blue woolen pelisse, tied on her mauve silk bonnet, and collected her gloves and scarf. "Let us go."

"I'm so glad you are coming," Emma said, looping her arm through Edith's as they made their way to the staircase. "I find that some of the others here make me quite tongue-tied, and I'm so glad to have someone accompany me that I dare consider might one day be a friend."

A knot in Edith's heart loosened. How long it had been since she'd had a female companion she might consider a friend. Since Maria, Lady Grantley's daughter, had married and moved to Scotland, Edith had had few people with whom she could share openly. Perhaps God in His provision had allowed this stay to be a time when she could find a friend, *be* a friend, even if He would not provide a renewal of old acquaintanceships.

She shook off the melancholy and offered Emma a smile. "I'd like that very much."

They joined the others in the hall, Edith murmuring her apologies for keeping them waiting.

"No matter," Lady Anne said. She turned to Mr. Bannerman, who was talking with one of Lady Grantley's servants. "Shall we go now?"

He nodded, and the party moved outside, where they were joined by another of the Grantley servants, an older man equipped with saws and ropes.

After a swift look at George, who had been joined by Miss Mowbray, Edith forced her attention back to Emma, who was the blushing recipient of Lord Sculthorpe's attention.

Ah. She swallowed a wry smile. So Edith's company had not exactly proved necessary after all. Never mind. She would enjoy the crisp air, and the sight of white-trunked bare trees, and the sensation of movement, especially after the hours spent sitting before.

And there was something rather lovely, indeed almost magical, about the mist-laden hills, the scrape of coolness on her skin, the tinkle of laughter, and the jingle of the harness as the large cart horse plodded behind them. Indeed, if it wasn't for the two persons walking ahead in the lead—one of whom seemed determined to hold the other's attention, with her nonstop chatter and giggles—Edith could think this afternoon jaunt most pleasant indeed.

"Oh, Miss Mansfield." Emma clutched her arm, forcing Edith's pace to slow. "Lord Sculthorpe was just saying about how he hoped there might be some interesting games this evening."

Edith glanced past Emma to where the dark-haired lordship watched them. "Yes?"

"I do not mind musicales, but I find the attendance of so many young ladies infinitely more diverting, and I would much prefer to spend time talking to them than merely listening to them."

Edith bit the inside of her bottom lip to hide a smile. Surely he didn't mean that to sound quite like it did.

He shifted and eyed Edith critically. "I say, Miss Mansfield, that is a pretty bonnet."

She reached up and touched a feather that was working its way loose. "I fear it is not terribly practical for such cool weather, but it's the warmest I had to bring with me."

"Practical or not, it suits you very well, don't you think, Miss Hammerson?"

Noting the downcast look in Emma's eye, Edith squeezed her new friend's arm gently. "I was saying to the other young ladies just how wonderful this particular shade of pink is for Miss Hammerson. Do you not agree that it matches her cheeks entirely?"

"Entirely," the young lord continued, his gaze returning to Emma with appreciation. "I say, Miss Hammerson, did you see that little squirrel? Quite a quick little fellow. Here one second, gone the next. I wonder . . ."

Edith slowed her steps, allowing the other two to walk on ahead. She'd seen the beseeching look in poor Emma's eyes, and Edith had no wish to draw Lord Sculthorpe's attentions for herself. She looked over the other young gentlemen in attendance and realized there was none of them of whom she wished to garner their notice in any particular way. None, except for—

No! She shook her head at herself angrily. Why did she keep thinking on him? Really, this was most ridiculous. She glanced up at the leaden skies, praying for the strength to overcome, when a cleared throat drew her attention to the elderly man holding the ropes, trudging quietly beside her, an Irish setter scampering at his heels.

"You might want to watch where you're walking, miss," he said, glancing at the muddy puddle ahead.

"Oh, thank you, Mr.—"

"Caddy, miss."

"Thank you, Mr. Caddy." She glanced at the saws he carried. "Have you a particular tree in mind?"

"Aye. I spied it a se'nnight ago. An old ash that fell down a few months back. I marked it so we could find it again. Should fit the great hall's hearth quite nicely."

"And Lady Grantley sees that it is lit on Christmas Eve?"

"That she does. Though with this year's ball, I think she wishes it to be lit the day afore."

He seemed disinclined for more talk, so she followed in silence until the party moved to a halt beside a fallen giant. A scarlet ribbon was tied around one of its branches.

"Aye, this be the one," Mr. Caddy said to the group's inquiry. "Now we just need to saw off the ends and attach the ropes to drag it back to the house."

"Any volunteers?" Mr. Bannerman asked.

"Surely you can't expect us to participate in such a menial task," Lord Sculthorpe scoffed.

"Why not?" He grinned, stripping off his overcoat. "Isn't that what you came here for?"

"Oh, but Mr. Bannerman, surely you have no wish to get dirty," Miss Mowbray protested.

"What is a little dirt between friends?" His gaze swept the gathered group, seeming to pause ever so slightly on Edith before turning to the man beside her. "Mr. Caddy, may I assist you?"

"I'd be glad for the help," the older man admitted, drawing the ropes and saw from the back of the horse.

The next moments were spent watching, the ladies gathered to one side under the protection of an aged tree while the men encouraged Mr. Bannerman and Mr. Caddy to their task.

Mr. Bannerman's coat and vest soon joined the greatcoat hanging on a nearby branch.

"Oh, he is such a fine specimen of a man," Miss Mowbray said with a sigh.

Edith couldn't help but privately agree. She'd known George Bannerman's shoulders to be broad—impossible not to, when playing side by side on the pianoforte—but she hadn't quite suspected he would appear so strong, nor to such advantage when stripped down to just his shirt.

Perhaps it was the marked attention of the young ladies, but eventually the other gentlemen also took their turns at the saw, exercise that soon saw their faces mottle to dark red and a glow of perspiration shine on their brows.

Mr. Bannerman moved to the side, offering encouragement to the others as they worked. He glanced up every so often, but his face was inscrutable, and it seemed he paid no more attention to her than anyone else.

"Foolish girl," she muttered under her breath, gaze dropping to study the muddied ground. *You reject what you still want.* But no, it hadn't been foolishness. Had been necessity. Had been familial obligation—

*Creak.*

She glanced up. Saw the branch above her quiver. Heard a shout. Then before she knew anything else, she was being pushed just as the branch above fell.

# CHAPTER 5

*Ooof!*

George slammed Edith into the ground in a dim sea of trembling leaves and twigs. Something heavy lay on his back, something had scratched his face, but he was barely conscious of it, aware of the woman he held in a desperate attempt to protect her from the falling branch. The woman who now stared at him with widened eyes and mouth mere inches away, in an expression that blended shock and fear.

"How dare you?"

And, apparently, anger.

She pushed uselessly at his chest, but the weight pinning him down refused to move. "Get off me!"

"I can't."

Maybe it was something about his wry tone that suggested truth, for she looked past him to the leaves he could feel crowding his head, and blinked, the anger draining from the honeyed depths of her eyes. "Oh."

For a moment they were trapped in an embrace he'd never dared imagine—and definitely never envisaged trapped as they were underneath a tree. Her breath whispered soft against his face, and a sweet . . . something wove between them that spoke of trust and hope and memories.

"I'm sorry if I hurt you," he whispered.

Her eyes filled, then closed, and she bit her lip. His heart grew sore.

Had he hurt her? He'd moved as quickly as he could, but perhaps she had been injured—by him and not the tree. Why did he always get things wrong?

"Edie?" He shifted an elbow, reached to touch her face. "Are you injured?"

The long lashes lifted, and he was once again drawn into the golden-brown gaze. "My head aches."

"I'm sorry," he said, regret knotting within. Why hadn't he just moved her instead of throwing her to the ground like a reckless brute?

"No, I—" She licked her lips. "I'm the one who is sorry."

What?

Just then the weight pinning him eased, and he was conscious of other voices, of movement, of the others who would no doubt be raising eyebrows at the most improper position in which George held Edith. He scrambled off and away, brushing aside twigs and leaves from his shirt as he fended off the inquiries as to his well-being.

He reached down and grasped Edith's hand. "Are you able to rise?"

"I think so."

He gently pulled her upright, and she was instantly surrounded by a cacophony of flustered exclamations, questions, and concern. She raised a hand to the back of her head. No doubt it must be throbbing.

"Oh, Miss Mansfield, do you have a headache? Oh, you should sit down and rest. Do you feel dizzy?"

Edith glanced up at him, distress in her eyes, which emboldened him to say, "If Miss Mansfield has no objection, I think it might be wise for some of us to return to the house."

"We should all go," Miss Mowbray declared.

Something passed across Edith's face that triggered a new rush of protectiveness within. "I think it would be better if the job of collecting the yule log could be completed, something which Mr. Caddy cannot perform alone." George glanced meaningfully at Lord Sculthorpe and Mr. Drake and tilted his head to the young ladies, which soon drew their chorus of assent.

"Bannerman is right. He and Miss Mansfield likely just need a little rest back at the house."

George gently squeezed Edith's hand, which somehow she'd not yet drawn away. "Do you feel able to walk back, or should a conveyance be summoned?"

"I'm sure I can walk." A smile flitted across her face. "I only had the wind knocked from me for a moment."

"Better the wind than the life," Mr. Caddy said. "Good thing this one"—he motioned to George—"was thinking so quickly."

"Yes." Her assent was mere breath as she stared up at him. "Thank you."

"I'm glad I could help in time." He smiled.

She blinked, then glanced down, her cheeks filling with a rosy hue. Then, as if noticing their hands were still united, she speedily withdrew hers from his clasp.

"I'll walk back with you," Lady Anne informed them in a tone that admitted no objection. "You should have someone walk back with you in case either of you feel dizzy."

"Thank you," Edith said, stumbling slightly then drawing herself upright once more.

"Are you sure you are well enough?" he asked quickly.

"Yes, I'm fine," she said, not looking at him.

He nodded and moved to collect his discarded garments and hat, then made his farewells to the others. "No doubt you will have this log at the house very soon."

"We might even beat you back," Mr. Drake called, "especially if you take the picturesque route."

George felt the tips of his ears heat, and he turned away, offering Edith his arm. But she merely shook her head and started walking with Lady Anne, as if determined not to allow any further speculation about them. He sucked in a sigh and followed close behind, leaving the others to the instructions of Mr. Caddy, which were loudly echoed by Lord Sculthorpe.

Walking behind the two ladies, George took a moment to stretch out his muscles, which were already protesting the endeavors of the past hour. Thank goodness his tailor had fashioned his coat for ease of wearing rather than mere style. But he was conscious now of an ache in his shoulder and upper back, something he would not admit for the world, but it was there nonetheless.

Small matter. He glanced at the slight figure walking ahead beside Lady Anne. Thank God he'd reached her in time. Thank God it had only been the branch and not the entire tree. Thank God the incident had resulted in only the slightest cuts and bruises and that it had not been anything worse. It could have been so very much worse.

"Thank You, God," he murmured.

A new revelation swept across him, and his feet stopped. Imagine if she had died. Not just today, but sometime in the past year. What if all his prayers and yearning frustration—and dare he admit, resentment?—had been for naught? He could not live another year without learning her heart. He could *not*. And after the way she'd looked at him just now, something inside whispered that she might not be opposed to his renewal of devotion. If only he could get the chance to speak to her alone . . .

"Mr. Bannerman?" Lady Anne called. "Are you quite all right there?"

"Forgive me." He hurried to rejoin them. "My mind was wandering."

Edith slid him a sideways look, but he couldn't decipher it. She remained so hard to read. She who, once upon a time, he'd been able to know her every mood, nearly able to discern her every thought simply by the light filling her features, or the way she worried her lip, or arched her fingers over the piano keys, or merely by her stance.

Did she think on him? Did she regret what she'd once said? Urgency pummeled his chest. He *needed* to speak with her soon. And alone.

Birdsong trailed across the air, nature singing of God's providence. Edith's pace slowed, then paused, allowing him to catch up to the ladies. "Oh, how lovely."

"A robin." He pointed to the tiny redbreast perched in the branch of a nearby alder.

They stood listening to its chirping calls for at least a minute, enjoying the sounds of nature's song, and a knot of tension in his heart eased. How wonderful was this world God had created. And if

God cared about the birds of the trees, as was written in the Scriptures, then surely it wasn't farfetched to believe that God had this situation with Edith sorted too.

He glanced down at her shining face. No need to guess her thoughts now. "It's beautiful, isn't it?"

"Very," she agreed.

Another look of intensity passed between them, broken only by Lady Anne's observation about the cooling air and the need to return soon.

She emphasized this by striding away, leaving Edith and George a few paces behind, sharing bemused looks. He offered his arm again, but she refused, yet seemed content enough to walk alongside him as they slowly followed in Lady Anne's wake. He struggled for the words to somehow introduce the topic nearest his heart, but somehow this still didn't seem the right time. Soon. He would talk with her soon.

He cleared his throat. "Are you sure you have suffered no ill effects from earlier?"

"Thank you, but I remain well." Her eyes slid back to him. "And you? I'm sorry I did not realize at the time, but you must have been hit by the falling branch. Are you sure you are uninjured, sir?"

Sir? "Please call me George, like you used to."

She shook her head, biting her lip, dousing his hopes.

He suppressed another sigh—propriety be hanged!—and answered her question. "I suspect I have some scratches and will feel this all tomorrow, but I cannot complain." He studied her, then added quietly, "I am so very glad that you are safe."

"And I, you." She glanced up at him, a frown marring her brow. "I'm afraid you do have a rather large graze."

His heart knew a double thump. Perhaps she did care after all. Hope hammered in his veins as she stopped and lifted a gloved hand to touch his right cheek. He trapped her hand there and took a moment to enjoy the surprise lighting her eyes, to trace her features once more in his mind, to enjoy the sweetness in the moment.

"Sir, please. What if Lady Anne turns and sees?"

"Then I'll say you're just concerned for my health." He leaned closer and said in a lower tone, "Perhaps you might even kiss it better?"

She blinked and immediately withdrew her hand. "No."

She turned and hurried to catch up with Lady Anne, but even as she moved, he thought he heard the words "Not today" float on the breeze.

He laughed to himself. Surely Edith couldn't be immune to him if she remained flustered at his nearness.

He followed more slowly, thinking back to the time when she had not been so missish with him, when she had owned an ease and candor that had led him to make that ill-fated declaration. Maybe this was his second chance, a God-given opportunity to restore things as heaven and nature intended. For she *should* be his.

His exhale puffed into a small white cloud, and he shook his head at himself. People didn't belong to others, no matter what certain members of society might think. And just because he believed it was only right and natural for Edith Mansfield to be perfectly matched with him didn't mean she believed the same. Even if they shared the same faith. Even if they had always shared a similar sense of humor. Even if they both valued family above riches, and kindness above comfort, and honor above—

"Oh!"

The loud exclamation and stumble hastened his steps to Edith's side. "Miss Mansfield?"

"Oh, forgive me. It is nothing," she gasped, rubbing her side.

"Hardly nothing," he disagreed, clutching her arm, as she seemed inclined to sink to the ground. "What is it?"

"Nothing but a stitch, I'm afraid." She held his arm, wincing.

"Try and stretch it out on the opposite side."

She leaned to the right, nearly toppling over, so he wrapped an arm around her shoulders to steady her.

"Is everything quite all right, Miss Mansfield?" Lady Anne called, hurrying back.

"Just a stitch."

"Oh." Lady Anne glanced between them and over to where the

house was situated, its stone-capped roof looming beyond a rise of trees. "It's still a little ways yet. And it's getting colder."

"I'll be fine in just a—ah!"

"Forgive me," George said, bending to sweep Edith into his arms, to her squeak of protest. "It's the only way."

"I can walk, sir," she said even as she glanced at Lady Anne.

"Yes. But as I'm sure your mother would prefer to see you before the light fades, you may find this is the only way."

"Mr. Bannerman is correct," Lady Anne said. "It is getting darker."

"But I don't need—" Edith's words faltered at his look, her petulant expression smoothing to resignation. "Oh, very well, then. Thank you, Mr. Bannerman."

"George," he murmured in a voice only loud enough for her to hear.

She glanced away and answered Lady Anne's concerned questions, leaving him more than a little nonplussed. When he'd prayed this morning for some method of reconciliation, little had he expected to be holding Edith in his arms again.

But this time there was no fear, no concern he might have accidentally harmed her. Instead, he was only conscious of how well she fit in his arms, of how stiff she remained with him, of the slight scent of lavender that rose from her hair. The scent tugged at his memories, pulled at his heartstrings, drew out a small sigh.

"Oh, I hope I'm not too heavy for you."

"Not at all," he lied. Admit his back was hurting? Never.

"Please." Her voice held a note of entreaty, forcing his gaze down to her eyes. "I am sure I can walk now. I would feel much better if I knew you were not encumbered with such a burden."

"I am hardly encumbered, my dearest Miss Mansfield."

She blushed and evaded his gaze, glancing at Lady Anne with wrinkled forehead as if worried what their companion might think.

"Miss Mansfield, surely you do not really expect Mr. Bannerman to forgo the opportunity to act like a hero?"

He chuckled and met Lady Anne's raised brows and shrewd eyes. "I'll have you know, Lady Anne, that today I have not been acting like a hero. I truly have been one."

She chuckle-snorted, a sound that made him laugh. Even Edith seemed to find the sound amusing, although her smile faded when she met his glance again.

"What is it, Miss Mansfield?"

"I . . ." She pressed her lips together, then exhaled quietly. "You have indeed been most heroic today, and for that I thank you."

Tenderness wound around him, but aware Lady Anne watched them avidly, he could not resist the words springing to his lips. "I beg your pardon?"

"I said," she said in a louder voice, "that you have been quite heroic today, and I am most grateful."

He coughed, the action causing his rib to throb. "Please excuse me. My hearing is not what it used to be when I was a younger man. Would you mind repeating that one more time?"

"I said," she spoke more loudly still, "that you are a true hero— oh!" She elbowed him in the chest, and he lowered her to stand again, where she glared at him, arms akimbo. "You heard me correctly the first time!"

"Forgive me, but they were such sweet words that I couldn't resist wanting to hear them again."

"Oh, you . . ." She shook her head, then turned so violently that her hat fluttered to the ground.

He bent, scooped it up, and meekly handed her hat to her.

She snatched it and marched away.

"What, no word of thanks?" he called.

"I think I've expressed my thanks enough to you already today, sir."

And with a huff and quickened pace that soon outstripped Lady Anne—whose offer to accompany her was met with refusal—she strode to where the path met the lawn encircling Grantley House. Relieved her earlier malaise seemed quite gone and she would attain the house within a minute, he slowly followed.

Lady Anne turned to study him, as if she found him quite diverting.

"Thank you for your company, Lady Anne," he offered.

"I don't know how thankful you really are, but it seems the re-

mainder of this Christmas house party will have additional entertainment value."

He inclined his head. "You might pray it ends more happily than
I deserve."

"What you deserve?" Again she made that strange half-snort,
half-chuckle sound. "I think anything where you might meet with
Miss Mansfield's favor will be more than you deserve."

"You have the right of it, ma'am."

"Hmm." She eyed him, then moved to loop her arm through his.
"In that case, I wonder what we should do?"

# CHAPTER 6

AT THE SIGHT of Lady Anne arm in arm with him, all that Edith had thought most miraculously certain suddenly turned to dust. How could he speak so tenderly to her one moment, then tease her so the next? And then to speak with bent head, in such a familiar, secretive way, to someone she'd begun to regard as a friend?

Edith swung her attention back to the steps of Grantley House, where her bedraggled appearance led to widened eyes and mouths as a footman drew near. "Can I be of assistance, miss?"

"Thank you, no," she managed to grit out. The only assistance she wanted was that which would ensure a swift passage upstairs and would hide her from the eyes of the chaperones—and Mama.

But alas, such a hope died as the door to the drawing room opened and Lady Grantley appeared, Mama's shocked face peering over her shoulder.

"My dear girl!"

"Edith, my love, what has happened?"

Edith found a smile, pinned it in place. "There was a slight mishap in the woods."

A collective indrawing of breath from the other parents and chaperones who had joined her mother and their hostess in the hall. "Never tell me you were attacked!"

"Only by a tree," she reassured.

"Oh, my dear!"

"Are you injured?"

"No, Mama. I was a little winded, but"—she would not admit to exactly how she had been saved—"but I am quite well now."

"And you were left to return alone?"

"No, Mama, there are others coming."

A deeper voice cut through the hubbub. "Miss Mansfield, there you are."

Edith pressed her lips together. Indeed, here she was.

Mr. Bannerman moved with ease through the gathered onlookers, whose gaping mouths and murmurs suggested his appearance was as remarkable as hers. He smiled at Edith, then turned to her mother. "Mrs. Mansfield, you must pardon my dishevelment. We"—he gestured to Edith—"have had something of an adventure this afternoon."

"I'm afraid I don't quite understand."

Edith studied the floor. Here he'd go, sounding off about his part in rescuing her, boasting of his heroics once again.

"There was a tree branch that could have caused more injury than it did," he said quietly.

"Injury?" Mama turned to Edith. "I thought you said you weren't injured?"

"And I am not—"

"Oh, we should summon the doctor at once!" Mama cried. "Margaret, please—"

"Send for the doctor," Lady Grantley instructed a footman, then patted Mama's arm. "Catherine, you need not distress yourself. Edith seems quite well."

"Oh, but how dreadful," one of the other mothers murmured.

"Not as dreadful as it could have been," Lady Anne said in a carrying voice. "If it hadn't been for the efforts of Mr. Bannerman here, that tree branch might have squashed poor Miss Mansfield flat."

"Oh my goodness!"

Edith grasped Mama's arm, whose paling face was reminiscent of the time when she had first learned of Papa's illness, and had taken to her bed for days. "I am quite all right, Mama. You need not be alarmed."

She glanced from where Lady Anne was gazing at the hero with an adoring smile on her face, to Mr. Bannerman, who for some reason seemed to still be watching Edith. She supposed she should give him full credit, although the words might taste like bile.

"Mr. Bannerman is the one who likely needs a doctor, seeing as he bore the brunt of the tree in his heroic endeavors."

All eyes swung to him, and his reddened face suggested he did not like the attention a whit more than she did. Now to escape before any more questions could be raised.

"If you don't mind, I think I shall return to my bedchamber and rest for a while."

"I'll send Dorcas up, and you shall have a hot bath."

"Thank you, Lady Grantley," Edith said while turning to her mother. "Mama? Would you come upstairs with me?"

"Yes, of course, my dear."

"I'll send the doctor to you when he arrives."

"Thank you, Lady Grantley, but that will not be necessary."

"Indeed it *will* be necessary," Mama said with a reversion to her stronger self. "But first, a bath and change of clothes."

They moved to the staircase. "Miss Mansfield?"

She closed her eyes momentarily, then turned, hoping her smile did not look as artificial as it felt. "Yes, Mr. Bannerman?"

"I . . ." He glanced at her mother and said in a lower voice, "I truly am thankful to God that the incident this afternoon was not nearly as disastrous as it might have been."

That deep look she had wondered over had returned to his eyes, causing an escalation in her heart's beating. It was becoming hard to breathe. "I am thankful for your assistance," she managed, hearing the words that sounded so cold and formal. She cleared her throat. "Truly." Her smile felt wobbly.

"I could not bear it if you had been—"

"Mr. Bannerman, please let my daughter be. She's obviously overwrought from this experience."

His eyes caught hers again, as if asking a question. She shook her head. No, she was not overwrought, but Mama was ushering her away, Lady Grantley was issuing instructions, and the perusal of all the spectators suddenly made her realize she was in danger of tears. She blinked them away, focused on placing one foot and then the other as she made her long ascent, then hurried to her bedchamber to join her mother and hide her heart's pain in her room.

———— ✦✕✦ ————

Upon her return downstairs—after a bath and a doctor-prescribed rest, which went a long way to securing both her own and Mama's emotional equilibrium—Edith found the others gathered in the drawing room, awaiting the dinner gong. She was instantly surrounded with enquiries as to her health from Emma and Lady Anne, and Miss Mowbray (resplendent in a beribboned gown one might expect to see at a London ball) a moment later.

"I am quite well, thank you," Edith said, genuinely touched by their concern. Then hoping to turn the subject, she said, "And how did the log retrieval go?"

"I don't precisely know why we had to assist in the first place." Miss Mowbray shrugged an elegant shoulder. "It hardly seemed a challenge for that Caddy creature."

"I'm sure Lady Grantley thought it might prove an interesting outing."

"Well, that certainly proved to be the case," Lady Anne agreed. "I've never seen a gentleman move quite so quickly before. Mr. Bannerman is quite the athlete, it appears."

Edith exhaled slowly. Resigning herself to being a witness to Lady Anne's ardent admiration of George Bannerman was not a high price to pay for being alive. And if he preferred someone like Lady Anne to herself, well, she only had herself to blame.

Conscious the others were looking at her, as if awaiting a response, Edith murmured, "I am very thankful he was not injured for my sake."

"But he was," Miss Mowbray said. "Look!"

Dread lined Edith's chest as she turned and obeyed. "Oh no."

Mr. Bannerman had just entered the room, his right arm in a white sling. He seemed to grow aware of her scrutiny and raised his head to look at her, offer a small smile, and shrug. Then he winced.

"Oh no," she whispered again. He'd been hurt for her sake—then had made a truly valiant sacrifice by offering to carry her home. The tears she'd thought vanquished upstairs made a sudden, sharp, stinging reappearance.

"Now, now, Miss Mansfield," Lady Anne said gently, "he's not badly injured. It is only a slight strain."

How did she know this? Why didn't Edith know this? Why hadn't he said anything instead of being intent on proving himself a hero? "I should never have gone today," she murmured.

"You are not responsible for what happened, nor for the stubborn pride of a man who refuses to speak on his injury. So said the doctor to Lady Grantley, anyway."

Oh. Edith gently clasped Lady Anne's hand. "You are truly kind." Guilt writhed through her midsection. It was little wonder he preferred Lady Anne to herself. Lady Anne scarcely seemed the sort to indulge in uncharitable observations about others or their intentions.

"He is a good man," Lady Anne said with a meaningful look that brought the heat to Edith's cheeks.

"Yes." She knew that. And did not blame Lady Anne for being enamored. Who would not wish to spend time with a young gentleman who truly lived up to that description? Apart from his chuckles at her expense this afternoon—which she could now overlook, as he must have been in *such* pain—he had always been gentle with her, had always proved kind and generous. Who could blame a young lady for not being aware of such a fact?

"Miss Mansfield."

Her heart thudded. She turned. "Oh, Mr. Bannerman, I did not realize that you were injured! I'm so sorry—"

"Why? You did not mean to hurt me, did you?"

She stared at him. Then recognizing the tease deep in his eyes, relaxed and smiled. "Of course not. It would appear you do not require assistance if you are intent on hurting yourself."

He chuckled. "The doctor said it probably was not the wisest thing to insist on carrying you back—"

"You carried Miss Mansfield back? Oh, how gallant you are, sir!"

Emma's voice drew awareness that they still had an audience. Edith took a step back, willing her face not to reveal the consternation his nearness drew forth. "Very gallant."

"Miss Mansfield." His eyes found hers once more, "I am hopeful that you would not mind if—"

"Ah, we are all arrived," Lady Grantley said. "Now, if the gentlemen could please escort the ladies into the dining room, we shall soon commence."

Edith knew a pang of disappointment as Mr. Bannerman inclined his head and moved away. She supposed she would have to go in with her dining companion from last night. She turned to Mr. Drake, only to see him holding his arm out to Emma, as if preparing to escort her.

"It seems we have been abandoned by our dinner partners." Mr. Bannerman's voice came from behind her.

She turned. "Alas. Whatever shall we do?"

He eyed her intently for a long moment, his gaze dipping to her mouth then lifting to her eyes again. "I would offer you my arm, but . . ." He shrugged, and a look of discomfort crossed his features again.

"Will you be able to eat sufficiently well?"

"I'm sure I can eat well—I confess our adventures this afternoon left me feeling quite ravenous. It's more the matter of whether my dining companion might deign to help me should the matter be required."

"I can help you," she said, then added softly, "I am in your debt, after all."

An instant of disappointment crossed his features before smoothing away into blandness as he gestured to the procession entering the dining room.

Her heart thudded strangely. Why had he seemed disappointed? Surely he did not—no. That was foolishness. Nothing could be gained by allowing hope to blossom where it would surely wither and fade.

She walked slowly into the dining room. This room, like many of those at Grantley House, was paneled in oak, from which hung paintings of ancient ancestors dressed in ermine and ruffs. Their expressions were such Edith was sure they must have intimidated many a younger person into strict behavior.

A footman pulled out her chair, and she sat next to Mr. Bannerman. Grace was said, and the first of the courses was brought out.

From the corner of her eye, she watched as her dining companion struggled to smoothly scoop the white soup with the spoon in his left hand. She glanced away, to where Lady Grantley sat at the head of the table in lieu of her deceased husband. Lady Grantley met her gaze with a nod, then resumed her conversation with Miss Mowbray's father. Edith frowned. The seating arrangements had to have been approved by Lady Grantley. Surely she hadn't—

"Is the soup not to your liking?"

"Oh!" She turned back to Mr. Bannerman, whose soup bowl had emptied. A glance back up revealed the amusement in his eyes. "I beg your pardon?"

"It is delicious soup," he said, eying her nearly full bowl.

"Apparently so." She hastened to finish, concentrating on eating elegantly, conscious his gaze weighed on her still. Why did he not speak?

"It seems this afternoon's exploits have fueled your appetite also."

She swallowed her mouthful with difficulty. "Mr. Bannerman, that is hardly the polite thing to say to a young lady."

"I beg your pardon?"

"One should not refer to one's appetites."

"Ah, I forgot. Young ladies are so very different to young men, after all."

"Indeed we are." Humor curled the edges of her lips. She glanced up, met his intense regard, and knew herself to be blushing.

She dragged her gaze away, glad for the interruption of the footmen clearing the table and bringing in the dishes for the next course.

When she had been served by her other dining neighbor, she turned her attention to her meal. The turbot was tasty, the entrees that followed designed to entice the senses.

Conversation flowed around them, the large porcelain epergne centering the table, allowing for a modicum of privacy. Surely she could eat this meal without attracting any more of the interested gazes that had followed her all evening. She simply needed Mr. Bannerman to refrain from any further startling observations or from looking at her in that deep way that made her wonder that he might not have feelings for Lady Anne Pennicooke after all. Perhaps then she might be able to sort out this confusing jumble of emotions and see her way straight again.

"Miss Mansfield."

"Yes, Mr. Bannerman?"

"I trust the lamb cutlets are more to your taste than the soup was."

"They are most enjoyable."

"Indeed." He paused, then said in a lower tone, "I am very glad for the chance to finally speak with you."

Her pulse increased its tempo. "Indeed?" Her voice sounded squeaky. She sipped her glass of watered wine.

"I was hoping you might honor me with an opportunity to perform with you again, should my godmother request it."

Oh. She was conscious of a pang of disappointment. That was certainly not what she had expected him to say. "Do you think such a request likely?"

"Quite likely, especially if I ask her to."

"And are you planning on doing so, sir?"

He smiled, a sight that curled warmth into the corners of her heart. "I think we both know the answer to that, do we not?"

Breath suspended. She returned her attention to her plate. "Was there a particular piece you wished to play?"

"I wondered how you might feel about performing 'Non lo diro col labbro' again."

Their duet of love, the prelude of which spoke of the sparks of burning eyes and passion. She swallowed and found his gaze again. "I'm afraid I have not played that for some time."

His eyes did not move from hers. "Neither have I. It seems we shall need to practice. Together," he added, as if subtly reminding her.

"One can hardly practice a duet alone," she murmured.

"Then you would not be opposed to the idea?" Was that hope lighting his eyes?

No. She was being foolish. Likely as not he probably just wanted an opportunity to expunge the memories. She studied the asparagus adorning her plate. "I think it best such a thing be postponed a little while."

"You do?"

The disappointment underlining his voice made her glance up. "At least until your arm is fully recovered."

"You are wise. Very well. We shall wait a little while longer."

She managed a fleeting smile, then resumed her study of her meal.

Wise she could scarcely claim to be, not when she knew spending time with him would only lead to sore hearts. No, she most certainly could not claim wisdom, not when she had been forced to reject the only man she had ever wished to marry.

# CHAPTER 7

LADY GRANTLEY CLAPPED her hands for attention, and the drawing room quietened. "I thought tonight we might try a different evening pastime, especially"—she eyed George—"seeing some of us are a trifle injured tonight."

George wondered just what she had in store. After his request to accompany Edith to dinner had resulted in underwhelming conversation from that fair lady, he hoped his godmother might have enough sympathy for him to see his cause promoted. But the ladies' departure from the table and the penchant of certain gentlemen for port had scarcely allowed time for him to speak with their hostess, and he'd been forced to hide his impatience.

"Now, I understand from Lady Anne that there are particular parlor games that are considered quite in vogue, so I thought we might engage in some tonight. Perhaps, seeing as my godson is indisposed, you might be willing to assist me in this first game, Miss Mansfield."

He quickly turned to see the young lady in question blushing but politely accepting the office. His eyes narrowed. Just what did Aunt Margaret have in mind?

"We shall play Musical Magic," she announced. "Edith, dear, are you familiar with this game?"

"Of course, ma'am."

Mr. Drake was sent from the room, and the young people gathered close whilst the chaperones and parents moved to play cards at several tables placed near the roaring fire.

"I think the object should be the urn on the mantelpiece," Lord Sculthorpe suggested.

"What about a rose from the vase on that small table?" Miss Mowbray said.

"Yes, a rose. And the objective?"

"He could give it to Miss Hammerson," suggested Lady Anne, who was proving to have quite a surprising romantic streak.

"An excellent notion," George's godmother agreed. "Call in Mr. Drake, then."

Mr. Drake was summoned, and Edith began playing the piano, loudly whenever he moved away from the vase atop the table, more softly as he drew near.

"Ah." Mr. Drake drew near the small round table and began touching the items displayed there: a shell, a smelling bottle, a painted miniature. Edith's music grew softer, softer, and then as he touched the vase, stopped.

"Is it the vase?" The music resumed. "The flowers?" It quietened.

Mr. Drake plucked out a rose, and the music ceased. "Yes?"

"Yes," the assembly chorused.

He glanced around the room as the piano playing resumed. "Am I to give it someone?" The piano grew softer.

Mr. Drake moved to the circle of chairs and began offering the rose to the various ladies there. Finally he offered it to Miss Hammerson, and the music ceased.

"Will you have this rose?"

"Yes," Miss Hammerson squeaked, her cheeks approximating the pinkish hue. "Th-thank you."

George smiled as the group burst into applause, wondering how many others would be maneuvered into such embarrassing, revealing positions.

"That was most enjoyable," his godmother said, glancing around the room with a broad smile. "I trust you can keep yourselves entertained while I attend to the older set."

"You can trust us," Lady Anne said, turning to face George with a look he could only regard as mischievous. Oh dear. During their walk this afternoon, he hadn't realized the lengths she might go to in order to assist him with his quest. Why had he not kept his mouth shut?

"Mr. Bannerman, do you think you could be our next player?"

"Of course." He pushed to his feet and moved outside to the drafty hall, doing his best to warm himself by the fire. He had a feeling that these next few minutes might prove interesting.

The door opened, and he was drawn back to the room, where he noted with surprise that Edith was no longer at the piano. Instead her place had been taken by a petulant-looking Miss Mowbray.

"Ah, here he is."

George moved around the room, the music swelling. He caught his godmother's eye and gave a small shrug and received a smile. He turned back to where the younger people were seated, noting the music quieten a little more, a little more. He moved into the center of the circle and began a slow procession in front of the seated guests, the music a little quieter each time until he stood before a blushing Edith, who did not look at him even as the music stilled.

"Miss Mansfield?" One swift glance up and down. "I wonder what I'm to do with you."

Miss Mowbray resumed playing as he puzzled out his dilemma. He knew well the purpose of so many of these pastimes was to encourage flirtations.

"Forgive me," he said to Edith, stretching out his hand. "I don't quite know what is expected."

She glanced at his hand as the music swelled again. So apparently he was not to ask her to stand, which must naturally preclude asking her to dance. What else might have been designed?

As he stood there, the music grew louder. Clearly he was meant to do something different.

Aha. Perhaps if he was to sit. He lowered himself to the floor, but the music did not entirely die away. He was not to stand, not to sit.

George bit back a grin and drew himself to one knee. No wonder

Edith's cheeks held such a rosy hue. The music stopped. He had it right. But was this the end of it?

The recurrence of the piano suggested not. What should he do? Edith was barely looking at him.

He reached across and gently clasped her hand. The music stopped.

He grew conscious of a strange intensity in the moment. Did anyone know just how near to the bone this struck? No wonder Edith refused to look him in the eye.

His heart hammering, George bent over her hand and pressed his lips to the back. The music resumed, but he was scarcely aware of that, instead aware of the way Edith's breath had caught.

"I don't mind this game," he murmured, in a voice only loud enough for her to hear.

She moved to pull her hand away, but he held it more firmly.

So not a kiss. Not a mere handhold. What else would these matchmakers decide on?

Of course.

Shaking his head at himself, he carefully withdrew the signet ring from his left hand's fifth finger, refusing to wince at his shoulder's pain. The music grew faint. He then glanced up at Edith's face, now looking more pale than pink.

"Miss Mansfield? Are you quite well?"

She bit her bottom lip and nodded, her dark honey eyes finally meeting his, watching him.

George gently pushed his ring onto her fourth finger, and the music stopped, and the circle broke out into applause.

"Took you long enough," Drake grumbled.

"My fingers are ever so sore," Miss Mowbray complained. "I do not think I want to play that game again."

"No," he heard Edith whisper. He turned to study her, and she plucked the ring from her finger and gave it back to him. "I do not want to do that ever again."

What?

His stomach grew tight as she rose and hurried to the fire, hands outstretched to the flames, and he tried to smooth away the disappointment her words provoked. He did not blame her for feeling disconcerted. Such a game had not felt like a game at all—it had felt much too real.

He exhaled and resumed his seat, mechanically answering the questions the others thought fit to ask, even managing a tight smile he hoped might pass for appreciation when Lady Anne asked delightedly if he'd enjoyed her ingenuity.

But that all faded when Edith moved from the fire to speak with her mother and Lady Grantley, then returned and collected her embroidered shawl. "Please forgive me," she said without looking at anyone. "I find the activities of the day have left me with something of the headache, and I am going to retire."

"Oh, but you can't," Lady Anne said with a swift look at George. He shook his head at her, but she continued. "Surely you do not want to miss out on the other games we've prepared."

"I have no wish to impair your enjoyment, but I fear it will not be quite so enjoyable for me."

"Of course not, especially if you are still tired," Miss Hammerson said softly. "Would you like me to accompany you?"

"Thank you, but I should not like to keep you from the evening's entertainments."

His spirits sagged as he studied Edith. Was she really so very tired from the day's activities, or was it the nighttime fare of which she'd grown weary? Apart from a few welcome moments at the dining table, she'd scarcely looked at him all night.

He watched her leave, an insistent tugging within begging him to race after her, to assure her that those moments earlier had scarcely been a jest to him. But would she reject him, as she'd so obviously done on their walk home? Others might call him heroic, but he doubted he had much courage to endure her rejection again.

*Lord, help her see that I love her still.*

*I love her.*

The words resonated in his soul. It had not passed, this feeling. If anything, today's misadventures had only served to reinforce the depth of his affections. And although she might treat him at arm's length, and at times with a measure of disdain, he suspected that might derive from embarrassment rather than any real sense of heart change. For those too-few moments when he'd witnessed the truth in her eyes—

"Bannerman? Still daydreaming, are we?" Lord Sculthorpe asked.

"I beg your pardon." He straightened, trying to recall what had been said.

"Perhaps he has something of the headache too," Lady Anne said, the mischief pronounced in her eyes.

Really, he must talk with her about this nonsense. It had obviously embarrassed Edith earlier. But wait—

"Forgive me, but you have the right of it. I'm afraid that I shall be of little use to others tonight, as I'm feeling quite tired." From their skeptical looks, perhaps he should mention the doctor again. "Dr. Graves was quite insistent I have an early night, and look, here it is now half past ten." Perhaps if he hurried he might still catch her—

"George?" His godmother now stood in front of him. "Are you feeling a mite unwell? Dear Edith said she was not feeling quite the thing, and so I wouldn't be surprised if you were feeling a trifle tired too."

"Forgive me. I have no desire to be rude. But I would prefer to find my bed soon." After he talked to Edith one more time and assured her he had nothing to do with tonight's tomfoolery. And maybe cleared up some other matters too.

"Of course. Well, good night, dear boy." She lifted a perfumed cheek for him to kiss, which he did before making his bow to the rest of the assembly.

"Good night, all. See you on the morrow."

He exited among a flurry of good-nights, and grasping his night candle from the table at the base of the staircase, he quickly lit it from the candle already aglow and hurried up the stairs. But when he reached the top, there was no sight of Edith. She'd disappeared, and he couldn't very well go visit the ladies quarters—his godmother would likely send him packing.

"Miss Mansfield?" he called, hoping against hope that she might hear him and return.

He startled as a footman stationed in nearby shadows made his way into the light. The footman cleared his throat. "Pardon me, sir, but Miss Mansfield went to her bedchamber a few minutes ago."

Of course she had. George sighed, but not desiring to engage the footman in any further talk, he nodded and walked slowly to his room.

He closed the door, touched his flame to light the lamp beside the bed, and sank into the armchair positioned by the fire. His disappointment grew, an aching, heavy thing. It seemed he was forever destined to play catch-up, to try to make amends, but for what he remained unsure. Should he perhaps speak to Edith's mother to discover where he'd fallen short? His godmother could not truly know the ins and outs of things—her guess was as good as his.

He stared into the fire a few moments longer, allowing his imagination to wander. If she had said yes to his proposal, they would have been married by now. She wouldn't be cloistered away; he wouldn't be frustrated, alone. They could be—

"Dear Lord, help me," he groaned, unwilling to let his mind stray any further.

Why had she refused him? Why were things so complicated still? "I've tried to talk with her," he told the room.

The furniture, the soft furnishings, remained silent.

He chuckled at himself—truly, what had he expected?—and released a weary yawn. Perhaps a good night's sleep might clear his brain and relieve him of these well-worn fancies.

A scratching sound came at the door. He moved to open it and saw the Irish setter that had once been one of Lord Grantley's favored hounds, staring up at him.

"Hello."

The dog moved past him, and George looked up and down the silent hall. He didn't recall seeing the dog in the bedrooms previously. A chuckle escaped. Was this God's way of helping him deal with his loneliness tonight?

He resumed his seat, and the dog sank his soft mahogany head into George's lap. "You're a friendly fellow, aren't you?"

A whine, and George scratched between the droopy ears, eliciting a rumble of delight from the canine's chest. "You like that, don't you?"

The dog settled his body over George's feet, allowing him to resume his previous posture and ruminations, but without the melancholy of earlier.

God was good. George knew that. He glanced at the Bible atop the table beside his bed and gently moved his canine companion to collect it. A minute later he reseated himself and began to read from where he'd left off this morning. The Christmas story was not simply one of joy and love. The heavens might have resounded with angelic chorus, but they too would soon hear of earthly pain. The mothers of the children slaughtered by a desperate king would scarcely have known that in a nearby village lay a Savior child, and naturally they would have grieved. Neither could the Virgin Mary have known her babe would live three and thirty years and then die on a barbaric cross.

He glanced from the printed page to the flickering flames. How pertinent that seemed tonight. He might live a life of virtual ease, enough that he might complain when things did not go as he'd prefer. But God had never promised his followers a painless existence. The Savior child had grown to be a man Who beckoned others to believe in Him, to follow Him, even as He trudged the road that led to His death.

The frustrations of earlier faded, and his momentary joys and fears grew dim. "Heavenly Father, forgive me for my self-interest. If I say I love her but do not do what You want me to do, then my words are mere air, and I am become as resounding brass or tinkling cymbal. Help me with this yearning. Help her with this pain. And please help me to trust You with this all."

# CHAPTER 8

AFTER A RESTLESS night where dreams blurred the evening's events with the all-too-painful past, Edith rose and was soon dressed. She stared at herself in the looking glass as the maid finished primping her hair, and sighed. Large, dark half-moons spread beneath her eyes, suggesting a weariness that made her look older than Grandmama in her last days.

"There, miss. You look very fine."

"You have done a wonderful job with my hair. Thank you."

"Oh, I enjoy dressing such smooth, dark hair. 'Tis no chore at all."

Edith's chin lifted. Perhaps this day would not bring any of yesterday's challenges. Surely they had to have been all faced by now. There could be nothing worse than last night's faux proposal. Had he intended to mock her, to make her wallow in regret? How could he do that after his earlier avowals of tenderness? It did not seem right, and so last night she had scarcely slept, trying to puzzle through it all.

She stood and dragged on a shawl. The window proclaimed an overcast vista of shaking trees, the morning air holding a coolness that even the fire seemed averse to warm.

"Ah, Miss Mansfield." Lady Anne stood at the top of the stairs. "I trust you slept well and are quite recovered from your headache."

Her headache? Oh. Her excuse to withdraw from last night's farce. Thank goodness for the clouded skies that layered new dimness inside and that might hide the embarrassment she could feel stealing across her face. "Thank you. I am better now."

"I'm so pleased. But I'm not surprised, really. This weather looks like we might yet have proper snow in time for Christmas."

"You think so?"

"Indeed. Yes, I have family members who are quite clever at predicting these things, due to their various ailments, which tend to flare whenever the weather changes. Perhaps you are like them also."

She frowned. Did Lady Anne mean to suggest Edith was like her aged relatives?

"In fact"—Lady Anne smiled slyly at Edith—"it seems yours wasn't the only head affected last night. Mr. Bannerman did not stay much longer after your departure, complaining he too had a headache."

"Is that so?" Had that sounded as bored as she hoped? Judging from Lady Anne's wrinkled brow, perhaps.

They reached the bottom of the stairs, and sounds from the breakfast room suggested the other guests were enjoying their first meal of the day. Edith followed Lady Anne inside and murmured her good mornings, then moved to retrieve a plate from the sideboard, which she soon filled with items from the warming pans. She took a seat at the far end of the table from George Bannerman, who was now freed from his sling, and focused on her breakfast, giving half an ear to the conversation around her.

"Good thing we collected our log when we did," Mr. Drake said. "The weather looks rather nasty today."

"I wonder if it will snow."

"Or perhaps there will be a blizzard, and we'll be trapped here for weeks."

Edith stilled. Trapped here for weeks? While that thought might have been welcomed a year ago, now it seemed as if being forced to stay mere days would prove too long. Mama had promised Lady Grantley they would stay until after Boxing Day, but Edith could not but wish they might be able to avoid that too. What if Mr. Bannerman resumed his hot-and-cold attentions? How long could she maintain this pretense that his actions did not dig at her heart?

"Edith?"

She started, then grew conscious that everyone was gazing at her. "I beg your pardon."

Lady Grantley smiled fondly at her. "I was hoping you would not mind assisting me today with the greenery."

Oh, dear heavens. Why had she ever agreed? "Certainly, ma'am, if you wish it."

"Oh, I do." Lady Grantley turned to look at the rest of the assembly. "Dear Edith has such a wonderful way with flowers and the like, and I'm sure these will be extremely pretty."

"Pardon me, ma'am," Miss Mowbray said, "but do you not wait until Christmas Eve to hang the greenery?"

Lady Grantley waved a dismissive hand. "That is only for the superstitious. And with all the preparations for the ball, its significance would likely be lost. Besides, I quite enjoy the amusement provided by mistletoe and the like and should not like to think my guests were missing out on some of the more enjoyable pleasantries of the Christmas season."

Edith could not look at the man seated beside their hostess. Would he wish to engage in some of these pleasantries? The thought that he might sent a delicious shiver down her spine, only to be ruthlessly quashed. He did not. He would not. No matter how gallant he had been. No matter how a tickling thought had wondered earlier if the reason he'd left the evening games had been less due to a headache and more due to her.

She shook her head at herself. Stupid, vain imaginings.

"Miss Mansfield? Do you not wish such traditions continued?"

"What? Oh no, no. Not at all, Miss Hammerson. I was thinking on something else quite entirely."

Miss Hammerson peered at Edith in a way that suggested she was not wholly believing, then produced a smile. "Then if you have no wish to see them continue, it surprises me that you so willingly participate in such rituals."

"Pardon? Oh, I don't mean—"

"I think decorating the house with festive greenery is simply a nice tradition and need hold no pagan associations if one does not wish it to," Mr. Bannerman said, glancing at Edith and offering a small smile. "After all, did not God create the greenery in the first place?"

She inclined her head as the table murmured agreement.

"One can choose to associate what meaning one wishes, or not," he continued. "Just as one can associate certain hymns as music from folk songs or an opera or something else entirely."

"Yes, well, that may be so," Lord Sculthorpe said with a look that suggested he'd never spared a thought on the origin of church music. "I'm simply looking forward to the mistletoe."

But Mr. Bannerman's words continued to resonate within. His discussion of meaning had felt deliberate. Was he suggesting she had perhaps misread things and could construct an alternative meaning to his actions? Or was she misreading things again? She winced. Now last night's "headache" did not seem feigned at all!

"Miss Mansfield? Are you well?"

Edith summoned a smile and spoke to her hostess. "I would be pleased to make a start on those decorations soon, if you have no objection."

"Of course." Lady Grantley glanced around the room, then rose, which saw every gentleman rise too. "I shall take you to the conservatory." She smiled. "It is a room of which I'm most proud, if anyone cares to join me."

The company followed her as one through the back of the hall to a door positioned beside the stairs. "Ready?"

A footman opened the door to a world of brightness. Gone were the shadows induced by the heavy timber paneling and furnishings of the other rooms of Grantley House. Instead, a space of light, of windows, and a profusion of plants met the eye. A tinkling sound and the soft chirp of small birds were carried on the warm, moist air that was redolent of flowers.

"Oh, this is lovely," Edith breathed.

"Is that a fountain?" Miss Mowbray moved to the center of the room, where a tiered stone edifice was surrounded by four curved benches. "Oh, look! There are fish!"

Edith joined the rest of the party as they surged forward and espied the small gold and silver fish frolicking in the water.

"I've never seen anything like it!"

"This was my little project this past year, after I was inspired by a visit to Carlton House. Prinny had a room built that was quite magnificent, complete with temple and flowers and candelabrum decorating the hall. It had the most lovely stained glass, too, but alas, I could not afford to emulate that, so I insisted the focus be on the windows and fountain. One does not wish to be too ostentatious, after all."

Edith bit back a smile and glanced up to find Mr. Bannerman studying her, his lips curved in such a way that suggested he shared her amusement.

"But even with all that glass, it does not feel cold."

"That's because it is heated."

No. Not decadent or ostentatious at all. Edith studied the black-and-white checkerboard floor, willing the burble of laughter in her throat to subside. She shouldn't laugh. Even if it seemed ridiculous that she and Mama could scarcely afford wax candles anymore and had to carefully measure exactly how far they'd melted to ensure they maintained appearances, thanks to the legacy of the Mansfield pride. She shook off the frustration and concentrated on the present. For this truly was a lovely room, and its contrast with the grayness outside quite remarkable.

"So I thought that Miss Mansfield, and any others who might wish to join her, might find this space quite suitable for the arranging of the evergreens." Lady Grantley gestured to a table surrounded by chairs. "I have found this quite a lovely place to sit and observe nature."

The birdsong grew louder. A question about such was put to their hostess.

"Ah, that would be the sweet canaries. They find this space quite welcoming also," Lady Grantley continued, a small pleat in her brow.

"You may be able to see them in the large cages over there. I used to let them fly around, but some of them flew a little too close to the chimney, which rather limited their flying ability."

"Oh dear."

A couple of smothered guffaws into coughs suggested some of the gentlemen found this amusing. Edith glanced away, only to encounter Mr. Bannerman's steady gaze. Her neck prickled, and she hastened her attention to her hostess.

"So, Edith, dear, do you think you can manage to create something in this paradise?"

"It will be my pleasure," Edith said sincerely. To sit here, amongst the sights and sounds of natural delights and be *warm*, was indeed a joy.

"I do hope you will not object if I should insist on joining you, Miss Mansfield," Miss Mowbray said.

"Of course not." It was scarcely hers to object to, though something of a surprise. Miss Mowbray had scarcely expressed any desire of wanting to further her acquaintance with Edith, nor given the impression of being willing to work. "I will appreciate the company."

A footman came in carrying heaped baskets of greenery, followed by another whose baskets were filled with ribbons and twigs of various sizes.

"Ah, here we are. Just set them down there," Lady Grantley commanded. "I declare, this looks such fun that I may have to join you also, my dears."

There was a murmur from the other guests, and before she knew what had happened, Edith was sitting at one end of the table, issuing instructions that seemed to be followed in varying degrees by the ladies—and a surprising number of gentlemen—who had elected to assist.

"We need to shape the willow wood into a circle and tie it off with ribbon. Then weave the holly and the ivy around the willow, tying it as best you can."

"The holly and the ivy," Lady Anne echoed. "I do think that may be my favorite Christmas song."

"The holly and the ivy, when they are both full grown,
of all the trees that are in the wood, the holly bears the
crown."

Edith listened, head bent, as Mr. Bannerman's rich voice echoed through the room, followed by softer voices that joined the refrain.

"O, the rising of the sun and the running of the deer,
the playing of the merry organ, sweet singing in the choir."

Sweet singing indeed. She'd always loved listening to his voice. She twisted a recalcitrant rosehip through a strand of willow wood.

"The holly bears a blossom, as white as lily flow'r,
and Mary bore sweet Jesus Christ, to be our dear Savior."

She drew in a deep breath, the song twining around her heart.

"The holly bears a berry as red as any blood,
and Mary bore sweet Jesus Christ to do poor sinners good."

The swell of others joining in the refrain prickled awareness she would be observed if she did not sing also, so she mouthed along as the next verse begun.

"The holly bears a prickle as sharp as any thorn,
and Mary bore sweet Jesus Christ on Christmas Day in the
morn."

The echoes of the chorus filled the room, resounding in Edith's heart. Memories, bitter and sweet, begged to be recalled as she contemplated those final words. Jesus Christ, her Savior, had been born, had suffered a crown of thorns, and died so she might live. Except she wasn't doing a very good job of living, save for living with regret. *Heavenly Father, forgive me.*

She gradually became aware of the sounds around her, the industry of busy fingers.

"I enjoy that Christmas song." Mr. Bannerman held up his half-finished kissing ball. "What do you think, Miss Mansfield? Will this suffice?"

She tried to speak. Couldn't. Swallowed. "I think you need more greenery."

"And definitely more berries, wouldn't you say?"

The berries one plucked when a kiss was stolen.

She ducked her head, held up her two circles, one placed upright at a perpendicular angle within the other. "You should be aiming to create a ball, which means using some of the other greenery to cover the outside and fill in any gaps."

"I've never understood why people use rosemary," Miss Mowbray said, frowning as she held up an aromatic stalk of spindly green.

"Rosemary is used to symbolize Mary, the mother of Jesus," Edith murmured.

"And it's used for remembrance." Mr. Bannerman said this with such an intent look that she had to glance away, as telltale heat flushed her cheeks.

"It certainly is warm in here," Lady Anne observed to no one in particular. "Poor Miss Mansfield is looking quite rosy."

"Speaking of roses," Edith said loudly to try to hide her embarrassment, "you may wish to thread through some rosehips also."

"But what about the mistletoe?" Mr. Drake protested.

"We add that at the end. Have you created your second circle yet, Mr. Drake?"

"Not yet."

"Perhaps you should finish that first, then."

His frown was quickly replaced with a knowing smile. "I suppose I should. The more kissing balls the better, I say."

Edith hid a smile and resumed her work. Now that her ball was looking more spherical, she needed to add ribbon to loop through the fruit that would adorn the kissing ball, leaving enough ribbon to twist into a loop above so it could be hung. She pushed a thin skewer through the hard pear, taking care not to pierce her finger. Then once the hole was created, she used the skewer to poke the ribbon through the pear. This she drew to the top, where she made the requisite loop, which she garnished with a big red bow. The addition of some mistletoe, complete with creamy berries, and her creation was done.

"Oh look!" Emma exclaimed. "How lovely!"

"That is indeed very pretty," Miss Mowbray said, laying aside her rather less impressive effort.

"Come now, Amelia," Lady Anne said. "Don't give up now. We need all the kissing balls we can make."

"Indeed we do," Mr. Bannerman said.

Edith shot him a look, but he seemed suddenly quite intensely focused on his creation.

"My dear Edith, that is simply lovely. Oh, you do have a way with such things." Lady Grantley held up the decorated ball. "I wonder where this would be best positioned?" She glanced around. "George?"

Mr. Bannerman looked up. "Perhaps it might suit the front hall so it can be admired by all who visit in the upcoming days."

"Hmm. That is an idea."

"Look!" Miss Hammerson held up her finished kissing ball.

"Oh, well done!" Mr. Drake exclaimed.

"I do hope it shall stay together," Miss Hammerson said worriedly.

"May I?" Edith said, drawing near. "If we just tighten the ribbons here . . . and here, I believe it will hold its shape for the twelve days of Christmas. It's really most charming."

And it was, with pink and silver ribbons, much like—Edith glanced at her friend's gown—exactly as Miss Hammerson's preferred attire. Edith smiled and looked up to encounter Mr. Bannerman's look of amusement. Had he noticed the same?

"Miss Hammerson has created a sweet something entirely apropos," he murmured, to that young lady's blush.

Edith eyed him. He seemed to be behaving today—mostly. It did seem unusual that so many of the gentlemen were willing to help with such things, but perhaps they were in agreement with Mr. Drake and thought the more mistletoe the merrier the party would be.

As if sensing her perusal, he glanced up. Smiled. Lifted his handi-work. "What do you think, Miss Mansfield? Will this pass the test?"

She moved unwilling feet to his end of the table, eying the abundant mistletoe berries with misgiving. A touch of the wreathed circles proved they would not come apart easily. In fact, it seemed well secured. And really, for a man, he had done quite a lovely job. "It looks very nice."

"Nice? Is that all?" He held it up, lifting his head to eye where the waxy mistletoe berries hung. "Do you think it will survive plucking?"

She blinked and stepped hastily away. "I'm sure you will be able to ascertain that, sir."

"You are sure?" he said, eyes intent on her. "You give me hope."

She gasped. "I did not mean to suggest—that is, please do not think I am going to be a willing participant, sir."

"Oh, I did not think that at all." He turned to Lady Grantley, and holding the ball up above them, he gave her a hearty kiss on the cheek, then plucked a berry. "There," he said with satisfaction. "I think this will do nicely."

Edith hastened to the other end of the table, confusion dogging her footsteps. Oh, why did he always fill her with consternation? And why had she lied about being unwilling? If only she could survive these remaining few days with her heart intact.

# CHAPTER 9

THE MORNING'S ACTIVITY in the conservatory had led to a proclaimed request from his godmother that more greenery be retrieved. George had volunteered, certain a walk might clear his head of the confusion induced by the earlier activity. Above, gray clouds threatened menacingly, their promise of rain, if not snow, having apparently hastened the request for more greenery. Beside him strode Mr. Caddy, and the visitor from last night panted by George's other side.

"He seems to have adopted me," George said, eying the red setter.

"Aye," Caddy said. "I suspect Rogan be thinking you look something like the master, being tall and lean like he was, and all."

"Rogan?"

"Means red-haired one."

"A more appropriate name never was." George ruffled the dog's auburn fur between his ears.

His thoughts returned to the conservatory and the actions of his godmother, who was proving to be as devious as Lady Anne in her machinations to bring George and Edith together.

Upon hearing his dismissal of Edith's concern that he might want to kiss her—had she really meant that? That look in her eyes suggested otherwise—Lady Grantley had insisted he hang it there in the conservatory, above a chaise lounge that was screened by large potted ferns yet still held a discreet view of the fountain.

"For who knows who may think such a place necessary."

"Who knows indeed," he had agreed gravely, to her shout of laughter.

"Oh, my dear boy, you need not look so grim. It has come to a pretty pass indeed if a young lady remains completely insensible of a young man's charms."

"You heard her. She has no wish to be caught under the mistletoe with me."

"Tosh and nonsense. Of course she does. But she doesn't quite know it herself, and it is *not* the done thing for a young lady to admit to owning such a desire, now is it?"

No. It wasn't. But though he had succumbed to his godmother's pleas and obeyed, ensuring quite a romantic setting should someone take it upon themselves to find the conservatory's kissing ball, he still had his doubts. Perhaps Edith would soften and he could see if his kissing ball might succeed in helping him win her favor. Amusement tweaked his lips. Now that he thought upon it, perhaps he *had* been a trifle heavy-handed with the mistletoe—the ball was positively dripping with it—but he'd not wanted to take chances. Hence the need to embark on a walk through the biting cold to retrieve what greenery they could in order to festoon the mantelpiece and staircase.

Caddy glanced up at the heavens. "It'll be white tomorrow."

"Truly?"

"Aye. I've seen it like this before. We best hurry."

An hour later, they had filled the cart with more yew and laurel branches. George had even dragged down another armful of mistletoe from an apple tree.

"Somebody be keen for kissing, I see."

George laughed, his breath clouding white in the frigid air. "You are an optimist."

"Hmm." Caddy looked at George sideways, a sudden speculative glance that made George wonder how much the old man really saw. "Still, it be a good thing to remove it from the tree. The tree has got a chance now."

"Is mistletoe a sucker then?"

"It be a strange plant, happy to leech off the life of another growing thing if it can."

"Sounds like some people I know."

"What's that?" Mr. Caddy eyed him.

"Oh, nothing. Merely thinking aloud."

He probably shouldn't be thinking about his cousin, but the description seemed most apt. Desperate to maintain a lifestyle Reginald could ill afford, clinging to others in the hope they might breathe life—or at least sink money—into ill-advised schemes, his agreement to a new life abroad had quickly descended into mystery concerning his whereabouts, thus necessitating George's absence from England these past six months. *Lord, be with Reginald, wherever he is*, he prayed.

His thoughts shifted to his father's estate, now his, and the similar challenges of assisting those who seemed determined to maintain the past at the expense of their futures. Since his father's death, George had been determined to do what he could to improve things for future generations, to ensure his sons—he winced, *Dear Lord, let her reconsider*—would not be faced with the same debts as he had. He needed finances to see things through, and a number of tenant farmers had refused his requests to modernize their practices, with their insistence that the old ways were best. He knew of others who disagreed, who were not backward in seeking forward, modern methods of agricultural practice, like the Duke of Hartington, one of the grandest residents of the country. But—his lips twisted wryly—one could afford to experiment when one had the finances to cover failure. George did not, so could not. Just like he could not afford failure on another front.

*Dear Lord, let her reconsider.* He wondered what Edith would say about his plans.

———✳———

That night after dinner—his attempt to sit next to Edith thwarted by the determined Miss Mowbray, who had insisted on talking about all manner of things he had no interest in, and who he suspected had no interest in farming—he joined the others in the drawing room, where their hostess had devised another series of games.

"Now, I know that there are some amongst you who are longing to inspect the mistletoe, so I trust you can manage to be decorous with such things."

A titter of laughter rang around the circle of young people. He glanced up; Edith looked away.

"Now, Amelia, you were speaking with me about an interesting game you would like to participate in."

"Oh yes! Truly, it is quite marvelous. It is a kind of reverse of hide-and-go-seek, where instead of everyone hiding as one person tries to find them, it is one person who goes and hides, and everyone must try to find them, until they are all hiding together, and waiting for the last person to discover them. That last person is in for the next game."

Mr. Drake frowned. "Is that not something of a child's game?"

"It is a game that people of all ages find amusing," she said with a degree of primness and tilted chin.

"Oh. Oh, I see! Well, in that case then . . ." He smiled at Miss Hammerson, who blushed. "So we'll need to find a hiding spot large enough for seven"—he counted the participants—"no, eight people."

"Yes! Isn't it marvelous?"

"So we are hiding in the dark?" Miss Hammerson said, looking worried.

"Oh yes, nothing to worry about. You shan't be alone."

"But what if we're hiding with a"—she blushed—"with a young gentleman?"

"Well, you'll have to manage as best you can, I suppose," Miss Mowbray said with a smile at George that raised the hairs on his neck.

Oh dear no.

"Does everyone go searching at the same time?"

Edith's question jerked his head up with surprise. Was she going to participate?

"Yes." Miss Mowbray looked at them all sternly. "But remember, this game will only succeed if people do not whisper and giggle and give the hiding spot away."

"I hereby promise that I shall not giggle," George said solemnly.

This garnered a swift half smile from Edith before she studied her slippers again.

"Oh, I'm so pleased Lady Grantley has agreed to this!" Miss Mowbray said, her clapped hands drawing their hostess to their circle again.

"My only stipulation is that you will all keep to the ground floor. There is to be no going up the stairs or engaging in unseemly conduct," his godmother said with a sharp look at the gentlemen.

"Of course, ma'am," George responded. "Any conduct shall be only that permitted by the presence of mistletoe."

"Very well, then. Oh, and I should prefer you to refrain from the conservatory, as I fear it may prove a little too dim."

But wasn't that the point?

"I shall remain here," she continued, "to keep your parents company."

It was decided that Lady Anne be allowed to hide first, her Christian name being closest to the beginning of the alphabet, save for Miss Mowbray, who insisted she needed to stay to direct how things should be properly conducted.

Lady Anne disappeared, and his fellow hunters began counting to one hundred. George glanced at the corner of the drawing room where the older generation continued their various reminiscences and card games and seemed most unconcerned about what their offspring and charges were doing. Perhaps his godmother had been busy appeasing others these past days.

"One hundred." Mr. Drake moved to the great hall and sang out, "Ready or not, here we come!"

He was followed by the others, save for Miss Mowbray, who hesitated at the door.

"I should allow you to go first," George gestured. "Ladies before gentlemen and all that."

"Oh no, sir. I couldn't let you do such a thing. We could go hunt together."

And be forced to hide together? Why did that thought not fill him with anticipation?

"Please." He gestured more firmly, relieved when she took the hint and preceded him into the great hall, from which various doors led to other chambers.

He was in time to see Mr. Drake slip through the door to the conservatory, accompanied by Miss Hammerson, both of whom seemed to have forgotten their hostess's instructions to not visit that room. Lord Sculthorpe tried the dining room, but George knew spaces would be limited there. Perhaps the library would prove a better bet. He glanced around, saw Edith slip through the library door, saw Miss Mowbray follow Lord Sculthorpe to the dining room, and knew he had to move quickly to avoid Miss Mowbray's company.

The library was dim, shadowed, but judging from the giggles ensuing from the desk in the corner, he thought he'd found his quarry. A squeal from without suggested Miss Mowbray was on her way and bade him hide at once.

He dived behind a large settee, only to encounter Edith's startled face as she tried to burrow behind the seat.

"The people one meets," he murmured.

"In the most peculiar places," she whispered back.

He grinned, the door opened, and they shrank down farther.

"I knew it!" Lord Sculthorpe said as footsteps creaked closer.

"Shh!" Lady Anne shushed from beneath a desk.

Lord Sculthorpe spied Edith and George and moved to join them, forcing George to inch closer to Edith. "Sorry," he murmured close to her ear. He caught a glimpse of her smile, and his heart swelled with hope.

They remained quietly hidden for another few moments before the door opened once again, admitting light and Miss Hammerson, who squeaked as Miss Mowbray entered just behind her.

"Quiet!" Miss Mowbray cautioned, hurrying to take her place behind another sofa.

George smiled to himself. This game really was rather an odd experience, but he couldn't argue with why they played it. From this proximity, he could smell Edith's appealing scent, something that reminded him of sweet lavender and roses. If he shifted ever so slightly he might even be able to touch—

The door thudded against filled bookshelves. "Oh, you have to be in here!" Mr. Drake said, to which the rest of the room emerged from their hiding spots with various cries of affirmation.

"It appears Mr. Drake will be our next hider," Miss Mowbray said.

"Excellent." He glanced over the ladies, then said to the room at large, "Well, you best all hurry back to the drawing room and count. I shall do my best not to be found."

This last was said with a wink at Miss Hammerson, which led George to wonder what that young man planned. Miss Hammerson seemed a sweet young thing, although perhaps a trifle naïve, and George had no desire to feel the need to chaperone the young couple.

They trekked back to the drawing room, where the young ladies assured their various elders that yes, everything was aboveboard and the young gentlemen were *so* honorable, and no, they had no wish to retire early and forgo such a thrilling game.

George watched as Edith nodded to her mother, then glanced at him, as if he'd been the subject of their conversation. He looked away, conscious as he did so just how much like a schoolboy he was behaving tonight. But he couldn't help it. His assurance seemed to leave whenever she was near, and he found himself questioning everything.

"Come on. That's one hundred," Lord Sculthorpe said.

This time, George held back, not catching Miss Mowbray's eye as the others surged into the hall, scattering behind closing doors. He noticed Edith move toward the ballroom and followed her there.

She moved to close the door, then jumped, stifling a cry as she noticed him. "Oh, you move like a cat!"

"Hush." He gestured to the far corner.

She nodded, and they gently closed the door.

Inside, the room's mirrored walls cast strange and eerie shadows as they silently moved to the farthest, dimmest corner. Edith glanced at him, offering a small smile, and he wondered what she was thinking. Did she think about the Christmas Eve ball, only a few days hence?

Would she permit him to dance with her, or would she ask him to keep his distance? He could only hope—

"Look! There." They saw men's shoes peeping from underneath the curtain and hurried to pull them back. "Mr. Drake. Hello."

"Quick, hide!" he whispered. "No, not here. Get your own curtains."

George stifled his amusement and gestured to the curtains nearer the wall, where the shadows were deepest. Edith nodded, and they moved silently to the window, drawing the curtains behind them.

From here the recessed window bays afforded further privacy. The shutters along the bottom had been designed long ago as additional house security but still permitted them to see through the clear panes at the top. The night wind looked quite wild, with flurries of—

"Is that snow?" Edith pushed her face to the glass, gazing out into the darkness.

"I believe so."

"Hush!" came Mr. Drake's voice.

Edith quietly chuckled, a sound low in her throat, and smiled up at George. "I never realized people took this game so seriously."

"That's because it's got a serious purpose."

"It does?"

He nodded, but before he could elaborate, the door opened and then shut as the patter of feet suggested they would be joined by another soon.

"What purpose is that?" Edith asked, shifting closer.

"This." He drew nearer, eyes intent on her, and bent his head—

"Mr. Bannerman!" Miss Mowbray sounded shocked. He'd not heard the pull of curtains. "Whatever are you doing?"

Nothing anymore, it would seem. "Miss Mowbray, you best hide quickly."

"So Mr. Drake is in here?"

"Surely you did not suspect me of conducting some secret rendezvous?"

Miss Mowbray's gaze swung from him to Edith, then back again. "I don't know what to think anymore."

Her words held a sting that might as well be a slap. "You have quite mistaken the matter," he told her in as firm a voice he could muster, considering they were still whispering.

But his words seemed to have little effect, judging from the way Edith shrank away from him. No. He didn't mean—

"Will you two please hush!" Mr. Drake cried.

Three people rushed in with shouts of laughter and insistent declarations that "you were the last one in" and "no, *you* were!"

Eventually the game was called a draw and then concluded, as the chaperones and parents seemed to waken to the fact of what might just happen to their dear charges when in the dark with young gentlemen, even if they be gentlemen of good quality.

Of what *might* happen, George thought wistfully as Edith was herded upstairs by a suddenly zealous Mrs. Mansfield, remembering how close Edith's lips had been to his.

How he'd struggle with his dreams tonight.

# CHAPTER 10

TODAY WAS THE day before Christmas Eve. Today would see the wrapping of small gifts to be distributed two days hence. Tonight would see the lighting of the yule log, and tomorrow night, the ball. The ball! Her heart fluttered even as tension tightened her midsection. *Please, Lord, give me a chance to make amends.*

Edith bit her lip and glanced out the library windows to where the white blanketing the trees and grounds had proved an early gift. "It looks so beautiful yet very cold," Edith murmured to her mother, seated beside the fire.

Mama glanced up from her book. "I'm so thankful we are not at home having to heat such a place and that we have no need to venture out of doors today." A sweet smile crossed her lips. "And that Margaret has such an extensive library."

"One can never have too many books."

"Indeed."

Dear Mama. She'd enjoyed these past few days reading and conversing with friends, so much so that they'd scarcely seen each other except at meals and in the evening. Lady Grantley's insistence that the young people be allowed to spend so much time together might have initially raised eyebrows, but everyone seemed quite relaxed and untroubled by such things now.

Everyone except Edith.

She could have sworn George had wanted to kiss her last night.

And not a kissing ball in sight! Even in the darkness of the ballroom, she had seen the way his eyes had focused on her lips, had noticed the way he'd leaned toward her. If they hadn't been interrupted, she might have finally known the thrill of his lips on hers. Again.

Shame twisted within. She should never have let him kiss her last year. Should never have—

"Ah, Edith, here you are." Lady Grantley moved into the library. "And Catherine too. I trust you are enjoying your stay?"

"It has proved most relaxing. Thank you, Margaret," Mama said.

"And you, Edith? I hope you'll remember to get some rest for tomorrow night's festivities?"

"I will endeavor to do so," Edith promised, motioning to the whiteness outside. "You do not think the snow will affect people's ability to travel to the ball?"

Lady Grantley's eyes widened. "You think people might be unable to attend?"

Remorse that she'd caused alarm softened Edith's tone. "You must forgive me for thinking about such practical matters, but—"

"Whatever shall we do? I had not thought we would experience such wild weather, let alone that it may preclude attendance at the ball!"

"Perhaps conditions will calm soon," Edith soothed.

"We shall certainly pray so. The ball simply must go on. You would be disappointed if it were canceled, would you not?"

This was said with such a significant look at Edith that she could not mistake her godmother's meaning. "I would be disappointed, yes," she owned. For shallow as it might be, she *did* wish George to see her looking her best. Perhaps it might induce opportunity to talk, to finally explain the terrible set of circumstances that had led her to utter those foolish, foolish words.

"I would hate to think the preparations for that would be for naught," Lady Grantley said, a crease between her brows.

"Perhaps it might be prudent to ensure the evening doesn't run too late," Edith suggested. "People may appreciate an earlier night, especially given the church service the next day."

Her godmother sighed, the worry knitting her forehead clearing. "Oh, you are such a sensible thing, aren't you?"

Just what every young lady longed to be called, Edith thought wryly.

"Edith is such a comfort to me," Mama said with a fond look. "These past months would have been ever so much more challenging if I had not had Edith's practical thinking and levelheaded ways."

Her throat tightened, and she clasped her mother's hand, giving it a gentle squeeze. Perhaps this enforced time at home had held a blessing in disguise.

"I'm sure Edith would prove to be quite the asset for a man seeking a capable wife, for someone who might happen to run an estate and needs a wife who can offer practical advice as well as speak to all manner of people."

Edith's cheeks grew hot.

Her godmother nodded. "Yes, well, if this snow continues, I think it would be wise to ensure the night ends early. Our neighbors must be able to be transported safely. We only have one sleigh, after all."

And ferrying everyone back to their homes with only one sleigh might prove an impossible task.

"Besides, I don't mind owning to you both that my first consideration is for the pleasure of my houseguests. And we have been such a merry company, haven't we?"

Edith nodded dutifully.

"Tonight shall be quite wonderful! Now, I wanted to ask you both if you have ensembles suitable for the evening."

"Of course," Mama answered for both of them.

"Good. Now, Edith, I hope you don't mind, but I would like to have a comfortable chat with your mother here."

A private chat? "Of course." She rose, placed a bookmark in her own book, and moved to the drawing room, from where she could hear lively chatter.

"Oh, Edith, come and join us," Miss Hammerson called. "This looks like such fun."

Edith moved closer to where a small table held a dish of raisins and almonds. The smell of brandy hung in the air.

"Join us," Mr. Drake said with a smile.

"Oh, do," Lady Anne said, adding, "You know it's said that whoever snatches the most treats from the bowl will meet their true love within a year."

Edith's gaze connected again with the man she'd once thought was her true love. She ducked her head. If only.

She joined the others around the table, needing to lean to reach the bowl. Brandy was poured over the bowl's contents again, and then it was set alight. Shivers prickled her spine.

"Ready? Go!"

Edith joined the others in the age-old chant.

> "Here he comes with flaming bowl,
> Don't he mean to take his toll,
> Snip! Snap! Dragon!
> Take care you don't take too much,
> Be not greedy in your clutch,
> Snip! Snap! Dragon!
> With his blue and lapping tongue
> Many of you will be stung,
> Snip! Snap! Dragon!
> For he snaps at all that comes
> Snatching at his feast of plums,
> Snip! Snap! Dragon!
> But Old Christmas makes him come,
> Though he looks so fee! fa! fum!
> Snip! Snap! Dragon!
> Don't 'ee fear him but be bold—
> Out he goes his flames are cold,
> Snip! Snap! Dragon!"

She snatched as many nuts from the bowl as she could, her nimble fingers soon amassing quite a small pile. The flames nipped and stung her fingers, but she joined the others in laughing at the excitement. Finally, the blue flames died away, and they were left with their piles, of which Miss Hammerson's was the greatest.

"Oh, well done to you," Mr. Drake said.

"Now you shall meet your true love," Lady Anne prophesied, adding with a sly look, "Unless you've already met him."

Miss Hammerson's cheeks pinked to match her gown, her swift upward glance at Mr. Drake confirming Edith's suspicions, making her wonder how long it might be until that enterprising young gentleman found Miss Hammerson underneath a kissing ball.

"I wonder who received the lucky raisin," Miss Mowbray said.

"The lucky raisin?"

"Lady Grantley said that one of the raisins contains a gold button, and whoever has that can claim a reward of their choosing."

Thus followed a frantic minute as everyone searched through their piles of raisins to find the button.

"Aha!" Mr. Bannerman held a small gold object aloft. "It seems I'm the fortunate one today."

"So what shall you claim as your reward?" Lady Anne asked.

He smiled, taking in the faces around him, before his gaze returned to rest on Edith's face. "Miss Mansfield, I wonder if you might do me the honor—"

She swallowed, heart thudding hard.

"—of taking a stroll with me."

"Oh!" What? He did not wish to claim the first dance tomorrow night? Disappointment bit with a savagery she did not expect. She sought to hide it with a small smile. "Well, of course."

"A stroll?" Lord Sculthorpe scoffed. "That's all?"

Mr. Bannerman bowed. "Hardly all, when such a stroll is to be enlivened with Miss Mansfield's gracious presence."

"If you say so," came his lordship's disgruntled reply, before saying sotto voce, "I wonder if that will involve strolling under a kissing ball?"

Edith could feel her cheeks flaming, and sought to change the subject. "Lady Grantley was saying some people might struggle to come to the ball tomorrow, due to the weather conditions."

This comment precipitated a general movement to the windows, from which they could see the bend and sway of the white-capped trees outside.

"It certainly is wild and windy," Mr. Drake observed.

"Perfect for staying indoors," Miss Mowbray agreed.

"I do hope conditions ease so we can make the church service on Christmas Day," Edith murmured.

"As do I," Mr. Bannerman said, claiming her attention once more. "After all, we would not be gathered together in this way, save for the birth of the Christ child, for Whom this holiday is named."

"Yes."

For a long moment she was caught in the hazel depths of his gaze.

When next he spoke, it seemed only for her. "The child Who grew to be a man, our Savior, Who died on a tree, Whose life and death and return to life again reminds us of grace and forgiveness and the second chances God gives."

A rush of emotion gathered behind her eyes. She ducked her head and bit her lip. Oh, she needed to talk with him, and soon. With his talk of second chances, the wisp of hope that had materialized days ago had sprouted wings. Perhaps God might allow a second chance for her too.

———◆✕◆———

That night after dinner saw the house party engage in another of the Christmas traditions.

They assembled in the great hall, where the yule log gathered several days ago sat in pride of place within the hearth. Lady Grantley retrieved a shallow wooden box from the mantelpiece, slid it open, and withdrew a sliver of wood.

"This remnant is from last year's yule log, with which we light this year's log and remember that the coming of Christ overcomes the darkness."

The candles were snuffed, save for one either side on the mantelpiece, whose flickering flames cast eerie shadows around the room. Edith inched closer to her mother and gently grasped her hand. *Heavenly Father, please let this coming year be a brighter one than the last.*

A spark from the flint, and the sliver of wood was soon aflame, and a footman bent to apply the flaming wood to the kindling beneath the massive log. A few puffs of breath saw the flames soar and the wood catch and burn. The company stood solemnly for long moments as the fire grew brighter.

Oh, how important it was to remember that goodness triumphed over darkness, that Christ's life was always there to light the way. Edith drew in a smoke-tinged breath, exhaled. Whatever happened this coming year, she need not fear; God would be with her still. And she'd remember this moment, that in the darkest hour, Jesus had triumphed over evil once and for all.

She shifted, the back of her right hand touching another. Strange warmth danced, and she glanced up. Sure enough, Mr. Bannerman was studying her, the electricity pulsing between them matched by the heat in his eyes. She jerked away, suddenly overwhelmed by the roaring emotion.

"Well, now that is done, I wonder if we should go to the drawing room and have some music." Lady Grantley turned to Mr. Bannerman. "George? Would you be able to lead us in some carols of the season?"

He cleared his throat, took a moment longer to answer. "Willing and able, ma'am."

"Very good." She waved a hand, encouraging everyone to go inside. "Please take a seat near the pianoforte. Let's sing in the season proper."

Edith drew in a deep breath and moved to sit beside her mother on a sofa that did not offer a direct view of the pianoforte—or its performer. She needed time to regain her composure, time to pretend his nearness didn't still affect her. She needed time to sort out the mire of emotion he always evoked—

"Miss Mansfield?"

Her head snapped up at his voice.

"Would you mind accompanying me?"

Oh no. His words might be innocuous enough, but that deep tone in his voice . . . Oh yes, she minded very much. How could she feign indifference with this audience when there was so much to be said in private?

"Oh, now that would be delightful," Lady Grantley said, gesturing Edith forward. "Please, Edith. I've always thought you made a wonderful pair."

She hoped the earlier yule-log episode might account for her hot cheeks. To refuse would seem churlish, so she dipped her head and acquiesced and moved to where Mr. Bannerman sat waiting.

"You are most unscrupulous, sir," she murmured between stiff upturned lips.

"Me? I simply requested your company. You are such an adept performer, after all."

This felt like a performance, that was true. If she could only reach the end without betraying her tumbling nerves.

"George? Edith? What song shall we sing?"

"Edith?" he said, eyes intent on her. "What do you think?"

She dragged her thoughts back to the matter at hand. "What about 'Come Thou Long Expected Jesus'?"

He nodded, as if he too remembered their previous performances of the song, then said, "This first song may not be familiar to everyone, but I hope by listening to the words you'll understand why we chose it."

He then played the opening chords and began to sing.

"Come, Thou long expected Jesus, Born to set thy people
  free,
From our sins and fears release us, Let us find our rest in
  Thee."

Edith joined in the second verse, her voice lifted in a harmony as they sang about Israel's strength and consolation. Then they moved on to sing about the birth of the Savior child and for His rule in their hearts and world. This last was like a sung prayer for those gathered, some of whom looked at her with puzzlement, listening to the performance of a Wesley song she was unsurprised not many knew.

The notes died away, and there was a smattering of applause before Mr. Drake said loudly, "Can we have something a little jollier, please?"

"Certainly." She turned to Mr. Bannerman. "Apparently we need to sing with more joy."

"That leaves only one choice, does it not?"

She smiled at the sparkle in his eyes and returned her attention to Lady Grantley and her houseguests. "I hope you know these words."

Mr. Bannerman began the familiar chords of "Joy to the World," and smiles lit the faces of those assembled.

> "Joy to the world, the Lord is come, let earth receive her king.
> Let ev'ry heart prepare Him room, and heaven and nature sing."

Mr. Bannerman offered a harmony in the second verse that added a new dynamic and brought a lift to her heart. Oh, how good it was to sing with him again. How good to sing praises to One most praiseworthy. How wonderful to remember the Lord had come to make His blessings flow far as the curse is found, to recall the glories of His righteousness and wonders of His love. Oh, how *good* it was to sing to God.

The music finished with a flourish and a demand for more.

"Oh, surely it is as if heaven and nature sing when you two sing together. We need another carol, please," Lady Anne declared.

Edith turned to Mr. Bannerman and murmured, "Do you sense 'Tidings of Comfort and Joy'?"

"I do indeed," he said with a grin that made her heart glow. "Do you sense an a cappella version?"

She smiled. "I do indeed."

He pushed back the piano stool and came to stand beside her, then picked up her hand and pressed it slightly, and they began.

"God rest you merry, Gentlemen, let nothing you dismay,
For Jesus Christ our Saviour was born upon this Day.
To save poor souls from Satan's power, which long time had
     gone astray.
Which brings tidings of comfort and joy."

Edith harmonized on the next two verses, adding a descant in the fourth, then blending harmoniously with Mr. Bannerman on the fifth and final verse.

"Now to the Lord sing praises all you within this place,
Like we true loving brethren each other to embrace,
For the merry time of Christmas is coming on a-pace,
And it is tidings of comfort and joy."

They held the last note, then bowed, and she grew suddenly conscious that he still held her hand, and he was now gazing at her again, deep into her soul, as if wanting to offer his own form of comfort and joy. No wonder everyone was looking at them with wide eyes.

"That was beautiful," Lady Grantley said, wiping her eyes. "Truly, your voices blending like so is a gift from heaven."

Edith's skin prickled. She withdrew her hand, curtsied, and hurried to her seat.

Mama held a tremulous smile. "Oh my dear, when George looked at you just now, it gave me such hope that perhaps there might still be a chance."

Perhaps there might be. God had performed more than one miracle at Christmas before. She dared peek across to where Mr. Bannerman stood with their hostess, talking in low, urgent tones. She needed to speak with him. Needed to. But how could she while the house was filled with curious guests? *Heavenly Father, please give me a second chance.*

Mr. Bannerman straightened, his gaze returning to fix on her. The rapid tattoo of her heart increased. She offered a smile, then ducked her head. Surely her mother would not mind if she and George were to take that stroll. And should they happen to pause under a sprig of mistletoe . . .

"You must speak—oh!" Her mother gasped and placed a hand on her midsection. "I do not feel quite the thing."

"Mother?" Edith rose and knelt beside her mother's chair. She was extremely pale, and her forehead held a sheen. Edith's chest grew taut.

"Forgive me, but I do not feel at all well."

"Do you wish to retire?" At her mother's nod, she continued, "Do you feel well enough for me to accompany you to your bedchamber?"

"Oh, but it appears someone wishes to talk with you."

Edith glanced at George. He did indeed seem to be moving toward her.

"You should explain things to him," her mother whispered, plucking at her sleeve.

Yes, she should. But she shook her head. "Let's get you upstairs and settled."

She held out a hand and assisted her mother to stand, refusing to glance in Mr. Bannerman's direction. She could not bear to see the reproach sure to be found in his eyes. Yes, she desperately longed to speak with him, but she loved her mother, and family must come first.

"Oh, dear Catherine." Lady Grantley fluttered to their side. "Whatever is the matter?"

"Mama needs to rest. She does not feel well."

"Oh my dear, of course! I wonder if it was the fish," she continued. "I thought it had rather a peculiar odor—but are you leaving too, Edith?"

Edith avoided the question, offering murmured apologies to their hostess, whose face held the distress Edith could feel churning in her stomach.

"I shall send for the servants and the doctor at once," her godmother assured.

"May I be of assistance?" a deeper voice asked.

She sucked in a breath, caught a trace of sandalwood, and dared look up into George's face. "Thank you, but—"

"I would be very thankful for your assistance, Mr. Bannerman," Mama said weakly.

"Of course."

His kindness toward her mother wrenched fresh appreciation toward him, especially when her mother seemed to falter halfway up the stairs and suddenly sagged against Edith. He wrapped an arm around her mother's shoulders and helped her up the stairs, all the while murmuring gentle encouragement.

Tears stung Edith's eyes. How considerate he was, how stubbornly helpful, how good. But there was no chance to express such sentiments, save for offering him a short word of thanks at the door of her mother's bedchamber, where they were met by the waiting housekeeper and a maid.

He inclined his head. "It's my privilege to serve you in any way, Miss Mansfield."

She bit her lip to stop the tremble, thanked him once more, and shut the door.

And later, after settling beside her mother, whose illness had resulted in a bout of retching that made Edith glad Lady Grantley had sent for the doctor—and that Edith had followed her conscience to put her mother's health above her own inclination—she drew a deep breath and slowly exhaled, noting the evening's events with a trace of irony. Family might come first—family, she thought wryly, always seemed to come first—but soon she *would* finally explain things to George Bannerman. *Please, Lord.*

# CHAPTER 11

———•⚬•———

THE PLATTERS OF savories and sweet pastries and cups of wassail punch held little interest. All he wanted was the chance to speak with Edith once and for all. Over the past few days he'd sensed a gradual thawing, something that had culminated in her permitting him to hold her hand during their final song last night, but he'd been proved wrong previously. His godmother had captured him immediately after the carol singing, which had precluded any further chance to talk then. And any hope to talk later had been dashed by her mother's sudden illness.

He'd learned that Mrs. Mansfield was feeling better today and had hoped Edith would make an appearance, but she had not. Concern had prompted quiet inquiry to his godmother, who had said Edith was well, merely resting before the ball. The knowing look in her eye had made him invent an excuse to be elsewhere. He did not want an audience. He wanted Edith, alone. Perhaps there might be time tonight.

His godmother moved from where she had been welcoming some of the local notables—today's milder weather having permitted travel to the dinner buffet preceding the ball—and spoke to the group where he stood.

But he couldn't speak—his attention focused on the entry, where another figure dressed in deep green made everyone else fade to insignificance.

His heart hitched. Beautiful. Edith was simply beautiful. Her hair held gold-red highlights, the gown draped her form to admiration, her cheeks and lips holding a rosy hue. His pulse scampered in his veins.

"George?" his godmother said. "I declare, you did not hear one word of what I just said."

"Forgive me. My mind was agreeably engaged elsewhere."

"One need hardly guess where," she said dryly.

He swung to face her. "I simply must speak to her."

"Then do so. None of us are getting any younger."

"You are quite right, ma'am."

She chuckled. "Oh, I do like it when gentlemen say that to me. It gives me such a feeling of confidence, even if it may be misplaced at times." She peered up at him. "You will speak to Catherine?"

"Edith's mother? Yes. I'll do so now."

"Good, good."

"Lady Grantley?"

Miss Hammerson stole his godmother's focus, so he turned to see Edith talking with her mother. He moved to join them, when Lord Sculthorpe placed a hand on his arm and requested his attention.

"Forgive me, Sculthorpe, but I really must speak with Miss Mansfield."

His lordship guffawed. "Bet that's not all you want to do with the pretty lady."

George forcibly removed his hand. "Please do not speak about her in that way."

"Oh, but it must be said. You are a sore trial to us all, Bannerman. Hardly got eyes for anything else save your Miss Mansfield."

And that was the problem. Despite the best efforts of his god-mother and Lady Anne. "She's not my Miss Mansfield," he muttered.

"Not yet anyway. Now, be a good chap and lend me your ear for a moment."

But George refused to be moved. "I'm sorry. I can be at your leisure as soon as I've had opportunity to speak with Edith and her mother."

"Edith, is it, eh? Well, if that's how you want to be."

"It is." How much wassail had the man had to drink?

"Well, good luck to you, I say."

"Thank you."

He moved to catch up with them, when a loud voice said behind him, "Miss Edith! Bannerman wants a word."

Edith turned, and the assembly stilled. This was certainly not what he desired. He bowed to her mother and said in a voice he hoped did not carry far, "Mrs. Mansfield, I am glad to see you are much improved from last night."

She inclined her head. "Thank you for your assistance."

"I hope you might be so good as to let me speak with you for a few moments."

"You wish to speak with me?" Her brows rose, and she glanced at Edith, then returned her attention to George, her gaze assessing. "Forgive my candor, Mr. Bannerman, but I really feel the person you *should* be speaking to is my daughter."

"Mama!" Edith hissed.

"Well, you certainly cannot carry on this way any longer, Edith. It's quite tiresome. You are neither of you children, nor will you ever have any until this gets sorted."

"Oh, Mama!" Edith's eyes looked as wide as his felt.

"Please, Edith." He faced her, silently begging her to look up at him, waiting until she eventually did. "I need to speak with you. You know we need to talk."

She bit her lip, but her gaze didn't falter. Eventually she said, "Very well, then."

"Ladies and gentlemen," his godmother announced, "we have a ball to begin."

The ball. A chance to hold Edith in his arms, however briefly. And then later, a chance to talk. This night would at last bring some resolution. *Please, Lord.*

The sound of musicians drew them into the ballroom, and he couldn't help but note Edith's quick glance at the alcove, the site of their almost-kiss two nights ago. She turned and caught his gaze, her cheeks pinking to a delightful color.

He drew closer and said in an under-voice, "I hope matters can be brought to a more satisfactory conclusion tonight."

The rosy hue deepened. "You shouldn't say such things, sir."

"No?" He smiled. "I simply refer to our talk later tonight."

"Oh."

That look she wore appeared awfully like disappointment. His chest knew a double thump of anticipation.

"Now, gentlemen, please claim your partner for the first two dances."

George turned to Edith. "Miss Mansfield, would you do the me the honor?"

She glanced at his outstretched hand, then up at him and nodded.

The next half hour passed as one of the most glorious of his life. Edith in his arms, smiling up at him as if she couldn't believe it either. Edith, laughing softly at his murmured compliments, the sound instilling hope that things might finally work out as they ought.

The music reached its conclusion, and they turned and applauded the musicians.

"May I procure you a glass of punch?"

"Thank you."

Edith's sweet smile held the promise of a kiss, and he hurried to fulfil his task. But when he returned, it was to see Lord Sculthorpe whisking her away to join him in a country dance.

Edith sent George a look of apology over Lord Sculthorpe's shoulder, a look that appeased him somewhat. He placed the glass on a small table, and contrary to his desire to simply watch the object of his desire, invited a young lady—the daughter of a local squire—to join the set that was forming. Better to fulfil his role as a gentleman than risk his godmother's displeasure.

Another dance passed, and another. But despite the fairness of his partners, none could compare to his Edie. She was lovely, she was sweet, and tonight, after their shared explanations, she *would* be his.

There was a break for a light supper, and then the dancing resumed again. But he'd lost all interest in dancing, in anything really, save for his upcoming talk with Edith. During supper, he'd snatched a few moments with Mrs. Mansfield and obtained her blessing, and now he was simply biding his time to share with Edith those things he'd been ruminating over for months now.

The last dance was called, and he rushed to claim Edith's hand. Three dances might be considered akin to a declaration in some circles, but as far as he was concerned, this was. "Please."

Edith nodded.

Their dance held the same joy as before, his rapid pulse as much induced by the sweetness of her scent drifting to tantalize his senses as it was in anticipation of their upcoming conversation. As the music drew to its concluding notes, he drew her apart and asked, "Are you ready to talk?"

She dragged in a deep breath. "Yes."

He grasped her hand, and with a nod to her mother, drew her from the ballroom and out into the hall where the yule log burned steadily. From behind him, Aunt Margaret clapped her hands for attention, then said in a carrying voice, "Tonight has been a wonderful celebration of the season in preparation for the quiet reflection of the Christmas Day church service tomorrow. I thank you all for coming and trust that my neighbors will have a safe journey home."

Edith paused. "Should we not stay?"

"Not if we don't want to be interrupted." He drew Edith toward the conservatory, as per his godmother's instructions.

"The conservatory?" he had questioned during their earlier conversation.

"Yes. Tonight. So you can talk."

"While the ball is on?"

"Well, as soon as you can steal away. I shall ensure the others are distracted by that silly hiding game, so you need not fear. Now, if you have any *nous* about you, you will slip in there as soon as you can and start your begging or explaining or whatever it is you must do to make that sweet girl listen to you."

He wrapped an arm around her and kissed her cheek. "You truly are the most devious of godmothers."

"And the best," she said tartly. "Don't forget that."

"And the best," he'd agreed, hugging her again. "And no one else will come in?"

"The footman will lock the room once you've slipped in. No one will have the key except me."

George hoped his godmother would remember this as he now twisted the conservatory door's handle and drew Edith inside, shutting the door quickly before they were spotted.

"What are we doing in here? Lady Grantley said this room is restricted."

"And so it is." He led her to where the fountain trickled peacefully. "To all except us."

Her eyes widened. "She knows?"

A sound like that of a key in the lock came. He exhaled. "Aunt Margaret wants us to be undisturbed. She said as soon as the neighbors have been sent home, she will encourage the others to participate in the hiding game."

"The hiding game?"

He nodded, and she released her hold on his arm, moving forward to sit on the seat near the fountain and fan herself. "I'd forgotten how warm this room is."

"Would you like a drink?"

"Thank you, no." She peeled off her gloves and kneaded her forehead, her posture one of defeat.

"Edith?" Should he have waited? Was she frightened to be alone with him? "I did not mean to concern you. I simply want to talk."

"George—"

She'd said his name!

"I want—no, I need to talk with you too." Her head drew up, her eyes shiny with tears. "I . . . I am so terribly sorry."

"My dear." He hurried to sit beside her and captured her hands in his, savoring the softness of her skin. "Please help me understand. Why did you say yes and then refuse me the next day?"

She sighed, a sound that could have been drawn up from her toes. "I could not say at the time. I wanted to write and explain, but my grandmother would not hear of it."

Her grandmother?

"Grandmama, my father's mother." She swallowed, looked down at their entwined fingers, then back up at him. "I don't think you ever met her, did you?"

He shook his head.

"She . . . she didn't want us to ever say anything, but I simply must. You deserve the truth."

He braced internally. *Lord, give me grace, and help me understand.*

"When we met two years ago, I . . . I was captivated. You were so kind, so smart and funny. You believed as I do. You were everything I thought wonderful—everything I still think wonderful," she corrected quickly, her dusky-sweet eyes steady on him. "And you know those times we spent together, times like last night when we'd play and sing—"

"And times like tonight when we'd dance together. Like we were made for each other."

She nodded. "Like that." She wet her bottom lip. "I had this sense that we were supposed to be together."

"As did I. Which is why I proposed, and was overjoyed when you accepted, and then devastated when you said the next day that you'd had a change of heart and could I please forgive you, but you must renege." He shook his head, the agony of a year ago still somehow raw. He lifted the corners of his mouth in a hollow smile. "See how those words pierced my soul, never to leave?"

Her eyes brimmed, and he regretted bringing up her pain. But if they were to truly move forward, the depths of their shared pain needed to be brought into the open. The time for hiding in shadows was done.

"I'm so sorry. I . . ." she dashed at a leaked tear. "I was so happy that night, and so was Mama, but when we went to speak with Father, he was not at all pleased."

"But why? I did not understand why he refused to see me when I wished to ask for your hand. I always thought he liked me."

"And so he did. Until"—she swallowed—"until . . ."

He pressed her fingers gently. "Until what, dearest Edie?"

"Until he told us he'd lost all his money and wanted no one to know."

George blinked. "What?"

"Father lost the Mansfield money in a series of bad investments, and his shame was so great that he grew extremely ill and would barely speak to anyone in those last weeks."

His heart stirred with compassion. "Oh, Edie."

"Mama was beside herself, sick with worry. She didn't want to advertise Father's misfortune and tried to plead with him that my being married to you would be a release of burden—" She broke off, her lips twisting wryly.

"I'm sure she didn't mean to suggest you were a burden," he assured.

"I know. Mama has been so patient. She's always been patient. She tried to explain that marriage to you would be best for me, but Father refused to listen and would not countenance such a thing."

"But why?"

"He said you would know from the marriage settlements how little he could truly offer, and he would not be shamed like that." She gave a bitter laugh. "The Mansfield pride has a lot to answer for."

"Oh my dear girl." He longed to draw her in his arms but still needed to refrain until further explanations could be sought and finally given. "You mentioned your grandmother."

She nodded, squeezing his fingers as if she could draw strength from him. "Grandmama came to stay in those last weeks before Father died. When she learned what had brought on his apoplexy, she was determined we would never speak of Father's losses again. She was always such a strong-willed person, that Mama and I could scarcely breathe in our own house without needing her permission. She would not countenance you, or any of our acquaintances, learning our circumstances and insisted your letters be returned. I'm so wretchedly sorry."

So that explained that. Her eyes, brimming with tears, drew forth forgiveness. One of the things he'd always loved about Edith was her consideration to others. Her duty to a strict grandparent was something he understood, even if it had been to his detriment. "And your family's house?"

"Grandmama had to pay down the mortgage, had to pay our household bills." She glanced down. "You cannot know the shame."

Oh yes he could. "My family has not always been judicious with finances either," he owned. At her quick glance up, he hastened to assure, "We are more secure now, and I have given your mother a reckoning of my account and assets." His lips twisted. "The estate's focus is on achieving farming success now."

"Farming? Truly? How wonderful that would be."

"You really think so?"

"Oh yes." Her eyes shadowed. "Not that I could ever admit to such a thing whilst Father and Grandmama were here."

"Forgive me. I was away, so cannot quite recall—is your grand-mother still alive?"

"She died this past June."

"Then please help me understand—why was nothing said then?"

She withdrew her fingers, bowed her head. "By that time so many months had passed that I felt sure you would want nothing more to do with me after I refused you. I knew myself to have wronged you, and I felt so ashamed." Another tear trickled down her cheek. "And then when Grandmama died and it seemed as if Mama and I were finally free of the promises we'd been bound to, I learned that you had gone abroad, and I could not chase after you anymore, especially as I was sure my behavior had given you such a disgust of me. I have sometimes wondered in these past days if you still hate me for what I did."

"Oh, Edie, never!"

"You say that now, but I know I could never forgive such unsteadi-ness of heart should our positions be reversed."

He drew nearer, dared to wipe away the tear quivering on her chin. "It's a good thing I am so forgiving."

She laughed but shook her head. "You shouldn't. We treated—*I* treated—you abominably."

"You, my dearest, sweetest Edie, did not. Although you still could."

She blinked. "I beg your pardon?"

"I once thought my heart broken, but that would be nothing compared to the pain I would feel if you were to tell me tonight you would refuse me again."

"What do you mean?"

He slipped from the seat to kneel in front of her, possessing her hands. "Dearest, sweetest Edith, I have never stopped loving you. I admit I wanted to leave the country because the pain of staying was too much to bear, and I welcomed the thought that family distractions might help heal my heart. But I never stopped loving you."

"Really?"

"Really." He picked up one of her hands, then the other, and kissed the backs of them. "I could never love anyone the way I love you," he added hoarsely.

"Never?"

"Never. You are the only one for me."

"But Lady Anne?"

"Was simply trying to promote my cause with you. Surely you did not think me enamored by her?"

"I wondered."

"Truly?"

She nodded. "I just could not fathom that you might still hold me in regard. Not when I'd hurt you so badly."

"Regard is such a weak word for the depths of my feelings, my love. There has only ever been you."

Her eyes seemed to fill with stars as a sweet smile lit her features. "Only me?"

"Only you," he repeated, gaze pinned on her. "Oh, my dearest, darling girl. I love you. I want to make you happy. Please do me the greatest honor and say you'll be my wife."

Her mouth sagged. "Really?"

"Really."

He waited, insides roiling. If she said no—

"Oh yes! Yes, please. Oh, George—"

Anything else was lost as his lips took passionate possession of hers. His arms drew her close as their kiss continued in a symphony of wonder, of yearning, of restored promise. Heat cascaded through his heart, pounding against his chest, while around them the warmth and floral fragrance and birdsong enveloped them in nature's embrace, as if heaven itself were sealing this moment with its blessing.

She pulled away first, a dazed expression on her face. "Oh, George."

He grinned at her blushing cheeks, at the way she patted down her hair. "I'm afraid, my dear Miss Mansfield, that you'll need to smooth your hair again."

"Why?"

He pointed above them, where his Christmas decoration hung sedately, the great strands of mistletoe promising many more kisses could be had.

"Oh dear." But her smile contained both invitation and promise.

He chuckled and drew close again for another lovely, long blissful minute.

"Was this what Lady Grantley had in mind when she said to use the conservatory?" Edith said a short time later, her head tucked up next to his as they listened to the nighttime song of the birds and splash of fountain, contentment wrapping around them as a cocoon.

"I rather expect so."

They shared smiles and another moment of awed wonder—how good was God?—then he drew up short. "Oh dear, I forgot."

"The others are still hiding!"

And their laughter filled the room and filled his heart with freeing joy.

# CHAPTER 12

A WONDERFUL, LANGUOROUS feeling seemed to have settled in her limbs. Edith stretched like a cat, keeping her weighted eyelids closed. What a delightful dream that had been, so marvelous in its detail. She pressed a finger to her lips and smiled. Her eyelids sprang open.

"Oh!" Her smile stretched. This was indeed real. George *had* proposed. He had kissed her—several rapturous times. A burble of laughter escaped. Oh, how she loved dancing at balls. Oh, how she loved Christmas kissing balls! She rolled to her side as memories from last night begged for attention. Dancing with him. The sweetness of his kiss. His whispers of ardor and promise. The security and strength she'd found in his arms. The feeling that the past months of uncertainty and pain were far behind.

She bit her lip, but her joy could not be contained. Oh, how *good* was God! Oh, how wonderful to know such grace! Even if not everyone had exhibited such a quality last night.

Another quiet chuckle released. She supposed she could not blame the other houseguests, for they had indeed been hiding for a *very* lengthy time awaiting Edith and George. Eventually they had given up, and Miss Mowbray had apparently grown most insistent that they be found—or so Lady Anne had said—and when the laughter from the conservatory finally caught their attention, Lady Grantley had succumbed to their pleas and unlocked the door, and they'd been found in their loverlike pose.

She hadn't cared a whit. Mama's look of delight at their explanation had covered any discomfiture demonstrated by the others, George's hastily murmured question to Mama receiving a warm hug in assent.

"Well, all I can say is, it's about time," Lady Grantley had said, a look of something like smugness creeping across her face.

Somehow Edith doubted that was all their hostess would say, but she didn't mind. The Mansfield pride had well and truly tumbled, but she knew how futile such a facade was now. There was no room for pride, not when life begged to be lived.

And what could it matter now, when today was Christmas, a chance to enjoy the Savior's birth, enjoy the exchange of gifts (George had hinted he had something rather special he wanted to give her), and a wonderful meal, all in the company of the man she loved, the man she knew without a doubt loved her too.

She stretched again, the lightness of her heart filling her mind and soul. Oh, how wonderful today would be!

→✕←

"Good morning."

She smiled and hurried down the last few stairs to where George waited. "Glad Christmas to you, sir."

He grinned, drew her hand to his lips, and murmured, "It would be an even gladder Christmas should you call me by my name."

Breath caught at the intense look in his eyes. "Happy Christmas, George."

"It is indeed, my love, because you are mine, and I am yours, and all shall know that this is so." He bent and kissed her. "Come to the conservatory with me."

"But do we not need breakfast before the church service?"

"This shan't take long."

Her heart hitched. That sparkle in his eyes . . .

Edith allowed herself to be led to the conservatory, where the sweet song of the birds and warm scented air proved heady contrast to the wintry white outside and beckoned them forward to revisit the place where their troths had been pledged.

"Dearest, darling Edith." He bent and kissed her thoroughly.

Oh, how sweet this was. How wonderful to hold and be held in such a way. Desire tingled through her veins, dazzling her senses. When she finally caught her breath, she managed to say, "Is that what you wanted to give me? I declare a degree of disappointment if you feel that such a thing needs to be given only once a year."

He chuckled. "I plan on making sure you never need feel any disappointment." He swiftly kissed her again, then withdrew a gold-wrapped package from his pocket. "I hope this will suffice."

Oh, how sweet he was. She accepted the gift and carefully removed the tissue paper to reveal a small box. Her heart beat even more loudly. She glanced up, saw his look of intensity, and smiled. Then she opened the lid. And gasped.

A delicate gold band held a posy of small pink and cream pearls, centered by a diamond and braced on either side by two more gold-etched flowers. "Oh, it is beautiful!"

"Then it is appropriate for you."

He drew the ring out and gently pushed it onto her fourth finger, where it glimmered in the light.

"Oh, it is perfect." She leaned up to kiss his lips. "Thank you."

"I'm happy you approve."

"How could I not? It is the most perfect betrothal ring in all of history." She smiled, tilting her head. "I'm surprised you would have such a thing with you. Have you made it your practice to travel everywhere with this ring?"

He chuckled. "When I learned you would be here, I ensured that it came with me. I'm so glad to finally see it sitting there on your finger."

Finally? She wrapped her arms around his neck and hugged him, drawing in his delicious sandalwood scent, wishing she could turn back the years. He must have bought this last year and decided to hold on to it despite her refusal. Oh, how special was this man. "Thank you for believing in us," she murmured against his cheek.

"Thank you for saying yes." He pressed a kiss to her hair, and the canaries resumed their song.

———•⸭•———

The church was crowded. It seemed the snow had not hampered any-one's efforts to attend, and Edith was conscious of George's near-ness throughout the Bible readings, and the sermon, and the songs. Mama had been delighted with the ring—indeed it seemed Mama would likely live in a perpetual state of delight these days—and Lady Grantley's renewed congratulations and well-wishes had been echoed by the other guests.

She sighed with pleasure, and George gently squeezed her hand and helped her stand as the next hymn was announced.

"How appropriate," he murmured in her ear.

She smiled and held up the hymnal. Oh, how true. Oh, how good was God. Oh, how wonderful to sing this song about her Savior next to this man who would soon be her husband. And she opened her mouth to sing.

"Joy to the world, the Lord is come, let earth receive her king.
Let ev'ry heart prepare him room, and heaven and nature sing."

# FAR AS THE CURSE IS FOUND

## AMANDA BARRATT

*Soli Deo Gloria*

*It is only with the heart that
one can see rightly; what is essential is
invisible to the eye.*
ANTOINE DE SAINT-EXUPÉRY

# CHAPTER 1

*November 1816*
*London, England*

EVEN THE SKY wept at the sight of him.

Dwight Inglewood, the Earl of Amberly, stared out the rain-streaked window of the carriage. London, that grand and fabled city, wore the raiment of a storm. Thunder growled. Thick clouds hung low in the sky. Rain pelted the carriage roof. Pedestrians, dark-garbed blurs of movement, hurried down cobbled streets. Wagons and carriages clogged the thoroughfares, their churning wheels splattering muddy water. Buildings bore the universal hue of washed-out gray, reducing even the finest architecture to something mean and shabby.

He yanked the curtain closed, enveloping the carriage in darkness.

As a boy, he'd feared the dark and what it might contain. Now, darkness had become his sanctuary. Night, his refuge.

He leaned against the velvet-upholstered seat, the steady drum of the rain lulling his taut nerves a fraction. Had madness besieged him when he'd first contemplated traveling to London? In Yorkshire the plan had seemed a simple one, a means of offering a salve for the wound he'd inflicted upon the lives of those who'd once been close to him. He would journey from Amberly Hall to Berkeley Square, gather what items he wished, finalize arrangements via the post for the townhouse to be sold, and return to the Hall.

In this act, there could be reparation.

He had steeled himself for the tightness in his chest, the prickle at the back of his neck, the acceleration in his pulse that would accompany his first departure from Amberly Hall in well over a year. Nevertheless, as it so often did, mental pain transposed itself into physical, regardless of how well he prepared himself.

The wheels rattled over the cobblestones. Time had become an immaterial thing, but he marked the passing minutes all the same. Five. Ten. The carriage stopped.

He had arrived.

Reaching out, he pushed open the carriage door. He hesitated, staring at the space where the closed door had previously blocked the light. Rain-scented air hit his face. Slick cobblestones and the gray facade of his townhouse met his gaze. He calculated the time it would take to walk from the carriage to the entrance. Thirty seconds. A minute. Couldn't be more.

The storm had darkened the sky. Rain fell in sheets. No one would be voluntarily strolling Mayfair today.

Hardening his jaw, he stepped out. Rain pinged against his cloak and the exposed skin of his face. His staccato footfalls matched the cadence of his heart.

The townhouse was a modest one, as Mayfair houses went, its pale stucco exterior marked with pilasters on either side of the black front door. Delicate iron balustrades framed the three windows on the third floor. In every window, the curtains were drawn.

He climbed the stone steps. At the door, he reached past the folds of his cloak to the pocket in his coat, where the key lay. He bent slightly and inserted it into the lock. The key stuck.

He drew in a sharp breath, glancing over his shoulder. A jagged streak of lightning split the sky, illuminating the street. Empty. For the moment.

He wrenched the key again. The door groaned open. Dwight slipped inside, closing it firmly behind him. He'd have relocked it, but Robbins, the coachman, needed to carry in the single trunk, as well as his own bags.

For a moment, Dwight stood, the weight of the key in his gloved fist, shadows surrounding him. Somewhere came the sound of squeaking and the patter of scurrying feet.

Truth be told, he far preferred the company of mice than a retinue of liveried servants lined up to greet him. Steps echoing, he crossed to the table where silver salvers containing calling cards had once been placed beside a vase of fresh flowers arranged by his mother. He fumbled in the semidarkness until he grasped a candlestick and stubby candle. A tinderbox sat beside it. Within a minute, a flame flared to life. He lifted the candlestick, holding it aloft.

Holland covers cloaked the furnishings and paintings, outlines of murky white. Cobwebs hung like gossamer threads, and dust floated in the air. Flickering candlelight illuminated the muted tones of the ceiling mural of Perseus and Andromeda. His gaze lingered on the figure of Perseus astride his winged horse, finding the beautiful Andromeda chained to the rocks, awaiting the sea monster who would devour her.

Mother had commissioned the mural when he was six. As a child, he'd not known why she'd chosen it. But the following years had snatched away any veil of innocence. For Mother, there had been no Perseus.

Even after both their absences—his to the war, hers to the grave— memories of her whelmed him afresh. Her bell-like laughter as she came down the stairs in an evening gown, her silk skirts rustling, the scent of violets enveloping him as she bent to give him a good-night kiss before setting forth for a dinner or ball.

Other memories. Her sobs echoing down the hall in the middle of the night. Like the cries of a wounded animal in a trap. He'd jumped out of bed, wanting to go to her, but his nanny held him back. *"No, Master Dwight. You mustn't disturb her. She needs rest."*

Years passed. Mother stopped crying. In the place of tears, a glassy haze owned her eyes. It wasn't until it had been too late that he'd learned of the laudanum that had robbed the spark from her gaze, stealing far more than just that.

Dwight sucked in a sharp breath.

*Desist.*

Enough of memories that would bring no one and nothing back.

He was in London because of two people he cared for dearly—her and Arthur. That was the sum of it. He'd do what he'd come to London to do and then return to Yorkshire. Never again would he set foot in this city.

For while he remained here, there could be no rest from the phantoms of his past.

—•✕•—

*Recall dimpled cheeks and sweet coos, and this night will soon end. Remember her warmth in my arms, each precious intake of breath as she sleeps, and I can forget their words, ignore their gazes.*

*Think only of her, and I can endure anything.*

Jenny Grey had run those words through her mind until they'd become as timeworn as the floorboards she now trod. Carrying a loaded-down tray, she wove her way through the crowded public house, the bitter scents of beer, gin, and ale mingling with stale sweat and cheap tobacco. Sputtering candles cast a grimy light. Perspiration slid down her back despite the drafts of cold air blowing through the room whenever a customer entered or exited.

Balancing her tray with one hand, she lifted a full tankard of ale and placed it in front of a blockish-faced man who sat hunched forward in his seat. He swiped it up and guzzled it down. She moved away. Her ears rang with the din of raised voices, raucous laughter, and the smack of a fist striking the bar. An ache throbbed in her temples. Pain drove talons into her lower back.

Only an hour more.

At the next table, a man pawed the tawdrily dressed woman perched upon his knee. She blinked sooty lashes up at Jenny in a gaze askance, before turning her attention to her lover and the gin Jenny placed before them.

Tray empty, Jenny hastened through the low-beamed room toward the long oaken bar. Customers sat on stools in front of the high counter, half-empty drinks grasped in their fists. Those at the bar weren't there for conviviality and were thus less likely to address her. They came to sate themselves and leave. The men at the tables were another matter.

Mr. Chadband, the proprietor of the Three Kings, refilled tankards behind the bar. His protruding middle strained against the buttons on his waistcoat. Upon second glance, one noticed the fasteners were not mere buttons, but teeth. Each one, Mr. Chadband boasted, had once belonged to men whom he'd brawled with and bested. A shiver crawled over Jenny whenever she looked at the yellowed appendages.

"What you doin' up 'ere, gel?" Mr. Chadband slid a tankard brimful with frothing beer in front of a man in a faded coat. "Customers just come in." Impatience flickered in his shrewd eyes. "Get on with it."

Jenny ducked her head and hurried toward the new arrivals. Two men had settled themselves at a corner table. As she approached, a hoot of laughter rang out. Tray beneath her arm, she stopped in front of the table.

"What'll it be, sirs?" She kept her words and gaze perfunctory.

"Well, now, lemme see." The man nearest her scratched his bristled chin. "I'll 'ave me a pint of ale. That is, 'less you're on offer, dearie." He leered.

She ignored the comment and turned to his companion. "For you?"

The man squinted at her. "Ain't very friendly, now is she, Bill?"

She pretended not to hear him, keeping her gaze on the space above their heads.

*Mama will be home soon, my sweet.*

"She ain't indeed." The first man shook his head, laughing. "He'll 'ave a beer, luv."

She spun and hurried toward the bar. Behind the counter, she worked to fill the tankards. Fizzing liquid swirled into the tarnished mugs. Bile no longer rose in her throat at the yeasty scent, but as she filled the tankards to the brim, her hands shook.

Tray high in one hand, she threaded through the tables. A solitary voice slurred out a bawdy tune. The groan of the door announced a new arrival.

She sensed the heat of their gazes on her as she set down the tankards. Her breath shuddered in. Keeping her gaze on the dirty floorboards, she turned away. A sharp tug on her apron strings jerked her backward. The empty tray clattered to the ground. She whirled around.

"Let me go." This time she met Bill's gaze with a direct stare. Her hair straggled around her hot cheeks.

"Now, lookie 'ere, missy." His hand snaked around her wrist. "I don't pay good coin to be ignored."

"You pay to drink." She'd learned not to let her voice tremble. "If you wish for something else, I'd be happy to get it for you. Otherwise, you're keeping me from the other customers."

The other man leaned back in his chair, chuckling. "Ain't you the 'igh an' mighty lady? Beggin' yer pardon, Yer Grace." He swept his hand in an affected bow. "Bill ain't learnt proper manners around the fairer sex." He grinned, flashing stained teeth. "Me neither, come to think of it."

Bill tightened his grip, ragged fingernails digging into the flesh of her inner wrist. She hid a wince. "If you don't let me go, Mr. Chadband will toss the both of you out on the street. And I wouldn't count on having all your limbs intact afterward neither."

"Is that so?" Bill sneered.

"Yes." She didn't break her stare, waiting for his grip on her wrist to slacken the barest amount so she could wrest free. "That is so."

"This ain't a very friendly place, Tom. Perhaps we'd best take our business where it's more appreciated." He released her.

Her wrist ached. Legs shaking, she bent to retrieve the tray. Footsteps clomped behind her. Something brushed her backside. A hand. She jerked, standing upright. The two men walked past her and headed for the door, chuckling. Bill glanced over his shoulder, shooting her a wink.

The door slammed. She stared after them, clutching the tray against her chest. The sensation of his hand on her lingered, making her want to scrub every inch of her skin.

As she had once before, when another man's touch had stained her. His hands had been clean, manicured, his pinky adorned with a signet ring. He'd smelled of bergamot. That day, he'd not coaxed her with sweet words or attempted to mask his real interest in befriending her. That day, he'd said not a word. The look in his eyes as he'd cornered her in the empty schoolroom . . .

"What's the matter with you, gel?" Mr. Chadband shouted. "We've got customers waitin'."

She pulled in a breath and fought to stop the shaking that had overtaken her, then walked toward the table of new arrivals. She couldn't afford to lose control of herself. The words she'd spoken to the men had been untrue. Mr. Chadband would do nothing for her. He'd made that a condition of the job—she must work hard and give him no trouble. In the months since she'd begun, she'd grown a thicker skin than she'd thought she could possess. Lewd words and crass insinuations barely penetrated the wall she'd built around herself.

Yet encounters with men like Bill were a painful reminder of how truly vulnerable she was. Would always be.

She approached the table, scarcely looking at its occupants. She did not need to see their faces to grant their requests.

"What will you have, sir?"

*Remember her warmth in my arms . . .*

"Pint of gin."

*I can forget their words, ignore their gazes.*

"Right away, sir."

*Think only of her, and I can endure anything.*

# CHAPTER 2

————◆✕◆————

EVERY FIBER OF his being craved air that did not smell of dust and the past.

After the bells tolled midnight, Dwight locked the townhouse door behind him and strode into the darkness. He'd remained inside his first night in London, listening to the sounds of the city and awaiting sleep that had not come. In Yorkshire, late-night walks had become his salvation. If he were to make his stay in London of any duration longer than a day or two, he could not deprive himself and expect to maintain his sanity.

His footfalls reverberated as he walked, cloak billowing in the wind. In Yorkshire, the air was scented with the sharp, earthy wind that blew over the moor. In London, every breath was tarnished with an undertone of smoke and grime. He'd never really noticed it, until now.

Though the city never truly quieted, a kind of stillness wrapped around him. He had no destination in mind, only a driving need to escape the confines of a place forever reminding him of the bygone.

On either side of him, the mansions of Mayfair slept, pale exteriors bathed in moonlight. Their rooms of gilded pretension were unoccupied now, as their owners forsook the city for their country estates. He recognized most of the houses, recalling the balls and dinners held there, the dances he'd shared with marriageable misses beneath glittering chandeliers, the rich wine, muted laughter, and unabashed luxury.

And Louisa. Always Louisa.

He clenched his jaw.

He'd be hanged before he let thoughts of her mire him tonight.

He quickened his pace, strides lengthening on the rain-glossed cobblestones, putting Mayfair behind him. Time passed. The murky glow from lampposts did little to penetrate the darkness. Fog whispered around him in tendrils and threads. He walked onward on streets that changed from cosseted grandeur to an underpinning of destitution overlaid by showy cheapness.

Covent Garden. As a young cove about town, he'd taken in many a performance at the district's theatres. At this hour, the Corinthian-columned entrances heralding an evening of enchantment lay cold and empty. Beggars hunkered in doorways. Beneath the vacant-eyed gazes of some lurked a feral desperation that would not hesitate to prey upon the weak.

Scantily clad women stood in the shadows of buildings, rouged faces and gaudy dresses announcing their availability for the right price. As he passed, one of the women gasped and drew back with a little shriek.

The fear in her gaze burned his back all the way down the street.

The fog-laden air held the scents of cheap spirits, human and animal waste, and decaying garbage. A drunk vomited on the side of the street. Dwight walked on.

He'd begun this walk in a veritable Olympus, only to find himself at the heart of an inferno Dante himself might have gained inspiration from. He did not fear for himself. His skill with the pistol he carried would protect him from harm. Yet what of those forced to eke out their livelihoods in such a place? Living each day with mankind at its basest and most pitiable crouched upon their very doorsteps?

In all the time he'd spent in London, had he ever stopped to consider such a thing?

With a sickening rush, he realized he had not.

In the distance, the mournful knell of a bell marked one.

He should return. To the ice-tipped solitude of the townhouse and another night likely as sleepless as the one before. He'd gathered and packed the items he wished to take with him to Yorkshire. A packet of letters penned in his mother's hand and tied with lavender ribbon. Her portrait. A lap desk once belonging to his grandfather.

Everything else would be sold at auction along with the house. He had only a few more rooms to search through, could be done with his part by the end of tomorrow, be on his way to Yorkshire the day after. His solicitor would see the sale carried out.

Dwight spun on his heel and started back the way he'd come.

Then out of the darkness, a scream rent the air.

———•✕•———

Shawl wrapped tight around her shoulders, Jenny hurried out the public house door and into the night, shoes slipping on the slick cobblestones. Another night's work was at an end. If only the coins wrapped inside the handkerchief in her apron pocket could offer them more than the barest survival. When she'd kissed Anna before leaving for the Three Kings, her nine-month-old daughter's skin had been too warm against her lips. She prayed it wasn't fever and that she'd return to find Anna sleeping peacefully.

Cold scraping her lungs with every breath, she reached the end of the street. Meager light illuminated the shadowy figures of two men. She pulled her shawl tighter and walked faster, head bent.

"Well, well, if it ain't little Miss 'igh an' Mighty."

Her heart jolted. She looked up. The men who'd been at the Three Kings stood a pace away, shoulder to shoulder, blocking her path.

She spun, grabbing her skirts in her fists, and ran. Heavy footfalls pounded behind her. She skidded on a slippery cobblestone. An iron grip grasped her arm, hauling her back as if she were no more than a cloth doll.

"We've been waitin' for you." Light cast wavering shadows on his bulldog-like face. The scent of sweat and the sickly odor of opium turned her stomach. She fought and twisted against his hold. His brawny arms pinned her tight, pressing her against his body.

A yellow-toothed leer curved the other man's lips. "Seein' as you don't know manners, we reckoned we ought to teach you some. Ain't that right, Bill?"

She scanned her surroundings, panic a sharp taste in her throat. No one would come to her aid, not at this hour and not in this part of the city. She had no choice but to fight her way out.

*God, please help me.*

How brittle the prayer seemed.

Summoning all her strength, she screamed and slammed her foot down on his. He yelped and reared backward. She shoved free. And ran. Plunging blindly forward, the sound of their boots echoing in her ears, her breath heaving in ragged gasps.

*Almost to the end of the street.* Her heart banged against her breastbone, her lungs burning. *Turn the corner and . . .*

Her feet flew out from under her. She spread her hands to break the fall.

She hit the ground facedown with a force that smacked the breath from her. Grit scraped her palms. She'd landed in a puddle reeking of rotten eggs.

Gasping out a breath, she pushed upward and fought to rise. Her feet tangled in her skirt. Footsteps crunched. The two men stood over her.

"Ain't so 'igh and mighty now, are you?" Bill yanked her to her feet.

She clawed and kicked and screamed as he shoved her against the side of a building, her head jarring against the brick. Pain slammed through her skull. His breath wafted hot across her face as he leaned in, hands sliding down her waist.

Unbidden, a tear trickled down her scraped cheek. No. This could not be happening again. She could not survive it a second time. Her mind went foggy, as if forgetfulness were the sole protection she had left.

*God. Please.*

A startled *oomph* penetrated the haze. Cold air replaced the heat of Bill's body against hers. Jenny raised her gaze.

A figure cloaked in black stood over the now-prone man. Like a specter rising out of the fog, garbed in a midnight cloak and hat. A mask, also black, concealed the left side of his face.

For a breathless instant, she stared at him.

"By Jove, 'tis a ghost!" Bill's companion gasped out.

The figure stood, gloved hand steadily aiming a pistol. "Get out of here." The words were a low snarl.

Bill's companion bolted, flinging a glance of wide-eyed terror over his shoulder. The man—it had to be a man—roughly nudged Bill's body with the toe of his boot.

Her lungs tightened. Was he dead? The muffled groan emerging from him denied it.

For the second time, she lifted her gaze to the man who'd rescued her. He towered over her, features inscrutable behind his mask. Bill's companion had called him a ghost. Fog swirling about him, she could almost believe it, if she believed in such things.

Could it be she'd been spared one fate only to fall prey to another?

He stared at her steadily, unmoving. A panther poised to strike. Her limbs shook, and her pulse thudded in her brain.

She would be no one's prey.

Steeling herself, she did the only thing she could think to do.

Jenny ran.

She strained for the heavy sound of boots as he pursued her, envisioned his cloaked form overtaking her and capturing her with a grip she could not escape. But only her own jagged breaths and stumbling steps met her ears.

After what seemed hours, she reached the building that was the closest thing to shelter she had in this vast and frightening city. She stumbled up the steps and down the corridor. Her hands trembled as she pulled the key from her pocket and unlocked the door. She stepped over the threshold, blinking in the light of a guttering candle. Mrs. Grimsdale, the woman who tended Anna while Jenny worked, snored in her chair. Jenny knelt beside the crate and lifted Anna into her arms, cradling her warm weight against her chest, kissing her downy curls.

"Mama's here, my love," she whispered, closing her eyes, breathing in her baby's sweet scent. "Mama's here and all is well."

# CHAPTER 3

SMOKE. CANNON FIRE. The groans of the fallen and dying. He'd stopped counting the hours. The world was a blur of red and blue uniforms. Reload. Aim. Fire. Reload. Aim. Fire. Flying bullets whizzed like deadly hail. The soldiers were trampling over the prone bodies—trampling because they had no choice.

Someone cried out. That voice. He knew it so well.

"Arthur!" he shouted. "Arthur!" Through the haze, he glimpsed Arthur's crumpled body. He dropped to his knees beside his friend. His breath stuck inside his chest.

*I promise to keep him safe, ma'am.*

He had to keep that promise.

Arthur stared up at him, eyes large in his ashen face. He'd been hit in the shoulder. Blood soaked through his uniform.

"Dwight," Arthur croaked.

Dwight yanked his shirt free from beneath his uniform, tore off the bottom, and tied it around Arthur's wound. "You're all right, Art. Everything will be all right." He hauled Arthur up, heaving his body over his shoulder with a grunt.

"Hold on, Art," he called, gripping his friend's body.

"I'm . . . holding . . ."

He ran through the smoke, the press of men, the vicious fight unfolding around them.

The ground shook. Fire erupted. The blast threw him airborne, separating him from Arthur like they were two dice in a cup. Pain. Blinding. Searing.

Darkness.

His scream jolted him awake. Dwight lurched up, gasping and shaking. Sitting forward in the center of the bed, sheets tangled around his legs, he dragged his hand through his sweat-damp hair.

Were the dreams to be his punishment for life, a ceaseless haunting of his spirit? His heart slammed against his rib cage. *Boom. Boom.*

It sounded like cannon fire.

He pulled in a serrated breath.

No bars or chains could be worse than the prison of his mind.

He sagged against the mattress, staring into the encompassing darkness. He'd find no more sleep tonight. He never did after the nightmares. If he was lucky, they woke him in the early morning, the pale light of dawn restoring a semblance of reason.

He was rarely lucky. After the dreams, the darkness he embraced because it shrouded him became his penance.

Stillness elevated every sound. A noise in the street below. The shifting of the house. His own rapid breathing.

London was making him worse than usual. If he were in Yorkshire, he'd have better control of himself. He needed the press of his fingers against the cool keys of the pianoforte, the abandonment brought by focusing on nothing beyond the blending of melody and harmony.

The day after the incident with the young woman, Robbins had returned from Oxford, where he'd driven the carriage to visit his cousin, and announced it had broken down on the journey home. That news had come four days ago. The carriage was still not in readiness. With his means of transportation unusable, and with no wish to return to Yorkshire via the public coach, Dwight had no choice but to stay in London until the carriage was in working order.

Each night, he walked the city at an hour when as few as possible would see him. Simply . . . walking, no destination in mind.

On the first night, he'd encountered her. First, by the sound of her screams, which he'd run toward until he came upon her. He recalled little about the men who'd accosted her, only that he'd rendered her attacker unconscious with a well-placed blow to the back of the head. He could still see her slight frame backdropped by a crumbling building, breaths coming fast, hair trailing down her cheeks like unspooled moonlight. How small she'd been. He'd forgotten how delicate a woman could be in comparison to his height. After the other man had fled, she'd remained still a moment, staring at him, gaze searching, as if she sought to find his.

He'd not much of one to find, unless one saw behind the mask.

Words had tumbled inside him. *Are you all right? Can I be of some assistance? What is your name?* In his former life, voicing any of those would have been easy. But they'd trapped inside his throat, and before he could set a one of them free, she'd fled. Lifting her skirts and plunging into the darkness. Vanishing, as if she'd been but a figment of unbridled fancy.

He didn't dare admit he'd walked the same streets again the following night, searching for her. Had he found her, he wasn't certain what he would have done. Introduced himself? *Ah, yes, I'm the man whose appearance frightened your assailants away. What was it the one called me? A ghost?*

He was thankful he'd been able to help her, but by the look in her eyes right before she ran, she'd been of the same opinion as her attackers. He'd become something to be feared.

The Amberly curse.

Each member of his family had owned their portion.

Apparently, fate had decreed this to be his.

————— ✛ —————

Head pounding and throat raw, Jenny dragged herself through the door of the Three Kings. She'd tried to get up yesterday but had only made it a few steps before a wave of dizziness sent her reeling. Somehow she'd managed to crawl back to her mattress, where she lay shivering and sweating with fever. Anna was feverish too. How she had cared for her daughter, she wasn't sure. It all seemed a blur—sponging

Anna's flushed cheeks with a damp cloth, preparing and feeding her gruel, and rocking her while Anna screamed and screamed.

Money for a doctor. If Anna worsened, somehow Jenny had to find it.

She couldn't afford to miss work again, though fever still burned her skin and ached in her joints. If she didn't work, they didn't live.

Mr. Chadband stood behind the bar, polishing a tankard with a worn rag. A few customers occupied tables—not as many as there would be in a couple of hours, and a blonde girl swept the floor, the bristles making a *swish, swish, swish* across the worn boards. Why was someone else sweeping the floor?

Jenny crossed the room, every step slow and painful.

*You cannot afford to be ill. You must not act ill or even allow yourself to feel ill. You have work to do. You have a child to support.*

The words bolstered her, and she greeted Mr. Chadband with her usual, "Good evening, sir," though it came out raspy.

He set the tankard and rag aside, regarding her in the dingy light. She straightened her shoulders. He must not think her unwell.

It burned to draw in a deep breath. "I'm sorry I didn't come in yesterday. I was ill. I'll work extra hours to make it up to you."

"That won't be necessary."

That was kinder than she'd expected. "Thank you—"

"Bella here'll be takin' your place." He drew himself up, the tooth buttons on his waistcoat straining. "Your services are no longer required."

She stared at him. She couldn't have heard . . . he didn't mean . . . "What?"

"You're dismissed." He reached into his pocket. One by one, he dropped five shillings onto the bar. They pinged as they landed. Five shillings. A week's wages. "Failure to report for work without notice means you don't work here no more. I knew when I agreed to take you on you'd be naught but trouble. I was right. You're jittery as a mouse, and you ain't friendly to the customers. Yesterday was the last straw."

She had to do something. This couldn't be happening. She couldn't accept this.

She took a step toward him. "Mr. Chadband." Shards of pain scraped her throat. "I'm sorry I missed work yesterday. I had the fever, and my baby did too. Please. I beg you to reconsider. I'll do anything you ask, but I must keep this job." If desperation had a sound, it was the tremor in her voice. "My baby and I need something to live on." She clasped her hands in front of her, as if in prayer. A gesture of complete helplessness.

Mr. Chadband coughed, pulling at his collar as if it itched. "Bella's my niece. She's been wantin' a job for a while now. She came by yesterday when you didn't arrive. I told her she could have it."

The brush of the broom against the floor had stilled. Tears slid down Jenny's cheeks. "Please, Mr. Chadband—"

His jaw hardened. "Enough. I won't have you in here wailin' like a pig and disturbin' the customers." His voice was cold. "Take your wages and get out before I call the traps."

In a daze, she picked up the scattered coins and slipped them into her apron pocket. She turned, glancing at the blonde girl who'd resumed sweeping. The girl couldn't have failed to hear the conversation. Bella didn't look at her.

Jenny trudged out of the Three Kings. Bitter wind scoured the early evening air. White-hot needles stung her lungs. For a minute, she stood shaking and lightheaded. Peddlers packed items into carts, closing their stalls for the day. A boy hung shutters on the building across the street.

*Dear God, what am I to do now?*

She owed every one of those shillings for rent, due in three days. Last week's wages had gone for food and heat. She'd nothing left to pay Mrs. Grimsdale to tend Anna—the woman had made it abundantly clear she took the task for sixpence a week, not for love of the baby. How would Jenny seek work with no one to care for her daughter?

Her head throbbed. Gritting her teeth, she made her way down the street, hunched forward against the icy wind.

*I'll go home and feed Anna, then hold her while she sleeps. Perhaps her fever will have broken by now. I'll think of something. Dear God, please. I have to think of something.*

# CHAPTER 4

⊶ ✠ ⊷

ANNA'S SMALL BODY convulsed as she coughed.

"Shh, now, my sweet." Jenny paced the floor, cradling her daughter against her chest. Her own teeth chattered in the chilly air, at variance to the fever burning her cheeks. They needed coal, but she couldn't afford any. She'd wrapped Anna in clothes and blankets, but the room was cold . . . so cold.

Was that why Anna's lips were blue? Because of the cold? Or was the cough and fever making them so? Anna coughed again, a thick, rattling sound that left her spent and limp against Jenny's chest.

"God," Jenny whispered through cracked lips. A cough spasmed her own body, and she bent double, Anna held against her. Tears trickled down her cheeks amid the hacking. "Please," she gasped. "Help us."

She couldn't count how many times she'd prayed that prayer over the past four days. At night before she slept. In the moments after she woke. During the hours she'd trudged to look for work, Anna in her arms. Over and over, she'd been told there was none to be had. Not as a seamstress, nor as a servant at a public house, nor as a charwoman. There had been a position as a scullery maid, and she'd done a thing that a month ago she'd have called horrible, unthinkable, and left Anna alone while she'd walked to the Mayfair townhouse to ask after it. But the starched butler at the door stated the position had already been filled. He'd followed his words by slamming the door in her face.

Anna needed warmth, medicine, and a doctor's care, or she might die. The truth pressed like a blade to Jenny's throat. She slipped her finger into the crook of her baby's closed fist. Usually, Anna grasped Jenny's finger with a grip so strong it made her wince at times. Now Anna didn't even stir.

*Oh, God.*

She could not watch her daughter die.

The Foundling Hospital.

Its name alone made her moan aloud.

What kind of mother even considered giving her baby into the care of others? What kind of mother could offer her child nothing?

Her chest contracted as a cough seized her lungs. She fought for breath and tasted phlegm. When it passed, she cradled her daughter, pressing their bodies together. For nine months, Anna had grown within her, and she'd pushed her daughter into the world in this very room. She'd been afraid to see her baby. Afraid when she looked into its face, she'd remember only the violation of the act that created the child. But the moment she'd held Anna, love had flooded her with a force unlike anything she'd known. Soul deep. Immutable.

She would give her life for the child in her arms.

*If she stays with me, she could die.*

What kind of world was it when the best gift she could give her daughter was to let her go?

Only for a little while. She'd find work, and then she would get Anna back.

Dully, she wondered how many mothers once thought the same.

She could not make this choice. But it had been forced upon her. Anna was hers and had been since the moment she first sensed the presence of life within her body. It was up to her to care for her daughter, even if the act left her shattered beyond repair.

"I'm sorry," she whispered against Anna's hair, tears sliding from her cheeks and landing onto baby-soft curls. "I'm so sorry."

Gently, she laid Anna in the box that was her cradle. Semidarkness coated the room. She picked up the blanket draped at the end of the bed. She'd knitted it from the softest yarn she could find. It had been the color of a robin's egg, but wear had faded it several shades and left it frayed in places. With trembling hands, she wrapped it around Anna. Everything in her wanted to draw this moment out and savor every touch, but there was no time. For her daughter's sake, she must sacrifice even these last minutes.

Anna in her arms, she left the room and descended the creaking stairs. The sky was starless, the street empty. A thumbnail of a moon hung like a splinter in the sky. Biting air burned her lungs.

She started down the street, Anna clutched to her chest. Her worn shoes slid on the cobblestones. She'd passed the Foundling Hospital when she'd first searched for work in London when Anna had been a slight mound beneath her dress, a flutter beneath her palm. Her feverish mind scrambled for street names. It would take her at least twenty minutes to walk—she must hurry. She broke into a half run.

Every step drew her toward goodbye.

Tears fell freely down her cheeks. Who would heed her at this hour? An insignificant girl running with a child in her arms. No one cared about her, least of all someone on a London street in the middle of the night. At least it wasn't day, when the gazes of the curious and censuring would have fallen upon her and shamed her all the more.

Each beat of her heart seemed to echo the same refrain. *How? To let her go and give her up, how can I do this thing?*

⸺✴⸺

Breath plumed from Dwight's lips, his strides long on the glistening cobblestones, his hat tipped low.

This would be his last walk in London. The carriage was ready, and he'd be on his way to Yorkshire at dawn. The items he wished to take sat packed by the door, and he'd drafted a letter to his solicitor with instructions as to the sale of the townhouse.

Every farthing would go to Mrs. Martin.

It was not in his power to see her son Arthur restored to her. But when he'd learned of her recent poverty, he'd grasped at the chance. Not to see himself redeemed in her eyes, for he would not have her know from whom the money came. Simply to care for her as Arthur would have wanted.

Movement caught his gaze. A shadow flitting across the street.

He peered into the darkness. Not a shadow. A woman.

Running with a bundle in her arms.

A sense of urgency pricked his spine. What reason would anyone have to be out so late, alone, and running?

He lengthened his stride.

She crumpled to the cobblestones.

He ran and knelt beside her. His breath caught. She lay motionless, face pale, eyes closed.

And in her arms . . . a baby.

The sight froze everything inside him. Had the fall harmed the child? Carefully, he lifted the bundle from her arms. An unnatural flush spotted the baby's round cheeks. Its eyes were open, but everything about the little one seemed listless. Blue tinged its lips.

The child was gravely ill.

Sheltering the baby in the warmth of his cloak, he looked down at the girl. Hair pale as moonlight fell over her shoulders.

It couldn't be. The woman he'd rescued? Impossible.

He stretched out his ungloved hand and laid it against her cheek. Heat radiated from her skin.

The young woman's eyes flickered open. She stared up at him with an unfocused gaze, wetting her chapped lips.

"I will not hurt you," he said quietly. "Please let me help you and your child."

"Anna," she murmured, struggling to sit up. A fit of violent coughing hindered her efforts. When the spell passed, she drew in a shallow, wheezing breath.

"If you hold the child, I can carry both of you."

She reached for the baby and cradled it against herself with surprising strength. "My sweet Anna," she breathed, or something like that.

He didn't have time to decipher the words. He had to get them out of the cold.

He lifted her into his arms. She was lighter than he'd anticipated, the angles of her bones pressing into him.

"Are you going to take her?" Fear stemmed from her voice.

He started down the street. "No one will take her." Somehow he sensed he must assure her of this.

"Then she will be safe?" The trembling in her body wrung something in him. Who was this woman, and what was she so afraid of? For the first time in recent memory, he did not assume himself to be the cause of the fear.

"Both of you will be," he said softly.

She relaxed, leaning her head against his chest. Cold stung his face, but he barely noticed it.

Moonlight guiding the way, he carried her home.

# CHAPTER 5

"YOU'RE SAFE."

It was far away. The voice. When Jenny cracked open her eyes, the room pitched like a boat in the middle of a storm. She closed her eyes again. She was hot. What was making her so hot? Something lay on top of her. A blanket. She thrashed and kicked, throwing it off.

"Shh. It's all right." Coolness covered her forehead, blessed relief from the heat. Where did the voice come from? Where was she?

"Anna!" She fought to sit up. Where was Anna? She saw something, a shadowy blur near her bed.

"Anna will be well. You must rest and get well too." Such a gentle sound. The closest thing to tenderness she'd heard in so very long.

Something lifted the back of her head. "Drink this." Bitter liquid filled her mouth, and she coughed, whatever it was running down her chin. The shadowy form was above her now. "You must drink it. For Anna." A spoon passed her lips a second time, and she tried to swallow. Again, a hand behind her aching head, lowering her down against soft pillows. "Rest now."

It was the last thing she heard before darkness again claimed her.

For three days, the fever gripped her. In those three days, Dwight scarcely left her side. Robbins had summoned a physician to treat both the woman, whose name he still did not know, and the baby, Anna.

The doctor had diagnosed both with fever and inflammation of the lungs, prescribing a tincture and recommending the room be kept warm and the patients wrapped in blankets to sweat out the disease. He'd suggested bloodletting, but Dwight speared him with a glare and said he'd not countenance butchery. When he'd taken ill with fever as a lad, a doctor had been sent for, and he'd had Dwight bled. From what he could tell, it had served only to weaken him.

After the doctor retreated, Dwight asked Robbins to find someone trustworthy to assist in caring for the woman and baby. Two hours later, Robbins returned with Mary Ellis, the daughter of a housekeeper whom Robbins had known in the days when the Inglewoods had taken part in the Season. When Mary arrived, Dwight had been holding Anna, trying to get her to take a dropperful of the medicine. He realized only later that for the first time since donning his mask, he'd been too preoccupied to care about either avoiding the other person or gauging their reaction. Whether Mary had been frightened of him at first, he hadn't bothered to ascertain. She'd set to work brewing a tea from some bark and herbs she'd brought, and had managed to get both patients to drink it.

Anna had begun to recover, the fever leaving her body after the second day, though her cough was still thick. Mary had left the sickroom to tend to Anna in the adjoining chamber, and as the candles flickered and darkness crept into the room, Dwight sat beside the young woman's bed.

When he'd carried her into the chamber, shouting for Robbins, the woman barely conscious, he'd tended the baby before turning to her. The woman's clothes had been wet and filthy from the grime of the street where she'd fallen. He'd undressed her down to her shift and clothed her in one of his nightshirts, which he'd warmed by the fire. She'd barely moved, and for a sickening moment, he'd wondered if it was too late and he was caring for a corpse. But he'd heard a low struggling breath, and exhaled a sigh of relief.

Now, she lay too still in the center of the bed. Everything was pale—the linens, her skin, the strands of her hair. Minutes ticked by, the shadows lengthening. His eyes grew heavy.

She groaned, and stirred on the bed. He sat upright, instantly alert.

"Please. No. I will work." She became more agitated, writhing and tangling the blankets around her. "Anna needs food." Her eyes opened wide, and she scanned the room with a frantic gaze. She lurched upward, coughing and choking. Her hair hung limp around her thin cheeks, and her eyes were hollows.

Panic vised his chest. It was like looking at his mother the month before she'd died.

"It's all right." As before, he tried to help her lay back down, but she struggled against him weakly.

Her unfocused gaze landed on him. "Anna. Where is Anna? Do you have her? Anna!" A cough racked her body, and he sat on the edge of the bed, supporting her as she fought for breath. When her coughing subsided, he brought the tea to her lips and helped her drink.

"Anna is safe." He placed his hand on her shoulder and eased her down against the pillows. She stared up at him. Her lips were pale and cracked, and her breath rattled when she drew it in. Was the fear on her face because of him or the twistings of her fevered mind? "Do not distress yourself." He kept his voice gentle. "Your child is well. We are caring for her."

"Who are you?" The question came scarcely louder than a breath. Before he could answer, her eyes fell closed. Her cheek turned toward the pillow.

He rose from the edge of the bed.

Mary came in. "I heard shouting."

"She woke and started calling for her baby."

Mary nodded. Wrinkles creased her dress, and shadows ringed her eyes. "Her fever still has not broken?"

He rested the back of his palm against her forehead and shook his head. "I'll let you know if there is any change."

"Yes, m'lord." She dipped a small curtsy and left the room. He resumed his seat.

*Who are you?*

Who was she? Did she have a husband somewhere, desperate with worry for his wife and child? Her slender hand bore no ring. Her voice was that of a gentlewoman, schooled in proper grammar, but her hands were rough, her nails ragged and chipped. He'd only grown more certain she was the same woman he'd come upon in the alley.

He'd seen enough of the world to recognize one who was truly alone in it.

She drew him. The truth of her life. Who she was. From where she had come. Her relationship to the child—mother? She looked almost too young to own the name. The reason she'd rushed through the streets carrying the baby?

There could be no denying she needed help. Though her hands showed the marks of hard labor, she'd not been well fed. Life, it seemed, had not been kind to her. In sleep, her features relaxed. But a faint crease remained between her eyes. As if even now she could not find peace.

Could he offer her refuge? For all he knew, she could be a criminal or a woman of ill repute. London's streets teemed with dissipation and desperate people. He could have unwittingly sheltered a person sought by the law.

Certainty settled inside him as he regarded the woman. Her features owned none of the hardness of one who'd lived a life of crime. Instead, they were almost . . . fragile.

Did a cord of communion bind all broken souls? Be that true or false, something pulled him toward her in a way he could not recall feeling since *before*. Undeniably, it shook him.

Whoever she was, from wherever she had come, if he could, he would help her.

# CHAPTER 6

JENNY OPENED HER eyes, blinking in the half darkness. She looked down at the length of the bed. A bed. White sheets. A room with indigo wallpaper and dark furnishings. She lifted her hand. She wore a shirt far too large for her, its sleeves rolled around her wrists. A fire crackled in a hearth to the left of the bed.

She swallowed. Dryness coated her throat.

Where was she?

Memories floated to the surface. Holding Anna while the baby coughed and then went limp. The almost physical pain of the decision to take her daughter to the Foundling Hospital. Running blindly through the soot-black night. Then . . . a male voice. What had he said?

Her gaze fell on a man standing at the curtained window. She must have made some sound, because he turned. Their gazes met.

Recognition jolted through her. That night in the alley, a masked man had rescued her.

The same man stood before her now, not six paces away. Then, garbed in a long cloak, fog clouding around him, aiming a pistol, he'd been a figure wrested from some dark imagination. Later, she'd asked herself if she'd simply dreamed the whole of it.

He wore no cloak now, simply an ordinary shirt and double-breasted waistcoat. A dark glove sheathed his left hand. Thick black hair tangled over his forehead in curling strands. A black mask covered the left side of his face. When she met his gaze, only the right eye looked back at her. There was no left eyehole in the mask he wore.

For the space of several breaths, they stared at each other.

Other memories wavered like shadows through her mind. He had been there for however long she'd lain in this bed. A deep, low voice had spoken to her, penetrating the haze of semiconsciousness. A hand had lifted her head and poured liquid down her throat.

*He had been there.*

Who was he?

"You're awake." It was the same voice that had spoken to her in the midst of the fever. Now, as then, it was low, gentle. At variance to his broad shoulders and imposing height. One slow step at a time, he crossed the space between them. She kept her gaze on him. As if by looking at him she maintained some control. Which could not have been farther from the truth.

He stood near the head of the bed. His right hand inched toward her. She drew back. His hand fell. Had he been about to touch her? "Have you still a fever?"

She shook her head.

Where was Anna? She strained for the sound of a baby crying but heard only silence. Was her daughter here?

The cold starkness of the other possibility grasped her throat and tightened it. "My baby." Her voice emerged gritty.

"Anna is safe." His lips moved—he was saying something else, but she didn't hear it.

Anna was safe. Her precious baby girl.

"Where is she?" She wasn't sure if she could believe him.

"She's sleeping. You may see her soon." Something akin to a smile edged his mouth. "That is her name, then? Anna?"

"Oh." She swallowed. "Yes. Her name is Anna."

Silence hung between them in uncertain threads. Outside, hooves clopped across cobblestones. "Can you eat something?"

She wasn't hungry, just tired. But in order to regain her strength, she must eat. She nodded.

"I'll have a tray brought in."

Vaguely, she wondered again how she had come to be in this man's house. Before she could ask, he turned, polished boots crossing the carpet. The door opened, clicked shut. Turning onto her side, she stared into the flames. Heat radiated from the hearth. She couldn't remember the last time she'd been in such a warm room. Burrowing into the blankets, she closed her eyes, the comforting sound of the fire lulling her.

Once again, the question rose.

Who was he?

———✳———

The fever had left her. Dwight couldn't remember the last time he'd been filled with such relief. As ill as she had been, he'd half expected a different outcome. But she'd eaten a bowl of broth prepared by Mary, who'd taken it to her. Afterward, she'd fallen asleep. With instructions to Mary to rouse him whenever she awoke, he'd retired to his room and slept deeply for the first time in days. Someone knocking on his door had awakened him, and Mary had said the young woman had woken and asked to see the baby.

He washed and dressed in a clean shirt, waistcoat, and coat, and made his way down the hall. The door to the bedchamber stood ajar. A soft voice drifted out.

"Look at you, my love. Are you crawling to Mama? Oh yes, you are. Yes, you are."

Through the crack, he saw the young woman sitting propped up by pillows while baby Anna crawled across the large bed toward her. "Such a big girl. Well done, Anna. Well done, my sweet." She lifted the baby into her arms and cuddled her close, kissing her cheeks.

The intimacy of the moment struck at his core. Mother and baby. Love given and received in its purest form. If only the rest of the world could be so simple.

He lingered outside, hesitant to enter the private moment. But he should not be standing in the corridor observing them unannounced. He rapped on the door.

"Come in," she called.

He opened the door. The young woman turned toward him. Though her face was still pale, it no longer held an alarming gray cast, and her eyes—a startling shade of lapis—were bright. Her hair hung in a thick braid over one shoulder. Anna grasped at its ends with tiny fingers.

"It's good to see you looking so well." He offered a slight smile.

No longer was she the frightened girl in the alley or the barely conscious woman in the throes of fever. Then it had not mattered who he was or how he appeared. Now, her health had returned enough for her to be aware of what she saw. He sucked in a breath, battling an overwhelming desire to flee.

There was a reason he lived in isolation from all but a few. New encounters were something he'd ceased to welcome. Yet here he was on the verge of one.

She gave an answering smile, hesitant and small. Several heartbeats passed. Her eyes met his. He tensed, expecting to read revulsion or mild shock at the very least. But she looked at him with a steady gaze. Cautious, yes, but without fear. "Thank you for caring for me and Anna. I do not know exactly how it happened, but I am grateful." She paused. "More grateful than I can express."

The genuineness in her voice and eyes, in those words of gratitude, unfurled something inside him. When had someone last thanked him?

When had he last done something worthy of thanks?

"I was glad to help." He paused. He'd conversed so easily once. Now, it took effort to form the words and voice them. Like pushing past a tangle of brambles to enter a clearing. "Glad I was there when you fell."

A shadow fell over her gaze, and she looked at Anna, still tugging on the ends of her braid. She absently disentangled the baby's fingers.

"I'm Dwight Inglewood," he said, realizing he'd not properly introduced himself. Not that omitting the *Earl of Amberly* qualified as a proper introduction, but somehow it didn't seem necessary to add his title.

"Jenny." Another pause. "Jenny Grey."

*It's a pleasure to make your acquaintance*, he almost said. A remnant from *before*. It had fallen from his lips like warm honey in countless ballrooms to countless young ladies and grande dames. But it was trapped behind the brambles and did not seem appropriate in these circumstances.

Deuce and blazes, he did not know how to greet her at all. Miss Grey? Mrs. Grey? Other than her name and her daughter's, what did he know about her beyond his own speculations?

Anna squirmed away from her place on Jenny's lap and started to crawl toward the edge of the bed. Jenny turned away from him to scoop the baby up. "And just where do you think you're going?" She playfully kissed Anna's round cheek and the baby squealed.

Dwight found himself smiling. When he'd first seen her, Anna had been so still. In the following days, as she'd coughed and battled fever, he'd feared she'd not survive.

To see her smiling and full of life . . . well, if miracles indeed existed, he'd count this as one.

Jenny settled the baby on her lap again. "May I ask how I came to be here?" A frown appeared between her eyes. "I'm afraid I'm a little hazy as to particulars."

"I was out for a walk. I saw you running. Then you fell, collapsed as if you'd fainted. I carried you here. You've been ill for five days."

"I see." The furrow deepened.

He had questions for her too. She had a lady's voice and elocution, but her clothes had been scarcely better than rags and her hands roughened by work. Would she answer them? In his experience, those with a past were loath to part with its secrets.

Still, he must know something of her. "What brought you out so late? I mean no impertinence, but you seemed in some distress."

She averted her face, looking down at Anna. The fire snapped. "I . . ." She raised her gaze. A troubled—no, haunted—look owned her eyes. "I've been unwell. One day I was too ill to go to the place where I worked. I managed to get up the next day, but when I arrived"— she stopped, moistening her cracked lips—"the man I worked for dismissed me. He'd already found a replacement. I could no longer afford for anyone to mind my baby, so I took her with me and tried to seek another position." She drew in a long breath. "I couldn't find one. Anna grew worse. Because I could not care for her, I decided to take her where others could. I was on my way when you . . ." Her words faded, and she didn't look at him.

She'd been on her way to abandon her daughter.

This young woman had bundled her child and run toward an orphanage or the workhouse because it seemed the best she had to offer. All she had left.

The rawness in her voice made it easier to break through the brambles. "Then I am glad I came to that street when I did. It's obvious you love your daughter very much."

Tears misted her eyes. "Yes. More than my own heart."

His throat tightened. In the past year and a half, he'd doubted the existence of love. The majority of humans were capricious, self-seeking creatures. Love was conditional, ephemeral, or not there at all. Yet it appeared before him now, written on this young mother's face. Love had spurred her to surrender her child in order to save her.

Could there be any greater sacrifice than that which required the rending of one's own soul?

He cleared his throat. "You may stay here as long as you wish. If there's anything you require, you need only to ask. Mary will attend you."

She shook her head, swiping a fingertip beneath her eyes. "I cannot accept anything more. I am a stranger to you. I will not impose upon your generosity for longer than tonight, if we might be permitted to stay that long. And I will see you are repaid in full for whatever expense you have incurred on our behalf—"

He held up his hand. "That won't be necessary. I wish for nothing from you and would refuse anything you offered. The recovery of you and your child is recompense enough." His words had come out firmer than he'd intended. Fault of his having used them so little in the past months. He cringed. "You should rest. I shall leave you now." He turned and crossed toward the door, sensing she watched him as he quitted the room.

In the corridor, he paused, staring at the blank spaces on the wall-paper where paintings had formerly hung. Dust floated in the air.

She'd said she would leave on the morrow. To go where? Her situation had not changed beyond her and the baby's physical recovery.

She had no husband. That much lay plain without her having to voice the words. Who was the child's father? Was he even among the living? If so, did the man care about Anna or her mother, or had he abandoned them? By all appearances, it seemed the latter.

Society would label Jenny Grey ruined and worthy of scorn. One who wished to uphold one's reputation did not associate with those of impure character.

But was her character impure? Those who condemned with a flick of a finger and a superior sniff were common enough among his class. He'd vowed never to follow their path. What right had he to judge what he did not know?

If she left, heaven knew what might become of her and her baby. Sickness and desperation had been merely allayed. Like shadows, they hovered, awaiting an opportune time to return. Six months hence, she could be back in the same desperate place. Only then, he would not be there.

Jaw set, he strode down the hall, determined to find a way to help her.

# CHAPTER 7

RISING FROM BED was harder than she'd imagined when she'd announced her intentions to leave. Jenny admitted fear had been at the root of those quickly spoken words. She'd vowed never again to be beholden to anyone, least of all a man. When last she'd been in that position, the results had shattered her. From that, she had still not recovered.

Though her cough had not completely abated and her legs wobbled when she walked, her daughter was well again. Jenny could begin once more to look for work.

And if her search proved as elusive as before?

It would not. She could not think that. What other choices lay before her?

*You may stay here . . .*

The man who'd taken her in held a mystery far surpassing the mask shielding his face.

Dwight Inglewood.

Despite his foreboding appearance, he'd spoken kindly to her. Smiled at Anna. She'd caught the genuine emotion in his voice as he'd said it was obvious she loved her daughter very much. And he'd offered to let her stay awhile longer.

Perhaps God had indeed heeded her desperate prayers.

But she could not remain with a man who was little more than a stranger. She knew nothing about him save his name and his disconcerting habit of walking the streets at night. Likely, this was his house. The bedchamber was finely appointed, though the cobwebs hanging from the ceiling and the dust coating the mantel gave evidence to its disuse. Of course, most of the well-to-do who owned residences in London only used them during the Season. What brought him here in the middle of November?

Pondering the man was a waste of time and energy, neither of which she had in abundance. The young woman named Mary had washed and pressed Jenny's clothes and left them over the back of a chair. Jenny crossed the room, focusing on putting one foot in front of the other. Halfway there, she stopped and took several slow breaths. She hated weakness in herself. Gritting her teeth, she slipped the too-large nightshirt over her head and picked up her dress.

By the time she'd finished, she was spent and breathing heavily. She made her way to the bed and sat on its edge. Mary had fashioned a bed for Anna out of a bureau drawer and soft blankets, and she had brought the makeshift cradle into Jenny's room last night. Anna still slept, curls golden against the creamy pillowslip, hands curled into tiny fists. Jenny's heart swelled.

Never again would she repeat the nightmare of that cold, dark room and the decision to give her daughter up.

But how could she be certain it would never happen? How could she be sure of anything in this hard, lonely life, least of all her own strength?

A knock sounded on the door. Had Mary brought breakfast? Last night there had been boiled chicken, potatoes, and preserved peaches—the best meal she'd eaten since the Carlisles. Jenny had wanted to wrap it in a napkin and save some for later, but hunger had overridden her willpower and she'd devoured every bite.

"Come in."

The door opened. Dwight Inglewood stood on the threshold. He wore a double-breasted coat of navy blue, beige trousers, and polished black boots. A black mask—the same one?—hid the left half of his face to just above his upper lip. What lay beneath it that he felt the need to conceal?

"Good morning." The formal greeting rubbed against her like velvet when she'd become accustomed to cheap wool. Since she'd woken from the fever, he'd spoken to her and treated her as a lady, when he must surely be aware she was not one.

"Good morning." She rose, standing before him in her worn gray dress, hair still in a loose braid down her back, tendrils falling around her cheeks. How untidy she must seem.

"Pray, do not get up on my account. I wondered if I might have a word with you."

"Of course." She sat on the edge of the bed. A chair stood near the wall at the opposite end of the room. Dwight carried it over. Before Mary had brought in Anna's cradle, the chair had sat beside the bed. Had he occupied it during her illness?

He sat, his right hand resting atop his gloved one, as if to cover it. He drew in a deep inhale, gaze on her. He'd a piercing stare, his eye a penetrating mix of blue and gray. She shifted. What had he come to say?

"Yesterday you mentioned you'd lost your means of employment. Where did you work?"

"I . . ." She swallowed. "I was a servant at a public house." Shame braised her cheeks. Though she was only nineteen, the regrets she carried were enough to buckle the shoulders of someone decades older. She'd been born in shame, and it had followed her through the passing years. Every landmark of her life falling in line after it, like dominoes.

His face showed no reaction—or perhaps the mask hid it. "Have you always done such work? If I may be so bold, you have the look of a lady."

A lady. She'd never been called that. Never thought of herself as such. She was a charity child, a governess, then . . .

"No," she whispered. "I was not always a servant at a public house."

"Have you family? Friends?"

She shook her head, voice barely audible as she answered, "There is no one." She couldn't bring herself to offer an explanation to this stranger. Her past was hers. To protect and to bear.

"And when I came upon you that night? Those men?"

"I did not know them." A shiver coursed through her. If he had not been there . . . "I fear I've not properly thanked you for coming to my aid."

"I did no more than any man of honor would have done." He looked down at his hands, as if she'd discomfited him. "Pray, forgive me, but are you often subject to such treatment?" His voice was quiet but with a hard edge.

Her breath shook when she drew it in. Fragments from that long-ago day flashed through her mind. Spots filled her vision. She fought for calm. "Not . . . often."

A minute elapsed. "I'm afraid I've not been forthright with you. My name is Dwight Inglewood, but I am also the Earl of Amberly. I have an estate in Yorkshire. Over the past two years, the number of staff employed there has been significantly reduced. At present, only four are in residence." He leaned forward. "I can offer you employment and a home for you and your child. Amberly Hall is a desolate place these days and has fallen into sore neglect. Robbins's sister, Mrs. Fletcher, currently handles the duties of both cook and housekeeper, an arduous task, as you can imagine. After training under her, you could in due course assume the role of housekeeper at the Hall, if such a position would suit you."

What manner of man was this? Masked man, earl. What other secrets did he hold? The directness of his offer startled her. He knew almost nothing about her—she had given him no letter of recommendation—yet he offered her a position at his home and the possibility of in time becoming the highest ranking female servant. Why? Why her?

She could scarcely grasp he was an earl, a member of the peerage, a man of title and estate. Was he in full possession of his senses? Other than the mask and his penchant for late-night walks, he'd not said or done anything suggesting he might not be lucid. And he'd cared for her and Anna while asking nothing in return.

What if he had . . . other intentions? She'd already been the prey of a man who thought because she was poor and friendless it made her virtue of no value and his for the claiming. She knew nothing of Lord Amberly, his family, his reputation. No knowledge was a poor kind of reassurance.

But wasn't she in danger wherever she went? The Three Kings had certainly been no haven. An unmarried woman without family living in the lowest parts of the city would never be truly safe.

Thankful he'd not pressed her for an immediate response, she faced him. "Why?" Perhaps a simple question could offer a window into his reasons. Although if one were a skilled actor, even the ugliest motives could be veiled.

"Because I've seen enough of the world to know its cruelties." His gaze held hers. "I would not wish you and your child to find yourselves in the circumstances you were in a week ago. I live a life of seclusion. I've no intentions of returning to London again. But if you can countenance a quiet life, I'd be glad to offer you a place at the Hall for as long as you have need of it. I can pay a fair salary and provide room and board. Your duties would be such that you could care for Anna."

Had someone asked her to leave London a month ago, she'd have refused. But a month ago, she'd had a means to earn her bread and had not almost given her child into the hands of strangers. She would be no more trapped by going to Yorkshire than she would be by staying in London. If there was one thing she knew how to do, it was escape.

*Lord, is this what You would have me do?*

Again, she searched his face, wishing she could read what lay beneath his enigmatic expression. He sat silent, rubbing his thumb in a circular motion along the fingers of his gloved hand. It wasn't her place to ask how he'd acquired his injuries, though the question tugged at her.

Though it seemed an improbable situation, what better option did she truly have? Fear, hunger, cold, coupled with endless hours of trudging through London seeking work there was no guarantee she would find.

She took a deep breath. "Very well, Your Lordship. I'd be most grateful to accept the position."

"You may regret it when you see the house." A half smile edged his lips.

Was he in jest? "I promise you'll find me a hard worker." She sat up straighter. Her physical state hadn't given much credence to those words. But she would show him she could work as hard and as long as he required.

He nodded, a brief gesture, as if the matter was settled. "We shall leave early tomorrow morning. You need another day to rest. The journey should take three or four days at the most, depending on the condition of the roads. If there's anything you wish to retrieve from your former lodgings, I can send my coachman."

"There are some things of Anna's." Little else. She'd sold almost everything to pay her way to London.

"If you write down the address, I'll send Robbins this afternoon." He rose. "We leave at seven. I shall not disturb you the rest of the day." He turned on his heel and abruptly left the room, the firm click of the door echoing in her ears.

Anna woke and began to fuss. Jenny stood and picked her up, gaze fixed on the door where Lord Amberly had exited.

The last thing she needed was to borrow another's secrets when already she held too many of her own.

✦ ✕ ✦

The journey lasted three days. Throughout the trip, Lord Amberly kept the curtains drawn, affording her no opportunity to view the passing landscape. The semidarkness of the carriage put her in mind of a tomb, and she was glad when they stopped to change horses or for the night. As his servant, it was not her place to question his preferences for darkness, nor engage him in conversation. Thus, they passed the majority of the journey in silence. She played with Anna and talked softly to her. Sometimes she fancied she caught Lord

Amberly smiling faintly at the baby's giggles and babbling, but he always retreated into the darkness too quickly for her to be sure.

Each night, they stopped at a coaching inn, and he ordered two rooms and dinner for them both on trays. He always escorted her to her chamber door, but she never saw him after, until the next morning. As they entered the inns, she noticed the way heads turned and gazes landed on the figure in the long black cloak and mask. He stood aloof, looking straight ahead and striding past them as if he neither saw nor heeded their gaping curiosity.

As a woman who'd carried the weight of an unborn child without a ring on her finger or a husband by her side, she knew the wounds the gazes of others could inflict. Whether one let the pain of them show upon one's face or barricaded it inside was simply a matter of management.

This morning, as he'd handed her into the carriage, he'd said they would reach Amberly Hall by nightfall. Her rough counting of the hours told her they must be nearly there. Anna slept, drool splotching the front of Jenny's dress. So much for making a tidy first impression on the other staff.

Who were they? Robbins seemed friendly enough, a man with a craggy face and plain speech. How long had he and the other staff known Lord Amberly? Did the earl have other family in residence? A wife? She'd never heard of Amberly Hall, nor of a Lord and Lady Amberly.

Likely Mrs. Carlisle would have had the answers and been aware of any circulating gossip. Of course, as a governess in her employ, Jenny had rarely been privy to the woman's prattle.

The carriage slowed, the crunch of churning wheels and horses' hooves muting, then ceasing altogether. She glanced at Lord Amberly. He sat staring at the curtained window, face hidden in shadow, lips set in a thin line.

A minute passed, then the carriage door opened. A young man in livery peered in, giving her a look of surprise. "Good evening, m'lord."

"Hello, William." Lord Amberly ducked low and climbed out of the carriage. He turned and held out his gloved hand to her—he wore gloves on both while traveling. Holding Anna, she placed her free hand in his. His leather-sheathed fingers kept a firm clasp on hers as he helped her alight.

The warmth of his palm penetrated through her chilled skin. When she stood on firm footing, she looked up. Wind tugged her hair into her eyes. "Thank you," she murmured.

He gave a brief nod.

Her breath stilled as she turned. Amberly Hall towered above her, a massive edifice of crumbling stone backdropped by a darkening sky. Dozens of windows stared back at her like empty gazes. Light glimmered from one; darkness shrouded the rest. Overgrown grass and weeds rustled in the sharp wind.

Never had she imagined a residence this vast and imposing. A house such as this held as many secrets as its master. She shivered, wind pulling at the ends of her shawl, holding Anna close. She glanced at Lord Amberly. He too stared at the house, a forbidding cast to his features.

He turned to her. "William will bring in your bag. Come."

She hastened to follow. The front door opened, and a woman came outside, carrying a candle. In the murky light, the flame cast a glow upon her features. Delicate wrinkles creased the corners of her eyes, her face framed by a ruffled cap. A chatelaine hung at the waistband of her apron.

"Good evening, m'lord." She bobbed a curtsy.

Jenny sensed the woman's gaze sharpening on her, and tightened her grip on Anna.

"Good evening, Mrs. Fletcher. May I present Miss Grey and her daughter, Anna."

Warmth emanated from Lord Amberly's body, and she pushed back the urge to lean into it. Though she'd been thankful for his protection on the journey, it was foolish to desire it now.

She dipped a curtsy, grateful the darkness hid the flush in her cheeks. Though she did not wish to begin her new employment on a basis of lies, Lord Amberly's introduction left no doubt of her status. Unwed and tainted by shame. "Good evening, ma'am."

"Miss Grey is to take a position at the Hall and assist you with your many duties."

"Is she now?" The woman's eyes narrowed. "Indeed." Like Robbins, the cadence of the North thickened her syllables. "You must have had a cold and wearisome journey. Come in by the fire. I'll make some hot negus." She opened the door.

Jenny stepped aside to let Lord Amberly and Mrs. Fletcher precede her, then followed them inside.

She blinked, adjusting to the light. A fire blazed in a massive hearth. The flames cast dancing shadows upon the stone walls and the finely wrought tapestry of red and gold that hung on the largest wall across from the hearth.

Lord Amberly and Mrs. Fletcher conversed in quiet tones. Jenny's shoes made little noise as she crossed the floor and stood before the fire, letting its heat warm her and Anna, who still slept. She inhaled her daughter's familiar scent, willing her own limbs to steady. Mrs. Fletcher's whispers rose.

"Know of her . . . child . . . risk . . . highly unusual . . ."

She stared into the flames, the flaring tongues of gold and orange blurring. They would order her to leave. Mrs. Fletcher would convince Lord Amberly he'd made a mistake. Would they turn her from the Hall tonight, leaving her to find her way in unfamiliar surroundings and bitter cold?

*Dear God, what will become of us?*

She began to shake. She should not have come. She'd made the decision in haste and journeyed to Yorkshire with a strange man to an unheard-of house, risking her and Anna's safety.

What price would she pay because of it?

"Miss Grey."

She turned at the commanding voice. Lord Amberly stood near the door, along with Mrs. Fletcher. The flickering light cast golden shadows onto his tall, cloaked form and masked face.

"Yes, m'lord?"

"You must be tired. Mrs. Fletcher will show you to your room and bring you something to eat. Do not hesitate to inform her if there's any way you might be made more comfortable. Tomorrow, after you've had a chance to rest, we will meet and discuss your duties at, let us say, ten o'clock. Will that suit?"

She wasn't to be dismissed, then. Jenny released a breath she'd not known she'd been holding. "Yes, m'lord. Thank you."

He made a gesture between a nod and a bow and strode across the great hall toward the stairs, ascending into the darkness without so much as a candle. Jenny shifted beneath Mrs. Fletcher's scrutiny. The dark hue of her dress and prim lines of her cap and apron lent a severity to her appearance, at odds with the soft roundness of her face.

"Well then." Mrs. Fletcher drew herself up, her words as brisk as her steps as she crossed the great hall. "Let's get you settled."

Jenny followed as Mrs. Fletcher climbed a flight of stairs, the wavering glow of her candle leading the way, their footsteps echoing on the wooden treads. A chill permeated the air of the second-floor gallery. On one side stretched a row of doors. On the other, portraits hung at intervals, candlelight illuminating women in rich gowns and stern-browed men in powdered wigs. Were these Lord Amberly's ancestors? Jenny didn't dare pause to study them as Mrs. Fletcher kept a steady pace, skirts rustling, steps muted on the carpet runner. Near the end of the gallery, Mrs. Fletcher opened a door and ascended a narrow flight of stairs. Halfway down the corridor, she stopped.

"I've put you next to Leah. She's the maid, a dear girl. You shall meet her tomorrow. You'll find your room in a bit of a state, I'm afraid. We did not expect you. It should suit for tonight, and we can give it a thorough going over in the morning."

If the charity school had taught her one thing, it was that if one caused extra trouble, one was unlikely to find favor.

"I don't wish to be an inconvenience. I'm here to work, and I intend to discharge my duties to the best of my ability."

Mrs. Fletcher made a slight *hmm* sound in the back of her throat. She shook her head and gave a faint smile. "You must forgive my impertinence, Miss Grey. I've become too long accustomed to my own company, I'm afraid, as have we all at the Hall. To see His

Lordship return from London accompanied by anyone, much less a young woman with a child, has taken me quite off my guard. You will pardon me, I hope."

"Of course." Jenny tried for a smile. "Please, you've no need to apologize."

"This is Lord Amberly's home. If he trusts you enough to bring you here, then I shall do my best to see to your comfort. His Lordship has not . . ." She glanced away, her words fading, and inhaled a sharp breath. "Well, then," she said briskly, bending toward the door and fumbling with her keys. "Let me show you your room."

As Mrs. Fletcher unlocked the door, Jenny stared down the length of the darkened corridor. As hidden as the man who owned the house.

No wonder Lord Amberly had gazed upon the Hall with such a grim countenance. The cold solitude of the floors below better suited a tomb than a place of residence.

In many ways, it reminded her of its master. Hidden. Empty. Hopeless.

A prayer welled up within her.

*Lord, if I can help him in some way, please show me how.*

# CHAPTER 8

As THE CLOCK struck quarter to ten, Dwight waited in the drawing room, a place he'd not entered in over a year, and questioned again the course of action he'd set in motion.

Offering employment to Jenny Grey had been a way of securing her and her child's welfare. He'd not hired an addition to his staff since the day he'd looked at the list of servants who'd departed, likely thinking their master insane, and determined the extent of his household—Robbins, Mrs. Fletcher, William, and Leah. He'd never intended to add or detract from that number unless circumstances absolutely required him to do so. Amberly Hall had been in a condition of gradual disrepair years before he'd become the earl. After Waterloo, he'd not been inclined to remedy that state of affairs. His staff maintained only their rooms, his, and, he assumed, the below-stairs kitchen. If a visitor happened upon the Hall, they'd have surmised its owners away on an extended journey.

In a way, that wasn't far from the truth.

Miss Grey would expect to occupy her time in some way. From the determined look in her eyes when she'd said she was a hard worker, he ascertained she'd think herself receiving charity if she didn't actually work. He surveyed the room, its furnishings white lumps beneath Holland covers, cobwebs hanging from the molded plasterwork ceiling, the trail of his boot tracks through the dust-coated floor.

Mother would be ashamed if she saw the Hall as it was now. Once, before the laudanum had stolen her thirst for life, she'd taken pride in the estate. In many ways, it had been a third child, as cosseted as he and his elder brother Henry. In those days, Amberly Hall's rooms were immaculate and tastefully decorated, flowers from her beloved hothouse adorning the tables, the rooms smelling of their soft fragrance and of polish and wax.

And if she saw *him* now? Would she recoil at the sight of her son's ravaged face? Dwight dragged in a breath past the tightness in his chest.

He would never know.

For which he was thankful.

A rap sounded on the door.

"Enter."

Miss Grey opened the door. A different dress garbed her diminutive frame, this one a shade of drab brown, the square neckline unfashionably high. Her pale hair was pinned in a simple knot at the nape of her neck. Her lapis gaze fixed on him.

He'd seen countless gemstones, but none as pure and startling as the shade of her eyes.

"You're early," he said, realizing how abrupt it sounded the instant the words left his mouth. "What I mean to say is . . . thank you for arriving so promptly."

"Good morning, Your Lordship."

The soft politeness of her greeting reduced him to a callow oaf. Had he been isolated from society so long he'd forgotten manners and good breeding?

Not forgotten, perhaps, but neglected to use.

Although what did it really matter? Once he informed her of her duties, they'd have little occasion to see each other. The other servants had grown accustomed to his moods.

Still, he found himself making a slight bow. "Good morning. Please." He yanked a Holland cover from a settee. Dust clouded the air. He coughed. "Sit down."

She crossed the room and sat on the edge. Her nose twitched, and she quickly covered her mouth and nose as she sneezed three times in succession. "Pardon me." She placed her hands in her lap. "I haven't a handkerchief at the moment."

He'd never heard anyone sneeze so quietly. Whenever Henry had, it had sounded like a great roar fit to spew his lungs out. Dwight fought to hide a smile.

When was the last time he'd had a smile to hide?

"Pray, don't apologize," he said in a stiffly formal tone that sounded altogether awkward. "Was your room satisfactory?"

"Yes. Thank you."

"I'll have William look out for something for Anna to sleep in. There ought to be an old cradle somewhere about."

"Thank you." She looked at him as if she meant it, as if she didn't see his mask or missing eye and gloved hand. As if she saw him simply as a man who'd shown her kindness. No more and no less.

She'd looked at him like that in London too. Perhaps that look had been the reason he'd brought her here. Upon an unfamiliar face, it was a thing he'd never thought to find. Curiosity, yes. Fear, of course. But never an equal regarding as a human soul.

He'd brought her here as a member of his staff. Their interactions must remain confined to that sphere. "As to your duties, I expect you've noticed the state of the house."

She nodded. Then she wouldn't try to deny how bad it truly was. Good. He liked honesty.

"Some of the rooms may be in want of more extensive repairs, but we shall leave those for the present. All are in need of a thorough cleaning. With the exception of the library."

One delicate brow rose. "The library?"

"Yes. It is to remain as it is. You should have no occasion to go in there."

No one would, if he had his way. He may be willing to restore the rest of the Hall, but that room would remain untouched.

"Yes, m'lord" was all she said.

"Leah, the maid, will assist you, as will William." Of course, it wasn't customary for a footman to perform such menial tasks, but he'd seen the way William and Leah looked at each other. They'd likely welcome the chance to spend time together. And the defined roles usually held by staff at a large estate had shifted at the Hall as their numbers decreased. Robbins cared not only for the horses but for the cow and chickens, as well as acting as a makeshift and not very good groundskeeper. "While you're working, Anna can stay in the kitchen with Mrs. Fletcher. I've already spoken with her, and she has agreed." Dash it, he sounded like his commanding officer. How could the arrival of one woman upend habits he'd held on to for months? "Of course, if you've some objection . . ."

"No." She shook her head. "I've no objections."

"You will receive forty pounds per annum, along with room and board. In addition to Sundays, you may have one afternoon off per week. The village is six miles down the road, but if you wish to go there, Robbins can drive you. Are those terms satisfactory?"

"Yes, m'lord."

His neck itched beneath the gentle pressure of her gaze. Though he was used to being stared at, he wasn't accustomed to being *looked* at.

"May I ask a question?"

He paused. "Very well."

Her brow crimped. "Has the Hall been in this state long? What I mean to ask is, was it always—"

"A great ruin of a mausoleum? No. It was not." His jaw tightened. The frankness of her question startled . . . and unnerved him. He'd heard how sharp his answer had sounded.

"I see. Will there be anything else, m'lord?" Her tone came out softer than before.

Deuce and blazes, could he not control himself? Doubtless she hadn't meant the words to be an affront regarding his neglect of the estate. His lack in yet another role he'd failed to perform.

He glanced away. "No. No, thank you. That will be all."

She rose. He braced his hand against the dusty mantel and stared into the cold, charred hearth.

The door opened, then clicked shut.

Leaving him in the only company he deserved.

His own.

———— ✳ ————

*Two Weeks Later*

The London house had sold.

Sitting at his desk, Dwight scanned the documents from his solicitor. The offer had been reasonable. As well as the house, the new occupants had purchased the majority of its furnishings, thus limiting the volume of items to be sold at auction.

The plan he'd laid the foundations for could now be put into motion.

Afternoon sunlight slanted across the glossy wood of his desk as Dwight retrieved a sheet of linen paper from the drawer and dipped his pen in ink. The empty page stared back at him. An emptiness that converged with memories he'd fought not to recall.

Arthur. Nine months and thirteen days younger than he. Always following behind on whatever adventure Dwight proposed. Best friends. Brothers by all but birth. They'd been nine and ten the time they'd snuck away and driven Father's curricle into York to see a group of traveling sword swallowers and doers of daring feats. Fifteen and sixteen when they'd thwarted Henry's plans to take his current lady love and her proper mama out in a rowboat on the Serpentine, by punching holes in the bottom of the boat. Seventeen and eighteen when they'd purchased commissions in the army, bursting with glory and victory, wooing the prettiest girls with their dashing regimentals.

He still remembered every nuance of the night before they'd left. They'd gathered at Amberly Hall for a farewell dinner. Dwight had taken a walk after the meal, the evening air crisp, light spilling onto the lawn. He'd found Mrs. Martin outside, arms hugged around herself, staring into the night. Tears glistened on her cheeks, and he'd handed her a handkerchief. After his mother's passing, she'd taken on the role, in a way. The rare times he'd sought a listening ear, he'd gone to her, not his father or Henry.

"Arthur would have made as fine a clergyman as his father, God rest him," she'd whispered, taking the folded square. "I could see him behind the pulpit giving sermons, couldn't you? It would have been a comfortable life. A good one."

He'd realized then what she had left out. It would have been a safe life. Arthur was her only son. Dwight had not convinced him to join the army. He hadn't needed to. Arthur had made the decision because Dwight had. Because they'd always done everything together.

"I promise to keep him safe, ma'am." How earnest his voice had sounded. "The two of us will do our king and country proud."

Mrs. Martin had wiped her eyes and given a wobbly smile. "I trust you, Dwight. If he'll be with you, I know all will be well."

They'd been twenty-four and twenty-five the day of the Battle of Waterloo.

The day he'd failed his promise to Mrs. Martin.

The pen clattered from his shaking hand, splotching the desk with a blot of ink. It spread and grew, a seeping stain. Blurring together with the image of blood soaking through Arthur's red coat. The most vivid thing he remembered before everything went black.

He pulled in a deep breath and picked up the pen. Nothing would stand in the way of him doing this thing—for Arthur, for their friendship, for a promise war had robbed him of the chance to keep. His quill scratched across the paper.

> *Dear Madam,*
> *I had the honor of being acquainted with your son, Lieutenant Arthur Martin. I served with him throughout his career, and a finer soldier could not be found in all of England. During our time together, he spoke often of you and his late father with gratitude for the love and devotion with which you brought him up. His willingness to serve and his loyalty to his comrades was admired by all who knew him, and I counted it a deep privilege to call him my friend.*
> *It is in his memory that I hereby bequeath you . . .*

He ended with . . .

*Make no attempt to seek out my identity or to thank me in any way. If you wish to thank me, do so by living your life in comfort and security as your son would have desired. Please accept, along with this gift, my best wishes for your health and happiness.*

*I remain most sincerely yours,*
*A friend*

Dwight reread the letter, blotted and folded it. He took up a fresh sheet and jotted a message to his solicitor, asking that the enclosed missive be delivered, along with information about the funds, to a Mrs. George Martin currently residing in York. After sealing and addressing it, he stood.

Rarely did he venture downstairs during the day. The uppermost room in the attic had become both home and haven while the rest of the house sat empty. Here, he created his own light. Or at the very least, a kind of forgetfulness. Music, once a youthful pastime, had become the cord by which he grasped that which eluded him. Peace.

But he needed to give the missive to William so it could be posted.

He descended the main staircase and entered the great hall. An airy freshness filled the house, despite the bleak winter days. The aged floorboards gleamed, the grate in the hearth shone, the cobwebs had been banished, and the tapestry had been brushed clean. A fire blazed, and the windows overlooking the front avenue showed not so much as a single smudge.

Miss Grey had not spoken in boast when she'd said he would find her a hard worker. She, Leah, and William were slowly but surely transforming the Hall. Even the air no longer bore the scent of must.

He shifted, rubbing his thumb across his gloved hand. Cobwebs and Holland covers were a great deal easier to hide behind.

Laughter rang out, followed by . . . singing. Curiosity drew him in the direction of the drawing room, the voices growing louder.

"And all the bells on earth shall ring,
On Christmas Day, on Christmas Day;

And all the bells on earth shall ring,
On Christmas Day in the morning."

The drawing room door stood ajar. Dwight paused outside of it. Leah, William, and Miss Grey stood in front of the mullioned windows overlooking the back of the house, cloths in hand, buckets at their feet, scrubbing the windows and singing as they worked.

Their voices blended, William's slightly out of tune, Leah's untrained soprano mingling with Miss Grey's softer tones. Sunlight filtered through the glistening and soap-splattered windows, shimmering upon Miss Grey's hair, turning it a rich golden shade.

They finished the song amid laughter.

"*You* were in the wrong key." Leah planted soapy fists on her hips and gave William a mock glare.

"I've never sang out of key in my life." William wiped his window with a dry cloth.

"You just did." Leah grinned. "Tell him, Jenny."

"I think I'd prefer not to have an opinion on the subject." Miss Grey's lips tilted upward. "But William was in the wrong key."

"Told you." Leah gave William a playful shove. "And Jenny would know. She's got a voice better'n either of us." She dropped her cloth into the bucket of water. "With the way we've been going on like larks all morning, it's made me think how close we are to Christmas. 'Tis less than three weeks away." Leah wrung out her cloth.

So it was. Dwight had forgotten.

"And how do you keep Christmas at the Hall?" Miss Grey asked.

"We don't. Not anymore." William rubbed at the window. "Not since . . ." He stopped.

*Not since Waterloo. Not since the master of the Hall had a face worth looking upon.*

Leah and William exchanged a glance laden with unspoken truth.

"Sing something for us, Jenny," Leah said quickly. "Help us pass the time, eh?"

Through the crack in the door, he saw Miss Grey bend to wring out her cloth. A spiral of hair slipped loose and dangled down her cheek. Dwight swallowed. He should announce his presence. But something rooted his feet and silenced his words.

"Very well. But this will have to be the last for today." Though her back was turned, he heard the smile in her voice. "Between all the scrubbing and singing, I've grown quite out of breath." She turned, laid a hand on her midsection, and closed her eyes.

"The holly and the ivy,
Now are both well grown,
Of all trees that are in the wood,
The holly bears the crown . . ."

His breath caught. Who in England didn't know this carol? Growing up, he'd heard it performed at parties, usually accompanied by the piano. Often enough for it to become ordinary. But Jenny Grey transformed the simple melody. What was it filling her voice?

His younger, less cynical self would have called it joy.

In music, he found abandonment, passion, forgetfulness. Yet never joy.

He listened, transfixed.

In the past year and a half, he'd sought little beyond solitude. There was no use in wishing his life different, for that would change nothing. If he could point to one desire, it would not have been the reclamation of all he himself had lost, but the restoration of his best friend's life. But as it was senseless to dream of what could never be, he'd chosen not to dream at all. Life had narrowed itself to the four walls of his attic room, the night-soaked moor, and pouring himself onto the keys until his fingers ached.

But in a moment of dawning certainty, he realized he wanted something again.

To know and be known by another.

As the final chorus of the song swelled onto the air, truth soaked through and chilled him to his core.

There was indeed something emptier than wanting nothing.

It was the futility of longing for the impossible.

# CHAPTER 9

THE MUSIC BECKONED her.

Jenny stood in the corridor of the servants' quarters, face lifted, eyes closed. From where it originated, other than the uppermost floor, she wasn't entirely sure.

But its source mattered less than its cadence.

Torn from the recesses of the soul, the notes came. Putting to rest her doubts that there could be beauty in pain. Fast and impassioned, the low tones lifted higher, the tempo at once speaking of freedom and sorrow, longing and despair, ending in a crescendo of poured-out anguish, each note reaching deep within her.

This was not the first time she'd heard the music. Rarely did a day pass without it reaching her ears. Sometimes it came in broken snatches, other times full melody. Leah and William seemed to take little notice of it, while she found herself straining for the sound. Every note a window into the enigma that was Lord Amberly.

She'd learned the rudimentaries of the piano to make her more suitable as a governess, but her efforts could at best be described as plunking out a tune in schoolgirl fashion. Lord Amberly played as if the keys were an extension of his hands. The vehicle by which the innermost parts of himself could find voice.

"Jenny!" Leah called.

"Coming." Jenny shifted her hold on a stack of freshly laundered tablecloths and headed down the corridor. She saw Lord Amberly little, but his absence regrettably did not extend to her wandering thoughts. She caught herself pondering his past, the scars he concealed, the life he'd led before their encounter. Since his abruptness the first morning at the Hall, she'd ventured no more questions.

Still, she wondered.

———✥———

Jenny stood at a window in the great hall, watching snow drift gently down, dusting the ground in a layer of unspoiled purity.

The first snowfall. In Lancashire, where she'd lived at a charity school, it rarely arrived before the first of the year. But when it did come and the students were released for afternoon exercise, she'd always been the first out the door, running ahead, face tipped upward, heedless of the cold. Snow made even the sparse landscape and squat gray school building fresh and new, could make her believe she stood in a forest of enchantment instead of surrounded by girls in drab uniforms and shouting teachers.

Footsteps sounded. She spun around, the past receding.

Lord Amberly came down the stairs. Warmth rippled through her, a sensation she could not account for.

"Good afternoon, m'lord." She dipped a curtsy.

He stopped at the bottom of the stairs. "Good afternoon." Though he wore the garb of a gentleman—a black coat and steel-gray waistcoat—he possessed little of a gentleman's polish. His hair was rumpled and in need of a trim, his right hand smeared with ink.

What a life of loneliness he must lead. Music was no substitute for the company of others. Or the feel of fresh air upon one's cheeks.

An impulse seized her. She rarely had impulses and acted upon them even less. Yet looking at him, recalling the haunted cadence of the music he played, only served to drive the impulse deeper. She did not need to go with him, of course. But perhaps . . .

"It's snowing."

"Oh." He glanced at the window. "So it is."

She pressed on. "Are you fond of snow?"

"I . . ." He cleared his throat, stepping closer. "I suppose I am."

"There's nothing so fine as a first snowfall. I must confess I've always found it quite invigorating. Perhaps you might enjoy a walk." She added a smile.

He stiffened. "I rarely go out-of-doors during the day."

"Why not?"

"It's . . . not something I do."

"Because of your face?" The instant the words left her mouth, she decided impulses were best avoided at all times. Now, he'd become angry, all her efforts for naught. Perhaps angry enough to dismiss her. She floundered for some way to repair the situation, but both her brain and tongue refused to cooperate.

His mouth opened, then closed. "Yes. I suppose it is."

He didn't sound angry. In fact, the words had emerged quieter than the ones before. So soft it seemed he spoke them to himself.

He was trapped. Trapped behind a mask in a prison built by no hands but his own. He'd saved her life, shown kindness to her and Anna, while asking for nothing in return.

When was the last time someone had done something unasked for him?

She took a deep breath. "Will you not come with me outside? Just for a few moments." She paused. "Please?"

He rubbed his thumb across his gloved hand. The mask hid so much of his features, leaving her too little to read.

A minute passed. Somehow, she sensed his future hung suspended in that minute. He'd set himself firmly on one path. Did he have it within himself to turn around?

"Yes."

It was more than she'd expected, that yes. But though it had been firmly spoken, she sensed it was still a tentative resolution. If she delayed to get her shawl or his coat, it might vanish altogether. She pushed open the heavy front door. He stood in the middle of the great hall, watching her.

"What are we waiting for?" She almost held out her hand to him, but at the last minute kept it at her side. He steeled himself—she saw it in the way he drew back his shoulders, tightened his jaw. Like a soldier preparing for battle. Then he strode toward the door, and together they stepped out into the snow.

A breeze swirled the fast-falling flakes, making them dance. Face upturned, she drank in breaths of the crisp air, snow falling on her cheeks like tiny kisses. Oh, it was glorious.

She turned. Lord Amberly stood beside her, hands tight at his sides, posture rigid, gaze fixed on the expanse of avenue stretching toward the road.

"Come." Lifting her skirts, she headed around the side of the house. "Come on."

Boots crunching on the snow-covered grass, he followed. She'd walked the grounds with Leah and William, so she'd a fair idea of where to go. At the back of the house, snow dusted the remains of what had once been gardens, white mingling with the green of overgrown, untended shrubs and flower beds. If she squinted, she could imagine herself in the enchanted forest of her childhood dreams, nature left untampered by the hand of man.

She stopped and faced him. "Now, do this." She closed her eyes.

"What?"

"Come on." She opened her eyes and laughed at his bewildered expression. "Try it."

Looking more than a little discomfited, he closed his eye. She did the same. "Lift your face toward the sky." She tilted her chin.

"Then what?"

"Breathe." She inhaled a deep breath, the pure air filling her lungs. "Now, breathe again. Feel the snow on your face. If you listen closely, you can almost hear it falling. Think of nothing beyond this moment." Her shoulders relaxed. Snowflakes tickled her cheeks, leaving damp tracks as they melted. Wind swept the air. Other than that, all was still. Still and perfect.

After a minute, she couldn't resist. She opened her eyes and peeked at him. He stood, face lifted toward the sky, his eye closed.

And she caught it. He wasn't smiling, but the curve of his lips had softened from that tight, pressed line.

He opened his eye. One side of his mouth edged upward. "For someone who insists we play the game, you aren't following the rules, Miss Grey."

Her breath tangled in her chest. "I was." A damp tendril of hair tickled her cheek. "I only stopped a moment ago." She swiped the strands behind her ear.

"So is this what one does when one ventures out into the snow? Contemplates?" He studied her, that disarming whisper of a smile on his face.

"Sometimes." A grin overtook her face—she couldn't have stopped it if she'd wanted to. "One of the things. Shall I show you another?"

"Why not?"

A giggle escaped as she crouched and scooped up a handful of snow, hands tingling from the cold. There wasn't enough to make a snowball. Not nearly. But she managed to pack a small one together. She stood. He watched her, standing a few paces away, the exposed side of his face slightly reddened in the cold.

"What do you intend to do with that?"

Blame it on the beauty of the gently falling flakes that transformed the stone house and untended gardens into a canvas for the magical. Or on the weight that had lifted from her shoulders, replaced with a girlishness she'd forgotten she possessed. Or on how, out here, the unspoken divide between them fell away and dissipated.

Snowball in hand, she pulled her arm back and threw. It smacked him in the shoulder, leaving a splotch on his coat. For a moment, he stared at her, as if unable to register what had just happened.

He cleared his throat. "Miss Grey."

She wiped her damp hands on the front of her skirt. "Lord Amberly."

She started to speak, but before she could, the smile bracketing the corners of his mouth became a full-fledged grin. "You have very good aim." He bent and scraped up a pile of snow, forming his own ball. He stood. "But I fear you chose the wrong opponent, because mine is even better." He made a move to throw the ball.

She shrieked, and ran. Footsteps crunched behind her. Snow blew against her cheeks, and her hair tugged loose from its pins and tangled around her face as she dashed across the lawn.

"It's only fair I should have a clear shot," he called.

Laughter spilled from her lips, mingling with her panting breaths. She glanced over her shoulder. He raced after her, snowball in hand.

She slipped, skidding in the slick snow. Down she went, landing on her backside. Her breath rushed out of her.

He ran up, halting in front of her, breathing heavily, snowball in hand. "Are you all right?"

A giddy laugh escaped, and she fell backward, lying with her face toward the sky. She was already snow-covered anyway.

"Why are you laughing?"

She only laughed harder.

He chuckled, shaking his head. "What is it?"

That she had no answer for, other than for the first time in a long, long while it felt good to laugh. A fresh giggle escaped. Better still was his laughter as it joined hers.

Perhaps they both needed to learn how to laugh again.

She held out a hand. "Do help me up."

He grasped her hand and pulled her to her feet. She stood, skirt heavy and wet, looking up at him. Flakes floated down and landed on her cheeks and eyelashes. Breath clouded from her lips. His eye was the color of grass after a summer rain, a rich, deep green. The remains of a smile hovered on his lips. Her heart tripped.

Laughter she could understand. But this? This swirl of strange emotions conglomerating in her chest? Those she could scarcely comprehend, much less reckon with.

For a moment, they stood, gazes caught, wind tugging the strands of his unruly hair. Even their very breaths seemed to fall in unison.

"Your hands," he murmured.

She looked at them. She hadn't noticed how cold they were and how red they had become. She shivered, the fragile moment between them broken. Until now, she hadn't felt the cold.

He took a step back. "We should go inside."

She nodded. Holding up her wet skirt so the hem didn't drag, she walked toward the house. The snow fell less heavily, the sky that had seemed so peerless before now a shade of washed-out gray.

Magic had faded.

Reality returned.

—✦—

A simple moment. That was all it had been. Throwing snowballs was a schoolboy's sport. Savoring the whisper of falling flakes upon his face was . . .

Joy.

A curious word. Dwight's life had held amusement, thrills, heady pleasures aplenty. Those fleeting minutes with Jenny Grey had been none of those things. When they'd laughed together, it had unraveled tension he hadn't realized he'd been carrying. Not only a lessening, but a gaining. He'd grinned and looked into her eyes, and lightness had cascaded through him. Not only because of the carefree abandon of the moment but because he'd shared it with her. She'd cared enough to invite him into it.

What could he give to her? He wanted to do something for her. Find a way to bestow upon her a measure of the joy she'd brought him.

Dwight knotted his cravat with a few deft twists. Morning sunlight spilled through the open curtains of his bedchamber.

He'd never been a man skilled in how to please the ladies. That had been Henry's domain. Aside from a few short-lived flirtations in his youth, there had only been one woman Dwight had truly cared to charm. He'd noticed Louisa's fondness for marzipan and gardenias, so he'd sent her both during their courtship. Spent hours attempting to write her verses. Upon their engagement, he'd bought her a ring from a London jeweler. Louisa had thanked him, but it had always seemed flat in comparison with the lengths he'd gone. Leading him to wonder more than once if perhaps he just wasn't enough for her.

But Miss Grey wasn't Louisa. She was a girl who reveled in the delight of the first snow, a woman he was beginning to . . . She was also a servant in his employ, a fact he'd do well to recollect.

The impropriety of flowers or some such token aside, he wanted to do something more.

But what would be meaningful to her? He rued how little he knew about her. One couldn't properly give a gift, a real gift, whilst lacking familiarity with the recipient.

He remembered Robbins carrying in Miss Grey's belongings after he'd retrieved them from her rented room. They'd barely filled a small crate, mostly baby whatnots. On the top, Dwight had glimpsed three small volumes. Books.

How far was he willing to go?

The question taunted him, reducing whatever loftiness his ideas had held to dross. Gifts of the gardenia and marzipan variety, even a gold ring with a perfect ruby, cost him little.

But his mother's favorite room? The place where he remembered her—and all that had died when he'd lost her—best?

In the past years, he'd taken pains to avoid the library. The very walls were rife with memories, some of his happiest. Since his return to the Hall after Waterloo, he hadn't once entered it. Nor intended to. It had always been her room. It seemed right for it to remain so.

Was that what his mother would have wanted? For the place she'd loved to be barred by a closed door, visited by none? Before the laudanum had overtaken her, she'd loved to fill the house with people and laughter, eschewing a quiet life as suitable for "old men and maiden aunts."

He recalled the serenity of Miss Grey's face as she'd tilted it toward the snow. Yes, he'd admittedly stolen a glance.

To share with her now as she had with him . . .

If he delayed, he'd reason himself out of it.

Dwight slid his arms through his coat, slipped his glove over his left hand, and strode from his bedchamber. He checked his pocket watch as he descended the stairs. Eight in the morning. Right about the time they'd be beginning the day's work. They'd finished cleaning the drawing room and dining room and were starting on the breakfast room.

His boots resounded on the floor as he approached the breakfast room. William stood on a chair, unfastening the drapes from the window and handing them down to Miss Grey. Leah knelt in front of the fireplace, cleaning the hearth.

"Good morning," he said from the doorway.

Three sets of gazes turned in his direction.

"Good morning, m'lord." William climbed down from the chair, standing in front of it like a soldier at attention. The others echoed greetings.

Dwight shifted. "Miss Grey, I was wondering if I might have a few moments of your time. There's . . . a housekeeping matter I wish to discuss."

Above the load of draperies in her arms, her eyes widened. "Of course." She deposited the draperies upon the breakfast table. "I shan't be long," she said before following him from the room.

"This way." He led the way down the corridor, turned down the next, aware of her beside him as they approached the library door. Reaching it, he paused.

She looked from the door back to him. Blinked.

"I thought it time you saw the library."

A frown appeared between her eyes. "But . . ."

He didn't finish her sentence. Ignoring the noose tightening his lungs, he turned the knob and opened the door. Held it for her. Tentatively, she stepped inside. Bracing himself, he followed.

*It's just a room.*

The library wore a veil of shadows. The scents of dust, old books, and . . . Of course he imagined it, his mother's violet fragrance washing over him. With firm steps, he crossed the carpeted floor and pushed back the closed curtains, flooding the space with light.

He turned.

Miss Grey stood in the center of the library, absorbing everything, a small, delighted smile finding purchase on her lips. He took it in, seeing the room through her eyes rather than the lens of his past. The books lining the walls from floor to ceiling. The windows overlooking the untended garden at the back of the house. The mahogany writing desk, coated with a film of dust.

Dwight walked toward her. "I thought you and the others might begin on this room next. As you can see, it's in need of it." He paused. "Perhaps you might find some of the books of interest to yourself. Borrow anything you like."

She looked at him for the first time since entering the room. "You mean . . . read the books?"

"If you wish. They're not doing anyone good sitting on the shelves collecting more dust."

She tilted her head. "I suppose not."

He motioned her forward. "Please. Have a look about."

She seemed to float as she crossed the room and ran her fingertips along a row of spines, leaving a trail through the dust. She slid one volume from the shelf. The spine crackled as she opened it. He came to stand behind her. She'd chosen a book of Shakespeare. *Hamlet.*

She turned. A smudge of dirt streaked her cheek. He closed and opened his fingers at his side to avoid reaching up and wiping it away. He'd laid his hand against her forehead when it had been hot with fever. Then he'd been conscious of little else but her welfare. What would it be like to touch her now? Let his fingers linger against the softness of her skin?

Her *unmarred* skin.

The ugliness of his scars stood all the starker in comparison.

He couldn't imagine anyone desiring to touch him.

"It's wonderful." Her smile deepened. "Thank you."

The sweetness of her words filled him, the pleasure not unlike the tingling warmth of a first sip of cherry brandy. "I wanted to . . ." *Please you?* Dash it, he couldn't say that. His unfinished sentence hung precariously in the air. Heat crept up his neck. "No matter."

"What made you change your mind?"

"What?" It was almost disconcerting, the way she could aim a question and hit him true in such a modulated voice.

"About the library. You said this room was to be left as it is." She replaced the book and faced him again, hands behind her back, gaze holding his. Pressing gently, like four days ago, when she'd asked him to walk with her in the snow.

He glanced away. "It was my mother's favorite room."

"You miss her, don't you?" The texture of the softly spoken question matched her gaze.

Had anyone asked him that before? Ever? Grief was something one donned mourning garb for. Black clothes and somber faces were to be the only visible expression. The day of his mother's burial, his father had looked him in the eye and, noticing Dwight's not quite steady chin, gritted out that he "had better not make an idiot of himself by behaving like a sniveling chit." Dwight had steeled himself by biting his lip so hard it had bled. When they tossed the first shovelful of dirt onto her coffin, he'd not shed a single tear.

"Yes." He cleared his throat, the word coming rough.

"What was she like?" A pensive smile touched her lips.

After the laudanum tightened its grip, she'd become a different woman. Almost as if he'd had two mothers. One full of life and beauty, the other a wraithlike shadow with a voice as frail as her body.

He remembered them both but could only bring himself to share about the first. "She was like springtime." He paused. "She loved laughter and music. Books. On rainy afternoons, we would take turns choosing one. Then we'd sit on the floor, just over there." He pointed to the corner nearest the window. "She'd read aloud for hours, novels, poetry, plays. Most times, I fell asleep listening to her voice, the rain on the roof." The memory floated over him, a wisp, a subtle fragrance, but potent nonetheless.

"That's lovely."

He swallowed. "She was lovely."

"When did she . . ."

"When I was eleven. She'd been . . . unhappy for some time. To this day, I still don't know whether she wished for death so much she chose to seize it herself, or if nature simply took its course." His throat thickened. "They found a laudanum bottle on the floor by her bed. Or so I heard the doctor tell my father. After it happened, I wondered if it was my fault. If I was what made her unhappy. If I could have saved her." He wasn't sure how or why the words had come, only that they had.

Strangely, as guarded as he'd become, he did not wish them back.

"The blame for her death is not yours to bear." She shook her head. "You were so young."

"And yet youth is no exemption from pain." He turned his gaze toward the window, staring at the unvarnished gray of the sky and the dying gardens as he tamped down the rise of emotion. Gathering himself, he turned back to her. She looked at him, expression gentle, sorrowful. Understanding.

It twined through him, that look. Soaking through him, burrowing deep.

Reaching the barren places of his heart.

# CHAPTER 10

SHE OUGHTN'T TO have let Leah coax her into spending their afternoon off shopping. It was now the second week of December, and Jenny hadn't yet visited the village. But Mrs. Fletcher had agreed to tend Anna, Robbins had announced himself free to drive them, and Leah had begged for Jenny's help choosing material for a new gown.

Of course, Jenny had no intentions of purchasing anything herself. She made do with her old dresses and one Mrs. Fletcher had given her, which she'd altered to fit her smaller measurements. But she let herself be swept away by Leah's debating over which muslin might suit her best. It was obvious the question really was, Which muslin might suit her best in the eyes of a certain footman?

"The green muslin would bring out the shade of your eyes." Jenny ran her fingertips over the lightweight fabric. "And it would not show wear as easily as the rose figured."

Leah bit her lip. "But the rose figured is so light and beautiful."

The bell above the door jangled.

"Good day to you, Mrs. Garmond," called the woman at the front counter. "Here to pick up your parcels?"

Leah studied the two bolts of fabric side by side. "Perhaps I ought to look at some ribbon before I make up my mind. You should see if there are any other muslins you like." She wove her way through the crowded shop toward the display of ribbons.

Jenny pulled a bolt of cream muslin with an aubergine print and laid it next to the others. Muted voices drifted to where she stood. She gave a quick glance over her shoulder. The back of the lady's bonnet and her dress of deep puce suggested an older woman of some distinction.

". . . the maid from Amberly Hall," whispered the woman behind the counter.

Jenny stilled.

"He still employs servants, then?"

"Indeed. Every so often, one of them comes into the village on some business or another. My son Frank, who works for the butcher, makes frequent deliveries to the Hall."

"Has he ever seen him?" the woman named Mrs. Garmond asked.

"Well, no. Of course, Frank never stays long. He says the place gives him the shivers. All overgrown and shuttered up. If I didn't know better, I'd say it was altogether abandoned." Warming to the topic, she neglected to whisper.

Jenny feigned interest in the fabric. It was Lord Amberly they spoke of. Despite the impropriety of eavesdropping, she couldn't check the urge to hear what they said.

"Perhaps it is. Perhaps he's not there at all, and his servants haven't bothered to tell anyone. And why would they, if the lazy things could continue to live off what's left of the money?" Mrs. Garmond tittered.

The woman behind the counter clucked her tongue. "I very much doubt that, Eliza. We would've heard if he'd passed on, surely."

"Though who can say how *alive* he is. No one's had so much as a glimpse of him since he returned from the war."

"Save for the Fishers' lad George. At least, George said he saw him. Stalking the moor in the dead of night, all dressed in black."

Jenny pressed a hand against her midsection. The bolts of fabric blurred together.

"More likely, George just had one too many at the Amberly Arms."

"But my Frank spoke to him the day after, and George hadn't had so much as a sip. 'Tis not the first time someone's said they've seen him either. Hugh Sturges saw him too. A great black shadow walking the moor when the moon was full. Like a dark spirit wrested from the grave."

"Perhaps it was not him after all, but his ghost."

The woman behind the counter *hmm*ed. "Whether it was human or not, Old Hugh had nightmares for days afterward, his wife said. Couldn't get the notion out of his head that the curse of the Amberlys had fallen on him. And what do you think? Hugh took ill with the pleurisy and died not a month later."

"Look, Jenny."

Jenny started. Leah stood at her elbow, holding a length of ribbon. "Wouldn't this match perfectly with the green?"

Jenny nodded, barely noticing the ribbon.

"Then I shall get enough of the ribbon to trim my old bonnet." Leah laid the ribbon atop the bolt of muslin. "How well they look together."

"Shall we take them up to the counter?" Jenny tried to infuse brightness into her words, but they came out sounding false.

"But are you sure?" Leah frowned. "That the green is the best choice?"

"You'll look beautiful." Jenny forced a smile.

Leah flushed. "It will be the nicest gown I've owned. Mrs. Fletcher has already offered to help me do it up." She lifted the bolt of muslin along with the ribbon and carried them toward the counter.

Mrs. Garmond and the woman behind the counter broke off their conversation as Jenny and Leah approached. They waited while Mrs. Garmond paid for her items. As she turned away, her gaze pierced Jenny. Jenny pressed her lips together. Without a word, Mrs. Garmond sailed out of the shop, the bell jangling in her wake.

Jenny stood in a daze while the woman behind the counter cut and wrapped Leah's ribbon and muslin. At last Leah paid for her parcels, and they left. Frosty air cooled Jenny's cheeks as they crossed the shop-lined street to where Robbins waited with the carriage. Inside, she sank against the seat, and the wheels jerked forward.

They'd spoken of Lord Amberly as if he were an apparition. They spoke, but they did not know. Not the truth. Not one jot of it. The man they called a ghost had stood beside her in the library and spoken of his mother with pain in his gaze and love in his voice, poured his heart into the music he played, treated her without judgment or censure. That day in the snow she'd not noticed his mask.

She'd seen only him. A man with a heart not unlike her own.

"Are you unwell, Jenny?"

Jenny glanced up. Leah studied her with a look of concern.

How long had Leah known Lord Amberly? Before or after whatever had happened that made him hide his face and retreat into isolation?

"While you were looking at the ribbons, I heard those women talking . . ." She relayed the conversation she'd overheard. Leah listened quietly as the carriage jostled along the rutted road.

"It's something we've grown accustomed to," Leah said when Jenny finished. "The whispers, the pointed glances, the mistrust. Though it was uncomfortable at first, the four of us scarcely heed it now."

"But why?" Jenny shook her head. "Why would they think those things?"

Leah sighed. "It's human nature to fear what one does not understand. And to come to conclusions about what one does not know the truth of. Mrs. Garmond dearly loves to gossip. I would not mind what she says."

"What happened to him?" The question fell from her lips like a breath. A question she'd turned through her mind countless times since he'd entered her life, but never voiced. She sensed Mrs. Fletcher would not speak of it, and there had never been the right moment to broach the topic with Leah or William. Of course one who held secrets would do well not to pry into the mysteries of others. But after she'd spoken the words, she did not regret them.

A darkness entered Leah's gaze. "Are you sure you wish to know?"

Leah's tone gave Jenny pause. Gone was the carefree girl with her head full of ribbons and her sweetheart. "I'm sorry. I should not have asked."

"I suppose if anyone has a right to know, it's you. None of us ever expected him to bring another to the house. It's been just the four of us for a good while now." She glanced away. "After Lord Amberly's father died, Captain Inglewood, as we called him then, was not the next to inherit the title. His elder brother was as worthless a scoundrel as I hope ever to meet, and when he broke his neck in a riding accident, few of us servants grieved him much.

"Captain Inglewood was in the army at the time, and his brother's death occurred just three days before the Battle of Waterloo. I started work at the house shortly before, so I was there when, several weeks after the battle, Captain Inglewood returned, now the earl. Of course, I did not see him, being a kitchen maid at the time, but those who did said he was terribly burned." Leah's voice grew strained. "He was engaged to a Miss Louisa Beresford, a lady of both family and fortune. I do not know exactly what happened, but sometime after His Lordship returned to the Hall, she came to visit. After she left, Lord Amberly was in a bad way. Robbins said he sank into a decline and could have very well ended up like his mother, God rest her."

"What happened then?" Jenny could hardly trust her voice.

Sadness filled Leah's gaze. "He rallied, but he never left the Hall or entertained guests. Just stayed up in the attic, with his music. We'd never been a large staff, but in the following months, most of the servants quit the place entirely. Throughout the generations, the family line has been marked by tragedy and cruel twists of fate, leading to whispers about some sort of a curse. After everything else, I suppose having a recluse for a master frightened them into handing in their notices. There was talk in the village about who the curse might descend upon next. Folk in these parts are a superstitious lot."

"But you never considered leaving?"

Leah shook her head. "Whenever I encountered Lord Amberly, he treated me with a civility I've rarely found among those of his station. And . . ." She drew in a shaking breath. "One night I was sent upstairs to mend the fire in his bedchamber. I was about to knock, when I . . . I saw him through a crack in the door. He stood in front of the fire, removing his shirt. I'd never seen him without his mask, had no idea what he concealed, but . . ." She blinked rapidly. ". . . his scars . . ." She lifted her chin. "That night, I realized. He's not a gargoyle or some curiosity to be gossiped about, but a broken and hurting man. As human as any of us and as worthy of compassion and kindness. Whenever I hear people talking as those women did today, I want to tell them they know nothing of what they speak." Her voice trembled. "I only wish he could see himself as he truly is, enough to open up his heart and live outside the shadows. I wish that, Jenny Grey." Tears filled her eyes. "But I fear the day may never come."

———————◆✕◆———————

Dwight descended the stairs to the sound of high-pitched wailing. In the great hall, he found Mrs. Fletcher bouncing Anna while the baby waved her tiny fists, face scrunched and red. "There now." Despite the soothing words, Mrs. Fletcher's tone had a mildly desperate edge. "It's all right, love. Your mama will be back soon." She turned, eyes widening. "Oh. Good evening, m'lord. Was there something you wanted?"

"Merely to give this to Robbins." He held out a letter, a response to his solicitor's missive detailing the auction of the remainder of the townhouse's furnishings. "Is he about somewhere?"

"Not presently." She raised her voice to be heard above Anna's screams. "He drove Jenny and Leah into the village, as it was their afternoon off. They should be back soon. If you set the letter on the hall table, I'll see he attends to it directly."

Dwight crossed the room and placed the letter on the silver salver on the low table. Anna's high-pitched wails echoed off the ceiling. He headed toward the stairs. Mrs. Fletcher paced the floor. "I don't know what can be the matter with the child." She shook her head, the ruffles on her cap fluttering. "I've tried everything I can think of. Her clout is dry as a bone, and I gave her some milk not an hour ago. Oh, I hope Miss Grey returns soon. I don't think my nerves can handle much more." Anna punctuated the end of Mrs. Fletcher's sentence with a particularly loud squall.

Dwight hesitated. The poor woman looked ready to burst into tears herself. He eyed Anna's flailing legs and puckered face.

"Mind if I try?"

"Would you?" Without waiting for a response, she passed Anna into his arms.

Though he'd held her during her first hours at the townhouse, it had been because there was no one else. And she'd been too weak with fever to do little more than whimper amid coughing fits and dreadful stillness.

How did one make a baby stop crying?

"Well, now, Miss Anna. What seems to be the trouble?" He looked her over, not exactly certain what one ought to look for. Mrs. Fletcher had already ascertained the state of her clout, and unless circumstances grew dire, he wasn't about to attempt a second check. She wore a soft, loose gown and knitted booties. Bootie, he corrected. One of them was missing. "Mrs. Fletcher?"

"Yes, m'lord?"

"One of her booties appears to be missing. Do you think you could find it?"

Mrs. Fletcher peered at Anna's small bare foot. "It must be in her cradle." She hastened toward the stairs.

In five minutes, Mrs. Fletcher was back down, and the bootie returned to Anna's foot. In ten, Dwight was seated by the fire in the drawing room, Anna's cries reduced to sniffles. In twenty, she lay fast asleep against his chest, lips pursed, making little sucking sounds. Tentatively, he reached up and ran a hand across her golden curls, the strands slipping through his fingers with gossamer softness.

"Sleep well," he whispered. From some faraway place came one of his earliest memories, his mother bending over his bed and tucking him in as she murmured soft words. *May your dreams hold only sunlight. May your life be free from shadows.*

The world was a harsh place for an illegitimate child. Quick to mete out judgment and slow to extend grace. What future awaited this precious little girl?

Who was the man who'd fathered this child, and where was he now? Did he know his daughter had lips like a rosebud and eyes of deepest blue, soft blonde curls, and ten perfect fingers? Did he deserve to know?

For that matter, was he even alive?

The drawing room door opened, and Jenny stepped in. "Mrs. Fletcher said—"

"Shh," he whispered. "She's asleep."

Jenny crossed the room, a smile softening her lips. "So she is," she said in a voice as quiet as his.

"She cries when one of her booties is missing."

"I know." She sat on the opposite edge of the settee. Firelight bathed the delicate contours of her face in a muted glow. "She always kicks one off in her sleep, then cries when she wakes up and her little foot is cold." She reached out and smoothed a hand across Anna's head. "Thank you for tending her. I hope she wasn't too much trouble."

"No." He swallowed, uncertain whether or not to put the emotions in his chest into words. "She's a treasure."

"She holds my heart in her tiny hands," she said softly. "Before Anna, I was alone. She gave me the first family I'd ever known. It should be the other way around, you know, mothers giving gifts to their children, but she gave me hope again, when I had lost mine."

He shouldn't ask. He was not entitled to pry into her secrets. But he wanted to understand her and to help her, if he could. So he would ask, and if she chose to tell him nothing, he would not press her. "And her father?"

She met his eyes, a tremulous set to her lips. A minute passed. He was about to speak, tell her it had been remiss of him to ask and he had no wish to tamper with her pain, but she began before he could.

"I never knew my parents. My first memories are of a foundling home. When I was a child, I was sent to a charity school. An apt name, as they never let us forget how beholden we were to their charity. At the age of seventeen, I finished my education and gained a position as a governess. The master of the house was often away on business, so I saw him rarely at first." She looked down at her clasped hands. "But when he was at home, I began to notice his . . . marked attentions to me. At the start, I thought it merely kindness, for which I was grateful, as his wife saw fit to show me little. But the longer it went on, the more uncomfortable I became. I did not want to lose my position, so I did my best to be civil and keep out of his way. But one night there was a party at the house. The children had gone downstairs with their mama to be presented to the guests. He came up to the schoolroom . . ." She swallowed, squeezing her eyes shut.

Dwight could hardly breathe for the fist of anger in his chest.

"After that night, I considered leaving. I almost did leave. But I had no family, no connections, no one in whom I could confide or seek advice. So I remained at the house. A few months passed, and I began to believe I was with child." Her knuckles whitened as she clenched her hands together. "His wife must have suspected my condition, must have noticed something. When her husband was away, she confronted me. When I told her who my child's father was, she raged at me to leave, or she'd summon the law and have me thrown into prison. I had enough money to get to London, so I went there."

She drew in a shaky inhale. "Obtaining respectable work was difficult without a recommendation. I knew no decent family would employ a woman in my condition as a governess, so I sought work as a seamstress. I found employment with a modiste until Anna was born. Shortly following my return after Anna's birth, there was an incident. One of the patronesses of Almack's commissioned a gown, and when it was delivered, she was dissatisfied with its quality. The lady herself came to the shop and voiced her displeasure. The modiste blamed me . . . dismissed me." She raised her eyes to his. "When a woman who lived near my lodgings told me the Three Kings was in want of a servant, it seemed my only option." She stopped. "I've never told anyone all of that. I don't know why I told you. You didn't need to hear it." She made an attempt at a smile, but tears glazed her eyes.

For a moment, he didn't speak, overwhelmed by the suffering that had marked this woman's life. What could he say that could even come close to being enough? Yet despite the brokenness, despite everything, she still laughed with him in the snow, lifted her voice in song, loved her daughter fiercely.

He'd known men the world termed strong—men of power and military prowess. He'd witnessed deeds of daring and courage on the battlefield, acts worthy of medals and speeches and grandeur. But he'd never before known a strength that could suffer so much and still keep going.

It awed him. And it shamed him.

In the face of the impossible, she'd done what he had not.

She'd lived.

———◦✕◦———

Like glass unable to bear the weight of a single crack, she'd shattered and told him everything. After Leah's revelation, to find him sitting by the fire cradling her sleeping daughter, then his gently spoken question . . . It had been more than she could bear. If she'd not known the depth of his suffering, would she have shared hers with such readiness? Sensing the rawness of his wounds, it had been easier to unbind hers.

When he reached out and placed his gloved hand over hers, fresh tears rushed to her eyes. The man before her was not one who'd treat such a touch lightly.

"I'm sorry. For all of it." His throat jerked. "No one's life should have to hold such pain."

The genuineness in his words undid her. Countless words and glances had met her over the years. The weight of censure at the charity school when the headmistress said her parents had been wicked and it was only due to the school's benevolence that she had any hope of becoming a good child. The shame of being the object of a cruel man's lust. The blow of judgment when Mrs. Carlisle dismissed her.

But never apology. Never understanding.

A sob escaped—half groan, half shudder—another fast on its heels. There in the darkness of the fire-lit room, she wept hard, wrenching tears. Pouring out the lack and sorrow and loss she'd tamped down in the battle of simply surviving.

He did not tell her to *shh*, to stem her tears. Nor did he say anything at all. He only sat beside her, his hand covering hers. Offering nothing beyond his steady presence.

She'd cried alone enough in her life to realize the magnitude of such a gift.

When she'd spent all she had within her, she drew her hand from beneath his and swiped under her eyes. A moment later, something brushed her hand. A handkerchief. She took the neatly folded square. It smelled of clean linen and sandalwood. She drew in a deep breath, the fabric a caress against her cheek. Even after she dried her face, she kept it in her hand.

"Thank you." Those simple words could scarcely hold the fullness in her heart.

He nodded.

For several moments, the fire crackled and neither spoke.

"What of your life?" she whispered. Here she'd wept for herself, when she'd so recently learned the scope of his pain. "Have you not also known the depth of suffering?"

Stillness hung between them as he regarded her. "I've known a great many things."

# CHAPTER 11

WIND MOANED OVER the barren landscape as Dwight strode across the moor that lay beyond Amberly Hall. Both the path and the hour were familiar to him, a refuge when the prospect of the nightmares proved too much for him to reckon with. On clear nights like this one, he didn't even need a lantern. Moon and stars lighted his way. To some, the moody darkness of the moor might seem an unwelcome prospect. To him, the uneven contours of the frost-glossed moorland with its hills and hollows soothed like a balm. Bracing air swept his face as he crested a hill.

What was it about Jenny Grey that made him question the foundations of the life that had become his new reality? Solitude. Seclusion. Separation. She'd given his empty house a heart again, and not only by chasing away the cobwebs and banishing the Holland covers. Now, laughter filled rooms formerly silent, and music beyond his own frustrated attempts could be heard throughout the house as she sang with William and Leah. Even Anna's crying breathed life where there had been a void.

She'd brought light where he'd consigned himself to darkness.

And he wanted more. Craving the forbidden like a prisoner craved open spaces. A joyful home. Children to love. A wife to cherish.

He'd seen the destruction brought about by a miserable union. Sullen silences punctuated by angry outbursts were all he recalled his parents ever sharing. As a young man, he'd eschewed love, believing it a weightless ideal. Then at the age of four and twenty, he'd met Louisa during Christmas leave from his regiment. She'd dazzled him with her effortless beauty, bestowing her charm on no man but him, their letters spanning the separation between them. During the Peace, when Napoleon was exiled on Elba, they'd become engaged. They would have been wed had not his father's unexpected death thrown the household into chaos, Napoleon's escape from Elba following close on its heels. He'd have married her before he left for Belgium, but she wanted a fashionable wedding at St. George's in London, a honeymoon in Bath.

The left side of his face tightened and tingled. A shadow of the searing agony that had gripped him for weeks following his awakening in a field hospital. He gritted his teeth.

The agony had faded to pain, the devastation left by the burns unbandaged and visible when Louisa had come to him during his convalescence at the Hall.

He remembered everything about that hour. The rustle of her skirts as she'd stepped over the threshold, the waft of her rose scent. He'd risen to greet her, uncertain as a schoolboy, heart thudding beneath his coat. In the haze of physicians and treatments and his fractured vision, he'd thought of her, dreamed of her. *Lived* on her. No matter the behavior of the rest of the world, Louisa would remain his constant.

He'd written to her that though his appearance was altered, his love for her had never been more abiding. She'd agreed to visit him in Yorkshire, accompanied by her mama.

He'd seen himself in the mirror. He'd known and yet he had not known the extent of the damage to his face. Somehow, he'd told himself, the strength of their love would hold steadfast.

One look into her eyes changed everything. In her face, he read the truth of his own.

He'd become repellent. An apparition instead of a man.

The echo of his words would forever haunt him. She'd somehow gathered herself and greeted him, but her voice was painfully strained. Her face pale. He'd tried to fill the silence but had floundered as he absorbed how the woman he loved was looking at him. After a quarter of an hour, she'd risen from the settee across from his.

"I shall leave you to rest. You must be tired." She gave a pinched smile.

She was leaving him. Panic and disbelief clamored in his chest. As she reached the door, he called out to her. Three desperate words. One final hope.

"I love you."

She turned, an ebony curl dangling against her cheek. For a long moment, she looked at him, lips parted slightly, her eyes a slate upon which horror and pity were writ in unmistakable letters.

Without a word, she opened the door. And left him.

The cracking of a stick jerked him from the memory. Clammy sweat had broken out beneath his shirt despite the cold. He stopped and glanced both ways, moonlight illuminating his surroundings in a waxen glow. He'd wandered farther east than usual, nearer the scattering of cottages that housed his tenants. He usually kept to the north and the heart of the moorland.

A gleam of light flashed.

Dwight tensed.

A small figure darted down the hill, carrying a lantern. Heavy breathing mingled with the baying of a dog. The flickering light of the lantern lifted, revealing the figure as a young boy. He froze, clutching the lantern, staring at Dwight from beneath a mop of tangled hair.

The boy's eyes widened.

In a split second, he ran, skidding down the hill, flying past without a look back, a scrawny dog at his heels.

"Stop!" Dwight called. If he could only speak to the boy a moment.

But the lad disappeared into the night, the bobbing glow of his lantern growing smaller and smaller.

The wind at his back, Dwight turned and strode toward the Hall.

That was what he did to people. What he would always do. His face was his reality. Even behind the mask the scars owned him.

Last night had been different. He'd touched Jenny before he could check himself, and she'd not pulled away. He couldn't remember the last time he'd initiated physical contact with another person since his injuries. Could recall even less the last time he'd wanted to.

She was lovely, but in a gentle, hidden way, deeper than the outward. She'd suffered so much, and he wanted to protect her. To earn her trust and keep her safe. To be the one privileged to listen to the things she shared with no one else, to share those things with her. To hear her laughter and let the music of her voice fill his heart.

To . . . love her.

He could not put himself through that again. Could not endure the sword thrust of rejection a second time. The coldness in another woman's gaze as he realized that though he offered everything he had, it was not enough.

Jenny was not Louisa. She saw him as he was and extended friendship. That in and of itself was a taste of joy. To press her for more might mean to lose her altogether. He must find a way to be content.

But the workings of the heart were like the composition of a masterpiece, not the winding of a clock. They did not alter into the right and proper form simply because one twisted them into submission. Theirs was a rare and beautiful mystery, and the fact that he'd ceased to be a whole man did not exempt him from their pull.

He would love her. In secret and in silence. Giving her his heart without asking for hers in return.

He was no fool. Hopeless longing was a mere shadow of love asked and received.

But even the bitterest futility could hold a kind of solace.

— ✕ —

"It will be difficult to find much greenery, but Leah and I shall do our best. Will you make sure William remembers to get the gold paper and red silk?"

"It's already on the list."

Voices filtered from the great hall as Dwight came down the stairs. Jenny stood near the door in conversation with Mrs. Fletcher. At the sight of him, both started like children caught in some misdeed.

"What's this about gold paper and red silk?" he asked.

Jenny flushed. Damp splotches marked her apron, and tendrils of hair had slipped loose and framed her cheeks.

"Nothing of consequence, m'lord," Mrs. Fletcher hastened. "Jenny and I have just been discussing a small celebration for Christmas Day. Of course, we intended to consult you before proceeding with any definite plans."

His mouth quirked upward. From the sound of things, consulting him had not been high on their list of priorities. "What did you have in mind?"

"Some festive decorations, a fine meal, music." Jenny paused. "Have you any objections, m'lord?"

How formally she addressed him. As if their conversation of a week ago had never taken place. Then she'd spoken to him as an equal rather than as an earl and her employer, shared pain bridging the divide between their stations. For him, nothing had changed. But of course she would revert to propriety's demands. Anything less would be seen as inappropriate, particularly in the eyes of Mrs. Fletcher.

He shifted, sensing their attention on him as they awaited an answer. As a boy, he'd looked forward to returning from school for the Christmas holidays. But like so much else in life, imagination proved sweeter than reality. Some years his mother had entertained and the house had blazed with candles, smelled of greenery, and sounded with laughter. Other times his parents had left him and Henry to attend a gathering at another estate, and the house was silent, the meal sparse. The last Christmas his mother had been alive she'd not left her room. He, Henry, and their father had sat around the table for Christmas dinner, the only noise the scraping of silver on their plates and the groan of the wind against the windowpanes. Two weeks later, her life had ended.

"If you do not wish to partake, perhaps we might still do so? Although I think you might enjoy it." Despite Jenny's modulated tone, he detected the persistent note that had become familiar. And not in an unpleasant way.

Perhaps it was time. After all, his staff deserved his gratitude. Last Christmas he'd done nothing to show his appreciation for them beyond an increase in wages. He could find some way to purchase gifts for each of them, enter into their festivities if they would have him.

"I think it a very fine idea. Please continue with your preparations."

"Then you will join us?" Hope lit Jenny's gaze.

She wanted him there.

"It would be my honor."

Her smile made him ache. Because when it fastened upon him, he imagined a future he'd no right to be conjuring.

"That's wonderful news, m'lord," Mrs. Fletcher said. Was it his imagination, or did she look between the two of them with a bemused glance?

Later, he'd rebuke himself for his wandering thoughts that would never come true. Now, stubbornly, he wanted to savor them.

"I'll leave you ladies to it then." He nodded, added a brief smile. "And I shall look forward to a happy Christmas."

Jenny's smile grew, and with it the light unspooling inside his chest. "We shall make certain it is."

# Chapter 12

FOOTSTEPS CRUNCHED. JENNY turned. Lord Amberly walked toward her, wind tumbling the strands of his dark hair. A thin layer of snow coated the hard ground.

She rose from her seat on the iron bench and dipped a slight curtsy. "Lord Amberly."

"Pray, sit. I did not intend to invade upon your privacy." Hands behind his back, he surveyed his surroundings. "I was merely taking a walk."

Before their walk, he'd said he was unaccustomed to going out of doors during the day.

Though he still wore the mask, there was a . . . difference in him. The darkness that had once mantled him had loosened. Lessened. Alterations not evident to the casual observer but unmistakable to her.

She resumed her seat on the bench, placing the volume she held on her lap. "Sunday mornings are a pleasant time for one."

"They seem to be. And you?" He took a step toward her, coming to stand by the bench in the center of the neglected garden.

She smoothed a hand across the worn cover of her Bible. "I like to take a bit of time on Sundays to read. As Christmas is in but three days, it seemed more appropriate than usual."

He glanced at the spine. A slight frown bracketed the corners of his mouth. "Are you religious?"

"Not really." She looked down at her clasped hands, pale against the black cover of the Bible, then up at him. More than walks in the snow or Christmas festivities or the courage to face the outside world, he needed the light of Christ.

*God, give me the words to speak to him. Open his heart to You.*

Since her first prayer for him, many more had followed. But there had never seemed the right moment to speak of such things, until now.

"That is, I prefer not to use that name. Religion is what I grew up with at the charity school. Sermons about the horrors of hell awaiting those who did not repent. Pamphlets about the fate visited upon wicked children. Endless catechisms we were required to recite perfectly or risk a ferule across the palm. Religion, even God, seemed full of anger, something to be feared."

"So you turned your back on it?"

She nodded. "Yes. I wanted nothing to do with a God of anger when cruelty already dominated so much of my life. But when I was thirteen, a new teacher arrived at the school. Every day during the hour for quiet studying, I noticed Mrs. Aldridge sat at her desk and read her Bible. One day I asked her why she found it so interesting, and she asked if she could read me something from it. I must confess I agreed only because I was eager to please her since she'd been kind to me. Would you like me to show you what she read?"

He'd listened in that quiet, watchful way of his. Now, he nodded.

The thin pages fluttered in the wind as she turned them until she found the place she sought. The page was tattered around the edges and water spotted. Tears. Both Mrs. Aldridge's and her own. Jenny cleared her throat. "'And we have known and believed the love that God hath to us. God is love; and he that dwelleth in love dwelleth in God, and God in him. Herein is our love made perfect, that we may have boldness in the day of judgment: because as he is, so are we in this world. There is no fear in love; but perfect love casteth out fear: because fear hath torment. He that feareth is not made perfect in love.'" She paused, meeting his eyes as she recited from memory. "'We love him, because he first loved us.'"

She kept the book open, hands resting on the well-worn page.

"When Mrs. Aldridge spoke of God, she did not seem afraid of Him. At least, not in the way we'd been taught. She painted a picture of a Father who sent His Son to earth as a babe, born to the humblest of families and in the lowliest of places, so He might grant us the gift of His eternal presence. A God who loved humanity in all its flaws and frailties enough to sacrifice His Son so we might live." Emotion lined her voice.

His jaw hardened. "I'm not quite sure I follow."

She tilted her head. "What do you mean?"

He walked around the bench to face her. "You, of all people, who have endured, who have lost such a great deal, how can you believe in the goodness of some almighty being while your own life has been racked with pain and suffering?" He stopped.

She drew in a breath. It was a question asked in earnest from the depths of both their pain. In the layers of his words, she heard what he did not say.

*How can you believe when a man stole your innocence? When you were nearly reduced to surrendering your child into the care of strangers?* And also, *How can I believe when I too have been faced with questions for which there seem to be no answers, loss for which there seems to be no remedy?*

"I have not always been certain," she admitted. "After I lost my situation as a governess, during the months of carrying Anna, the darkness seemed too great for anything, even God, to overcome. Some mornings I lay in bed uncertain if I could summon the strength to get up, asking why God would allow such devastation into my life when I'd done my best to please Him." She pressed her lips together, remembering the emptiness of those days. "It seemed He had abandoned me as surely as my earthly parents. But as time went on, I realized our circumstances are not a reflection of His love. In spite of everything, He is the one certainty we can cling to. He sees each broken part and loves every last piece." Thickness gathered in her throat. "And though I've known the darkness of suffering, there have been other moments when I've sensed His provision. So in answer to your question, yes, I still believe. Not in this world or my happiness in it, but in Him." She closed the Bible and wrapped both hands around it. "And you?" She searched his gaze. "Where does your faith lie?"

She sensed tension radiating from the stiffness in his shoulders, the tightened lines of his face. Had she been wrong to speak thus to him?

No. Whether he opened his soul to it or not, she cared for him too much to keep back the truth.

Wind riffled the barren tree branches. She shivered in the cold. He stood in front of her, boots planted on the frostbitten ground, form black against the gray landscape. Silence weighted the air. She'd not fill it. She'd said enough.

"Up until last year, myself. Now?" He shook his head. "Nothing."

She rose, skirt trailing the ground. She took a step toward him, pressing the Bible into his gloved hands. "Please," she whispered. "Read this." Then she turned away, hastening toward the house before he could reject what she had handed him. Her legs shook, wind blowing tendrils of hair away from her stinging cheeks.

She cared for him. How slowly it had begun until the truth of her heart lay before her. His scars, his woundedness, his strength, and his hidden tenderness. All of him, even the parts she did not know.

*Father in heaven, mend his soul and make it Yours.*

✦ ✕ ✦

A shout pierced the silence.

Dwight shoved back his chair. He strode from his bedchamber, threw open the door, pounded down the stairs. Shouted words ricocheted through the house.

"Where is he? I'll drag him from his hole meself." The voice was male. Angry.

Dwight burst into the great hall. William blocked the path of a stocky man. "I must insist that you leave. His Lordship does not receive visitors."

"There he is." The man lunged past William, a bull breaking free from his cage. Wiry hair stuck up in wild tufts from his balding head.

His coat was ragged, unbuttoned, the loose shirt beneath stained. Raw fury sizzled in his gaze. "The black devil himself."

"Is there some way I might be of assistance?" Dwight fought to keep his voice calm.

Footsteps clattered down the stairs. Jenny rushed into the great hall, Anna in her arms. Mrs. Fletcher followed.

"I'm going to have to ask you to leave, *sir*." William fisted the collar of the man's coat, as if to drag him bodily toward the door. The man fought the footman's grip, shoving him off, charging forward.

"You put a curse on my son. He wouldn't eat after he come back that night, starin' glassy-eyed into nothin', jumpin' if you so much as come up behind him. He done told me what he saw. You! Stalkin' the countryside in your mask. What're you hidin', you hound from Hades?" He made a sound between a shout and a sob. "He's dead now. My poor little lad. Went missin' two nights ago. Found him in the bottom of the old well on the Linton property." His face twisted. "Who's to say you didn't put him there yourself?"

It started as a burning in his gut, spread to a coldness seeping into every pore.

"That isn't true!" Jenny's voice echoed through the great hall. Anna started to wail. "He did not kill your son. You have no right to come here and say such things."

"Get out of my house." Dwight gritted the words. "Or I will call the constable."

"The village is cursed because of you!" The man's words reverberated off the ceiling. "'Tis time someone took matters into his own hands and said *enough*." He reached inside his coat.

Time stilled. Metal flashed. He raised his arm, pointing a pistol directly at Dwight.

Dwight lunged with all his strength, grasped the barrel, and twisted. A shot exploded. Someone screamed. The pistol clattered to the floor, skidding across the wood. A sickening crack. The man hit the floor with a heavy thud. Smoke hazed the air. William stood over the fallen man, gripping a poker.

"Lord Amberly, are you hurt?"

As if through fog, he saw Jenny rush toward him. He stared at her blankly, shook his head. Behind her, Mrs. Fletcher held her hand to her mouth, eyes wide.

Robbins surged through the front door, breathing heavily. "What the deuce happened?"

With measured steps, Dwight crossed to where the pistol lay and picked it up. The handle was sweaty from the man's grip. "Robbins, ride straightaway to the village and fetch the constable."

"Yes, m'lord." Robbins turned. The door shut behind him.

Dwight blinked. The sharp scent of smoke hung in the air. "Is he breathing?"

William nodded, the poker he'd struck the man with still clutched in his hands.

"Go upstairs. Fetch my pistol." His voice sounded as if it came from inside a long, dark tunnel. "We'll need to guard him until the constable arrives."

"What can I do?" Jenny asked. She rocked Anna, the baby's cries gnawing at the frayed hold he had on control.

"Nothing. Tend to her. Take Mrs. Fletcher with you."

She stared at him, the tendons in her neck tightening, the pallor of her face making her eyes all the brighter. Then she nodded. He looked away as the women left.

William brought the pistol, which Dwight grasped as they awaited the arrival of the constable. The man on the floor wakened with a groan, blood trickling down one side of his head. Realization flickered across his liver-spotted face. "Not a move, not a word," Dwight ordered, voice low.

It might have been an hour, was probably less, before the front door opened, bringing in a gust of cold air, Robbins, the constable, and another man. Mud tracked across the floor as they strode in.

"Lord Amberly? Thomas Horton, parish constable." He gave a perfunctory nod. Dwight recalled seeing the man in the village in prior years.

"Thank you for coming."

The man who'd attacked him struggled to his feet with a grunt.

Droplets of blood splattered the floor. "He murdered my son. I know he's the one that done the deed. When I confronted him, he struck me down." His eyes slitted. "Black as coal, he is, down to his bones."

The other man, likely the constable's assistant, took the man by his arm. "Steady on. Never fear, you'll have your say."

"Is there someplace we might speak?" the constable asked.

Dwight led him into the drawing room. Briefly, the constable questioned him, after which he asked to speak to the other witnesses—William, Jenny, and Mrs. Fletcher. Dwight waited outside the door.

At length, the constable exited, pausing in the corridor. "He'll be taken into custody. You'll be required to appear as a witness at the trial. We'll contact you if we require further information before then."

Dwight nodded. "I'll show you out." He led the way into the great hall, several sets of footsteps behind him. In the great hall, the constable's assistant guarded the man, whose name, Dwight had learned from the constable, was Ezra Miller. His son's name was Ben. The constable had assured him the circumstances of the lad's death would be inquired into. That was the first question Dwight had asked.

The constable took hold of Ezra's arm. "You'll be coming with us, my man. And I'd advise you to go quietly."

"The last of the Amberlys, you are." Ezra turned, gaze landing on Dwight. The hatred in the man's eyes seared him. "Pity there be a last at all."

The door shut. For a moment, the room was silent.

Sensing the gazes of his staff upon him, Dwight forced words to come. "Thank you for your assistance this afternoon." His voice sounded strange, shaky. "Pray, forgive me. There are matters requiring my attention." He turned on his heel and strode toward the stairs.

He didn't stop until he'd reached the attic and locked the door behind him.

# CHAPTER 13

———◆✕◆———

THE MOMENT THE man had aimed a pistol at Lord Amberly's heart was one her own would never forget. Hours later, Jenny's breath still faltered with every intake.

Another moment, too, would never leave her. The one when Lord Amberly had met her eyes afterward. To look upon his face was like gazing into a void from which all light had vanished.

While Mrs. Fletcher tended Anna, Jenny went down to the kitchen and prepared tea—black, the kind he preferred. She lifted the tray in both hands and ascended the kitchen steps. Onward, she walked through the house and up the stairs. The nearer she drew to the attic, the harder her heart pounded.

She could not leave him alone. The venom of the words the man had spoken seeped through her, leaving a chill.

*The village is cursed because of you . . . My son is dead . . . Pity there be a last at all.*

Oh, Dwight. He had done nothing to justify such hate. Why did the world always seek to torment those who were different than they?

She reached the attic door, its aged wood shut tight. A barrier, severing him from the rest of the world. Would that forever be the way he managed pain, by locking himself away from everything and everyone?

Drawing in a breath, she shifted the tray to one hand, then lifted her fist and knocked.

No answer.

"Lord Amberly?" She knocked again. "Are you there? I've brought you some tea."

Still, nothing.

"Please open the door."

A minute passed. The door scraped open. Dwight stood inside. He'd shucked his coat and waistcoat, his cravat missing, his shirt open at the throat. His hair fell over his forehead, the strands disheveled, as if he'd raked his fingers through them. His gaze met hers, still lifeless. As if refusing to feel at all had become the only way he could endure.

"May I come in?"

He stepped aside to let her pass.

She crossed the threshold, uncertain of what she'd find. The room was paneled in wood and pitched low, holding teetering stacks of crates and boxes at one end, paintings draped in cloths, a cracked lantern upon an old desk.

On the opposite end of the room sat a mahogany pianoforte. Though the instrument was not as large as the grand piano owned by the Carlisles, its quality was unmistakably fine. Crumpled wads of paper littered the floor.

This was his sanctuary. From this room, the music came. Those broken snatches of melody drifting like smoke through the house. Fragmented and anguished, much like the man who created them.

She turned to him. He stood near the door, staring out the single window at the opposite end of the room. Tendrils of fading light fell across the floorboards. "Where should I set this?"

"Just . . . there." His voice was cracked. He gestured to the desk.

She crossed the room and placed the tray upon the desk. Then she faced him. Twilight bathed his features. The marked pain upon them wrenched her to the core.

Heaven help her, she couldn't let him suffer alone. Who would speak truth to him if she did not?

Her steps echoed as she walked toward him. Though her legs shook, calm suffused her mind. "You must not listen to the lies."

At her words, his head, which had been lowered, hair tangling across his brow, lifted. He stared at her, so much of his mien, so much of *him* hidden behind that terrible mask.

"You are not who they say you are. You are not cursed or a monster or any of the other brands that have been placed upon you."

"I beg you." His voice was low. "Do not."

No. Light must shine upon darkness.

"You are a man of tenderness and noble heart. Did you not save me and my child, offer us shelter and rescue? Did you not care for us when we were ill, as if we were as close as blood? Did you not fight a war for the sake of king and country?" She took a step closer, throat tight. "Anyone who cannot see beyond your mask is not worthy to know you at all." Tears filmed her eyes, her words a whisper. "You are not your scars." She reached up and placed her hand against the masked side of his face. It was smooth, slightly warm from the heat of him.

*Please. See yourself as I do.*

Her fingertips trailed downward to the taut skin of his jaw.

In a blinding instant, he jerked back. "Go." He flung his hand toward the door, breathing ragged.

"Please." Hot tears slipped down her cheeks. She shook her head. "Listen—"

"Go," he repeated, voice dark. "My life is none of your concern."

Tears coming so fast she could scarcely see, she rushed past him and out the door. Above the roar in her ears, she heard it shut with a cold click. The most final of sounds. Down the stairs she fled, stumbling in her haste.

At the bottom of the steps, her legs gave way. She crumpled, resting her head on her bent knees. Her shoulders shook.

Darkness had won.

Sorrow yawned deep.

—✕—

Though twilight still traced the sky, a darkness as thick as night encompassed the whole of him. Dwight slid down the wall and sank to the floor.

*You are not your scars.*

She'd uttered those words as if their truth ran soul deep.

He was. And would ever be. They branded him as surely as a searing iron, a ceaseless reminder of what he had become. His flesh the vehicle that drove him from the realm of humanity and into the shadows. Making him the subject of schoolboys' tales and village gossip. He'd heard the doctors when they'd first unwrapped the bandages, their murmured *"What a pity."* When he'd first beheld his ravaged face, he'd made no sound, said not a word. But the breath had left his lungs, replaced by a chasm slowly sucking him downward.

This was his reality. Another loss to add to the column stretching from the day he'd glimpsed his mother's colorless face as she'd lain in bed, hands folded across her breast, lips motionless and waxen.

Only this loss had left him among the living. He'd summoned gratitude, told himself he could still continue as before. Then came the day when Louisa visited him, her rejection cutting like a knife through the layers of his future.

When he'd received the letter from Arthur's mother, the paper creased and tear stained, casting blame upon him for her son's death, the last vestiges of hope had died. More than the pain of his own injuries, Arthur was gone. The Martin family forever robbed of a son and brother.

That had sealed it. What good had Dwight been to anyone? He'd been unable to save those closest to him—his mother, his best friend. Even his father and Henry. Though his relationships with both had been strained, they'd still been family.

He'd tried to drown the silence with music. But his attempts to soothe the emptiness had fallen like dust to the ground.

Worthless. His life, encapsulated in a single word.

Jenny Grey had given him a glimpse of hope again. He'd even begun to imagine a future beyond the confines of the Hall. And secretly, a future with her.

*"The village is cursed because of you."*

Ezra's words chanted through his mind. Dwight did not believe in curses, but a weight of darkness had rested upon his family, as one loss after another befell them. Now, the latest. A child's life had been heaped upon his head. Ezra was crazed with grief and likely speaking from the depths of it. But his accusations remained.

Dwight lowered his face into his hands, resting his forehead on his palms.

Why did he loathe himself so much? Why did he feel the need to hide his face? The world was harsh, and in it he felt fragile. Life and the people he'd trusted had pierced him deeply. Isolation seemed the only remedy.

Had he unwittingly caused a boy's death? He'd shut himself away so as not to inflict his presence on society. Had that not been enough? Could he not be allowed to live in peace, alone, untampered with? Could he never be free?

Desperation surged through his chest. With a visceral groan, he tore the mask from his face. It fell to the ground. He rose and crossed to the piano. A candle in a silver holder rested on the floor. He lit it and laid his tinderbox aside. The flame flickered as he carried the candle to the window.

Drawing in a shuddering breath, he held it aloft. Against the backdrop of darkness, his reflection was an overlay. He did not look away after the first glance, but took it all in. The puckered, angry skin lacing the left side of his face like raw meat, the void of his missing eye. Recalling what was not visible, the scars covering the rest of his body.

Life held no future but this.

*Our circumstances are not a reflection of His love.*

For a long moment, he stared at his face in the candlelight.

Beneath the burden of darkness, his soul felt fractured. Empty.

*He sees each broken part and loves every last one . . . I still believe . . . Not in this world or my happiness in it, but in Him.*

Light fell upon the music rack, littered with ink-blotted pages of his scribbled attempts. He swept them aside.

The small Bible sat on the mahogany stand, worn and ordinary. He'd absently placed it there after she'd given it to him. He set the candle on the bench and picked up the book, the faded cover smooth against his hand.

The expression in her eyes as she'd handed it to him, shining with emotion, full of hope.

*Please. Read this.*

Her face rose again, as she'd stood before him less than an hour ago, tears in her eyes, touching him as if she could unmake his wounds by the gentleness of her hand.

He'd lost her. The woman who'd stolen his heart with the beauty of hers had sought to help him. He'd pushed her away.

How could he mend this? How could he mend any part of life's brokenness? How could he mend himself?

He stared down at the book in his hand, the truest prayer he'd ever spoken falling from his lips and onto the empty air.

"God, I offer myself to You. Alone, I am nothing."

# CHAPTER 14

HEAVINESS PRESSED UPON her shoulders as Jenny entered the great hall. A fire snapped in the hearth, and tapers cast flickering outlines upon the walls. Light and shadow braided together. Like life.

Leah stood on a stool in front of the mantel, a basket of greenery at her feet. Had it only been yesterday they'd gathered it, breathless and laughing as they went in search of holly?

Holding her skirt with one hand, Leah climbed down. "When I came back from the village, Mrs. Fletcher told me what happened." She sighed. "I know Christmas Eve isn't until tomorrow, but I had to keep busy."

"It looks beautiful." Deep-green leaves and red berries garlanded the mantel. With what joyous expectation they'd planned to keep Christmas. Jenny had spent the morning making mincemeat pies with Mrs. Fletcher while Anna sat on a blanket in the kitchen, playing with the wooden blocks William had carved for her. In view of the day's events, their holiday anticipation seemed lusterless and empty. "Truly, Leah."

Leah's keen gaze took in Jenny's face. "What is it? I can see by the look of you that something is not right." She walked to the stairs, settling herself on the bottom step. Jenny followed.

How could she begin to sift through her emotions at the thought of the man upstairs? For so long, she'd tried to hide their existence. Now, after everything . . .

She could not deny how deeply she cared.

"I went upstairs." She kept her gaze on her clasped hands. "I thought I could find a way to reach him, but he wouldn't listen. He told me to go, said his life was none of my concern." She faced Leah, blinking back the burn in her eyes. "I'd begun to think God brought me to this place to show him how to live again, but how can I when he pushes me away? They say the family is cursed, and there he is upstairs, cursing himself by his inability to realize the truth about himself." She shook her head. "I should leave. Perhaps it was a mistake I came here at all."

A bittersweet smile softened Leah's face. "You love him, don't you?"

Jenny shook her head, blinking back tears. Remembrances bled into each other. His quiet presence beside her sickbed. The way he'd brought her to his home and given her a place in it. His hand over hers as she'd released secrets she'd held close too long, his softly spoken *I'm sorry*. The gentle way he cradled her child in his arms.

She'd known the world as little else but cruel. Yet in the most unexpected of places, in a man who kept so much locked away yet had shared himself with her, she'd found trust. Honor. Tenderness. She swallowed. "I love him because I see him better than he sees himself."

"He cares for you too. I've noticed the way he is with you. The way I imagine he was before . . ."

She couldn't believe Leah's words, no matter how much she wanted to. "All my life I've been told who I am and what my place is. When Lord Amberly asked me to come here, it was as if he saw beyond my past. How could I not care for him? But these feelings change nothing. I will never be more than a servant."

"You are more than a servant." Leah reached out and placed a firm hand on Jenny's. "You are a woman who has done so much here for us all. I believe God brought you to us. Why, I don't know. Whether for him or for you, I can't say. But I do believe He has a plan. And when it looks the darkest is when we have to trust the most." She squeezed Jenny's fingers and stood. "Get some rest. It's been a long day." Leah's footsteps were soft as she climbed the stairs.

A hush fell over the room, broken only by the popping of the fire. The remainder of the Christmas greenery sat in its basket, candles glowed, and the scent of polish and aged wood hung in the air.

She had to get up, move forward, continue on with life. She had to feed Anna and put her to bed. Mrs. Fletcher was likely weary of tending her.

Still, Jenny lingered.

Christmas and the New Year would soon be here. What did her life in the dawning year hold? For so long, she'd whittled the future down to the span of making it through another day. At Amberly Hall, she'd begun to hope again. She must not let that hope die. Right now, she could do nothing for Dwight. Except pray. For him. For herself.

She bowed her head, resting it against her clasped hands.

*Be with Dwight. He needs You so. Grant us both Your presence this Christmas.*

◆•✕•◆

Dawn spilled through the window. Dwight lifted his head. Cramps knotted the back of his neck. He'd fallen asleep sitting on the floor, Jenny's Bible in his lap. How late had he read? Time had slipped by without his notice as he'd pored over the well-worn volume and wept over the holy words.

This was the succor sought by his empty soul. The ever-elusive peace he'd tried to grasp. These pages were the well from which one could drink and never thirst again, the pearl worth selling all in order to possess. The light to permeate the deepest darkness.

To vainly seek redemption was perhaps the greatest futility of his life. It waited, an undeserved gift, for the poorest of sinners to embrace. Last night, he had.

Without the scars, devoid of the darkness, would he have reached this place?

He stared at his left hand, freed from its glove, the furrowed skin a reminder of the life he'd led. Now, with the help of God, he would chart a new beginning. His scars were part of that. But they were not and would never again be the whole of him.

He stood, easing the kinks in his muscles. It was Christmas Eve. In the past week, with the help of Robbins and Mrs. Fletcher separately, he'd chosen and purchased gifts for his staff. A novel called *Emma* and a shawl for Mrs. Fletcher. A gold watch for Robbins. Fabric for a coat for William and the sum of ten pounds, for Dwight had every reason to believe the young man would need to buy a wedding ring in the year ahead. A cloak for Leah and a pair of sewing scissors.

And for Jenny, cloth a hue of rich blue, to match her eyes, and a silver chain with a cross pendant. Would she receive the gifts after what had passed between them yesterday?

More than that, would she accept his apology and grant him the chance to begin anew?

He'd little right to ask it of her. Yet what he must do was unmistakable. What he must offer lay plain.

She would see him as he was.

Then the choice would be in her hands.

# CHAPTER 15

Dwight's heart hammered as he stood in the drawing room. He'd waited for another woman in this very room, heart a drumbeat in his chest, gaze on the door, running words through his mind. After she'd left, he'd vowed *never again*.

The time had come. He sensed it in his spirit.

No matter what followed, this woman was worth the risk.

The door opened with a soft creak. He turned. Jenny stood on the threshold, hands clasped at her waist. Uncertainty weighted her gaze, her face pale.

"Mrs. Fletcher said you wished to see me."

He nodded, words cleaving to the roof of his mouth. Sunlight streamed through the windows, falling upon her.

She was so beautiful, her quiet radiance evident even in the midst of her hesitancy. He ached to draw her into his arms and press his lips against her hair, her face, her mouth. But could anyone take pleasure in such a touch from him?

He'd asked God to help him gain freedom from the shackles he'd bound himself with because of his scars.

Was grace strong enough to grant even that?

"I wish . . ." He grasped for words. ". . . to ask your forgiveness for my behavior yesterday. I was wrong to ask you to leave." He swallowed. "As I have been wrong about a great many things. Some time ago, a woman I cared for hurt me deeply. After that, I made myself a prisoner in my isolation. But nothing guarantees we will be spared pain, no matter what steps we take to lock ourselves away. You showed me that. It's because of you . . . and because of Christ that I can answer the question you asked not so long ago with a different answer. I believe, and my life is no longer my own."

She raised her hand to her lips. Were those tears shining in her eyes?

"I want to thank you for all you have given me. And to . . ." He sucked in a jagged breath.

Could he do this? Once done, it could not be taken back.

And whatever her response, it would stay with him a lifetime.

Perhaps the greater part of love was not in its being received, but given. An unconditional act of offering everything, asking nothing.

For her, he would offer this. Himself, no barriers between them.

With shaking hands, he removed the mask. Let it fall to the ground. Then raised his head.

Her gaze met his. She made no move or sound, her face a little paler. A fist tightened around his throat.

He'd stripped the mask away, and with it the layers wrapping his heart. Only the core remained. Before her, he stood bare. Vulnerable. But to be truly whole meant to be both of those things, in spite of fear.

In the silence, she regarded him. A single tear slipped down her cheek.

Then she walked toward him, sunlight a veil around her. Overwhelmed, he bent his head, unable to look at her this close.

Something brushed his jaw, feather soft. She lifted his chin. Gaze to gaze. He couldn't breathe. Tears slid unheeded down her cheeks. She tilted her face toward his.

Gently, her fingers whispered against his scarred skin. With a tenderness that made him ache, she touched what he'd kept hidden, the soft pressure of her hand lingering against the side of his cheek.

Her touch broke him. For in it was grace.

He placed his hand over hers, twining their fingers. Then lowering her hand, still held in his, he lifted it once more. Brushed his lips against her knuckles, head bowed low, this act of fealty the truest he could offer. A tear of his own fell and landed against her smooth fingers. Her indrawn breath was the only sound. How long they stayed like this he could not account.

In that moment, she was all he knew.

———◦✕◦———

The path of an altered life would not be an easy one. But with the help of God, Dwight would walk it, seeking Him for strength.

When he'd told Mrs. Fletcher and Robbins about his plan, astonishment evidenced itself upon their faces. But he glimpsed the smile creeping around Mrs. Fletcher's mouth, Robbins's nod and quick acquiescence. Everything lay in readiness now. Robbins's trip to the poulterer's had produced eleven geese. Each of his tenant families would receive one.

Dwight recalled from boyhood that Christmas Day service began at nine and ended at ten. Everyone should have left church and returned to their cottages by now. Robbins had told him the parish had a new vicar. Dwight intended to call upon him soon, take his place in the family pew, but that would keep for another day.

He stood in the great hall as William and Robbins loaded the carriage. Jenny came down the stairs. She'd been the first he'd shared his plan with, and the way her eyes shone had been approval enough for him. She held Anna, the baby's fingers gripping a wooden block.

"Happy Christmas." Jenny smiled. She wore the brown dress that had once been Mrs. Fletcher's, ringlets framing her cheeks. She was beautiful in whatever she wore, but he couldn't wait to watch her eyes light up when he gave her his gift. The other gift, the one he'd worked on long into the night, he'd share with her later.

"Happy Christmas." He managed a smile in return. William passed, hauling another load to the carriage, the open front door carrying in a gust of cool air. The strangeness of it hitting both sides of his face would take some getting accustomed to. He wore a patch over his left eye, but he'd not don the mask again. He was through with hiding. Those he met would see him as he was, and it would be up to them to accept or reject.

Still, his stomach knotted, the muscles beneath his right eye twitching.

"If they know you, they will not fear you," she said softly.

"I wish I shared your certainty."

"Then do." Her resolute gaze met his. "I will pray. And you will be strong."

William trooped in. "Everything's ready, m'lord."

"Go." Jenny reached out and clasped her hand over his. Her touch steadied him. "I'll be here with Mrs. Fletcher, preparing a feast fit for the Prince Regent." She smiled.

Though he wished she could come with him, this was something he must do alone. At the door, he turned. Jenny stood, watching him, Anna in her arms. Giving him courage, bidding him onward.

He followed William outside. The sky was colorless, the air brisk. He climbed into the carriage, and the horses clip-clopped down the avenue.

Far too soon, the carriage stopped. He disliked admitting he'd never met a single one of his tenants, save when his father had been the earl. Since he'd returned from Waterloo, his solicitor had traveled to Yorkshire twice a month and dealt with all matters concerning the tenants, a service for which he was paid handsomely. This state of affairs had not lent itself to the estate's prosperity. It made every one of these unannounced visits all the more difficult. And necessary.

*God, please guide me.*

William opened the door, and Dwight exited the carriage. They stood before a stone cottage, smoke curling from its chimney, the yard well tended. William unloaded one of the baskets from the back of the carriage.

"This is the Summersons' place."

"Thank you, William." Dwight reached for the basket. "I'll take it."

William nodded. Basket in hand, Dwight hesitated. Ahead stood the door. A family lived within, their dwelling on Amberly land.

Since becoming the earl, he'd made many mistakes.

Today was the beginning of amends.

Some were made in secret—like the gift to Arthur's mother. Dwight's solicitor had written with news that the gift had been received with the benefactor's identity still unknown to the family. Dwight prayed he'd find a way to enter their lives again. Not as their benefactor, but as the friend he'd once been.

Other amends were made by facing shortcomings straight on and purposing to be a better man.

*If they know you, they will not fear you.*

Jenny's words an echo, he approached the cottage. He lifted his fist and knocked. The door swung open. A middle-aged man stood inside.

"Mr. Summerson?"

"Yes?" Mr. Summerson's gaze narrowed, distrust evident on his weathered face.

"I'm Lord Amberly."

Mr. Summerson said nothing, one hand holding the door. A frown creased the man's brow. Whether of disbelief, anger, or disgust, Dwight couldn't tell.

He gave a brief smile. "I don't wish to interrupt your holiday. I simply came to offer my compliments of the season. And to give you this goose." He held out the covered basket.

Mr. Summerson made no move to take it.

If he left now, he'd be no closer to earning Mr. Summerson's trust. No nearer to rebuilding the shambles of the past to forge a better future.

"I . . . believe I knew your brother. Was he not second footman at the Hall some fifteen years ago?"

Mr. Summerson nodded. "Aye. Joseph."

"Yes, that's right. I recall he taught me how to play bowls one summer. We were grateful to have him in our employ. He left and moved to York when I was away, I believe. Is he well settled there, do you know?"

"He owns a shop now. Has a wife and three children. My eldest daughter, Charlotte, lives with them."

A little girl appeared in the doorway. "Who's that man, Father?" She stared at Dwight.

Mr. Summerson glanced at the child. "I thought I told you to stay inside." His tone was gruff but not unkind.

"But I wanted to see who it was." Her dress was wrinkled, her curly hair not quite combed. "What's wrong with his face?" One of her front teeth was missing, making her lisp.

Dwight bent down, meeting her at eye level. "My name is Lord Amberly. I live in the big house down the road. I fought in the war and was wounded. That's why my face looks like this."

The girl blinked wide brown eyes. "Does it hurt?"

"It used to," he said. "Not as much anymore."

"Why are you here?"

"That's enough questions, Emma," Mr. Summerson said. "Go see if your mother needs help."

"Yes, Father." She ducked her head, peering at Dwight shyly. "Will you come and see us again?"

"Perhaps." Dwight smiled, standing to his full height again.

She scampered into the house, her chatter drifting out to them. "A man is out there with Father. His face was hurt in the war, but he seems very nice. He said he might come again."

"Is she your daughter?"

Mr. Summerson gave a low chuckle. "Our Emma is five and full of questions."

"She's a dear child." Dwight paused. "In truth, Mr. Summerson, I came to offer my apologies for my absence these past months. I'm aware my management of the estate has not been what it should. I intend to remedy that."

Mr. Summerson's frown deepened. "I heard about the Miller lad. Word is Ezra came to the Hall, tried to take revenge."

"I can assure you I had nothing to do with the death of Ben Miller," Dwight said quietly. "The constable is in the midst of an investigation. I'm deeply sorry for the family and will aid his wife and remaining children in any way I can."

Mr. Summerson rubbed a thumb across his chin. Then he nodded.

Dwight held out the basket. Mr. Summerson took it.

"When your grandfather was earl, I heard he used to hold a supper for his tenants at the Hall." He met Dwight's gaze, a challenge in his eyes. "Perhaps you might revive the practice."

"Would you come?"

Mr. Summerson nodded. "I just might."

"Then I just might do that." Dwight held out his hand.

After a pause, Mr. Summerson clasped it in a firm grip. "Happy Christmas to you, m'lord."

"Happy Christmas. My best to your family for the New Year."

Dwight walked back to the carriage. Robbins leaned down from his seat. "How'd you fare?"

Despite the cold, a sense of purpose warmed Dwight from within. "It went . . ." He paused. "It went well. It did indeed."

# CHAPTER 16

As she carried in the platter, Mrs. Fletcher's smile was brighter than the flames wreathing the plum pudding. They all clapped as she placed the pudding before Dwight. Sitting beside Leah, Anna in her lap, Jenny looked at the smiling faces around the dining room table, her heart full. Anna, sensing the excitement, clapped her little palms together and laughed, her wide smile revealing one tiny tooth.

"Now, don't any of you be getting your hopes up," Mrs. Fletcher said as blue flames flickered and danced atop the pudding. "I haven't made one of these in . . . heavens, I don't know how long. I might have misplaced my knack for it."

"Don't believe a word of it." Dwight grinned. "Her puddings are renowned throughout the county."

"Well, they say the proof of the pudding is in the eating." William winked at Leah.

Mrs. Fletcher made a move toward the stack of small plates, and Leah rose to help her. "Permit me." Dwight stood. "You ladies have done more than your share of serving today. It's time I had a turn."

Mrs. Fletcher hesitated. "Well, if you insist."

"Ah, sit yourself down, Alice." Robbins leaned back in his chair. "You've been to-ing and fro-ing enough to make my head spin."

Dwight sliced the pudding and passed around plates bedecked with slices of the fragrant, speckled sweet. As he handed Jenny her piece, their hands brushed. A fluttery brightness filled her. She ducked her gaze to Anna.

Perhaps society might find it irregular, an earl taking Christmas dinner with his servants. But as they'd talked and laughed amid the passing of dishes and serving of roast beef, potatoes, and flaky Christmas pie filled with succulent poultry, nothing had seemed more right.

After handing around everyone's plates, Dwight reclaimed his seat. Mrs. Fletcher, who'd been laughing at some joke of Robbins's, leaned forward as Dwight lifted his fork and swallowed a bite.

"Perfection."

Robbins's eyes fell closed as he chewed. "Now *that's* a Christmas pudding. Ever had its equal, Miss Grey?"

Jenny tasted the pudding. She'd never eaten plum pudding before, but this was indeed delicious. Dense and warm, rich with fruits and spices. "I can't say that I have."

Mrs. Fletcher looked relieved as she sampled her own slice. "They say if a cook can't do a Christmas pudding up good and proper, she's no cook at all."

Silver clinked and laughter flowed as they savored the pudding, followed by slices of mincemeat pie. Though this was a meal few others could surpass, Jenny's gaze and attention wandered away from it and back to Dwight again and again. The timbre of his voice as he and Robbins reminisced about a stubborn colt Dwight had tried to tame in boyhood. The sincerity with which he praised Mrs. Fletcher after the final bite of pudding. The half smile lingering about the edges of his mouth as his gaze met Jenny's.

She'd been so proud when he'd returned from visiting the tenants. He stopped at the Millers last, he'd said. There had only been Mrs. Miller and her young daughter home. They'd greeted him with distrust and had not accepted their goose. Dwight had assured Jenny he'd let them remain at the cottage if they wished to do so. On his way back to Amberly Hall, he'd met the constable on the road, who'd said the investigation into Ben Miller's death was at an end. After assessing the site of the old well on the abandoned Linton property and questioning Mrs. Miller, the constable had concluded young Ben had been out at night searching for his dog, as the animal frequently broke its rope and wandered from home. The boards covering the well were old and rotted, and Ben had fallen through. Jenny was saddened but thankful Dwight bore no blame. He needed no more obstacles to overcome.

When plates sat empty, the fragrance of the meal a warm remnant in the air, Jenny turned to William and Leah with a knowing look.

"Shall we do it now?" Leah whispered.

Jenny nodded, a smile tugging on her lips as she stood and handed Anna to Mrs. Fletcher. William and Leah pushed back their chairs and joined her.

Dwight turned from his conversation with Robbins. "What's this?"

The three of them looked at each other. Leah spoke up. "In my family, it's rather a tradition to sing carols after Christmas dinner."

"We did promise you music." Jenny took her place between Leah and William at the end of the table.

"And we're not half bad," William added.

Leah wrinkled her nose at him.

Dwight leaned slightly back in his chair at the head of the table. "Then by all means, proceed."

"Ready?" William asked.

Jenny drew in a slow breath.

"Joy to the world; the Lord is come!
Let earth receive her King!
Let ev'ry heart prepare Him room,
And heaven and nature sing."

The words flowed, their voices blending in harmony. As she sang, not once did she take her eyes from Dwight. He listened, gaze thoughtful. The words held meaning for him now. Not merely a carol sung at Christmastide, but an encompassing of the miracle of Christ's birth in all its wonder and promise. The stanzas welled through her, brimming with fresh hope.

"No more let sins and sorrows grow,
Nor thorns infest the ground;
He comes to make his blessings flow
Far as the curse is found."

When they finished the last stanza, applause filled the room.

"That was . . ." Dwight paused. ". . . truly wonderful."

Jenny smiled. William said something to Leah, making her blush. Anna tried to wriggle away from Mrs. Fletcher, holding out her arms to Dwight. He swept her up, laughing as she grasped the folds of his cravat with her tiny fingers.

In all the Christmases of her life, those at the charity school, the one she'd spent with the Carlisles, and the last, when she'd been with child and alone in London, the Christmas of 1816 stood out with a radiant glow.

The only thing imperfect about this day was that it must end.

———◆✕◆———

Joy filled the remainder of that Christmas Day. They'd moved to the drawing room, and Dwight had announced he had gifts for all of them. After they'd opened and admired them, Leah said, with a regretful look, that they'd nothing for him. Emotion in his voice, he'd said they'd already given him more than he deserved or could ever repay.

After the others had left, Jenny hoisted a sleeping Anna into her arms, her daughter's head cradled against her chest. Dwight stood by the fireplace as voices and footsteps drifted from the corridor. He met her gaze and smiled.

"It was a wonderful day." She returned his smile. "A Christmas never to be forgotten."

"And I'm grateful to all of you for it." Sincerity lined his words.

Her cheeks warmed. She brushed a lock of hair away from Anna's forehead. Yesterday there had been no room for awkwardness. There had been a rightness to the intimate moment between them. Indeed, when she'd taken the first step, it was as if a divine hand guided her in every act that followed.

But now? How did he view her? The tenuous question, one she could scarcely ask, tugged at her, begging an answer for which she was hardly entitled.

She loved him. Of that her heart could not be more certain. There would be no sweeter joy than a future at his side. But perhaps God intended her part in his journey to go no further than helping him live again. Could she accept that when the sound of his voice, his hand on hers renewed dreams she'd thought forever lost to her? The act that had conceived her daughter had blackened her girlhood hopes of love and made her doubt she could give herself to any man without fear.

Then she'd come to know a man whom life had scarred. It had left him broken and changed, as it had done to her. But love reached beyond those wounds and into them.

How could she bear the shattering if she was forced to let him go? The answer rose soft within her.

With fortitude from God on high. He'd carried her through storms before, and as long as she remained on this earth, there would be storms ahead. His arms were strong enough for this.

She sensed Dwight regarding her and lifted her eyes. The ache of meeting his gaze pierced too deep. She must settle her feelings, reorder them, before she faced him again. "Well," she said, tone too bright, smile unwieldy. "Good night then." Anna in her arms, she moved toward the door.

"Wait." Scarcely more than a breath, that single word. But it stilled her as if he'd said a thousand. She turned, their gazes colliding in the flare of candlelight.

"Don't go."

⸻ ❊ ⸻

Before the night was through, he had one last gift to give her.

In the midst of the loss the years had brought, he'd never asked for nor expected miracles. Until he'd been given one. Grace had renewed his soul and love awakened his spirit. He deserved neither but would reach for both.

"Would you join me upstairs for a few moments?" He swallowed, throat dry. "There's something I wanted to show you."

She stared at him, lips parted, eyes wide with confusion. Anna lay asleep against her chest. "Let me just put Anna to bed first."

"I'll wait for you."

Minutes passed like hours as he waited for her in his attic room, standing by his piano, scanning the sheets sitting on the music rack.

At last there came a soft knock at the door. He crossed to open it. Hesitancy flickered in Jenny's eyes as she stepped over the threshold. Shadows fell across the floor, candlelight gilding the space. He took in the sight of her, her intermingled strength and fragility, vowing never to do anything to make her fear him.

"May I play something for you?"

She nodded.

He seated himself at the piano and rested his hands against the keys. He met her gaze. Drew in a breath, stilling the clamor within much as she'd taught him to do that day in the snow.

And then he began. It was the piece he'd been composing since he'd first sat down in a vain attempt to silence the voices of his past and mend his soul with music. Only it had an end where it had none before. The notes wept from his fingers as he poured them out, low and fast and dark.

If music told a story, this was his.

He played the familiar notes, the ones he'd known for so long they'd become a part of him, the anguish of each one bleeding onto the air as his fingers flew across the keys.

The cold stillness of his mother's chamber, her hair jet against the pillowslip, her eyes closed, his eleven-year-old self standing at the foot of her bed, hands by his sides. Helpless. Arthur's gasped-out words: *I'm . . . holding . . .* Louisa's final glance of pity and rejection. The wind howling across the moor as he strode into solitary darkness night after night.

Then the tempo shifted. Moments of laughter. The sweetness of a sleeping child against his chest. Quiet words of thanks. Broken ones of sorrow. Smiles brimming with joy. Undeserved gifts. The brush of her fingertips against his face. Light breaking through.

The cadence of it all wove through the music until the final notes fell from his fingers.

He rose. She stared at him with wonder on her face.

He'd speak the words, even if their rejection would inflict deeper scars than those upon his body. Even if he risked losing her because of them. He refused to live a single day under the shadow of another regret. Whatever happened, Jenny Grey had given him more than he'd ever deserved.

"There's something else I wanted to say . . ." His heart beat like a captive thing. ". . . to tell you."

"Yes?" Her voice came a bit breathless.

"I love you." He said it slowly, tasting the rightness of the words. He could have said so much else, told her in a dozen different ways. Yet these three words bound into a single truth encompassed the sum and measure of his heart.

A choked sound escaped her throat. And then they were coming toward each other, meeting in the center of the room. She looked up at him. "I love you too," she whispered.

Another miracle, those words. Love in and of itself was one. For it to be echoed was a second, as overwhelming as the first.

"I never want to hurt you. Would never ask anything of you that you were not willing to give." He needed her to know this. Though the scars she carried might be less visible than his own, they were in no less need of gentleness and healing.

"I know." She nodded, eyes wet. For a moment, silence fell between them.

"Dwight." His name slipped out in a ragged sigh. "I would very much like for you to kiss me. That is . . ." She paused, face flushing. "If you wanted to."

Oh, but he did. Slowly, he lowered his head and brushed his lips over hers. Loving her with every breath, through each tender kiss. He pulled her against him, holding in his arms she whom he cherished most in his heart.

Lord willing, she would become his bride. Anna, his daughter.

Together, the three of them, a family.

Indeed, they would be blessed.

Very.

# WONDERS OF HIS LOVE

## ERICA VETSCH

# CHAPTER 1

*Haverly Manor*
*Oxfordshire, England*
*October 1814*

DID A TURTLE ever protest the restrictions of its carapace? Did the canary resent the cage, no matter how gilded, and imagine soaring through the sky? Did a sheep long to leap like a stag and escape the paddock?

Cilla played another series of arpeggios on the pianoforte, letting her mother-in-law's monologue about her various aches and dissatisfactions drift around her. This day varied little from those that had come before it, for weeks, months. For nearly a year and a half now.

Actually, if she were honest, the sameness had covered all her life. She was Lady Priscilla Haverly, dutiful, soft spoken, accommodating, and always steering toward the safest path. Such it had always been, and such would it always be.

Why, then, did she have these stirrings of rebellion against the known and familiar? Who had planted these seeds of revolution that had recently sprouted in her heart and mind?

Her hands stilled on the keys, and she stared out the music room window at the parterre gardens surrounding Haverly Manor, now beginning their decline toward winter hibernation. Designed by Capability Brown more than fifty years before, the grounds were still some of the most beautiful in all of England.

At least she'd been told so many times by the dowager.

The gardens were much like Cilla's life. Regular, orderly, planned out. No real spontaneity or serendipity. Nothing unexpected ever happened there.

"What a dreadful autumn it has been." The Dowager Duchess of Haverly sighed and shifted her bandaged foot on the pillow. "This ankle has been such a trial. I pray neither of you have to suffer what I have endured these past few weeks."

Cilla recognized her cue. "What may I do to help?" She rose, heading toward the chaise upon which the dowager reclined. "Do you need the cushions adjusted?"

"I need this infernal break to heal properly. It's cost me too much time and enjoyment already." The older woman frowned, jabbing in the direction of her injury with a sharp finger. "I am glad that it was I, and not you, Charlotte, who fell down the stairs, though I could wish it hadn't been on the eve of my trip to Gateshead to see Sophia. She was no doubt devastated that I couldn't come to her."

Cilla's sister-in-law Charlotte looked up from her book, one hand resting on the swell of her unborn child. In three months she would meet either a son and heir or a delightful daughter. "Did you say something, madam?"

A long-suffering sigh hissed through the dowager's lips. "Charlotte, when will you put down those dusty old history books and take part in the conversation?"

Cilla sent Charlotte a sympathetic look as she bent to arrange the pillows. "Perhaps a cup of tea would be the thing? I understand Cook was making some pastries today. Would you like me to ring for the parlor maid?"

"I don't want pastries or tea. I want you to listen to me." The dowager thumped the upholstery beside her. "I have had an idea that will help take my mind off my pains, and it involves you both, so please at least pretend to listen."

Charlotte closed her book, and Cilla perched on the edge of a chair. When the dowager became imperious, there would be no peace until she'd had her say.

"Yes, madam?" Charlotte asked. Cilla's sister-in-law always called the dowager "madam," as did her husband, Marcus, the duke. They all did. Even Cilla's deceased husband had called his mother "madam." It seemed to suit her better than Mother or Your Grace or even, as she had once suggested, "Mother Dowager."

"Because Sophia decided to humor Mamie and take her to the seashore, I was done out of the fall house party I had planned in order to introduce Sophia to some eligible suitors. I'm only thankful that no invitations had been issued. It would have been so deflating to have to renege. Of course, then I had my little accident, so I wouldn't have been able to attend the party anyway."

Not this again. For weeks Cilla had heard little else but how Sophie had foiled her mother's carefully laid plans. Cilla tried to be gracious, knowing her mother-in-law was disappointed, and tried to remember that her injury caused her pain, but as the days wore on, it had become all Cilla could do to hold her tongue. How she wished she could escape the house like her romp of a sister-in-law, even if only for a little while.

"However, now that my foot appears to finally be on the mend, I think we should turn our thoughts to the Christmas season. I propose we host a house party in December. Something small and intimate, perhaps half a dozen guests, plus our family. We can have a few evening entertainments, some daytime outings. What do you think?" Though she asked for their input, she spoke as if the party were *fait accompli.*

Cilla glanced at Charlotte. This was the first time in the weeks since the dowager had taken a nasty tumble down the staircase at the dower house that she expressed interest in anything outside her own woes. Perhaps it would be just the thing to shake her out of her doldrums.

A Christmas party.

Cilla's own interest stirred. Was this the tonic she needed for her restless and dissatisfied spirit? Something to break the monotony of her days?

"What a wonderful idea, madam." Charlotte slipped a strip of paper into her book and set it aside. "I'm sure Marcus would approve. He spoke just yesterday about inviting the Whitelocks to join us for the holiday."

The dowager grimaced. She thought the Earl of Whitelock a plebeian upstart ever since the Prince Regent had seen fit to lift him from the ranks of common soldier and gift him with a title. His wife, Diana, was the daughter of a duke, therefore eminently acceptable, but Cilla doubted Evan—the earl—would ever come up to scratch where the dowager was concerned.

"Why Marcus should collect such odd personages for his friends, I shall never know. It's like he cannot help himself."

Charlotte grinned. "It's one of the many reasons I love him. He collected me, after all, and I am odd by most people's standards."

"Humph. You wouldn't be if you would only submit yourself to my careful guidance." The dowager's mouth puckered like a drawstring bag. "You are constantly speaking your mind, refusing to conform. Such behavior is a death knell in proper society circles. I don't know why Marcus encourages you to think so boldly. I wish you would be more like Cilla. She never says a word out of turn. From the moment she entered the Haverly family, she has been a model of rectitude."

*Meaning, I never talk back, never exert my will, never step out of line. At first I did it to maintain the peace and because I truly thought you would show me the way to be a proper duchess. Then it became a habit. I've suborned my will to yours for so long, I feel pale, with as little substance as a wraith.*

And yet a stubborn flicker that had flared to life in the months following the death of her husband, Neville, and the birth of their daughter, Honora Mary, refused to be doused.

But what good did it do to have even a small desire to think and do for herself? She had nowhere to go, no real place in society. Even her status in the Haverly family seemed undefined. She felt more like a paid companion to the dowager than a daughter of the house. For Cilla, life stretched before her as one of continually serving her mother-in-law, deferring to her stronger will, waiting to grow old.

Such was the life of a widow who almost became a duchess.

"I shall craft the guest list carefully." The dowager narrowed her eyes, staring at Cilla. "Only a few guests outside of family, but those invited will be of the highest character. Perhaps an eligible bachelor or two to liven things up?"

She raised her brows, and Cilla fidgeted. Eligible bachelors?

Would that be the answer to the restlessness she felt? A way to escape the doldrums of living with the dowager?

The idea of remarriage held little appeal, especially one engineered by her mother-in-law. Cilla's first marriage had been arranged by others. And though the marriage had not been unhappy, if she wed again, it would be for love, not status or security.

"There is more." The dowager sat up straighter, forgetting in her haste to wince and moan as she moved her foot. "Charlotte, it is beyond time you and Marcus had your official portraits painted to hang in the gallery here. It should have been done right after your wedding, but Marcus hardly remains home long enough for anyone to pencil sketch him, never mind sitting for a portrait. But Christmas is different. He'll be here for the month, and that's plenty of time for a painter to capture both your likenesses in oils."

Charlotte shook her head. "That's a very nice thought, madam, but I cannot sit for a portrait in December. I'm due to deliver in January. I refuse to be rotund in my official portrait." She patted her baby affectionately.

"Pish tosh. You will sit to have your face painted, and the painter can complete the portrait using a model wearing your dress. And I've found just the man to do the work. Lady Tringall recommended him. His name is Hamish Sinclair. He's Scots, but that can't be helped, I suppose." She adjusted her fichu and shook her head, as if lamenting the man's poor lot in life to be born north of the border. "He is not yet a member of the Royal Academy of Arts, which is a mark against him. Still, he can't charge the same prices as an RA member, can he? Anyway, we failed to have Neville's portrait done, and now it's too late. I refuse to make the same error again."

Cilla stood and went to the window, opening the sash to the crisp afternoon air. The room felt confining and stuffy. Every room did lately when the topic of her late husband arose. Neville Haverly had been the heir to the dukedom, but he had died before he could inherit. His portrait would never hang in the Haverly gallery, taking its place in the line of dukes. Hers would not hang beside his as his duchess.

She had married well, as per her parents' wishes. She had been a good daughter, a good wife, a good daughter-in-law. In the natural course of events, she would have become a good duchess, and had her husband lived long enough, she would have hopefully supplied him with a son to inherit.

She had given birth to Neville's child after his death, but to the dismay of the dowager, the baby had been a girl. So Cilla wasn't even the mother of the heir. Honora Mary was now ten months old, and Cilla couldn't imagine her life without her precious girl. But it left Cilla with an undefined role in society.

"The portraits will be my Christmas present to the pair of you." The dowager reeked of satisfaction with herself and her plans. "And the party can be your gift to me."

A Christmas party.

At least it would be something Cilla could anticipate.

Perhaps something exciting would happen. Something wondrous.

After all, it would be Christmas, the time of year when miracles were supposed to occur.

---

*Oxfordshire*
*December 1, 1814*

*This commission will surely be better than your last, for it canna be any worse.*

Hamish Sinclair gripped the baggage rail atop the mail coach— the only space left aboard the conveyance—and fought to stay aboard. Cold mist swirled around him, cutting visibility and driving the cold into his bones. He hardly dared release his hold on the railing in order to blow into his fist. If he suffered frostbite to his fingers, he would lose his only means of supporting himself.

The man crowded next to him eyed Hamish's well-worn cape, and his gaze paused on the red, royal-blue, and dark-green tartan muffler knotted at Hamish's neck.

The Sinclair plaid. That coupled with Hamish's dark-red hair were a dead giveaway to his heritage.

His fellow traveler scowled and tried not to let their shoulders touch.

Which was laughable, considering they were packed in like apples in a barrel.

A stone structure emerged from the mist ahead, and the coach slowed. As they drew abreast, the horses stopped and the coach lurched, jerking the passengers forward. Hamish grabbed the railing once more, sliding forward in spite of his efforts and knocking into the driver.

"Humph," the man protested, righting his hat. "This 'ere's where you said you wanted to get off."

A gatehouse. Gray stone, with gables and corbels and arched windows. His hands itched to draw it. What must the building look like in summer, with ivy and roses climbing over it?

The iron gates were shut.

His prison for the next month?

Hamish jumped down, and the coachman tossed his belongings after him. "Careful. That's full of glass bottles." He stopped the driver from throwing the wooden box, instead climbing halfway up to take it himself.

When his belongings lay on the damp grass beside him, the mail coach took off, leaving him on the verge. Shouldering the pack, he grasped the leather handle of his supply box. Hopefully, the crates he had shipped from his last place of work had arrived before him.

Hamish had gone only two steps when the gatehouse door opened and a man stepped out, wiping his hands on a towel and chewing vigorously.

"You the painter they're expecting at the big house?" he asked.

"Aye, Hamish Sinclair." He set the box down to offer his hand.

"Name's Canby. Where's your horse?" He looked down the road, but the mist had swallowed the mail coach.

"I've no horse, nor carriage either. Is it far to the manor?"

"A fair stretch of the legs." He unlatched a small gate set into the larger ones. "You'll pass a house on the left of the road, big enough you'll swear it's the manor, but that's the dowager's house. Keep on around the bend, and you'll see Haverly right enough."

Hamish thanked him and set off. Should he go to the servants' entrance? He thought not. When he had first started out as a portrait painter, he'd behaved as a servant, trying to be unseen, keeping quiet in the presence of his "betters," since that was what he was used to. But no more. He'd found if he arrived with confidence, as a professional and a gentleman, he was treated with more respect.

He didn't have a defined place in society. Servant, tradesman, or gifted guest, each depended upon how he carried himself and the tenor of the household.

What would the Haverly family be like? A duke and duchess. By far the highest ranking peers he'd been commissioned to paint.

Perhaps having them as his clients would raise him in the estimation of the jury at the Royal Academy. Of course, it wouldn't help his latest application, which lay with the jurors at the moment. But in the future? *Please, Lord, don't make me go through the application process again. If they turn me down this time, should I assume it's Your way of saying stop trying?*

If he had known this commission was in the offing, he would have delayed his application to include the Duke and Duchess of Haverly's portraits.

He had no appointments after this one, and at the first of the year, if he didn't gain acceptance into the Royal Academy of the Arts, he would be forced to take up a position that held little appeal.

The letter lay heavily in his pocket, an offer of employment at the Stratford Ladies Academy.

Teaching painting to giggling girls. He groaned as he trudged on. Why had watercolors suddenly become the fashionable pastime of the female elite? Becoming a painting instructor marked the end of a serious artist's career.

But it would put a roof over his head and food in his belly.

Frustration quickened his pace, and he marched with force. Why did he have to spend so much time chasing his crust when all he wanted to do was give life to the images crashing about in his head? The world was a riot of colors, shades, intensities of light. He wanted to experiment with techniques, with subjects, wanted to capture the world as he saw it in vivid pigment and sweeping brush stroke.

But without the status of an RA membership and the fat commission work that accompanied it, he would never have enough laid by to paint for his own pleasure for any length of time.

What he really longed for was a studio in London, regular exhibitions of his art, and the freedom to travel the country with his easel and palette.

Of course, every artist in England wanted the same.

"Get your head out of the clouds, Hamish Sinclair. Get on with the work a'fore you."

Where was this house? He'd walked a fair piece, and still nothing. The lane curved, and in the distance, a lake lay like a pewter charger, dull and flat under the gray skies.

He raised the collar on his coat. The Duke of Haverly must like his privacy to live way out here. Hopefully, he would be amenable to paint, both his looks and his temperament.

Striding on, Hamish finally reached the dower house. The same gray stone as the gatehouse, with symmetrical windows, early Georgian. And large. In the distance the manor itself appeared through the mist.

What a pile. The house spread gracefully, and unlike the gate and dower houses, the manor was constructed of red brick with many white-trimmed windows. Perhaps the dower house was the original manor, and this had been built later? It would be a dream to paint, set as it was in such perfect surroundings.

His boots crunched on the gravel, and his breath puffed in white clouds. "Getting soft, Hamish. Too many days spent at your easel and not enough walking the countryside." At least here at Haverly there appeared to be a fair patch of countryside to walk, should he be granted the time.

The mist changed to raindrops as he mounted the front steps. His arrival couldn't be more inauspicious. He used the brass knocker. *Be confident, and don't let them cow you, no matter how high their rank or their instep.*

Within moments, the right-hand door opened. A somber, lined face greeted him. "Yes?"

"Hamish Sinclair. I'm expected." He smiled, but not too broadly. The next moments would determine how his stay here would go. "The portrait artist?"

The butler looked him over from dark-red hair to scuffed boots. Not only scuffed but bearing more than a few splashes of dried paint.

"I see. Yes. Please, come in. I shall see if Her Grace is home." The butler stood aside, holding the door. He frowned, suspicious, as if almost ready to tell him to go round the back.

Hamish stepped inside, lowering his collar and loosening the tartan scarf at his throat. What a foyer. What must this hall look like on a sunny day when beams would stream through the skylights more than three stories overhead?

"This way, if you please."

Hamish followed the butler into a reception room of mint greens and golds and creams. Restful, but it needed a bit of bright color to liven it up. It felt cold. Perhaps a splash of crimson or coral here and there to wake it up?

"Wait here."

Hamish took the time to study the paintings in the room. A still life of flowers on a table, a landscape of some cows in a pasture. Nice work, though not unusual in composition or subject matter in either case. He squinted at the brushwork on the landscape, uncertain in the dim light, but confirming his suspicions as he scrutinized the techniques up close. If this wasn't a Gainsborough, he'd eat his palette knife.

The door opened, and a gray-haired woman entered, leaning upon a cane. In spite of this impediment, she had an imperious tilt to her head and moved well enough. Curls clustered on either side of her round cheeks, and her eyes were bright as shoe buttons. Her black dress seemed to swallow what little light came through the windows from the dreary day outside.

She reminded him of the ravens he'd seen at the Tower of London. His mind sketched a few quick strokes, creating a caricature, and he disguised his private amusement with a small cough. *Please don't let her be the duchess I'm supposed to paint.* He'd be hard pressed to smooth the prunes-and-prisms pucker from her expression.

The butler announced her. "Her Grace, the Dowager Duchess of Haverly."

"Hmm." She studied Hamish. "The painter?"

"Your Grace." Hamish bowed. "Hamish Sinclair." The dowager, not the duchess. He smiled.

She gave an acknowledging nod. "You are younger than I had hoped. Have you enough experience to capture likenesses accurately? Lady Tringall praised your work, but I've begun to have doubts. Perhaps I should have sought a more well-known artist for such an important commission."

He stifled a sigh. This was familiar ground. "Your Grace, may I suggest a conditional agreement? If I dinna produce paintings that meet with your approval, you will owe me nothing." How often had he been forced to make the same promise in order to secure a commission? "However, if you choose not to purchase the portraits, they will be mine to keep." To safeguard against someone claiming they were not up to standard and refusing to pay but displaying the portraits afterward. He'd learned his lessons the hard way.

"You must be quite sure of yourself. It's tantamount to bragging." She took a seat in a chair near the fireplace as if it were her throne.

"If I wasna confident in my abilities, I couldna expect you to be confident either. I will do my best for you, and I am certain my best is verra good indeed." And he was. Of all the things he doubted in his life, his ability to capture a likeness in paint wasn't one of them.

The door opened once more, and a woman came in.

Hamish felt a jolt in his chest, and his lips parted. Quickly, he catalogued her features.

Skin of alabaster, delicately winged brows, high cheekbones, and pale-golden hair. Large blue eyes, pink lips, and a slender neck.

What a delight she would be to paint. Whatever her husband

looked like, her portrait would arrest attention and demand to be noticed. *Portrait of the Duchess of Haverly* would be the centerpiece of any gallery showing. He'd need to dress her appropriately though. Her current attire of pale gray was too tame and matronly for such an exquisite countenance.

"Ah, Cilla, do come in. The painter has arrived. Please guide him through the gallery so he may see the previous dukes and duchesses and get an inkling of what I require of him. I would take him myself, but I cannot manage the stairs." The dowager rose to her feet, stacking her hands atop her cane, her limp far more exaggerated than when she had come into the room. "Mr. Sinclair, you'll be expected to work quickly and well. I want to reveal the portraits on Christmas Eve night."

Twenty-four days.

He would prepare his canvases tonight, provided his supplies had arrived.

What pigments should he mix in order to capture the faint hint of rose in the fair duchess's cheeks?

———✦✕✦———

Cilla's mind had been elsewhere when she entered the reception room, but the painter had scattered her thoughts. He looked every inch a Scotsman, from his auburn hair to his tartan scarf to his sturdy boots. She could imagine him striding the hills of the Highlands in a kilt, the wind tossing his red locks, his eyes keen on the horizon.

She shook her head. What ridiculousness. He had probably grown up in Jedburgh or Kirkcudbright and never seen the Highlands. It wasn't like her to even notice a man's appearance, and here she was spinning imaginary stories about this one on first glance.

"If you'll follow me, Mr. Sinclair." Just today she and her mother-in-law had moved temporarily into Haverly Manor from the dower house in order to be on hand for the preparations and party. Cilla had been on her way to find the butler to see about sending a message into the village, when the dowager had ordered her to give this tour. And Cilla had obeyed without a protest.

Typical.

Having secured permission to plan one of the party evenings, Cilla had opted to hire a troupe of actors to perform sketches and soliloquies. And though the dowager had rolled her eyes and scoffed, saying she had no desire to have such plebeian and suspect individuals as actors in her house, Cilla had persisted quietly—quite out of character—and prevailed. Charlotte had taken her part, expressing enthusiasm for the project.

This small bit of independence and rebellion felt good, and Cilla held the warm glow of it to her chest. Perhaps she was capable of making her own choices and standing up to the dowager after all.

"The gallery is on the first floor at the back." She'd show him through quickly and still have time to send one of the footmen to town. She only hoped the acting troupe wouldn't have already booked an engagement for the night she'd chosen or left the village altogether. They had been performing for the last two weeks at the village pub, and they were said to be quite good.

"Aye." He walked beside her up the staircase. He wore a tartan waistcoat, and he had flecks of paint on his trousers and shoes. No wonder the dowager had expressed doubts. Not many would have the confidence to come into her august presence in less than their absolute best. But he didn't seem cowed by the dowager.

Perhaps she should take notes.

"Have you painted portraits for a long time?" The question seemed vacuous, but it was all she could think of to break the silence. What did one say to an artist?

"Aye, getting on for ten years now." His Scots accent wasn't unpleasant, as if he'd worked to make himself more understandable to the English ear. But *for* still sounded like "fair" and *now* like "know."

She stopped before a pair of white-painted doors. "This is the gallery."

He opened the door and held it for her to precede him. As she passed, her nose pricked with unfamiliar scents. Chemical smells, almost medicinal. Perhaps from his color compounds and paints?

The gallery spread in long wings to the right and left across the back of the house, and paintings hung in measured ranks on every wall. Weak light filtered through the net curtains. "The Haverly family line in England dates back to 1066 and the Norman invasion. William the Conqueror awarded land to his favorite barons, and eventually the baronies became duchies."

Mr. Sinclair clasped his hands behind his back and studied the first Baron Haverly. The painting was dark, on wood, with the baron attired in black robes with gold trim. Overall, the portrait was flat and severe.

Without a word, the artist went down the row, quickly with the older paintings, and slowly as they approached the more recent ones.

When they arrived at the portraits of her father-in-law and the dowager, his brows rose. "Sir Joshua Reynolds. Most impressive." He stroked his cheek, narrowing his eyes. Backing up a few steps, he said, "An interesting composition."

Cilla bit her lip, for Mr. Sinclair was looking at the dowager's portrait. A youthful dowager, newly ascended to her title as Duchess of Haverly. She was thin, pretty, with large doe eyes. As if she'd never heard harsh speech or made a demand in her entire life. Two Cavalier King Charles spaniels cavorted at her feet, and over her shoulder, one could see a bucolic countryside setting.

"'Tis a shame about the pigments. Reynolds could paint, but he couldn't mix color. Not lasting color. All his skin tones turn white within a few years. And he did insist quite often on painting his subjects in garb from ancient Greece or Rome."

Cilla had often wondered at this aspect of the dowager's portrait. The white flowing garment seemed inappropriate for the dowager, even as a young bride.

"So you don't propose to paint the current duke and duchess in Roman toga or Grecian gown?" she asked.

"Nay." He paused. "Unless you desire it?"

"I have no say." She put her hand to her chest. "Though I doubt Marcus or Charlotte will wish it. In fact, Lady Charlotte, the duchess, has already chosen a gown for her painting."

His head swiveled away from the portraits to face her. "Are ye no' the duchess?" He coughed. "I mean, are you not the duchess?"

She drew in a breath. "No. I'm . . ." How should she describe herself and her non-place in society? "I was married to the heir, who passed away before he inherited. It is his younger brother and wife who are the duke and duchess."

He pursed his lips. "I see."

Was that disappointment she read in his eyes? Eyes that were not green as she had thought, but hazel. Why would he be disappointed that she wasn't the duchess? Surely she was mistaken. "Perhaps I can show you to your studio now?"

"Certainly." He made a small bow and indicated she should lead the way.

They climbed to the third floor of the huge manor house. When she had lived there, she and Neville had shared their own apartments on the second floor, looking out on the lake. Those rooms would be used by the Earl and Countess of Whitelock when they arrived for the party.

On the third floor, they passed the open door to the nursery, and Cilla paused. The nurse, a young woman named Agatha, held Honora Mary on her lap, playing pat-pat with her hands. Honora Mary giggled and squealed.

The painter dug inside his jacket and produced a slim sketchpad and pencil, and in a few lightning strokes, he captured the moment. Cilla stood fascinated as line by line, shading by shading, he put in the light from the screened fireplace, the edge of the rug, the wispy halo of Honora Mary's curls. He had caught the likenesses perfectly.

Cilla studied the drawing so quickly and skillfully done. "How did you learn to draw like that?" Though sketching and painting had come into vogue as proper pursuits and talents for society women, Cilla had no ability in that direction whatsoever.

Mr. Sinclair shrugged, flipping the book closed. A small pang touched Cilla's heart as the drawing disappeared.

"I dinna remember not knowing how to draw. I have studied, apprenticed to several master painters, both here and on the Continent, but I've always been able to draw what I see."

What would it be like to possess such a talent? It wouldn't even have to be drawing or painting. What if she could sing or be more than just proficient on the pianoforte? What if she had a flair for design like Marcus's friend Diana, Countess of Whitelock, or a head for study like Charlotte, or a natural ability to nurture and care for others like her sister-in-law Sophie?

What if Cilla's only talent lay in her ability to do as she was told and allow others to direct her life?

"I didn't realize the duke had children." Mr. Sinclair put his thumbs into his waistcoat pockets. "Will he want a portrait of her, do you think?" Hope tinged his voice.

"Honora Mary is my daughter." Cilla smiled at the nurse. "And perhaps, if you have time and think you can get her to sit still long enough. Agatha, I'll return in a while to put her down for her nap."

"Yes, ma'am." The nurse bobbed her lace cap.

At the far end of the hall, Cilla opened the door to a small, dark room with a single window that faced north. Two large crates stood in the center of the space. "The dowager has assigned this room as your studio. Your sleeping quarters are next door."

He shook his head, stepping into the rectangular space. His boots rang on the wooden floor. "No, this willna do at all. 'Tis smaller than a cabinet. That's no' a proper light source." He pointed to the small square of glass high up in the wall.

She tugged on her lower lip. "The dowager says this is where Sir Joshua painted her portrait and the duke's. She specifically set aside this room for you."

"That may be, but I'm not Sir Joshua, and I do not use his techniques. It may have been the done thing to keep a studio dark and control the light source thirty or forty years ago, but I need natural light and space to paint. These canvases will be large, and the duke and duchess will prefer more comfort than being stuffed into a small room that will smell of paint and turpentine." He folded his arms across his tartan waistcoat. "I'm afraid I'll have to insist."

She could see his point. Three weeks or better cooped up in this room would drive her mad. Where could she put him that wouldn't interfere with the dowager's carefully laid plans for housing their guests during the party? What room had light and space but wouldn't be in use during the entertaining? Dare she make a change without consulting the dowager?

"Perhaps . . . there is one place." She stepped out of the small room and retraced her path toward the nursery, stopping about halfway down the hall. "Will this be better?"

He opened the door she indicated and stepped inside. Even on this dull, dreary day, the room was light and airy. A bare expanse of board floor, whitewashed walls, and a plain marble fireplace. The tables and chairs had been pushed to the side and draped with a cloth. "Aye, this is better." He turned a full circle in the space that must be four or five times the size of the smaller room.

"It was once the schoolroom, though it hasn't been in use since Sophie . . . Lady Sophia, the duke's sister, outgrew it. If this will suit, I'll ask the dowager, and I'll send a maid up to dust and sweep and lay a fire. And Rodbury, the butler, will see that your supplies are brought here."

He seemed barely to hear her, as if already planning the space, studying the angle of light through the windows, holding his hand up as if already at the easel.

# Chapter 2

——◆◃✕▹◆——

The preliminary sketches had gone well, as had his first meeting with the duke and duchess. They were a handsome couple who had an affectionate air for one another. Hamish tamped down his disappointment that Lady Cilla wasn't to be one of the subjects of this commission and got on with the work.

Up in his new studio, he studied the drawings he'd created the night before in the formal parlor. The dowager had stood at his elbow, scrutinizing each stroke of his charcoal. When he'd finished the first sketch, he'd raised questioning brows at her. He'd had to smother his chuckle as she humphed and told him she supposed it would do. The woman had more prickles than a hedgehog.

The duchess, Lady Charlotte, made an excellent subject. She had strong features, and when she smiled, her entire face seemed to glow. It would not be difficult to capture the intelligence in her eyes. Though she was clearly in a delicate condition, Hamish would be able to complete most of the portrait with a model sitting in for her.

His Grace, Marcus by given name, had distinctive hair, long and clubbed back in a queue. Could he be convinced to let it lie free on his shoulders for his portrait? His eyes would be the most difficult to capture. They were knowing eyes, observant and keen. Hamish would have to work to ensure they did not seem calculating.

Together the portraits would be most striking. A satisfactory commission in spite of the dowager's clucking.

As the evening of preliminary sketching progressed, Hamish had surreptitiously drawn the dowager; the parlor maid; Rodbury; Tetford, the housekeeper; and finally, when he couldn't resist any longer, he'd sketched Lady Cilla.

Or a version of her. All evening she had kept her chin down, her movements small, had deferred and served the dowager. She seemed timid and . . . cowed? There was no fire in her, no interest in her eyes, as there had been when she had looked at her daughter or had shown him the family gallery.

But in his drawing, she held her chin at a confident angle, and certainty stared out from her beautiful eyes. There was firmness in her expression on the page that wasn't evident in her demeanor in the drawing room.

Perhaps someday he would take this sketch and create the painting he had seen the moment he first laid eyes upon her.

Or perhaps he would consign it to a drawer when he took up the teaching position that lay ahead of him.

He flipped the sketchbook pages until he found the one of the duke and stepped to his easel. Late last night he'd stretched canvas onto a frame and primed the surface. He ran his fingers over the dried primer, feeling the rough tooth. Perfect. With the sketch for reference, he used a bit of charcoal to outline the composition of the painting, positioning the duke slightly to the right of center. He had just finished the bones of the background when the duke spoke from the other side of the canvas.

"Am I on time?"

"Your Grace." Hamish rounded the easel and bowed. "You are indeed." He had prepared the studio, erecting the backdrop he'd chosen, a deep velvet curtain the color of merlot and a lyre-back Sheraton chair for the duke to rest his hand on. The rich walnut of the chair would pair nicely with the duke's clothes. His Grace had opted for a black jacket with a golden waistcoat and snowy linens, buff breeches, and tall, shining Hessians, complete with white tassels.

"I feel sadly overdressed for this occasion." He allowed Hamish to position him so the light fell across his face just so. Hamish looked

WONDERS OF HIS LOVE

at his own attire, brown paint-spattered trousers, a cream shirt with sleeves folded up to bare his forearms, and his scuffed boots.

"I assure you, Your Grace, I will wear a jacket when the duchess sits for me." He positioned the duke as he would appear in the portrait. The duke's hair was gathered at the nape of his neck, and Hamish decided to let it be. The style suited him.

The duke shrugged. "Don't fear the duchess will censure you. She's not a high stickler. She'll be more interested in learning about you and your work and what books you've read than what you're wearing, if I'm any judge."

Hamish opened the high folding table he used to rest his palette upon and, putting his finger over the stopper, shook a bottle of pigment he'd mixed last night to redistribute the oil. The easel had been adjusted so the canvas sat nearly on the floor to bring the area where he would paint the duke's face into easy reach.

He picked up his favorite brush and dipped it into the pigment, dropping a dollop of paint onto his palette and loading the brush.

"Is it all right if I talk, or would you prefer me to remain quiet?" the duke asked.

"By all means, talk. It can get quite tedious for you to have to stand still and silent for such a long time." *And your conversation is sure to be much better than that of the three whining sisters of my previous commission. Their petulance drove me to distraction.*

"Good. I have a proposition to put to you, and I hope you will agree to it."

"Yes, Your Grace?" Hamish blocked in skin tone.

"Lady Cilla will be the one to model for the duchess when the time comes."

Hamish's head came up. So he would have an opportunity to spend more time with Lady Cilla after all.

"However, I would like you to not only paint her sitting in for Lady Charlotte but also, if you could do it without her knowing, I should like you to paint her portrait. If you complete the duchess's portrait first, we can provide a ruse for Cilla's painting . . . say Lady Charlotte changed her mind about what gown she wanted and could

Cilla sit for you in a different dress?" The duke held his head still, but his eyes slanted to Hamish's. "Would you have time to paint Cilla as well as the portraits you've been hired to complete? I should like to present it to her as a Christmas gift if possible. By rights, she should have been the duchess, and she should have had her portrait hung in the family gallery."

A chance to paint Lady Cilla, not as a stand-in but as herself. The composition of the painting was already in his mind. But three formal, high-caliber portraits in just over three weeks? Could he do it?

How could he not?

"Yes, Your Grace. I would be honored." Even if he had to paint round the clock, he would get it done.

"Will it be any trouble to keep the portrait from her until it is completed?"

"Nay, milord. The dowager has ordered me to keep all the paintings secret from you and the duchess until she can present them to you on Christmas Day."

"Ah, trust my mother to try to control even this." He looked heavenward and sighed. "Still, we'll humor her. She'll enjoy the unveiling that way."

Hamish returned to his work, but his mind spun. Lady Cilla had filled his thoughts to an uncomfortable degree over the past two days. He would need to guard himself. Their worlds lay far apart. He would paint her and leave her behind, and he would not seek to trifle with her feelings or allow her to trifle with his. She would be a subject who just might make his name among the top portraitists of his time, but nothing more.

———————•✕•———————

"Why does it have to be me?" Cilla smoothed the raspberry satin of the dress Charlotte had chosen for her portrait. It felt so strange after all the black and gray and navy Cilla had worn over the last year. "I would think having one of the maids sit in for you would be sufficient?"

"Here, put this on." Charlotte handed her a lacy white shawl. "The Dowager has spoken. She says you need to take my place because you will pose like a lady, and some of the maids will not." She shrugged. "You know how it is when she gets an idea in her head. There's no dissuading her."

Cilla accepted her fate and headed up to the schoolroom studio, her heart pounding oddly against her stays. Why was she so unsettled? She was merely sitting still for an artist to paint the dress she wore. She was a placeholder. It seemed fitting for her situation. Not the duchess, but a passable, temporary substitute.

Her maid followed her up the stairs to act as chaperone.

Mr. Sinclair was waiting for them, though they heard him before they saw him, as he whistled a light tune to himself from behind his easel.

Cilla cleared her throat, and the music stopped. His bright hazel eyes met hers.

"Oh, aye, good day, Lady Priscilla. Come in." He wiped his hands on a paint-stained rag, smiling in a friendly way that sent trickles of sensation along her skin.

Her throat closed up as she recognized the feeling. Attraction. Of being very aware and alive in the presence of a man.

Heat rose up her neck and into her cheeks, and she lowered her chin, taking deep breaths. Why must she be so fair complexioned, showing every emotion, whether wanted or not? And how could she have feelings of attraction for a . . . for a painter? For a man who would be here for less than a month and then be on his way.

*Don't allow your head to be turned, Cilla Haverly. You're a respectable widow and mother, not some flighty debutante or simpleton ready to fall for every handsome face you see.*

All that was true, which made these unaccustomed feelings all the more startling. She shook her head and stepped into the room, grasping for composure. Feelings were flighty and unreliable, and these too would soon pass. She just needed to ignore them.

Though Mr. Sinclair was handsome, and she couldn't be blamed for noticing, could she?

"I've got your place all ready." Mr. Sinclair indicated the chair where Charlotte had sat to have her likeness painted. "If you'll allow me to pose you to match what I've already completed?"

"Perhaps if I could see what you've done so far, I would know how best to sit for you?" She was bursting with curiosity, as was the rest of the household.

"Ah, I am most sorry, but the dowager has decreed none shall see the paintings but herself until they are presented." He shrugged, spreading his hands in appeal.

Once again the dowager had spoken. Cilla stifled a sigh and arranged her skirts as she sat in the chair. Mr. Sinclair waited until she was seated properly before reaching for her left hand. A frisson went from her fingertips to the top of her head.

"Rest your elbow on the arm of the chair, and hold this fan with the other, letting it dangle a bit?" He raised his brows to see if she understood. "And if you'll allow me?" With quick movements, he adjusted the shawl about her, lowering it to reveal more of her neck and shoulders.

Again, heat surged along her veins. She inhaled sharply, and the scent of linseed oil, paint, and, strangely, pinewood caught her attention. His cheeks were ruddy, and the cuffs on his trousers damp. Had he been tramping in the woods?

She wished she had gone with him. Peace was to be found in the woods, stirring up the fallen leaves, brushing against the pine and laurel, drawing in deep breaths of cold, clean air after being shut up in the house. Cilla had been so busy with plans and duties for the party, she'd not gone for her customary afternoon walks.

Mr. Sinclair studied her with a critical eye, and she struggled to keep her chin up. Was he pleased with what he saw? Or did he see her at all? Since she was only here to have the dress painted, perhaps he didn't even notice her.

Cilla's maid took a chair near the door, setting her mending basket on the floor and removing a lace cap and needle and thread. She looked so young and sweet, one would never know that she'd made her living as a streetwalker in Covent Garden not more than

six months ago. Charlotte and the dowager were making real progress with their reforms. And more than just retraining and equip-
ping "unfortunates" with life skills, Charlotte was also teaching them
about their need of being washed inside too. Every week they assembled for Bible reading and discussion.

It was Cilla's favorite time. The girls were so eager to learn. It
amazed her that in a Christian nation such as England, there could
exist anyone who hadn't at least the rudiments of a biblical education.
And yet these ladies devoured the new information.

Mr. Sinclair resumed his place at his easel, and from her angle, she
could see nearly all of him. He arranged several bottles of paint in a
row on a high table at his elbow.

"Are you comfortable?" he asked, his eyes not straying from his
work.

"Yes." *Unless you take into account that my stays feel too tight and the
sound of your voice does odd things to my circulation.*

"Please dinna move if you can help it, but feel free to talk if you
wish." Humor laced his voice. "I will admit, there are times when my
subject has near driven me mad with constant prattling, but I somehow think that would not be the case with you, Lady Priscilla."

Given his permission, she could think of nothing to say. She really
was behaving like a gauche debutante.

"Do you like painting?" She winced. Of course he must like it.

"Painting and drawing, yes. It's what I was born to do and why I
had to leave home."

"Where was home?"

"An estate near Dunbarton, on the Leven River. My father was the
stable master, and my mother was a weaver. Or I should say, they *are*.
They both still live there. Much to my father's dismay, I chose not to
become his head groomsman with the hope of becoming stable master myself one day. He's waiting for me to fail as an artist and come
home to take up the job he thinks best for me." There was a hint of
frustrated bitterness in his words.

"How old were you when you left?"

"I was a brash sixteen summers with riots of color and images filling my head. I could always draw any likeness, and I was caned as a boy in school for using any scrap of paper and ink for making pictures rather than letters and numbers."

Cilla tried to imagine venturing out on her own at sixteen, and her glance flicked to her maid. She most likely would have ended up like this girl had. It was different for men. They could earn their living in respectable ways without needing anyone to give permission.

"How did you begin to paint? It's a far stretch from boyhood sketches to portrait painting, is it not? You mentioned training with established artists?"

"I got myself to London and apprenticed. Which means I was a personal servant for no wages. But my governor did teach me the rudiments, and he took me to Italy with him, where I saw great masterworks. Eventually I managed to find a paid position with an Irish painter. When he passed away, he left me his tools, but without a patron, I couldn't afford to paint for a living just yet. I went to work for a colorist, which was perhaps the best thing I could have done. I learned to mix my own pigments and about the chemistry of color." He continued to add paint to the canvas, looking over at her from time to time. Sunlight streamed in the windows, spilling over his shoulders and the canvas, creating a corona around his head and picking out the deep red tones of his hair.

Hamish Sinclair was so different from Neville, who had possessed sharp features and dark-blond hair with a touch of curl he always tried to quell with pomade. Neville had been conservative in dress, in speech, in emotion. He had been conscientious, punctilious, and reserved.

A model husband and heir who took his duties seriously, molded from birth by his parents to succeed.

And Cilla had patterned her behavior after his. Duty first, and carried out in the proper, dignified manner.

Neville had seen the world in black and white, with rigid lines that governed behavior.

Hamish Sinclair spoke of vivid color and images tumbling in his head.

"So now you make your way in the world as a painter. Has your father relented at all?" she asked, aware that she might be trespassing on more personal territory.

"He has not, and he may be nearer getting his way than I would like. I have submitted my latest efforts to the Royal Academy, and I am awaiting their judgment. If I canna earn admittance to the RA, I shall be forced to either take up an appointment as painting instructor at a girls' academy in Stratford-upon-Avon or go home to Scotland and the stables."

She widened her eyes. "You make that sound as if a trip to the gallows would be preferable. Why would you take up such a position in a school if you didn't wish to become a teacher?" Teaching was the one skill Cilla possessed, and she loved it, whether it was instructing the new housemaids in their Bible classes or teaching them to read and write.

"One must earn one's crust. It is difficult to make a living and get commissions important enough to subsist upon if one isn't a member of the Royal Academy. It has become something of a badge of honor, a credential. Daft as it may seem, portraitists must have that credential in order to command more than a few pounds for a painting."

A wistful longing drifted through Cilla's chest like a breeze, stirring the discontent she tried so hard to keep stifled there. "Teaching position or not, I admire your freedom, the ability to cross the country exercising your abilities, meeting new people, doing what you love. You were able to break free of the mold others had planned for you and embrace and explore your talents."

Did she sound as jealous to him as she did to herself?

# CHAPTER 3

"GOOD MORNING, LADIES, and welcome to Haverly." Cilla addressed the newest arrivals from London. Thin, wary, a couple defiant, these women were on the cusp of changing their lives if they wished to do so.

"This is Lady Priscilla. She'll be helping to instruct you while you're here." Dorothy Stokes, Aunt Dolly to all who knew her, pulled her gloves off finger by finger.

Their cheeks were red with cold, and one young girl wiped her nose with the heel of her hand. They had few belongings, and their clothes were mostly tattered and patched. Some had fading bruises. One exception, a striking woman in fine clothes, held herself apart. She must have been one of the higher-paid girls, a mistress or kept woman perhaps? Cilla hoped her adjustment wouldn't be too difficult.

"The first thing is to get you warm and fed. Tetford, our house-keeper, will show you to the servants' dining room for a meal and then to your rooms. There are uniforms on your beds. The house seamstress will see to alterations if they're needed." Cilla smiled. "I know this is all strange and new to you, but you'll soon settle in. Aunt Dolly and I will see to assigning you your duties, and your training will begin later today."

"House rules are simple," Tetford said, her expression stern. She wasn't really mean, but the housekeeper was brusque. "Attend to your duties, be respectful of the family that is housing and training you, and under no circumstances are you to fraternize with the men who work and live here."

It had to be addressed, but Cilla winced at the tone. "Ladies, we appreciate you coming, and we look forward to a positive experience. If you are willing to work and learn, you will leave here with skills and references that will allow you to find honest employment in domestic service in even the best houses in England."

The door behind them opened, and a gust of air swirled in. Hamish Sinclair stepped over the sill, removing his hat and stomping to remove the rime of snow on his boots. He stopped when he saw the ladies.

Cilla's breath hitched. His eyes were bright, his cheeks ruddy from his morning walk. Each day this week, he had left the house early and tramped through the woods for a good hour before returning . . . not that she had gotten into the habit of watching his comings and goings. He looked hale and masculine.

The new ladies showed no interest. How could that be? Couldn't they feel the attraction, the fascination of this man? Perhaps they were all tired, or they had taken Tetford's warning to heart.

"Good morning." His brows rose, looking from one to the other before letting his gaze rest on Cilla. "I apologize for the intrusion." Edging sideways, he skirted the group. "Will I see you in the studio a'fore long?" Easing his plaid scarf from around his neck, he unbuttoned his coat. His tartan-patterned waistcoat covered a dark-blue shirt. A sketchbook peeked from his coat pocket, and Cilla wondered if he slept with it. She'd never seen him without paper and charcoal near to hand.

"Yes, I'll be up directly, if that suits you?" She did a mental scamper around all she had to do today. "In perhaps an hour? Guests are arriving tomorrow, and there's still so much to finish." Including the entertainment for the evening—the acting troupe Cilla had hired.

Mr. Sinclair bowed and headed down the hall to the green baize door that separated the servants' domain from the main house.

"Who is that?" One of the girls leaned over to watch him disappear.

Tetford cleared her throat. "Mr. Sinclair is an artist hired to paint the portraits of the duke and duchess. He's not your concern." She motioned for them to head up the back stairs. "We're wasting time."

Cilla hurried to her room. But the dress she was supposed to wear was nowhere to be found. In its place, a vibrant blue satin gown hung in her dressing room. The fabric was rich, heavy, and to her mind, gorgeous.

"What's this?" she asked her maid.

"Her Grace changed her mind about which dress she wants for her portrait. She wants you to wear this one instead." The servant shrugged, as if the choices of her employers were beyond her ability to understand.

"What will Mr. Sinclair say? He's already put in so much work on the painting." Would he have to begin again, or could he paint over an entire dress and make it look right?

"Her Grace was most insistent, milady." The maid moved to help Cilla change.

The dress was so beautiful, Cilla couldn't fault Charlotte for preferring it. A radiant color no one could miss, it was nothing Cilla would ever be bold enough to choose for herself. Her mother had dressed her entirely in pastels until her marriage, and after that it was subdued, matronly colors and then mourning clothes. A dress like this would not allow one to blend into the background.

Yet she felt a surge of confidence in this beautiful gown, and a wistful bit of longing. What if she were the sort of woman who *would* wear an ensemble like this? Confident, strong, sure of herself and her opinions? Someone like Charlotte?

Entering the studio, she heard a lightly whistled tune. Was he even aware that he hummed and whistled while he worked? It was such a happy sound, the sound of someone who was content with his vocation. "Mr. Sinclair?"

"Ah, right on time, milady." He rounded the easel and stopped, looking at her from hair to hem.

He blinked and smiled, rubbing his hands down his waistcoat. "Well, that *is* a change."

"Do you like it?" Cilla touched the slick satin. His reaction was gratifying to her woman's heart. It had been a long time since a man had looked at her with admiration. "I hope you don't mind the switch. Did the duchess inform you?"

"Aye, she came by the studio this morning. She's not the first of my commissions to change her mind halfway, so don't spend a minute upset about it. The new look will paint up beautifully, but I'll need to mix some new pigments. It willna take long. You dinna have to sit still while I work, though I would ask you to stay on that side of the studio so as not to view the painting. I would hate to disappoint the dowager."

Cilla took the opportunity to move about in the dress, enjoying the whisper of the fabric and the heaviness of the skirts. There wasn't much to see in the studio, since she couldn't look at the paintings in progress. A few crates and tables that held various tools of his trade. Her maid sewed in her chair by the door.

There was one crate with the top loosened, and she slid it to the side. A row of paintings stood on edge with spacers between to keep the canvases from touching.

Mr. Sinclair was busy, his back to Cilla, again whistling a soft tune. She removed a spacer and lifted one of the paintings. Soulful eyes stared back at her, a young girl with round cheeks and a full lower lip. She wore a maid's cap and carried a tea tray, though only part of the tray showed. In the background, more indistinct than the girl, a pair of women sat together in a drawing room, waiting to be served.

Those eyes. What a striking portrait. Who was the girl?

Curious, Cilla removed another painting, this one of an old man sitting on an upturned bucket, lighting a long pipe. He leaned against a stable wall, and a horse looked out over a half door above him. In a brilliant use of light and shadow, the artist had captured every weary line of the old horseman's face, every cobblestone of the yard, even the light in the eye of a bird pecking some fallen grain. And in the distance, a rider in a top hat and breeches ambled away on a gray horse.

In the third painting, a highborn lady stood before a long mirror, but she was a bit blurred and unfocused. It was the abigail kneeling behind her to mend her hem who stood out in sharp relief.

Mr. Sinclair cleared his throat, and she whirled, guilt washing over her. Embarrassed to be prying, she lowered the painting. It wasn't like her to overstep her bounds, but she had been so curious and drawn in by the first piece, she had to delve further.

"I'm sorry. I should have asked." She caught herself ducking her chin and forced herself to look him in the eyes. If she was going to do anything about always fading into the background, she would start by owning what she had done. "These are amazing. Are they your work?"

"Aye." He took the canvas from her, glancing at it before sliding it back into the crate. "Done when I had big aspirations. But they're not what the paying public wants to see."

"Why ever not? They're so different."

"People who buy paintings want to be the focal point of the paintings. I call these the Army of the Unseen. The butlers, tigers, maids, and grooms of the world are the centerpieces of these portraits, and they canna afford to buy paintings." He shrugged. "I was trying to say something with my art, but those whom I was targeting were na ready to listen."

"That's a shame. They're beautiful. Perhaps you haven't shown them to the right buyers."

He gave a forced laugh. "You could be correct, but if the right buyers exist, I dinna know where." With a slap, he put the top back on the crate. "The pigments are ready. Shall we proceed?"

When she resumed her seat and arranged herself in the usual position, he frowned and tilted his head. "Starting the gown over means we can choose a different pose. May I?" He touched her shoulder, sending a tremor along her skin through the silk as he turned her to face left instead of right.

"Can you really make such changes without affecting the parts you've already done?"

"Trust me. The painting will look fine."

This time his fingertips grazed her chin to set it at a new angle, and she shivered. Not that his hand was cold—quite the reverse, actually. But when he touched her, even as impersonally as now, she felt as if she were jolted awake from a deep sleep. Her heart pounded, and her palms sweated.

What was wrong with her?

———◆✕◆———

He should have made certain that crate was firmly fastened. It was his fault the paintings were available for her to see.

With quick slashes of the charcoal, he drew her face and form on the pristine canvas. She gave no inkling she was aware that the portrait he now created was of her, not the duchess.

That dress. The color was striking, and it favored her complexion perfectly. He had a moment of doubt, a rarity with him. Would he be able to do her justice with his painting? Could he capture the ethereal beauty, the inner strength he perceived? She had survived the death of her spouse and raising a daughter alone and still managed to maintain a sweet disposition. Even while under the thumb of the dominating dowager. In rare moments, a flash of rebellious independence lit her captivating eyes, hinting at what may lie beneath the mask. Would he be able to convey through paint and pigment, brushstroke and technique, the woman behind the perfect features?

He'd spent far too much time contemplating Lady Priscilla Haverly. And not only when she sat for him. She invaded his thoughts as he tramped through the woods, when he heard her down the hall in the nursery with her daughter, when he laid his head on his pillow at night.

What was it about this woman, so far above his station, that fascinated him so?

"Who were all those young ladies in the back foyer when I came in?" He asked a question to keep his thoughts from straying into dangerous areas. "New staff, I assume? Brought in to help with the house party?"

Cilla shook her head. "New staff, yes, but not for the party. It's a ministry of the duke and duchess. They bring women in need of training from London and give them the opportunity to learn and change their circumstances. The women are former streetwalkers and Cyprians, caught in a terrible way of living. We try to offer hope and skills to change their lives. Along with spiritual teaching." She raised her brows, as if appealing to him to understand. "So many women are trapped in a way of life not of their choosing."

The wistfulness in her voice resonated. Did she consider herself trapped? She was in such an indefinable role here. Widow to the man who never became the duke. Mother to a girl child who would never inherit. To what did she look forward? Remarriage to another titled gentleman? Or forever wearing the willow for her dead husband?

A vision of a new painting flashed across his mind. Of Cilla in sharp relief, serving the dowager. One of the Army of the Unseen.

"And is your program working?" He had heard of Magdalen Hospital in London, of course, for the reforming of prostitutes, but he'd never heard of the landed gentry becoming involved personally.

"Yes, we've already graduated our first group. And the duchess's sister, Miss Pippa Cashel, is keeping watch and checking in on the ladies in their new positions. She works at a rescue house in the city and makes the referrals here to Haverly."

A sound at the door drew his attention. The nurse, Agatha, stood in the opening, bent at the waist, holding the hands of the child. Honora Mary's laughter entered the room before her, a smile splitting her face.

"Mistress, may we come in?"

Cilla looked to him for permission, and he nodded. Setting aside his brush, he picked up his charcoal and leafed through his notebook for a clean sheet. He still needed to paint the child's picture for her mother. Though she hadn't formally asked, he would do it for her as a gift.

The baby high-stepped in front of the nurse, hands held firmly, squealing with each step.

"She's a happy child, is she not?" he asked. "I hear her often."

"I hope she's not a distraction or nuisance. I can ask the nurse to keep the door closed if you like." Cilla held her pose, but her eyes followed the baby across the room.

"Dinna think of it. She's no trouble." He enjoyed the homey, happy sound, so different from his usual work environment. Stepping around the easel, he squatted and sketched the baby from her cherubic curls to her stocking feet. She stared at him, babbling, even tilting her head as if to see if he understood.

"May I see it?" Cilla asked. "You draw so quickly, and you capture likenesses so easily. I've never seen anyone do what you do."

It chuffed him to hear her praise. "You can have this one. Though if you'd like, I could draw a better one later, with more time. Pen and ink, not charcoal."

"You're so busy, I hate to ask, but I would appreciate a drawing. She's growing so quickly. I would love to capture her at this age."

She took the notebook from his hand, admiring the sketch of her daughter on the top page. "May I?" When he nodded, she flipped through the other drawings.

She'd find an odd collection there. The newel post in the foyer, a corbel on the summerhouse eave, one of the duke's favorite hunters, a pair of foxhounds from the kennel. He'd captured the housekeeper, Tetford, hands on hips with her mouth slanted in her habitual look of suspicion. Cilla leafed through his quick sketches of the tweeny maid carrying a can of water up a flight of stairs, and one of the bootboy, arm-deep in one of Marcus's boots, a cloth in his hand.

Sketches that would become the framework for future installments in his Army of the Unseen series. Though there were no buyers, he felt compelled to paint them anyway.

"Milady." The nurse eased Honora Mary to the floor and let go of her hands. "Aunt Dolly poked her head into the nursery to let me know a new group of ladies had arrived from the city. Will one of them be assigned to the nursery?"

"I don't know at this point. Once they've been fitted for their uniforms, and Tetford and Dolly have a chance to interview them, they'll assign—"

A crash interrupted her, followed by a moment of silence. A piercing wail filled the room. Cilla leapt from her chair, but Hamish reached the child first.

The baby sat in a pool of oil, paint thinner, and splashes of color. She had crawled to his paint table and tried to pull herself up by the cloth, dumping the entire contents down on herself as she fell. One of the jars had broken and lay not far from the baby.

He didn't hesitate. He lifted the child, holding her against his chest and crooning to her. "Ah, lassie, dinna fash yersel. 'Tis just a bit of paint and the like. Let's go look out the windee. There's no need for such a stramash." He took her over to the window, bouncing her lightly as he patted her back.

At Cilla's look of incomprehension, he realized he'd slipped into his Glaswegian accent.

"Oh, your clothes." She wrung her fingers. "I'm so sorry."

Glancing down, he took in the thick dabs of paint dotting his shirt.

"'Tis not the first time I've gotten paint on my clothes. Dinna worry. There's no real harm done."

The baby stopped her wailing, staring up at him. One splayed hand reached for his beard, and he leaned back, laughing. "Oh, no, lassie. 'Tis one thing to have paint on my shirt. Another altogether to have it stuck in my beard."

The nurse stood by, a stricken look on her young face. "I'm so sorry, milady. I should have been watching her."

Hamish waited. The nurse had been inattentive, and in most houses, this would earn her a scolding.

Cilla took a deep breath. "As Mr. Sinclair said, there's no real harm done, though we will need to replace his ruined clothes." She gave an order to her maid. "Please go get a footman and one of the tweenys. Tell them what happened, and have them bring the appropriate para-phernalia to see to the debris."

Her maid hurried away, and Agatha shifted from foot to foot.

"Take Honora Mary to the nursery. She'll need a bath, and it will be easier to remove the paint if you don't wait until it dries." Cilla spread her hands toward Hamish. "I am so sorry. We'll right the mess quickly."

"Nothing was damaged that canna be repaired." He picked up a drop cloth and held it out to the nurse. "Wrap her in this so you dinna ruin your own clothes."

They had just returned to the portrait painting, with Cilla once more seated before him, when a familiar tapping step sounded in the hallway. The dowager, her face grim, hitched into the room, leaning heavily on her cane. She stopped when she saw the mess on the floor and crossed her arms. "The things I am forced to do while injured. That last flight of stairs was nearly my undoing. This has been a day of utter disappointment. Not only has Sophia written to say she cannot come home for Christmas—and isn't it just like her to put Mamie Richardson's wishes and needs ahead of those of her own mother?—sickness in the house indeed." She paused, her mouth puckered, as if she had tasted raw vinegar. Then she shook her head. "Cilla, I hate to tell you this, but the entertainment you planned for tomorrow night . . ." She huffed. "I tried to tell you, but you wouldn't listen. You insisted on going your own way, and look what's happened."

"What's wrong, madam?" Cilla's lower lip disappeared behind her teeth, and uncertainty painted her words.

"I told you not to hire *actors*. People who make their living in the *arts* aren't to be trusted."

Hamish winced, but when Cilla turned stricken eyes toward him, he shook his head and winked at her.

Her lips parted, and in spite of the dowager's scolding, she coughed to cover a laugh.

"Why are they not to be trusted?" he asked the older woman.

The dowager seemed to remember he was there, though if she realized she'd insulted him, she gave no indication. "The actors Lady Priscilla hired for tomorrow night have taken her money and run. They aren't to be found in the village. They've packed up in the night and slunk away. Now we've nothing to amuse our guests. How is this going to look? The very first evening? Are we supposed to sit around staring at one another?" Her mouth pinched like a seamstress holding pins between her teeth. "This is what you get for not following my advice."

"Are you certain they've gone?" Cilla's shoulders slumped. "Perhaps they had another engagement and will return tomorrow?"

"They didn't pay their bill at the inn. They're hardly likely to come back under those circumstances. It's a disaster, I tell you." The dowager left no one in doubt as to who should bear the blame.

Hamish stepped forward. "Perhaps I may offer a solution? I would be willing to create silhouettes and caricatures of your guests tomorrow, for their amusement, if you like." Though he would prefer not to mingle with the party, he felt compelled to come to Cilla's aid.

Cilla's reaction made whatever sacrifice he had to make worth it. She glowed, bestowing a smile on him that had his heart doing irrational things. "Would you? That's most gallant."

The dowager sniffed. "I suppose we have no choice. As long as it doesn't distract you from the work you've been hired to do." She eyed him in his Honora Mary–painted clothes. "And I hope you will make yourself presentable before you meet the guests."

He bowed, picking up a rag to wipe his hands. "I shall endeavor to do my best."

The look Cilla gave him as she went with the dowager out into the hall warmed him through.

Her silently mouthed *Thank you* rang in his heart as if she'd shouted the words.

# CHAPTER 4

CILLA SAT ALONG the wall in the drawing room, listening to the various conversations of the family and guests. She stacked her hands in her lap. She wore a dove-gray gown, a plain string of pearls, no adornment in her hair, and did her best to blend into the background.

The Whitelocks had arrived, Evan and Diana, along with their two precious little ones, Cian and William. The earl fidgeted with his cravat and fussed with his cufflinks, but the countess was elegant and refined, at ease as a house party guest.

The dowager had invited several local guests for the evening as well. Mr. and Mrs. MacAllister who lived in the village, the new Baron and Baroness Richardson, and the vicar. The baron and his wife were a bit of a challenge to like, but they were behaving well tonight. Mrs. MacAllister was sweetness itself, and the vicar always had a lighthearted story to tell.

One guest who drew Cilla's interest was Reginald, Lord Athelson. He was staying through the holidays, and if she didn't miss her guess, he had been invited by the dowager as a possible husband for Cilla. Lord Athelson was perhaps a dozen years her senior, with silver at his temples. He was tall, lean, and with narrow lips and a clipped manner of speaking.

She supposed he was eminently suitable. He was a member of the peerage, though of a much lower rank than Neville had been. He was a man of impeccable manners. He was of independent means, rumored to be quite wealthy.

And he had the dowager's approval, not something easy to acquire.

Glancing at the ormolu clock on the mantel, she stifled a sigh. This evening was to have been her contribution to the house party entertainment, the acting troupe. But her grand idea had collapsed before it had a chance to amuse anyone. She should never have put forth her opinion and tried to do something on her own. Not only had she risked and earned the dowager's disapproval, she had also proven her mother-in-law's assessment of Cilla's capabilities as a hostess right. She should have stayed in a support role in the proceedings, the place for which she was best suited.

At least the evening wasn't a total disaster. Thanks to Hamish—in the privacy of her mind, she had decided to call him Hamish rather than Mr. Sinclair—they had a novel entertainment planned, something unusual and interesting.

The clock chimed, and the drawing room door opened. Hamish presented himself, a wooden box beneath his arm, precisely on time.

Cilla's heart thudded against her stays, and her mouth went dry. He had certainly heeded the dowager's command as far as his attire for the evening. He wore a short black jacket with silver buttons, a white shirt, and . . . a kilt. Dress brogues laced up his calves, which were covered in thick wool socks, and a sporran purse hung from a silver chain at his waist. A stag-antler knife hilt stuck up from one sock.

Conversation ceased as he walked toward Marcus and Charlotte and bowed. "Your Grace." The pleats on the kilt moved in a mesmerizing way. Cilla couldn't stop staring. How could bare knees and plaid pleats be so masculine?

"Sinclair. I understand you're going to provide a bit of amusement this evening?" Marcus said.

"If it pleases milord. May I begin with the duchess?" He held up the box, flipping it open and revealing it to be a writing desk.

Within minutes he was seated at a table, Charlotte in profile before him. Deftly, he cut black paper with a pair of small shears, and her silhouette appeared. He held it up for Charlotte, who laughed and took it. He'd captured her perfectly, from the slight upturn of her nose to the serene brow to the shape of her coiffure.

"Most skillful, sir. You are going to be much in demand this evening." Charlotte smiled, lighting her whole face.

Marcus helped her rise and motioned for Mrs. MacAllister to have her turn.

Hamish's ability proved quite popular, and one after another, the guests took their turn. Even the dowager suffered to have her silhouette crafted.

"If you like, I can mount your family's silhouettes in a long frame for you." Hamish sorted the profiles on the tea table.

Marcus nodded. "But it would be incomplete. Come, Cilla. It's your turn."

Why was she so nervous? It wasn't as if she hadn't spent several hours in Hamish's company, sitting for him as he used his talents.

Still, she was as self-conscious as a schoolgirl at her first party as she took the chair.

Hamish lowered his scissors and paper and opened the writing desk. Pulling out a small folder of stiff paper, he opened it and withdrew a silhouette. "I've completed Lady Priscilla's. I'll confess to practicing a bit before I came down. 'Tis been a while since I cut profiles, so I worked on a few." He laid out a row of black shapes.

Everyone crowded around. There was Cilla's, but also in the row were Honora Mary, with her curly locks, and two youngsters that had to be Cian and William, the children of the Whitelocks. The nursery at Haverly had never been so full.

Charlotte and Diana praised Hamish's work, but Cilla sat still.

Hamish had gone to the nursery and created the children's silhouettes using them as models. But he'd made hers from memory. Or perhaps from one of his sketches? In either case, he hadn't needed her to sit for him to catch her likeness.

Why that should warm her heart and shorten her breath, she struggled to understand.

What was it about him that his arrival into her life should make her feel as if dawn were finally appearing on the horizon after a long, dark night? He would be here such a short time. Would she still feel this alive and vibrant after he'd gone?

The thought of his leaving caused an ache in her middle.

*Oh, you're being ridiculous. It isn't as if you're in love with him. You've only known him a few days, and anyway, he's in the way of a tradesman. The dowager would never give her permission, even if Hamish should offer for her.*

Not that he would. He was an itinerant painter. How could he pursue his career and travel the country painting portraits and maintain a family residence somewhere?

Though there was that teaching position. That was stable employment, wasn't it?

No, if she was wise, she would discipline her mind, keep her feelings in check. If she allowed herself to indulge in fancies concerning Hamish Sinclair, she would only increase the sense of restlessness and discontent she'd been struggling with the past few weeks.

◆※◆

Hamish would be the first to admit that it was nice hearing praise of his silhouettes. Even the dowager had been complimentary when he'd handed hers over.

"Your Grace, shall I continue?" he asked the dowager.

"Yes, yes." She clapped her hands, and the conversations died. "I know you're all enjoying the evening's entertainment, and I'm pleased to say we're not finished yet. Mr. Sinclair?"

He rose. "With the dowager's help, I've written the names of each guest on these slips of paper. While I realize that some of you are better known to one another, I'll ask you each to take pen and ink and write one word beside each name that describes that person. From your lists, I shall endeavor to create a caricature of you. Dinna take a long time over your descriptive words. This isna meant to be laborious, just a wee bit of fun."

One of the footmen was ready with pots of ink and quills, and everyone fell to their list making.

While they wrote, Hamish studied them, already forming images in his mind. He was curious as to the dynamic in the room. Though Marcus and Charlotte were the ranking members, the duke seemed unbothered that his mother was so bossy. Hamish liked the Earl of Whitelock. He'd heard the story of how he gained his title, and Hamish could see the soldier beneath the earl. And he liked the way the man's eyes rested lightly on his wife, as if still bemused to have such a fine creature for his own.

Cilla was a riddle. She kept to the fringes, saying little, and her dress . . . Hamish frowned. If it had been created to make her disappear in a group, it could not have been more perfect. Dull gray, with no adornment.

And yet she was still the most beautiful woman in the room. She could be wearing sackcloth and her quality would shine through.

If only she was clothed in the dress from earlier in the day. She was made to wear every shade of blue.

"I'm finished." Baroness Richardson handed him her paper. "I did my best, but it's difficult when you don't really know people. I was told this was a friendly area, but either people don't entertain much, or we're not being invited." She shook her head, as if such a thing couldn't be right, but Hamish wondered after listening to her waspish tone.

Either she and the dowager would be best friends or at daggers drawn, they seemed so alike.

The pages came back to him, and once he'd gathered them up, he turned his chair and the table his writing desk was open upon so his back was to a wall.

"Now, Cilla, if you wouldn't mind," the dowager said. "Perhaps a bit of music will fill in the time while Mr. Sinclair works?"

Hamish paused, his pen held over the inkwell. He followed Cilla's progress across the room, noting her bowed head and the way she pulled her shoulders in, as if to make herself smaller.

Why would such a beautiful, kind, interesting person be so . . .

timid? Did no one else here appreciate her fine qualities and tell her so? Did they not notice how her voice quickened and her face grew lively when she spoke of helping the women brought from London to train as domestics? Did they not see how she caressed her daughter's cheek, or how she paused before answering a question, as if she wanted to get her response just right before speaking?

He glanced at the dowager. Perhaps living always at the beck and call of such a demanding woman leached the will out of Cilla? She should get away, escape the control of another, and forge her own path.

Though how could she do that, other than through marriage? Did her brother-in-law give her a stipend? Was it enough for her to live on away from Haverly?

"I'll turn pages for you." Lord Athelson unfolded his long frame from his chair and followed Cilla to the pianoforte. He stood close, almost leaning over her, his head near hers.

Hamish frowned. Who was that man? Did Cilla know him? The dowager beamed, as if she were getting her way, a bit of calculation narrowing her eyes. Of all the guests, Lord Athelson was the only bachelor. It wasn't difficult to see that he had eyes for Cilla and that the dowager approved.

*Get back to your work, Hamish. The doings of the aristocracy are no concern of yours.* He dipped his pen into the inkwell once more and began the caricature of the Duchess of Haverly.

Cilla played softly, with a delicate touch. But Hamish, who was no musician himself, was disappointed. She played with no soul, no fire, no change in tone or tempo.

And Athelson remained at her side. At one point, he put his hand on her upper back, and it was all Hamish could do not to jump up and swat it away.

*Stop being ridiculous.*

Putting his head down, he tried to ignore everyone and lose himself in his work. Consulting the lists, and watching the guests, he created the caricatures, mindful that he should not allow his personal feelings to color the sketches.

Ninety minutes later, it was time to reveal the caricatures. He was satisfied with all but one.

"You've captured Charlotte perfectly." The duke held up the picture of his wife as a beautiful fountain, words and ideas flowing out of her.

The duke had been more difficult. He was portrayed as a book, but the book had hinges and a lock. Hamish had sensed the duke was a man of many secrets and responsibilities. Hamish must have caught it right, because the duchess nodded when she saw it, and the duke sent Hamish a javelin look.

Lord Athelson had been a struggle. Hamish had been tempted to portray him as a narrow lamppost or as a thin, placid cow, but he'd refrained. Instead, he had drawn the man as a fox sunning himself on a grassy slope. Hamish had tried not to make him look sly, instead giving him an intelligent glint.

Each recipient seemed pleased with their likeness.

The last one was Cilla, whom he had drawn as a white rose, delicate and sweet, protected beneath a bell jar. It was safe, conservative, and, if he admitted it, boring. Of course, the dowager loved it.

"Absolutely perfect. I must say, you're coming up trumps, Mr. Sinclair, much better than I had hoped. Now, if your portraits are as good, you shall be handsomely rewarded." She looked at him over the top of her reading glasses, reminding him that he had entered into an agreement where, if she was not satisfied, she would owe him nothing for the paintings.

He bowed, acknowledging their respective situations. Though the dowager had refused to have her likeness captured in caricature, Hamish could see her as a satisfied cat on a satin pillow, servants all around her holding bowls of milk, toys, and treats.

Cilla took the rendition of herself from the dowager's hand and studied it. When she flicked her lashes up and caught Hamish looking for her reaction, he locked eyes with her. Was she pleased? Disappointed? Indifferent?

Her lower lip disappeared behind her teeth, and she studied the paper again. A tight smile and a small nod was all he got.

If only she knew of the drawing he'd completed before he'd come downstairs, the one hidden under the blotter of his writing desk. In it Cilla was portrayed as a bright butterfly, rising above a flower garden and outshining the blooms for color. She had broken free of the restraints of the chrysalis the dowager had wrapped her in and soared with a will of her own wherever she pleased. Was he being fanciful, ascribing to her wishes and dreams that she didn't have, dreams he only had for her?

In any case the drawing had been too personal an image for anyone else's eyes, and he had decided to keep it for himself.

With his part of the entertainment done, he packed his tools. The duke followed him to the door.

"Thank you for tonight. I appreciate you being so generous with your talents."

"My pleasure, Your Grace."

"How is Cilla's portrait coming along?" He kept his voice low.

"Very well. It will be done by Christmas Eve." Especially since even late at night, Hamish couldn't stop working on it. Or just sitting and staring at her likeness.

"Do you ride?" The duke opened the drawing room door before the footman could perform the duty.

"Your pardon?" The question caught Hamish off guard and yanked his mind off Cilla.

"Do you ride? We're planning a hunt tomorrow. Not a full hunt, but a trial. If you ride, I would be pleased if you would join us. You might like the opportunity to get out of the house for a while."

"I'd be honored. Thank you." He had ridden all his life, being the son of a stable master. "However . . ."

"If you haven't brought the appropriate kit, don't worry. I'll have my valet bring you breeches and boots tonight. We're of a size, you and I."

Hamish thanked him again and escaped to his studio. After lighting a lamp, he sat on a stool before Cilla's portrait, the butterfly caricature in his hand.

"You're a fool, Hamish Sinclair. Keep your mind on the work, else you'll become a thrawn de'il. You should be thinking about your application to the academy, not a bonny aristocrat. Or you should be preparing yourself for teaching lassies at a girl's school, which is more likely."

He thought about crumpling the drawing and tossing it into the rubbish bin, but at the last moment he tucked it back into his writing desk.

# CHAPTER 5

"I'm glad you're going to go, Cilla. You've been cooped up for so long. I wish I could participate." Charlotte patted her rounded belly. "Enjoy some fresh air and sunshine for me."

"Diana will keep me company on the ride, and we'll tell you all about it when we get back." She checked her riding habit in the morning room mirror, adjusting the short veil. A thrum of excitement vibrated across her skin.

"I do hope you'll make Lord Athelson feel welcome. He won't be familiar with the terrain, so he will need someone to attend him." The dowager spoke diffidently, but she stared at Cilla. "He is such a nice man, don't you think?"

So Cilla had been correct in the dowager's motives for inviting Athelson.

"He is very nice." And so he was. He had been most punctilious in his behavior toward her last evening. That he sparked no interest in her wasn't his fault.

And evidently she sparked no interest in Hamish Sinclair. He saw her as a white rose? The caricature he'd created of her was so pale and bland as to be almost insulting. The bell jar? And yet those who'd viewed it said it was a wonderful representation of her. Couldn't he at least have made the rose red, given her some color?

When they reached the stables, grooms held saddled horses, the animals stamping in the cold air, jetting steam clouds with every breath.

Their shoes rang on the cobbles, heads stuck out over half doors, whickering softly, and the clock bell in the cupola chimed nine times.

Hamish stood beside a tall bay, holding the reins, looking resplendent in hacking jacket, breeches, and tall black boots. His hat sat at a rakish angle, and he bowed slightly to Cilla when he caught her staring at him.

She was reminded of his painting of the groom in the stable yard after the master had ridden away. It made her look more closely at the stable hands here.

Marcus strode to the center of their small party. Six riders would make up the field—the two ladies, Marcus, Hamish, Evan, and Lord Athelson.

"The huntsman has taken the dogs out into the field to await us." Marcus took the reins from his head groomsman. "This is a young pack of hounds, and we've decided that we'll have a drag hunt today. No live quarry, just a trail laid by one of the lads early this morning for the dogs to follow. As we're hunting with such a small pack, there will be no whippers-in. The huntsman will have charge of the pack, and the master will lead the field. Everyone ready?"

Cilla patted the silky nose of her mare, Trickster, admiring the shine of her black coat, even under these cloudy skies. The groom gave Cilla an impersonal leg up into her sidesaddle, and she adjusted her skirts and fitted her boot into the stirrup. Trickster sidled, shaking her head and jingling the bit.

"Thank you for taking such good care of her. She looks fine." Cilla made sure to compliment the groom. He tugged his forelock and slapped Trickster on the neck.

It felt good to be back on her horse. The mare had been a gift from her husband when they married, and together Cilla and Neville had ridden over the Haverly property, back when her husband had been the heir and expected to inherit everything he saw. They had visited the farms and tenants, the shepherds and the craftsmen that called the estate home.

After Neville died, there was no one to ride with, and she'd only gone out a few times.

A groom tossed Hamish aboard, and he landed lightly, gathering his reins and finding his seat with a minimum of fuss. He patted his mount's withers, rubbing up his neck and under his mane in a friendly manner that made Cilla smile.

Lord Athelson was another matter. He inspected his mount from nose to tail, twitched the saddle cloth, fiddled with a rein, and tested the girth. With a frown, he tightened the buckles.

"She d-d-doesn't like it t-t-too t-t-tight, sir," the groom stammered.

"I've been riding since before you were born, and I know my business. I don't want the saddle slipping halfway over a jump. Now, be a good lad and remember your place." Athelson sent a sharp look the groom's way, and the young man subsided.

Finally, Athelson mounted, using a block, fussing and shifting in the saddle. His horse turned in a sharp circle, pushing her nose out and trying to grab the bit. Strawberry was usually a quiet, reliable ride, but perhaps the combination of the cold and a new rider had her feeling chippy this morning.

"Let's go." Marcus led the way out of the yard at a walk. Cilla allowed her body to fall into the rhythm of her horse, tugging her gloves on tighter and keeping her back straight but supple. Hamish drew alongside, his cheeks ruddy with the chill.

He smiled at her, and her heart did a flip.

"'Tis a grand day for a hunt, is it not?" His eyes seemed especially bright, his hands light on the reins, his seat secure.

"Yes."

Before she could say more, Lord Athelson nosed his mare between them. "Lady Priscilla, allow me to ride with you. I'm a member of my local hunt club and well able to look after you." He ignored Hamish, keeping up a prattle about his estate, the house, his solid financial footing.

A few minutes into his monologue, Cilla realized he was filling her in on information she would need if he were to offer for her, reasons why it made sense for her to accept.

And they were indeed all sensible reasons, pragmatic and rational. Enough time had passed for her remarriage to be not only unremarkable but expected. Her parents would approve of Lord Athelson. The dowager clearly did. And so on.

Suddenly Cilla was fed up to the back teeth with the prosaic, rational expectations of everyone around her. She kicked Trickster into a canter, riding to the front, leaving Lord Athelson midsentence. Her bad manners should probably make her feel guilty, but she didn't in the least today.

Her movement encouraged the others to quicken, and soon they arrived at the field where the master and the huntsman had assembled the pack.

Hamish drew up near her, and she watched him reach inside his hacking jacket for his sketch pad and pencil to capture the scene. Marcus spoke to the master, who nodded to the huntsman.

"Trot along, boys!" the huntsman called to the dogs, and they spread out ahead of him, heads up. The huntsman gave a small blast on his horn, and if this had been a real hunt, it would have alerted any fox in the area that he was now quarry. But since this was a drag hunt, the dogs were only searching for the scent trail that had been laid down for them.

"Leu—in!" The huntsman gave the order, and the dogs spread out, noses down, tails lashing the air as they quartered, seeking the smell they were after.

The riders fanned out behind the master, and when a cry went up from one of the dogs, the race was on.

Cilla thrilled to the pace, the sound, the movement. Icy wind whipped her veil against her face, but she leaned into it. Trickster caught her exuberance and pricked her ears, lashing her tail as they approached the first fence.

They soared over it with ease, and Cilla drew back on the reins a bit, lest she outpace the master, which would be a *faux pas* hard to live down.

Everyone seemed to be going well. Diana and Evan were both excellent riders, and of course Marcus could ride anything. Lord Athelson still struggled with his mare. She held her head high and tried to bolt, and then she balked at a fence, nearly flinging Athelson over her head. He turned her in a sharp circle, and when they were lined up with the fence, he kicked her hard in the belly.

Cilla frowned, but the mare cleared the fence and galloped on, tail swishing.

Hamish was in a class by himself. He and his mount seemed to be one. He sat still in the saddle, balanced, the pair flowing over the hedges and fences as if they weren't there, his reins light, palms pressing his horse's neck over the jumps.

Cilla couldn't get enough of watching him.

They followed the dogs into a patch of woods and approached a barred gate a bit higher than the other ones they had leapt, with a downslope on the far side. The approach was narrow, and they would need to take turns. Mindful of the dowager's instructions, Cilla slowed to warn Lord Athelson.

She held up her hand as she trotted Trickster, and Athelson pulled his mount up near her.

"There's a bit of a fall away on the far side I thought you should know about. And the ground is muddy."

His nostrils pinched, and he frowned. "I can see that. I'm not a novice, you know."

Abashed at his crisp tone, Cilla nodded and went ahead of him. It wasn't a dangerous fence if you took care.

Marcus jumped first, and when Hamish saw the duke's landing on the far side, he trotted his mount up to the gate to give him a good look at the situation before turning back. A sensible thing to do when one wasn't familiar with the course.

"It's soft, so be careful," he warned Cilla.

She nodded. Trickster was a capable jumper, surefooted and trustworthy in spite of her name.

Hamish jumped his horse, letting the reins slip through his fingers as the gelding plunged down the slope on landing. Cilla let out a breath.

He pulled up halfway down the hill, turning back to watch, raising his hand for her to come ahead.

Giving Trickster plenty of space to see the gate, and lots of encouragement, Cilla cantered down the wooded lane. With ears pricked and head up, Trickster sailed over the bars, landing well out and emerging into the sunshine, snorting. Cilla patted her warm neck.

"Well done." Hamish's grin of approval warmed her through. "My father would approve. He's a keen eye and a stern word for sloppy riding."

"That explains your excellent equitation." She smiled, feeling as if she had thrown off a heavy cloak. What was it about him that the smallest compliment made her hum with pleasure?

Lord Athelson and Strawberry were next, and the gray mare fought him all the way. Cilla waited for him to pull her up and get her settled, but he didn't. Instead, he popped his boot with his riding crop and kicked hard. Strawberry's nostrils flared, ears pinned back, and halfway over the jump, she twisted. When she landed, her head went down between her knees while at the same time she kicked her back legs. Athelson flew over her withers, somersaulting in the air and rolling down the hill in an ungainly heap.

Marcus was off his horse quickly, handing the reins to Cilla, while Hamish set out after the kicking, bucking Strawberry. Hamish's horse was much the faster and overtook her before she'd gone too far.

The huntsman and the master waited in the field below, the dogs gathered around, eager to continue the trail.

Lord Athelson slowly sat up, his face a mottled blue and white. His hat had gone one way, his crop the other. His stock appeared to be trying to climb into his left ear. Mud splattered his breeches and boots, and a smear ran across the back of his hacking jacket.

Marcus grabbed him under the arms and hoisted him to his feet while Diana brought her mount alongside Cilla's, having completed the jump successfully.

"Are you injured, Reginald?" Marcus asked. He strode down the slope and retrieved the man's hat, smacking it against his leg to loosen the dirt.

Lord Athelson closed his eyes, took a deep inhalation through his narrow nose, and smiled tightly. "Only my dignity. Is the mare all right?"

The tightness in Cilla's middle eased when he asked about the horse. Hamish arrived, leading the mare, who had white ringing her eyes and her ears laid back. He gave his reins to Cilla and hopped to the ground.

"Easy, lass. Easy. Nay harm done." He approached Strawberry, hand raised, his voice soothing. The mare pricked her ears, stamping her foot and snorting, pulling back against his hold. Easing slowly toward her, the Scotsman crooned in what Cilla assumed was his native tongue.

Strawberry let him touch her quivering muzzle.

After a few moments, the tension in the gray mare released, and she shoved her nose into Hamish's chest. Hamish checked her over.

"She seems sound." Without drawing attention to it, Hamish ran the stirrup leather up and loosened the girth, resetting the saddle cloth and saddle. He refastened the girth, but not as tightly as Lord Athelson had back in the stable yard.

Lord Athelson returned his hat to his head and took the reins.

"Milord, would you prefer my mount? I can take the mare," Hamish offered.

Umbrage colored Athelson's tone. "Of course not." He eyed Hamish as if he were an offending servant.

"Shall we continue, or has everyone had enough?" Marcus asked.

"We should complete the hunt if we don't want to confuse the dogs, right?" Evan asked. "You said they were a young pack in training. Calling them off the scent before they reach their prize might send the wrong message."

"Athelson?"

"Let's proceed." He accepted Hamish's boost into the saddle, and he patted the mare's neck. "I'll attempt to stay with this girl for the remainder of the ride."

Cilla had to give him credit. He was trying to gather his decorum.

Hamish leapt aboard without benefit of a leg up, and Cilla turned away.

If she had any sense, she would be considering the dowager and Lord Athelson's plans instead of mooning over an itinerant artist who would be gone in a fortnight, no matter how kind, capable, or handsome he may be.

—◆✕◆—

Hamish balanced his weight over his stirrups, heels down, hands low and quiet, exactly as his father had taught him. Getting out of the studio and onto a horse made him feel good. Though he tramped through the woods every day, he hadn't ridden in a while. He'd probably feel it tomorrow, but it would be worth it.

He followed Lord Athelson, who had spent much of the day either battling his horse or putting himself between Hamish and Cilla.

There was no denying Hamish still felt the sting of Lord Athelson's attitude. He was the hired help, nothing more. The aristocrat had treated Hamish like a servant from the moment they'd met, and he'd done everything he could to drive home his point during this ride.

*Lord, I am struggling. I know You put me in my current situation, and You didn't make a mistake. Help me be content, not to be critical of another, and to remember that You love Lord Athelson as much as You love me.*

As much as his father's instruction about riding ran through his memory, his mother's instructions about how to pray and how to treat others rang even stronger. She had always reminded Hamish that God loved even people who annoyed or frustrated or were unkind, and He had commanded Hamish to love them too.

Some people were easier than others to love.

His eyes found Cilla, composed and steady in the saddle, as ethereal and delicate as crystal, glowing with good health. Her eyes had a sparkle he hadn't seen often, and never in the presence of the dowager. Out here in the fresh air, she was vibrant, with a touch of freedom about her he never saw in the house.

She would be easy to love. If he admitted the truth to himself, he was half in love with her already. Or at least the idea of her, a quiet, beautiful, kind woman in whom he sensed a banked fire waiting for something to fuel it into a bright flame. He fancied himself blowing on those coals and bringing a blaze to light.

Which was so much twaddle. He wasn't in a position to coax any woman's feelings, much less one so far out of his reach. She had been married to the heir to a dukedom, after all. And who was he? A stable master's son with some artistic ability.

The pack had followed the trail well, running the scent to its termination and being rewarded with many pats and much praise. All the horses had behaved, even Athelson's mare, now that the girth wasn't unpleasantly tight. With the sun standing nearly overhead, the party made their way back toward the stables.

They had to cross a rock-strewn stream below the manor house that, while it flowed rather quickly, wasn't terribly deep. However, when the huntsman's horse and the pack leapt into the water, one of the dogs let out a loud yelp, thrashing and crying.

The master was off his horse and splashing through the icy water before Hamish realized what had happened. The large man grabbed the animal by the nape before it could be swept downstream. Foxhounds were large, athletic canines, and the master struggled with the panicked dog. Hamish jumped to the ground to help him get the animal onto the bank.

"Easy, girl. Easy." The master laid the dog on the grass, holding her neck down to assess the damage. "She must have hit a boulder under the water when she jumped in." He ran his hand down her near foreleg, and when he reached the elbow joint, the dog cried out.

"Is it broken?" Hamish held the dog's hindquarters.

"Difficult to say." The man's face was a mask of anguish. He clearly cared for each of the dogs in his pack.

"Perhaps you should put the poor thing out of its misery." Lord Athelson drew his mare alongside, looking down and blotting out the weak sunlight. "Surely you brought a pistol?"

"Oh no." Cilla was off her horse, slipping the reins and kneeling beside Hamish. Her shoulder brushed his, and she reached out to pat the trembling dog. "There must be something we can do."

The master motioned for Hamish to hold the dog, and he stood. "Your Grace," he called across the stream, where the rest of the riders and dogs milled. "I'll stay here to see what is to be done. Let the huntsman take the rest of the pack back to the kennel, and I will meet him there."

"Right. Do you want me to send anyone back for you?"

"No need, Your Grace." The master was already bending over the injured foxhound again.

"I'll stay with you," Hamish offered.

"As will I." Cilla continued to stroke the dog's flank.

"Really, Lady Priscilla, this is no place for you. Let me escort you back to the house." Lord Athelson leaned from the saddle, offering his hand to help her stand. "Let the servants deal with this unfortunate incident."

Hamish wanted to smack the man's hand away, but he refrained. Cilla's expression grew stiff.

"That's most kind, but I prefer to stay." Her voice held a firmness Hamish hadn't heard before. She wasn't rude, but she left no one in doubt as to her wishes. Some of that suspected fire sparking to life?

"Very well." Athelson scowled and turned his mare, booting her in the ribs to encourage her to cross the water.

Hamish felt down the injured joint, and the dog whimpered. "I think it's dislocated. If we can reduce it quickly, she might make a full recovery." And before anyone could stop him, he grasped the leg, pulling sharply and feeling the satisfied click as the elbow returned to a normal position. The dog's wail cut off sharply, and she lay panting on her side.

The master startled. "How did you do that?"

"I've been around dogs quite a bit. My father's best friend is a master of hounds in Scotland. He taught me a thing or two." Hamish unpinned his stock, unwinding the white cloth from around his neck. "We'll just bandage this to keep the swelling down and get her onto one of the horses for the trip to the kennel."

When the leg was bound, Hamish assessed the three horses. The dog was quieter now that her joint was aligned, but it would be an unpleasant journey getting her home.

"My horse won't carry her. He's hotheaded and young." The master fondled the dog's ears.

"Trickster can carry her, but I don't know that I'm strong enough to hold a grown dog." Cilla rubbed her hands on the grass.

"I'll take her." Hamish gathered his reins and leapt aboard.

After an initial struggle, the dog seemed to realize they were trying to help, and she went limp across Hamish's lap. The ride back to the kennel was slow, and though he urged the master and Cilla to go ahead of him, they refused.

When they reached the yard, grooms took the dog, and Hamish slid to the ground, his legs numb.

The kennels were adjacent to the stables, and Hamish and Cilla followed the grooms.

"I want to see her bedded down." Cilla accepted Hamish's arm.

"Lady Priscilla, I've been waiting for you." Lord Athelson rounded the corner. "The dowager requests your presence immediately." He held his chin high, looking at Hamish along the side of his nose.

Cilla paused, biting her lip.

Much to his disappointment, she slipped her arm from Hamish's and gathered the skirts of her riding habit. "I shall come at once."

She sounded more like a servant than Hamish ever had.

# Chapter 6

Hamish strode along the path to the estate chapel, hands in pockets beneath his cloak, blowing out frosty breaths. Around him, some of the servants from Haverly Manor trundled along. The carriages had already gone ahead with the members of the household and their guests, leaving the servants to walk the quarter mile to church.

He didn't mind. He'd been offered transport in a wagon that carried the higher-ranking servants, but he'd opted to walk, a chance to clear his head and prepare for the service.

Snow had fallen overnight, a few inches that would most likely be gone by afternoon. Even now, bits of snow slipped from tree limbs to land in the soft drifts.

The church was larger than Hamish had envisioned, and already nearly full. He looked down the nave. The Haverly family sat in the front pews on the left, and he easily picked out Cilla's silver bonnet and dark-gray cloak. She sat between Athelson and the dowager.

Hamish took a seat in the back, only steps from the door under the balcony. He settled into the corner of the pew.

The organist began to play, and music swelled out and filled the sanctuary.

Light slanted through the stained-glass windows, creating rainbows of color across the heads of the congregation, and Hamish's fingers longed to paint the scene. Ahead of him and across the aisle, the new ladies brought for training from London sat together. How often had they been able to attend church in the past? He acknowledged that he knew none of their stories, but he envisioned a painting of them in a row, dressed in their new clothes, each one eager to make a good impression, to change their lives.

They were in the perfect place for that. If God changed them from the inside out, they would be truly changed forever.

The vicar took the pulpit, and Hamish focused his attention.

"Do you feel unseen? Do you wonder if God knows you? How can He see you amongst so many people, people of greater importance and stature than your own?"

It was as if the vicar was speaking right to Hamish and no one else.

"As we continue in this Advent season, I would like you to consider the arrival of our Savior. He was not born to the aristocracy. Quite the reverse, in fact. He was born to a carpenter and a maiden of no renown. He arrived in lodgings that didn't belong to his parents. He arrived in a stable. And the coming of the King of Kings had no fanfare, no procession, no royal announcement . . . until the angels appeared. But to whom did the angels come? To the privileged and wealthy? No, they delivered their message to a group of servants spending the night out on a hillside, caring for a flock of sheep." He looked from one face to another. "Heaven rejoiced to spread the good news through some of the least-considered citizens of Bethlehem. God saw those shepherds. Knew their names, their stories. And He chose to bless them, the small, not the great, with the birth announcement."

Hamish drew a picture in his mind of that dark night, the burst of light, the appearance of the angels. The shepherds in rough-woven cloth and battered sandals, with unkempt beards.

Unseen even in the presence of others.

"Never forget, God cares about the humble. God sees them. No one remains unseen to Him. No matter how you feel, He sees you. God sees you, God hears you, and God loves you. He loves you so much, He sent His Son to earth as a fragile child, to Joseph and Mary, who had no standing or rank, in order to save you. If you are wondering if God sees you and hears you, the answer is yes. He not only sees you, but He cares about you, and He is in control of the smallest parts of your life, making no mistakes in your circumstances."

A twinge of guilt pierced Hamish's conscience. He had been feeling forlorn and forgotten, as if God was not concerned with the minutiae of his life. Behaving as if God didn't see him. He had even stopped praying about getting into the Royal Academy.

*If I don't pray about it, then if I am disappointed, it won't be because God doesn't love me or want me to have this. It feels selfish to pray for something for myself. And I didn't want to presume upon God. But could a child of God presume upon his heavenly Father? If God already knows my heart's desire, it is ludicrous to think I could hide it from Him.*

He wanted to squirm over this error in his thinking.

*Is it wrong to pray about things that I want rather than things that I need?*

An image of Cilla's face filled his head.

He had not prayed about Lady Priscilla Haverly at all.

Should he? And if so, how should he pray? If God already knew his heart, and Hamish believed He did, then he should talk to Him about it.

"I have chosen a rather unconventional hymn for our choir to close with. I know that while Isaac Watts intended 'Joy to the World' to be in praise of the Lord's second coming, the words also apply to His first. Please listen carefully, especially to the phrase that reminds us of the "wonders of His love."' The vicar motioned to the choir director. "God's amazing, wonderful love is yours, no matter your rank or the amount of money you have, whether you work for yourself or work for others. No matter who you are, God sees you and loves you and sent His Son for your salvation. Let that be your theme this Advent season."

When the service was over and people began to file out, Hamish remained in his seat. The Haverly party would exit first, following behind the vicar as they came down the aisle. When the dowager was abreast of Hamish's pew, she said, "Why did he spend so much time talking about God seeing us? Of course He sees us. He's God, after all."

Cilla's lips twitched, and she caught Hamish's eye.

286

His heart lightened.

Then Lord Athelson blocked his view of her, taking her arm and leading her outside.

The gulf between himself and Lady Priscilla Haverly yawned as widely as ever.

God might see him, but it was clear that Lord Athelson would prefer that Cilla not.

—•✕•—

"I've never seen any paintings like them. Each one tells such a story." Cilla leaned back in the window seat in Charlotte's private sitting room. "Hami— I mean, Mr. Sinclair makes me see things in a way I never have before." She had thought about those paintings so often over the past few days . . . and she'd thought about Hamish. More than was proper.

She didn't miss the look that passed between Charlotte and Diana. A blush started up Cilla's cheeks, and she bent to fiddle with the buckle on her shoe to hide it. She shouldn't talk so much about him if she didn't want others to think anything was amiss, but she couldn't seem to help it.

Hamish Sinclair was interesting, handsome, talented, kind, and he treated her like a person with a mind and will and desires. He had come to her rescue about the entertainers that first night of the party and had never once chided her for the way her plans had come to naught. When she sat for him in the portrait studio, he asked her opinion and thoughts on all manner of things and never made her feel silly or unimportant. When she had opted to stay behind during the hunt to help with the injured dog, he hadn't questioned her decision or told her it wasn't her place.

"He certainly did a nice job on the caricatures." Diana filled the silence, holding her teacup with both hands and blowing the gentle steam rising from the brew. "And he was very generous when I asked if he could do a few sketches of the boys."

"I'm eager to see the portraits. I wish the dowager hadn't insisted they be kept from us until Christmas Eve." Charlotte leafed through a book, but she glanced up at Cilla frequently. "You've spent the most time in the studio. Do you get a sense of how the paintings are coming along?"

"They're sure to be beautiful. The blue gown will look fabulous with your coloring. I liked the red one, but I love the blue." Cilla drew her feet up onto the bench, glad that the dowager wasn't there to criticize her posture. That blue gown had come to symbolize something for Cilla. She felt like a different person when she wore it. Though she knew she was only sitting in as a model for Charlotte, she pretended Hamish was really painting her in the blue dress. "Perhaps when the modiste arrives, you can choose something like it for the party."

"I am still amazed the dowager agreed to a fancy dress party for Christmas Eve. And that she sent for costumes for all of us." Charlotte put down her book and went to her writing desk. Stacks of invitations lay in short piles, ready for the footmen to deliver them in the morning. "She's invited half the parish."

"What do you think you'll choose for a costume?" Diana asked.

"I'll have to see what the selection is. It puts me in mind of our masquerade party last winter. I wore green and gold to that one, and Marcus said he liked it."

"Evan would wear his military dress if he could." Diana laughed. "He's a soldier first, a gentleman after."

Would Hamish rather wear his kilt and sporran? Would he be invited as a guest to the party? Or would he stay in the shadows until time to reveal the portraits?

Two days later, when the modiste arrived with trunks of clothes, Cilla could hardly contain her excitement. Two rooms in the attics had been set aside, one for the men, one for the women, and the costumer, a tiny woman with skin like a dried apple, showed off her wares.

"You can see, dere is everytink you could vant." Her German accent was thick, but she spoke slowly, in contrast to her movements, which were quick as a bird's. She held up dresses, flicked hems, adjusted collars.

Cilla stood near the door, her hands clasped under her chin. The dowager sat on a plush chair in the center of the room, her cane leaning against her leg, smiling. If the costume choices were any indication, her Christmas Eve ball was going to be a success.

"Charlotte, we should start with you first. Something concealing of your condition. I'm of two minds whether you should even be seen at this late stage in your confinement, but Marcus has insisted, and I have had to give in." The dowager shifted in her chair, clearly ruffled by not getting her way.

Charlotte drew a dress from one of the trunks. The gown had a green skirt embroidered with golden harps and cherubs.

"Zat vun is inspired by Christmas itself," the modiste said. "Holly und candles und angels, ja?"

"It would suit you so well, Charlotte, with that high waistline and the generous gathers." Diana touched the velvet sleeve. "What could be more fitting for a Christmas Eve ball than to go as Christmas itself?"

"Shall I try it on?"

And thus began a flurry of dressing behind the screen and then parading. The dressmaker had brought two assistant seamstresses, and there were three on staff at Haverly, the head seamstress and two in training. They stood by ready to perform alterations as needed.

Cilla waited her turn, admiring the fabrics and colors.

The dowager tapped her cane on the floor, and everyone quieted. "We need something suitable for Cilla. I think one of those might do." She used the cane to point to a trunk of gray, black, and brown dresses.

"Oh, no," Diana protested. "Cilla, don't you want something bright and colorful?"

"Humph." The dowager cleared her throat, leaving no one in doubt that she felt Diana had overstepped. "Cilla has never worn 'bright and colorful.' Pastels suited her when she was younger, and now that she's a mature widow, it would be unseemly for her to appear in anything frivolous."

Which made Cilla feel in the sere and yellow. She was twenty-four, not eighty-four.

A spark of rebellion flickered to life in her heart. "It won't hurt to try on something different, will it?"

Diana didn't wait for the dowager to weigh in. Snatching up a ruby-red gown with a gauzy white overskirt embroidered with silver snowflakes, she drew Cilla behind the screen.

Studying herself in the mirror, she turned this way and that, admiring the swish and sway of the dress, the way the lamplight glinted off the silver threads.

"That's unsuitable." The dowager's lips drew in. "Cilla never likes to draw attention to herself. You shouldn't force her to dress so boldly."

"Madam, Cilla is right here, and she is free to give her opinion. No one is forcing her to do anything, unless you consider yourself, who is trying to force her to dress in something akin to widow's weeds. Next you'll insist she go about veiled in black."

The room froze at Charlotte's tone. Everyone looked from the dowager to Cilla.

She took a short breath. Was fire about to rain down?

"Lord Athelson commented," the dowager said, frosty voiced, "that he appreciated the womanly and demure and subdued way in which Cilla dressed. You do want to please him, do you not?" She pierced Cilla with a stern gaze.

Did she? Force of habit almost had her agreeing, giving in to the dowager's wishes, to Athelson's wishes. But that flicker of rebellion wouldn't be snuffed.

The warm look in Hamish's eyes when he painted her sitting in for Charlotte's portrait flashed through Cilla's mind.

She straightened. "I want to please myself. I like this dress, Diana, but there is another that caught my attention." Without waiting for the dowager's permission, she drew out a luminous blue dress. It had peacock feathers down the back that formed a train that swept the ground. Peacock feathers adorned the bodice as well. It was bold, beautiful, and well out of Cilla's character. In a small way it reminded her of the blue dress of Charlotte's portrait . . . or rather the feelings the dress engendered in Cilla when she wore it.

"Absolutely not." The dowager slammed the tip of her cane into the floor. "I forbid it."

"Forbid it?" Cilla went cold in her core. This was too much to bear.

"Madam, I am not a child. I can certainly please myself when it comes to what I wear, especially to a party."

As soon as the words were out, she regretted them. The dowager's complexion mottled as her face hardened.

"You're becoming headstrong, a very unpleasant feature in a young woman. I never would have expected such rebellion from you, Priscilla." The dowager rose, using her cane prodigiously. "I hope you don't come to regret this choice. I put a lot of thought into the choice of Lord Athelson, and if you display the sort of wayward determination of your sister-in-law and her friend, he might not offer for you. I'd hate for you to be the object of comments and gossip in the parish by behaving so out of character."

Doubts assailed her. Was the dress too much? Was she becoming headstrong? Cilla put the iridescent gown back into the trunk and folded her hands. As always, she felt that impending sense of doom should she cross the dowager. As if any decision she made on her own would prove disastrous.

"What would you suggest, madam?"

"That's more like it." The dowager settled back into her chair. "Something subdued and tasteful. Perhaps something in silver, or if you want some color, lavender?"

"I haf sometink in purple. It is inspired by ze English iris flower?" The seamstress hurried to pull out a dress of deep lavender with touches of white. "Vill dis do?"

"That's perfect. You say you like flowers, Cilla," the dowager said. "You will look just right in this gown."

Charlotte and Diana said nothing, but Cilla caught their disappointment.

Turning to the servants who waited for them to finish so their jobs could begin, she smiled. "Thank you so much for helping us today. Frau Becker, you've brought beautiful costumes, and you are very talented. You've quite an eye for design and color." Cilla held her hand out, indicating the seamstresses. "We'll try not to make the process of alterations difficult for you all. Perhaps we could make up a roster of who should come to the sewing rooms at what time. We can get everyone in and give you plenty of time to finish before Christmas Eve?"

The women nodded, but they looked to the dowager and Charlotte. "That sounds like a workable plan," Charlotte agreed.

As the ladies of the house made their way down the stairs, the dowager had one last word. "Cilla, what has come over you? Speaking to the servants that way. One does not ask a servant to perform the duties for which they are being paid. One tells a servant what one wishes, and it is the duty of the servant to obey without question. If you ask, you give the help the idea that they may refuse the order."

*Which might be why you never ask me to do anything. You tell.*

She looked once more over her shoulder at the peacock dress. It would have been nice, but it wasn't to be.

Dissatisfaction slowed her steps. What would Honora Mary say to her mother if she knew of today's goings on? She would say Cilla talked big, but when push came to shove, she always gave in to the dowager.

Cilla excused herself from the ladies and returned to the dressing room. It wouldn't hurt to look at the peacock dress one more time, would it?

# CHAPTER 7

WITH THE BALLROOM closed in order to decorate for the Christmas Eve fancy dress ball, the dowager elected to use the music room for an evening of country dancing and party games.

Cilla stroked her hand down her velvet gown. The Prussian-blue dress with white lace trim was the most daring thing in her wardrobe . . . which wasn't saying much. But it wasn't the dress that unsettled her. She felt as if she were on the cusp of something big, something she had been longing for but hadn't known she wanted.

And she feared that if the moment presented itself, she would somehow botch it or retreat from it, as she had the dowager when it came to her choice of costume.

Would that moment have anything to do with Hamish Sinclair? Her face heated at the thought.

"Don't you look nice?" Diana looped her arm through Cilla's. "You're positively glowing." She eyed Cilla shrewdly. "Is it love that's put the bloom in your cheeks?"

Cilla laughed. "You're in love yourself, so you think everyone else must be in love to be happy?" She squeezed Diana's arm. "I am happy for you. I only hope to one day find someone who looks at me the way Evan looks at you."

Diana scanned the room, stopping on Reginald Athelson, who stood beside Whitelock. "The dowager is quite taken with Lord Athelson. And he seems quite taken with you."

"If you're asking if he has made me an offer, the answer is no." Cilla tapped her foot as the small ensemble began to play.

"And if he does?"

Cilla was saved from having to answer by the approach of the man of whom they spoke. Lord Athelson bowed before her. "Will you do me the honor? The dowager has appointed us top couple for the first dance."

And as always with the dowager, she had not asked Cilla what she might wish. "Thank you, sir." She took his hand and allowed him to escort her, because it was the polite thing to do.

"You look different this evening. Have you changed your hair?" He frowned.

"No, sir."

As other couples lined up, she tried to think of something intelligent to say. But her mind and thoughts were elsewhere.

Today, Honora Mary had taken her first steps all by herself, and Cilla had been there to see it. And her first thought had been to take the child down the hall to Hamish's studio so he could see the new accomplishment for himself.

Later, when she had gone to find Charlotte to show her Honora Mary's new skill, Charlotte had wanted to speak with her regarding something else.

"Cilla, I'm glad we have a little time alone."

That Charlotte, who was most forthright, sounded hesitant put Cilla on her guard. "Yes?" Had Charlotte somehow discovered her growing regard for Hamish Sinclair? Had Cilla failed to sufficiently disguise her interest when speaking of his paintings? Was this the warning that she had felt coming and had dreaded? The warning she felt she might just need?

"It's about Lord Athelson."

Relief coursed through her, and she struggled not to let it show. "What about him?"

"Do you like him?"

"Like him? He seems pleasant enough, I suppose." Cilla bounced Honora Mary on her hip.

"The dowager seems quite determined that you take Reginald Athelson's suit seriously. She mentioned this morning that she didn't understand why the man was dawdling, unless it was that you were so reserved with him that he thought you might refuse. In fact, I heard her tell Lord Athelson that it was just your way, not to be put off, and that she was sure you would be agreeable to the match."

"She said that to him?" Cilla stopped bouncing the baby. "In front of you?"

"Well, not exactly in front of me. I was in the library, and she brought him into the room to talk. I was behind a shelf, and I didn't know what to do. But how I found out is beside the point. What are you going to do?"

What was she going to do? She hadn't given Charlotte an answer, because she didn't have one.

Now, Lord Reginald grasped her fingertips and guided her down the lines of dancers, turning elegantly on the toe of his dancing shoe at the far end, bowing to her curtsy. He was quite good.

Evan and Diana were next, and the rest of the dancers moved up the line until it was time to break into fours.

As entertainments went, the evening was quite pleasant, except something seemed missing for Cilla.

And she knew what it was. Or rather who it was.

During a break from the dancing for refreshments, she watched the maids perform their duties well. This new group of ladies had caught on even more quickly than the first, and she was proud of them.

When the music started again and the dancing resumed, Cilla couldn't face it. Nothing felt right, as if her skin was too tight, or that the house and the guests and the entire Christmas season were closing in on her. She needed time to think, to sort herself out.

The conservatory was mere steps from the music room. It was her place of calm and solace. The room was warm, heated like a Roman bath, with hot water in pipes under the flagstone floor. Condensation beaded on the glass panes and ran in rivulets down the windows. On very cold nights, braziers were lit along the paths, but tonight the room was illuminated only by the intermittent stars.

The Haverly conservatory boasted palm, banana, and citrus trees, as well as many ferns and exotic flowers, all planted in great containers. Cilla had enjoyed making over the conservatory when she was first married. Neville had indulged her love of flowers, though he had neither shared nor understood it. One reason Cilla loved the conservatory so much was that the dowager never came here. It had been Cilla's alone until she had moved to the dower house. Now it belonged to Marcus and Charlotte.

The palms stood silhouetted against the night sky, and faint moonlight drifted through the mist that gathered along the path. Rich scents of loam and green things filled her nose. The flagstones wove a gentle curve through the center of the long room, and she made her way to the bench she had placed there. In the far corner, a small fountain splashed, soothing her frayed nerves.

"Good evening." The voice, coming out of the darkness, made her jump.

"Oh," she gasped. "Good evening, sir."

Hamish stepped from the shadows of a mango tree. "I hope I'm not disturbing you."

"No, not at all." Although he did disturb her. Her senses were alerted, and the vast room seemed to lack a sufficient amount of air. She fidgeted with her hands until she realized she was doing it. Where was her serenity tonight? It wasn't normal for her to feel this agitated and . . . reckless? "I'm glad you are enjoying the conservatory. It's my favorite place."

"I can see why. All these plants, growing and expanding and blooming." He shrugged. "I confess—I come here as much for the warmth as for the plants. That and the green. My eyes become starved for green once winter sets in."

"I feel that way too. When the last leaf falls outside, though I love to see snow on bare tree branches, I miss the green." How could she be both so uncomfortable and so at peace in someone's presence?

In spite of the closed doors, the music drifted through, and Cilla's brows rose. A waltz? She hadn't realized a waltz would be on the dance list tonight.

Hamish's teeth gleamed in the moonlight. He bowed deeply. "May I have the honor?"

"What, here?" She laughed. Again that reckless sensation swept over her.

"Sometimes you have to seize enjoyment where you find it."

She took his hand, and he put his other palm on her waist. In moments they were moving down the stone path together. It was a slow waltz, and with each second, each step, she gave herself up to the pleasure of the moment.

The faint smell of linseed oil, turpentine, and paint came up from his jacket, and Cilla knew she would forever think of him if she smelled the combination in the future. His shoulder was solid under her hand, and he moved with purpose. As they danced toward the far end of the conservatory, away from the doors and the sound of the music, his steps slowed.

He stopped and stared down into her eyes, his expression solemn, but with a fire in his look that sent her heart cavorting and shortened her breath.

"Ah, lass, what are we doing? What are you doing to me?" His burr brushed her skin, and before she could formulate an answer, his lips came down and met hers.

A roaring started in her ears, and she leaned into him. Warmth trickled through her like water as his arms tightened. She'd never kissed a man with facial hair before, but his whiskers were surprisingly soft. With closed eyes, she drank in the taste and feel of him, her hands bracketing his face, feeling cherished and exhilarated all at the same time, safe and in peril all at once.

She never wanted it to end. How could he make her feel possessed and yet so free? She wanted to melt into a puddle and fly right up into the rafters. Nothing made sense, and she didn't care a bit.

When she thought she might faint, he withdrew, breaking the kiss. Her hand dropped to his chest, and his heart thundered under her palm, his breath choppy. He'd been at least as affected as she, hadn't he?

Her tongue came out and tasted her lips, and light flared in his eyes, but he gently stood her away from him.

"I apologize, milady. I had no right. I've overstepped my bounds." His lips were stiff, as were his movements as he stepped back, nearly leaving the path. "I trust you can find your way back to your party?" With a short bow, he strode away, leaving her empty and shocked.

She stared after him, his kiss still fresh on her lips. What had happened? She felt popped like a whiplash, one moment soaring, the next collapsed of heart.

The discontent, the longing, the restlessness she'd felt for weeks had evaporated in his arms, only to roar back at his departure.

Who was this new woman she was becoming?

And why on earth had this new woman fallen in love with a painter with whom she had no future?

——✕——

Hamish capped his bottle of linseed oil, tucked it into his supply case, and closed the lid. With a rag, he wiped the windowsill and his easels, and then he leaned down and scrubbed his boots. The studio was tidy, his tools and paints packed. Only one brush and his pot of varnish remained on the table. He'd fussed and cleaned and packed all morning.

Anything to keep busy.

The paintings were finished, draped beneath clean sheeting. A woodworker from the village would arrive tomorrow, Christmas Eve day, with the carved frames that had been commissioned, and Hamish's work would be done.

But before the framer came, there was the final inspection with the dowager. Hamish slipped his plain silver-cased watch from his pocket. She had said to be ready by noon, but he had a suspicion she would be late. The festivities had gone far into the night last night, and she had probably stayed for the entire evening.

Last night.

Hot chills ran over his skin. That description made no sense, and yet it was the best he could concoct for the sensation that overwhelmed him every time he thought about kissing Cilla Haverly.

Exultant and abashed, thrilled and anxious. What had he been thinking?

He *hadn't* been thinking, only feeling. Feeling the rightness of being with her, of holding her close, of desiring to make her feel special, unique, precious, and protected. In that moment, he had wanted her to know that she mattered, that she had a place, if not at Haverly, then in his heart.

His heart. That space in his chest felt as if it were being crushed by a giant fist.

Because there was no future for him with Cilla. She was aristocracy; he was a tradesman. Her mother-in-law had organized her future with Lord Athelson, someone of her own class and station.

Cilla would no doubt accept Athelson's offer, which was certain to come, and Hamish would depart with only her memory to cherish.

He lifted the covering from the painting of Cilla. Commissioned by the duke, it did not come under the heading of the dowager's gift. If she didn't approve the portraits of the duke and duchess, those paintings were his to keep. The portrait of Lady Priscilla Haverly would stay here at the manor regardless.

It had finished even better than his mind had envisioned. Kindness and intelligence shone from her blue eyes. He'd added just a touch of violet and then thinned ultramarine until it was barely opaque to capture the reflection along her lower lids. Her lips were soft and pink, and as he looked at them, he remembered the feel of them beneath his, the soft sigh she had breathed out, the way her hands had come up to cup his face.

*Stop it. That way lies madness. Discipline your mind if you can't discipline your heart, you fool.*

Cilla looked like she could emerge from the portrait walking and talking.

Her hair glowed like the golden riches of Croesus, like the palest honey, like the most brilliant sunshine . . . ah, he was rhapsodizing and running out of comparisons. In truth, nothing compared to Cilla.

Like the lovelorn swain he was, he replaced the sheeting, removed the painting from its easel, and set it against the wall next to his crate of personal paintings. The duke had not given instructions that Cil-la's portrait be shown to anyone in advance, not even the dowager. Hamish wanted to please the duke, who seemed an upstanding fellow and who had treated Hamish well.

Pleasing the dowager was another matter. Thus far, only getting her way quickly and utterly seemed to satisfy her. She wasn't mean-spirited, just bossy and completely convinced she knew what was best for every person she encountered.

And she kept Cilla tethered to her with her domineering ways.

He noted steps in the hall, with the extra click of the cane she used when she wanted to draw sympathy. He'd realized early on that when no one was watching, she didn't need it to get around and didn't even limp. Yet another way she had of getting Cilla and the rest of the ladies to wait upon her.

Raking his fingers through his unruly hair, he moved from behind the paintings.

"Mr. Sinclair, are they finished?"

"Yes, Your Grace. They're ready for your approval." He wiped his hands on his thighs and reached for the first covering. "Shall we begin with the duke?"

The dowager backed a few paces—with the cane hooked over her forearm—and studied the portrait. Her expression gave nothing away. With an imperious flick of her hand, she indicated he should remove the sheet from the next one in the row.

"And here is the duchess."

Pursing her lips, she tilted her head, looking from one to the other. She moved forward, again without the aid of her cane, and took in the details.

"If you are satisfied, I will apply a thin coat of varnish to them. When they're dry, I'll get them into the frames and move them to the ballroom for your presentation tomorrow night."

She gave a single, curt nod. "I am satisfied with your work."

His tight muscles relaxed. The commission was the largest of his career, and the paintings would hopefully be a feather in his cap when it came to garnering more work.

But the dowager wasn't finished. "Before we settle the accounts, there is another matter."

Her expression made him wonder if she had drunk fresh vinegar. Sour as pickling.

"Your Grace?"

"I have come to the realization that you have been taking liberties you shouldn't."

Shock hit him broadside.

"People here may think I'm too old to notice or to remember what being young is like, but they would be wrong. I see the way you are around Lady Priscilla, and I see the way she looks at you. Neither of you is fooling anyone, and I am here to tell you it stops now."

Heat prickled across his skin.

"Lady Priscilla is my son's widow, mother of my grandchild, and she will not carry on in this house with the *help*. Is that understood?"

"Your Grace—"

"I am not finished." This time she banged the tip of her cane on the hard floor. "You will not interfere with my plans for my daughter-in-law, nor will you turn her head with romantic notions of a forbidden dalliance. I cannot imagine what she was thinking last evening, sneaking off to rendezvous with you in the conservatory. It was plain as a pikestaff, when she returned all flustered and starry-eyed, what had been going on."

Flustered and starry-eyed? So his kiss had affected her as much as it had him? Hope burst into flower in his chest, but one look into the dowager's frosty eyes withered the bloom.

After a pause, her face softened a trifle, but her words were still forceful. "I suppose you cannot help yourself. Lady Priscilla is born of a quality you probably don't encounter often. It is to be expected that a man in your position might develop a *tendresse* for someone like her. You will soon recover from this fleeting fancy, I have no doubt."

A *tendresse*? A fleeting fancy? Her words relegated his feelings for Cilla to mere infatuation, a momentary heart bumping that would evaporate once he departed.

The dowager actually patted his arm. "See, I can be understanding of young people's feelings. But let there be no mistake in what must happen. If you imagine yourself in love with Lady Priscilla, you will do what is best for her, which is not to trifle with her feelings or endanger her carefully planned and safe future."

Her Grace being "understanding" was harder to stomach than her being stern and dictatorial.

"Your path and Lady Priscilla's lie far apart. Her future is here at Haverly until she remarries someone of her own station. Your behavior is encouraging her to become reckless and rebellious, most out of character for her. You must cease, for both your sakes. Are we in agreement then?" She asked it as if the answer was obvious.

He nodded, his jaw too tight to let out any words, which was just as well. To be upbraided by this woman and told to stay where he belonged, in the lower ranks, was both humiliating and infuriating.

"Excellent. I shall expect the paintings to be in position by seven o'clock tomorrow evening in the gallery." She paused. "Oh, and this arrived for you yesterday. I meant to have it sent up and forgot." With a shrug, she handed him a letter and marched out of the studio.

Feeling bludgeoned, he read his name on the front of the envelope. It had to be from the Royal Academy. No one else would send him a letter, and he had left word with his application that he would be at Haverly Manor through Christmas Day if they should need to contact him.

The letter had been franked in London. He turned the envelope over, and a roaring sound started in his head. The seal had been broken.

Had the dowager stooped to reading his mail? Or was he doing her an injustice? Seals *could* be broken by accident.

And yet he was feeling raw enough at her upbraiding to ascribe any dark motive to the woman.

His hand shook as he opened the letter.

"Mr. Sinclair, we regret to inform you . . ."

He didn't need to read further. The opening was identical to the previous two he'd received. Balling the letter in his fist, he hurled it at the rubbish bin. Like his artistic ambitions, it fell well short. Once again he had been refused entry to that exclusive club, and with that failure, the one last sliver of hope to have anything to offer Cilla died.

He would have to go to Stratford and take up the teaching position. There was no other choice, because after Christmas Day, he was without another commission.

# CHAPTER 8

CILLA NODDED TO the young woman who carried in the tea tray. This trainee was doing particularly well, according to Tetford. She was bright, quick, and only needed to be told once how to do a thing. High praise from the housekeeper.

Returning to her needlework, for which she had little enthusiasm, Cilla let the conversation flow around her. She wanted to converse even less than usual with their guests tonight. And who would blame her if they knew the truth? Her mind and heart were centered solely upon Hamish Sinclair and that kiss!

She swung from giddiness and giggles to mortification and muttering. How was she supposed to feel? How was she supposed to act? Hamish had not made an appearance since last night, and she certainly wasn't going to chase him up to the studio to ask for either an explanation or for a repetition. Though she would dearly love to repeat that kiss . . .

Thoughts of him had invaded her dreams. The romance of the encounter, the starlight, the music, the dancing . . . and being kissed by him. If she was truthful, not just being kissed by him, but kissing him right back! Again she had the sensation of being awakened from a long slumber, as if she had been frozen in place for a long time, and only come to life when he walked through her door.

Had she felt this way for Neville? She had loved him, she was sure of it. But her love for Neville had felt . . . expected. He had been chosen for her by her parents and his, and she had dutifully become his wife, and she had loved him because it was what she was supposed to do.

But falling in love with Hamish was the very definition of unexpected.

That thought brought her up short.

Love?

Was she in love with Hamish Sinclair?

It certainly felt like it.

Bleakness entered her chest. What good did it do her to be in love with him, when nothing could come of it? He would only be here a few more days. She would remain behind, caught in this strange limbo of widow, mother, daughter-in-law.

She didn't have the responsibilities of being the wife of the almost heir to the dukedom, but she also had no freedom to be anything else.

Shackled by convention and circumstances.

"Lady Priscilla, would you do me the honor of a stroll through the conservatory?"

Cilla jerked her thoughts to the present, surprised that Lord Athelson had approached without her notice. A stroll through the conservatory?

Heart bumping, she caught Charlotte's eye from across the room. Her sister-in-law frowned, biting her lower lip and placing her hand on Marcus's arm. With a slight incline of her head, she indicated Athelson, and Marcus's gaze sharpened.

"Yes, of course." Setting aside her needlework, Cilla rose.

Not the conservatory. Anywhere but there. She wanted nothing to mar or overlay her memories of that place.

But Athelson wasted no time, walking slightly ahead of her to open the doors to the greenhouse. The familiar, loamy, floral scents rolled over her.

This evening, the servants had lit the hanging lanterns along the path, both for light and warmth, and Athelson offered his arm to Cilla, tucking her hand into the crook of his elbow and covering it with his own.

Glancing up at him, she waited for what she feared was coming. He was stiff, as if freshly starched. When they reached the bench halfway along the room, she stopped. This was far enough. She sat and arranged her skirts.

"Lady Priscilla, I am a man of both title and possessions." He clasped his hands behind his back and paced. "I have a superb home and estate that brings in fifteen thousand pounds a year. I have a townhome in London and a seaside home in Brighton. I possess a good name and a good fortune. What I do not possess, however, is a wife to grace those homes or my life."

She gripped her hands in her lap, trying to keep her despair from showing.

"I could not have been happier when I received the dowager's invitation to this house party, and her suggestion—her strong suggestion—that I consider getting to know you during my stay. She claimed you were beautiful, biddable, and would be amenable to a proposal from me. I have certainly found the first two to be entirely correct. Dare I hope you will be true to the third?"

A chill crept up her spine. Biddable? Amenable?

"I assure you, it will not be a burden to assume responsibility for you and for your daughter. She will have the best governesses, the best training for her station in life, and when the time comes, we can select a suitable husband for her. She will be treated as I would treat my own children, should God bless me with offspring." He paused, and a tinge of color hit his cheeks. "If that isn't too bold a statement at this juncture."

Honora Mary. Her adventurous, adorable daughter. Lord Athelson had her future planned out, though he had never laid eyes upon her.

Anger replaced the chill in Cilla's bones. She no more wanted Lord Athelson to choose her daughter's husband than she wanted the dowager to select one for her, Cilla.

Hamish's face flashed through her mind. He had never once told Cilla what she should do, what she should wear, what she should think. He had asked for her opinion, talked to her as if what she said mattered, as if she was capable of making choices and having preferences.

He had seen her. The real her.

She felt as if Lord Athelson only saw her as her mother-in-law had portrayed her, and if she accepted his offer, her awakening sense of independence would return to slumber forever.

But refusing him would put her in direct opposition to the dowager, and more than that, it would mean she would continue here at Haverly with no real place.

Refusing Athelson guaranteed nothing in regard to Hamish. The artist had not offered for her and probably had no plans to do so.

But should that matter? She must make the decision that was best for herself and for Honora Mary, regardless of anyone else.

"I can see I have caught you by surprise. I am a patient man. Perhaps you would like a day or so to consider my offer?"

Cilla grasped at the lifeline he had thrown her, even as she chided herself for taking the safe way out yet again.

"Yes. Thank you. It is a big step, and I must be sure I am making a sound decision."

"Perhaps you can inform me of your decision tomorrow evening at the party? I am certain the rest of the guests and your family would enjoy celebrating with us."

He seemed supremely confident that after a day's consideration, she would accept his proposal.

———————— ✦✕✦ ————————

Hamish finished tapping the wooden wedges into the corners of the frame to hold the canvas tight and set down his hammer. Turning the painting was a matter of muscle and leverage, since it was nearly as tall as he.

"Let me help." The Duke of Haverly's hands grasped one edge of the frame.

"Thank you, Your Grace."

They leaned the painting on the easel and stepped back.

Cilla's beautiful eyes looked out serenely, and Hamish felt a stab in his chest.

"I came to inspect the portrait, but I can see there was no need." The duke took in the work, resting one finger on his chin. "You will go far in this world with talent like that."

Bitterness coated Hamish's tongue. "If by far, you mean a girls' school in Warwickshire, then you are correct."

"Ah yes. I heard about your latest disappointment regarding the Royal Academy. I don't know what they are thinking, the old fools. I suspect they are intimidated by the abilities of better and younger artists and are seeking to protect their position by denying applications of people they fear."

How did the duke know about his latest missive from the RA? Had the dowager not only read Hamish's mail but passed along the contents? Did the entire manor know he was an artistic failure?

"Whatever their reasons, they hold the power, and they give or deny as they wish." Hamish picked up his hammer and his box of staples and wedges, and he tucked them into his box of tools. "After three attempts to gain entry, it's clear I dinna produce the type of paintings they wish to display."

"If they could see this one, they might change their minds."

"I'm happy you're pleased with it." He felt it was his best work, but he was biased and could not be objective about anything pertaining to Cilla Haverly, even her likeness in oils.

"Cilla mentioned to my wife that you have other paintings here? She spoke most highly of the collection. I enjoy good art. Would you allow me to view them?"

It warmed him that Cilla had spoken well of his pictures, but having anyone see them was a risk, especially someone of the aristocracy. They weren't exactly flattering to the upper classes.

Still, he had something to say with his art, and if the duke wanted to listen, so be it. Art was meant to be shared.

"They're in here, Your Grace." He dug out his hammer once more and pried the lid off the crate. "You might recognize a pair of them, since I painted them while I was here."

One by one Hamish lifted the canvases, leaning them in a row along the baseboards of the studio until all eight were lined up.

And one by one the duke bent, picked up a painting, studied it, and moved on to the next. He said nothing, but as he went down the line, he took more time with each painting, until he held the last, a picture of Tetford, his housekeeper, instructing a parlor maid in the art of laying a proper tea tray. The dowager stood in the background, though if one didn't know who it was, one would never guess, because her face and form were indistinct, part of the setting. It was the young maid's face that stood out in sharp relief, and the housekeeper, caught in a rare moment of kindness as she moved a teaspoon from one side of the tray to the other.

"These are quite compelling. What are your plans for them?" Marcus placed the painting in the row and backed up a few paces to look at the collection as a whole.

"Plans?" Hamish shrugged. "I've no plans."

"Then why paint them? Surely you wish to show them?"

"Where, milord? I have no gallery, not even a home in which to display them. I painted them because . . ." He paused. "I painted them because I felt compelled to tell the story of those people who are all around but are rarely seen. That's the name of the collection: Army of the Unseen."

The duke nodded, stroking his chin. Finally he returned to the portrait of Cilla. "I wonder if you realize how much of yourself you reveal in your work."

"All artists reveal their worldview through their work." Hamish leaned against the empty crate. "'Tis a topic much discussed amongst painters, especially after they've had a pint or two." He chuckled.

"No doubt. However, when I look at this painting, I wonder if you realize how loudly you're speaking." He sent a piercing look at Hamish.

"What do you mean?"

"I mean, if you have painted my wife in this same manner, I shall have to call you out to settle things."

Hamish straightened. "Milord?"

"Do you realize the expression on Cilla's face is one of love? You have painted her as you see her, or as you wish to see her, looking back at you with utter love in her eyes."

Hamish's mouth went dry, and heat swirled in his ears. An uncomfortable tightness gripped his chest muscles. Had he really done such a thing?

"Anyone with half an eye can see it." His Grace took Hamish's measure, his expression unreadable. Hamish bowed his head.

Was this the point at which the duke would throw him out of the house? Did he think Hamish had somehow sullied his sister-in-law's reputation?

If he chose, the duke could ruin Hamish's career. He would never get work again, and the school would rescind its offer of employment.

Would even his father accept him back home if he found out his son had taken such liberties with a woman of Cilla's standing?

When Hamish raised his head, the duke was smiling.

Smiling?

"She's an easy woman to love, isn't she?" He put up his hands. "Do not misunderstand me. I love Cilla like the sister she is to me, but I understand how you might succumb to stronger feelings for her. Do you intend to offer for her? If so, I hereby give my permission and blessing. Charlotte and I have been watching you both this past month, and it's easy for anyone to see how you feel about one another."

Words fled from Hamish's head. He could hardly believe what the duke was saying. After a moment of looking a complete cake, he was sure, he managed, "But I have nothing to offer someone like her."

The duke raised his brows. "It might surprise you that I know quite a bit about you. I wouldn't have someone to stay in my home without gathering some information about him. You are a man of integrity, honor, and considerable ability. Though the Royal Academy has declined your application, that has more to do with internal politics than your skill as a painter. I've been giving this matter some thought and discussing it with my wife."

Hamish liked how the duke included his wife in his decision-making. He seemed to value her opinion and input. And from what Hamish had observed, the duchess was well learned and well spoken, with a high intelligence.

"What you need is a patron with some influence." The duke picked up the picture of the lady's maid. "More than one even. I propose that I become that patron, and I am certain that Whitelock will join me. When we return to London next month, I intend to mount a showing of your artwork. Either we will rent gallery space, or we will open Haverly House on Cavendish Square for the event. You can show your Army of the Unseen paintings alongside the portraits of myself and my duchess, and if Cilla is amenable, her portrait as well. I'm certain a showing would garner you new commissions. You will surely have, with patrons and publicity, the means to support yourself through your painting, and not only yourself, but a wife and child too?"

Hamish sagged against the crate once more, his knees giving out. "Milord." He shook his head. "I canna quite take it in. You would do that for me? I canna ken why you would do such a thing."

"I must say, you're a cautious fellow. Most men would already be shaking my hand. I wish to become your patron because I think your work deserves to be seen, that an injustice has been done denying you entrance into the Royal Academy, and that you would make Cilla a good husband. You make her happy. I don't think she realized she was unhappy until you arrived. She was caught in a sort of stasis, and now she's become alive. Charlotte told me Cilla has begun pushing back against the dowager, albeit on a limited scale, and we're both glad to see it. My mother is a strong woman who enjoys getting her own way altogether too much."

"The dowager has informed me in no uncertain terms to leave Lady Priscilla strictly alone." Hamish writhed inwardly at the chastisement he'd received.

The duke shrugged. "Don't worry about my mother. I'll put my foot down if need be."

Hamish stood and offered his hand, his heart thudding hard at the thought of his new future and what might come to be. "I canna thank you enough, sir. If you're willing to take a chance on me, I'm willing to accept your offer."

"I wouldn't advise waiting too long in regard to Cilla. I believe Athelson has already made his case to her."

A chill rippled through Hamish. What if she'd already accepted? What if she preferred Athelson to himself, regardless of what the duke thought? Or what if she cared for him but wouldn't defy the dowager? She might prefer safety and convention over a paint-spattered Scotsman.

# CHAPTER 9

———✠———

THE CHRISTMAS EVE party was only hours away, and Cilla couldn't settle to anything. Lord Athelson's offer weighed upon her mind, but not as much as thoughts of Hamish Sinclair.

Tonight he would present the portraits, and tomorrow he would leave the Haverly estate forever. Her chest ached at the thought.

She wandered around the dressing room she shared with the dowager. It would be nice to return to the dower house, where at least she had her own private space. Or would it? Returning to the dower house felt like a retreat and a return to the status quo.

Which was unbearable to contemplate. She wasn't the same woman who had moved into Haverly Manor for a Christmas party just three weeks ago.

But how could she maintain the change? How could she keep from sliding backward into her old routines and customs?

Accepting Lord Athelson's offer was the safe route, the one that would cause the least amount of discord with the dowager, the option that society and convention would approve.

But what of her wishes? What of what her heart wanted?

She had to *do* something different if she wanted to *be* something different.

Determined to ride this wave of recklessness as far as it would take her, Cilla squared her shoulders and planted her flag in the sand. The transformation must start tonight.

Hours later, with the clock having chimed seven a quarter of an hour hence, and already late for the party, Cilla took one last look at her reflection in the mirror in her boudoir, meeting the eyes of her abigail, who stood behind her, hairbrush in hand. Together they had moved her belongings out of the shared dressing room and into her bedroom before the dowager came upstairs to dress in order to have some privacy for the transformation.

"You look beautiful, milady."

If Charlotte's stories of the Roman Empire were to be believed, Cilla was about to cross her Rubicon.

"Thank you." Gathering her courage, she picked up her fan and headed downstairs to cause a stir.

Thankfully, the hallway into the ballroom was empty but for the footman stationed there. Cilla formed her expression into a pleasant smile, forcing her wobbly knees to function.

When the footman held the door for her, his eyes widened, and he broke protocol by grinning broadly. Covering his mistake, he smoothed his face and nodded.

Voices, light, and music came from the ballroom, and Cilla held herself proud and walked in with more confidence than she felt.

For a moment, no one noticed her entrance, and she wondered if she were here at all or if this were a dream . . . or nightmare. One in which, in spite of her best efforts, she would remain unseen.

Then Charlotte, in her green-and-gold Christmas-inspired gown, turned and spotted Cilla. Her jade eyes widened, as did her smile, and she came forward, hands outstretched. She embraced Cilla, brushing her cheek with a kiss.

"Darling, you did it. I'm so proud of you. Look at you." She stepped back, taking in the peacock gown, the curls, the aquamarine and diamond necklace. Cilla's maid had pinned a trio of peacock feathers into her curls with a diamond brooch, and her fan was of feathers as well.

Diana hurried over.

"How? I thought . . ." Diana stopped.

Cilla shrugged. "I changed my mind. The lavender dress was nice, but I decided it was too tame for tonight's celebration." Did anyone else notice that her voice shook?

She looked over the crowd, not admitting to herself whom she hoped to see. There must be fifty people here. All the house-party guests and many from the surrounding area. Was Hamish here? What would he think of her choice of costume?

"Come. We'll greet the dowager with you." Charlotte linked her arm through Cilla's on one side, and Diana did likewise on the other. "Best to get it over with right away. Strength in numbers."

The dowager sat on a chaise that had been set on a low dais along one wall. Dressed in her customary black, with polished jet beading, her mouth was a flat line and her eyes fierce. Her cane rested at her side, and as Cilla approached, she lifted it and stacked her hands atop the gold-and-glass orb-handled top.

"Madam, doesn't Cilla look beautiful tonight?" Charlotte spoke first. "Her gown will be the talk of the district."

"That's what I'm afraid of," the dowager hissed. "Everyone is looking at her. What happened to the dress I chose for you?"

Trying to work some moisture into her mouth, Cilla swallowed. "I changed my mind. I prefer this one."

"I see. And you give no regard to my preferences? I, who am only ever trying to do what is best for you? You're making a spectacle of yourself in that ridiculous garment."

*I refuse to wilt. I refuse to cower. I am a grown woman, and I can wear what I want.*

"Madam, I have given nothing but regard for your preferences since the day we first met. I have no desire to hurt you, but it is beyond time I made my own decisions. I am an adult, a widow, and a mother. I do not need someone telling me what to do." Cilla kept her voice low, aware of the crowded room. She took a seat beside the dowager and put her hand atop her mother-in-law's. "I know you will say that when I try to assert myself, no good comes of it. And that may be. But if I rise or fall with my choices, they will at least be my own."

The dowager jerked her hand away. "What has come over you?

What will Lord Athelson say at the way you're displaying yourself in that costume? I know what it is. It's that painter." She shook her head emphatically. "Get any notions of that man right out of your head, Priscilla Haverly. Don't be more foolish than you have to be."

"Mother!" Marcus stepped up and put his hand out to Cilla. When she stood, he put his arm around her shoulders. "You are the one making a fool of yourself. I have given you quite a bit of leeway over the years, but this is too much. Cilla looks beautiful, and I for one am proud of her. She is correct. She doesn't need anyone telling her what to do. She's smart, capable, and qualified to make her own choices without a lecture from you."

Though the dowager gaped, Marcus appeared not to care. He turned Cilla and motioned for Charlotte and Diana to follow him. He led them through the crowd, motioning for Charlotte to sit. "I'll get you some refreshments."

"I'll help." Diana followed him.

Cilla wanted to laugh and to weep, but mostly she wanted to sit down somewhere quiet. She had done it. She had defied the dowager in front of a roomful of people, and she hadn't backed down. Grateful as she was for Marcus's support, she hadn't even been tempted to fold in the face of her mother-in-law's opposition.

Charlotte lowered herself carefully into one of the chairs, her hand on her rounded stomach. "That was brilliant. I can hardly believe it. Bravo!"

Cilla sank into the chair opposite, her hands trembling.

"How do you feel?"

Shaking her head, Cilla shrugged. "I don't know. I feel . . . free. Does that make sense? Of course it doesn't. It's not like I have been a prisoner here at Haverly."

"Do you think you've been a prisoner of your fears?" Charlotte accepted a glass of punch from Marcus. "Of being afraid to share your thoughts and wishes for fear of being wrong or being ridiculed? Or having to fight to have them in the face of a stronger personality?"

How did Charlotte know? "You have a way of getting to the heart of a matter, don't you?" Cilla took a cup from Diana. She sipped the punch, puckering at the tartness but grateful for the refreshment. "The truth is, I've been feeling disquieted for some time. For too long, I have been content to drift along, living in the dower house, at the beck and call of the dowager, with few responsibilities and fewer ambitions." As she said it aloud, she felt ashamed at her own spinelessness. "I have let others make decisions for me my entire life because that felt safe and easy. My parents, Neville, the dowager, and to a certain extent, even Marcus have directed my life. It is beyond time I made my own choices. What kind of example am I setting for my daughter? I feel, over the past few weeks, as if I have awakened from slumber to see myself and my way of life for the first time."

"Wonderful!" Charlotte clapped. "I'm so happy for you."

"Now that revolution has begun," Marcus said, leaning against his wife's chair, "what are your plans?"

"I've nothing firm in mind, but I do know that I must move out of the dower house. You've been most generous with your stipend, Marcus, and I will use some of it to procure a house of my own." She had never for a single day of her life lived on her own. The thought excited and scared her in equal measure.

"Do you wish my help in finding a place, or would you prefer to look on your own?"

Gratified that he had asked instead of taking over for her, she said, "Thank you, Marcus. I will accept your aid."

"Before you go too far with the plotting and planning, perhaps you had better see how the evening plays out." He took her empty cup and placed it on the tray of a passing maid.

"Oh, that's right. There's Lord Athelson to deal with." She drew her fan through her fingers.

"Amongst other things. Have you forgotten that tonight is when the dowager plans to reveal the portraits?" Marcus turned to his butler, who had appeared at his shoulder and whispered something Cilla couldn't hear. "Everything is in readiness in the gallery, I'm told. Let's get this presentation over with. Charlotte?" He helped her rise.

Lord Athelson appeared at Cilla's side, as if he'd been hovering nearby. "Lady Priscilla, allow me." He bowed and offered his arm. "I

must say, you look . . . different this evening. That is . . . I don't know
that I . . . are you quite sure about your ensemble?" He bumbled to
a stop, his neck reddening above his collar. His choice of costume
resembled a Puritan preacher. At least she hoped it was a costume.
Or was unrelieved black with only a white neckpiece his version of
proper evening wear? He could not have looked less flamboyant or
less interesting.

When the rest of the party guests were making their way upstairs,
Lord Athelson guided her toward the back of the group. "Lady Priscilla, I do hope you are ready to give me your answer to my proposal.
I know the dowager is eager to make the announcement just after the
portraits are viewed."

Was she? Cilla's determination strengthened. How like the
dowager.

"Sir." She kept her voice low. "I am sorry, but I cannot marry you.
I realize the honor you have done by asking for my hand, but I must
decline." She was sorry. Not to be saying no, but that saying no would
disappoint him. She was under no illusions that he was in love with
her or that she was breaking his heart, but it would be a blow to his
pride to have her decline an opportunity to fall in with his plans.

He raised himself to his full height, his face going pale and his
eyes bleak. "You're refusing me?" The words came out quite loud, and
heads turned. People paused on their way up the stairs.

Cilla sought patience, looking up at the darkened skylight of the
foyer. "Lord Athelson, I have given the matter much thought, and I
have made up my mind. I am sorry. Perhaps you would like a moment
or two to compose yourself? I'll leave you in peace." She removed her
hand from his arm, gathered her skirts, and made her way toward
the gallery. She passed several guests, smiling at them and nodding.
"Isn't it exciting? I can't wait to see the finished paintings. The artist is most talented. I'm sure you'll enjoy his work."

"Lady Priscilla, you'll regret your decision." Lord Athelson's voice
filled the foyer.

She stopped and turned on the landing. "Perhaps, but the possibility of regret will no longer keep me from making my own choices."

If she hadn't been so unsettled and anticipating seeing Hamish again, she would have laughed at the startled expression on Lord Athelson's face. With a lighter heart than she would have imagined possible when she set out from her bedroom tonight, she entered the well-lit gallery.

Taking charge of her life and making decisions for herself could become quite addictive. Loving Hamish had set her free, and she would always be grateful, no matter what else happened.

At the far end of the gallery, the dowager appeared to be putting on a brave face, making the best of the evening in spite of the upsets she'd suffered. The poor woman was going to have at least one more when she learned that Cilla would not become Lady Athelson, but it couldn't be helped. If one would be bossy and try to order and organize someone else's life, one must be prepared for disappointment when they kicked over the traces and refused to be compliant with one's dictates.

It would do the dowager good not to get her way all the time.

Her heart kicked.

Hamish.

Resplendent in his Highland kilt. He couldn't have looked more different from Reginald Athelson if he tried. Candlelight raced along his burnished red hair and lit his eyes. They locked with hers, and it was as if an invisible thread flew from him to her, locking them together.

People moved between them, cutting off her view of him, and she shouldered her way through them in a most unladylike and, for her, unaccustomed manner. But she didn't care. She had to be near him. She didn't stop until she had gotten to the front of the guests and stood mere feet away so she could gaze her fill at the man she loved.

The portraits hung on the wall, covered in white sheets, and she frowned. There were three of them, not two. Had he painted a new portrait of the dowager? It would be like Cilla's mother-in-law to commission one of herself, to make tonight's celebration about her.

Before she could ask, Marcus beckoned her to cross the open space. "Stand here." He pointed to a spot beside Charlotte. "Please."

The dowager poked Marcus in the arm. "What is this?" She glared at Cilla. "Aren't you supposed to be with Lord Athelson? Where is he?"

"I don't know, madam. I left him downstairs. I must warn you not to make any announcements on my behalf regarding Lord Athelson. I have heard his proposal, and I have declined the honor of becoming his wife." She didn't flinch in the face of the dowager's growing displeasure.

"Easy there, madam." Marcus took his mother's arm. "You look as if you've bitten a wasp."

This was supposed to be her grand moment, and Cilla felt badly for ruining it for her. "Madam, would you like a chair?"

"Leave me be. We'll talk about this later. We have guests." The dowager pulled herself together, imperious to the end. "If you're intent on ruining your life and disregarding my attempts to forestall a catastrophe, I'm hardly in a position to change things at the moment, am I?" She motioned to the footman hovering nearby.

"Lords and Ladies, ladies and gentlemen, if we may have your attention," he called out.

Conversations ceased.

The dowager cleared her throat and composed herself. "Thank you all for coming tonight. To get the festivities started, I would like to present my Christmas gifts to the duke and duchess." She flicked her hand toward Hamish, shooting him a scowl, and he and the footman grasped the sheet covering the first painting.

Marcus's portrait was striking. The likeness was uncanny. He was painted in full, with a rich backdrop of merlot velvet drapes and a picturesque landscape visible through a window that brought Marcus forward in the piece. He looked commanding and strong.

Just as he was in real life.

A round of applause went up from the guests.

Then it was time for Charlotte's painting.

Cilla thought she knew what to expect, but when the sheet dropped away, she froze. There sat Charlotte, in the lyre-backed chair, in the gown of raspberry satin. The white shawl draped her creamy shoulders, the lace painted in remarkable detail. She had been painted smiling, her face alight with intelligence, against a backdrop of book-shelves loaded with beautifully bound books.

But what of the blue dress she'd changed her mind about? The dress that Cilla had sat in so many times?

While the guests clapped again, Marcus took Cilla's arm. "There's one more. A gift from Charlotte and myself. I hope you like it."

The sheet dropped from the third painting, and Cilla stared, unbelieving.

◆—►✕◄—◆

Hamish couldn't quite breathe. Did she like it? Did she hate it? Why wasn't she moving or speaking?

Cilla stood immobile, the duke clasping her arm lightly.

The dowager leaned on her cane, her mouth agape. "Oh my."

The applause was quite loud this time, led by Marcus.

"What do you think?" he asked Cilla.

But Cilla was no longer looking at the painting. She stared at Hamish.

Was it his imagination, or did her expression match the one in the painting? Was she looking at him with . . . love . . . in her eyes?

She seemed to come to herself, giving a little shake. "Marcus, it's wonderful. What a surprise. I had no idea." She reached out to squeeze the duchess's hand. "You had to be part of this, Charlotte, pretending to change your mind about the dress, and I believed the entire charade."

"We wanted it to be a secret. You do like it, don't you?"

Cilla looked at Hamish again. "I love everything Hamish paints."

She had called him Hamish rather than Mr. Sinclair. Did she realize the slip? The dowager certainly had, because if looks could cause death, he would be a corpse in that instant.

Before she could say anything more, people approached to view the portraits up close and to speak with him.

The dowager fielded many compliments on her choice of artists, and Hamish wondered if it choked her to say thank you.

Lord Athelson was conspicuous by his absence. Where was the man? Surely he would be there to comment on Cilla's portrait at least.

Hamish spied him near the doors, half a head taller than most of the men there. He looked strained, with pale cheeks and bleak eyes.

Or was that how he always looked to Hamish? Lord Athelson's gaze followed Cilla, darting between her and the portrait.

Cilla. Hamish was stunned by her appearance tonight. She wore the most arresting color, with peacock feathers in her hair and in a cascade down her back. Even more beautiful than in the blue portrait dress. She moved amongst the guests with more animation and purpose than he'd ever seen her have before. What had given her such confidence?

When could he see her alone? He had so much to tell her, so much he hoped for, but there were all these infernal people around.

The duke tapped him on the shoulder. "You will be my guest tonight. Would you please escort Cilla? I've had the staff seat you next to her at dinner, but there will be dancing first."

"Yes, Your Grace. And thank you."

The duke smiled. "The rest is up to you. Make the most of your opportunity."

When they went back down to the ballroom, Cilla was on his arm. He couldn't have been more proud.

The dowager nearly choked when he nodded her way. Poor old duck. It must gall her that the portraits were such a raging success when she must wish him on the far side of the moon right now.

He barely refrained from winking at her.

"Are you pleased?" he asked Cilla.

"I'm stunned. And honored. It's . . ." she laughed. "How can I say it's a beautiful painting without sounding vain, as I am the subject of it?"

"It *is* beautiful, and it's a true likeness. I've never seen a more exquisite woman in my life. I thought so the first time I met you, and I think so even more now." He squeezed her hand. "There is so much I need to say to you. Tell me it isn't too late."

"Too late?" She turned those amazing blue eyes on him.

"Lord Athelson?"

She pressed her lips together, as if smothering a smile, and dipped her chin. "There is no need to worry about Lord Athelson. Not now, not ever again."

The knot in his stomach eased, and his heart hammered in his chest. The music began for the first dance, a waltz, and he gathered Cilla into his arms. She held her skirt in one hand, and they swung into the dance.

Two turns about the ballroom, and blissful as dancing with her was, he couldn't stand it any longer. "I must speak to you," he whispered against her temple.

At her nod, he led her from the ballroom and into the conservatory. If he ever became rich, he would have one of these attached to his house. Cilla clearly loved the place, and he could imagine spending many peaceful evenings with her surrounded by tropical plants and moonlight.

Walking right down to the far end, he turned to face her, taking her hands in his. Starlight caressed her skin, and he caught a whiff of her perfume. It swirled through his head, stealing his thoughts.

"Hamish, thank you for the painting. Thank you for helping me to see myself both as I was and how I could be. I feel free and confident for the first time in my life. I've made a few decisions, and I have you to thank for the courage to do so."

"Decisions?"

"I'm going to move from the Haverly estate and establish my own home. Not far away, because I want Honora Mary to grow up close to her family. But I cannot stay with the dowager any longer. It's not good for her, and it certainly isn't good for me."

"I see. That's grand, but could we talk about this later?" he asked.

She jerked as if he'd smacked her. "I'm sorry. I thought you wanted to speak to me."

"For truth, lass, I'd rather be kissing you." He drew her into his embrace, locking his arms around her waist and bringing her up against him.

A slow smile emerged on her lovely face, and he gave in to the temptation that had been plaguing him all evening.

This second kiss was even better than the first, if that was possible. It rocked him right to his boots. Her little sigh and murmur of surrender shot fire along his veins, and he deepened the kiss, wanting to meld them together forever. When starbursts showered behind his eyes, he released her lips, brushing his along her temple, her cheeks, her forehead, her hair. He inhaled the sweet scent of her skin. "Ah, lass, what you do to me. I havna been my own man since I first laid eyes on ye."

Her breath came in satisfyingly short gusts, and her hands tunneled into the hair at his nape. "Hamish. I've been so miserable."

"No more than me, lass. I know by rights I shouldna ask, that we're far apart in social standing, but I'm bold enough to at least speak my heart. Lady Priscilla Haverly, I love you with everything I am and have. I promise, if you'll have me, I'll work my fingers tae the bone tae provide for you and your bairn. If you'll dare, will you marry me?"

She didn't make him wait. The words were barely out when she threw herself deeper into his embrace, wrapping her arms around his neck and hugging him fiercely. "Yes, yes, oh my, yes."

He kissed her hard, his heart soaring, promising her without words that they two would become one and that he would love her without restraint for the rest of his days.

A long time later, he held her gently, her cheek against his chest, his chin on her hair. The peacock feathers tickled his nose, but he didn't care. His boots didn't even seem to touch the flagstones beneath them.

"Do you think I'll like being a schoolmaster's wife? Does the position come with housing, or should we look for a place in Stratford?" She spread her hand over his tartan waistcoat on his chest. Could she feel his heart thudding there?

"Ah, well, about that teaching position. Things have changed a wee bit." He told her about the duke's generous offer of patronage and the plans being laid for the new Season in London.

She leaned back in his arms. "Isn't that just like Marcus? Oh,

Hamish, I'm so happy for you. Now you will be able to do what you love, and those old crusts at the Royal Academy will be begging you to join."

He hugged her again, dropping a kiss on her nose. "I find now it matters na so much if they never accept me. I've got your love. I need nothing else to be happy."

# CHAPTER 10

CHURCH BELLS RANG out across the kingdom on Christmas morning, but none sweeter than those of the Haverly Manor chapel. Cilla walked arm in arm with Hamish up the church steps. If it wouldn't have been unseemly, she would have rested her head on his broad shoulder.

When they entered the nave, Cilla paused. Where should they sit? The dowager was already in the Haverly pew in the front, sitting as if a fireplace poker had been sewn into the back of her gown.

Whatever Marcus had said to her while Hamish had been proposing, it had a profound effect upon the woman. She had received the news of the betrothal if not warmly and graciously, at least politely.

Marcus and Charlotte passed them in the aisle and took their places up front with the dowager, as did the rest of the family.

"Let's sit here." Cilla indicated a pew halfway back.

"I sat with the servants last time." Hamish let her precede him into the row.

"And I sat with the duke and duchess. But now we're just us. We can sit where we choose."

The dowager turned in her seat, opened her mouth and then closed it, pivoting to face the front again. Her days of dominating Cilla were through, but it would take time for both of them to adjust to their new roles.

Cilla took in little of the service. Sitting here with Hamish, his shoulder brushing hers, sharing a hymnal, it all seemed so unreal. Her heart sang, even when the lump in her throat prevented her from joining in. Being in love was a truly wondrous thing.

After church services and Christmas breakfast at the manor, the family gathered in the music room to exchange small tokens. First there were the gifts to the servants. Marcus and Charlotte had sent hampers to all their tenants earlier in the morning, but the house servants received their gifts just before the family and guests.

The room was filled with people, even little people, as Marcus and Charlotte had insisted that the nursery inhabitants join them. Cilla had Honora Mary on her lap, and Hamish had his sketch pad out, capturing the moment.

The dowager seemed to be coming to terms with the new way of things. She had even come up with a gift for Hamish, a fine pen and ink set.

And he had a gift for her.

"Your Grace, I hope you like it." He passed her a square parcel.

With a sniff, the dowager tore the paper and held up a small canvas. She didn't say a word, but she blinked rapidly.

"What is it?" Evan Whitelock asked, both Cian, his adopted son, and William, his heir, on his lap.

The dowager turned the painting around. It was of herself, holding Honora Mary, her namesake. Her face was soft, loving, and gentle, and Honora Mary's curls were a halo about her head.

Cilla caught Hamish's eye and mouthed, *Thank you.*

He nodded and quietly passed the dowager his handkerchief.

Cilla looked around the room at her family and guests. She didn't even feel like the same woman she had been last fall when the dowager first broached the subject of a Christmas party. At the time Cilla had wondered if holiday festivities would be the tonic she needed to carry her out of the doldrums.

But it hadn't been a house party she'd needed.

No, it was love that had freed her.

Wondrous, wondrous love.

# EPILOGUE

—•✕•—

"I'D HAVE TO say the showing is a success, if we're judging by sheer number of people in attendance." Marcus had to speak loudly to be heard over the din. "It's been like this all week."

Hamish shook yet another hand and directed the man congratulating him to his assistant at the desk in the corner. He shook his head. He, Hamish Sinclair, now had an assistant, and that assistant was taking bookings for new commissions at an alarming rate.

"The publicity you and Whitelock put about might have something to do with it." He blew out a breath. "With all the work rolling in, I'll be painting well into the summer to catch up."

They stood in the gallery space rented by Marcus and his friends on Piccadilly near Hatchards bookshop. The duke had procured the property with remarkable quickness. He must frequent the area often to have known of its availability.

Hamish had insisted Cilla have charge of what painting should go where, his only contribution being that her most recent portrait in the peacock dress must be the centerpiece of the exhibition.

And so it was. It hung on the back wall of the long room, opposite the doors, begging people to come closer to examine it. And without fail, her lovely likeness drew people into the room.

"Brilliant of you to place it there and to rope off the center of the room so nothing stands between it and the entryway," Marcus commented when he followed Hamish's gaze. "And you've lit it most effectively with those reflectors."

Along the right-hand wall of the gallery, Cilla had hung the Army of the Unseen series, and it was here most of the people lingered. Already the collection had garnered the interest of the newspapers and caused quite a stir amongst the artistic community. Some scoffed, others praised, but no one was without an opinion.

"My favorite, of course, is this one." Marcus indicated the newest of the portraits. Charlotte, his duchess, looked out from the painting with serene eyes, holding the new heir in her arms, one Anthony Marcus Haverly. "My mother had a fit about the name, but Charlotte, with her love of all things historical, threatened to name the boy Octavius, and the dowager stopped her complaints."

"He's a fine little chap." Evan Whitelock clapped Marcus on the shoulder. "Thankfully, he looks like his mother."

Marcus laughed. "I suppose you prefer your family portrait best?"

Hamish had created portraits of both of his patron's families. The little boys had painted up most effectively. They played on the floor with a spaniel, while their parents held hands above them, much in accord.

When the crush dwindled, he found Cilla with the dowager. The older woman had melted a bit in her resistance to the idea of his and Cilla's marriage, especially in the face of his newfound success in London. She was now taking credit for their relationship and his "triumph," as she put it. If it hadn't been for her, after all, he never would have come to Haverly.

He supposed he did owe the old duck.

The front door opened again to let in more people, and this time a ripple went through the room.

Hamish turned, and Cilla let out a gasp. The dowager snatched up her fan, though it wasn't really warm, and stirred the air hard enough to disturb her iron-gray curls.

"Is that—" Hamish cut off, not believing his eyes as Marcus and Evan went to greet the newcomers.

"It's the Prince Regent," Cilla whispered.

"And the president of the Royal Academy, Benjamin West."

"You sound more in awe of West than the Prince of Wales," the dowager said. "Go on—make your bow!"

Hamish started forward with Cilla. Was this really happening? A nervous chill skittered across his chest.

"Your Highness, may I present Mr. Hamish Sinclair, and his wife, Priscilla," Marcus said.

Hamish bowed, and Cilla dipped into a deep curtsy. "Your Highness, 'tis an honor." He straightened, and though he tried to center his attention on the Royal, he couldn't help but notice Mr. West's careful study of Cilla's portrait.

"Haverly here told me of your exhibition, and I had to see for myself." The prince rocked on his toes, his belly burgeoning out over his breeches in an alarming manner. "Most interesting, yes."

"Would you like a tour, Your Highness?" Hamish asked. He rubbed his palms on his thighs.

"Too right, I would, but not by you. I would prefer the company of your lovely wife." The Prince Regent guffawed, but he also leered a bit. Hamish's hands fisted, but Marcus shook his head briefly.

"Cilla and I would be happy to accompany you, Your Highness. Did you know Cilla was my sister-in-law?" Marcus drew the prince away, and Hamish relaxed a fraction. Marcus would watch over her.

Though, Cilla could take care of herself pretty well these days. She'd blossomed into a woman of strong character these past few weeks.

Mr. West went down the row of the Army of the Unseen, tapping his chin thoughtfully when he took in the last one in the collection, the portrait of Tetford and the maid with the tea tray. "You've shown some real talent here. Where did you train, if I may ask?" He had a faint American tinge to his voice, testament to his Pennsylvania birth.

"I'm an autodidact, much like you, Mr. West. I worked for a few painters and a colorist, but I've no formal training."

"Ah, a man of independence. I like that. You aren't overly influenced by anyone else's work that way." He continued to stare at the painting.

They were interrupted by the Prince Regent's return. "I say, these are quite good. I would like to have you visit Carlton House. It's devilish hard these days to find someone who can capture a good likeness, and I want you to paint my portrait. West here can paint a portrait if he has to, but he prefers his landscapes, don't you, old chap?"

Cilla put her hand over her mouth behind him, her eyes wide.

A royal commission? And requested . . . or should he say demanded . . . right in front of the president of the RA?

"A most excellent idea." Mr. West nodded. "I was just going to request that Mr. Sinclair submit a new application to the academy. His work is certainly of that caliber."

Hamish raised his brow. "Thank you, Your Highness. It would be an honor to paint your portrait. If you'll have your secretary send me the particulars, I am certain we can get it done soon." He turned to Mr. West. "Sir, I appreciate your offer. I'll talk it over with my wife, get her opinion, and we'll think about it."

Hamish bowed and backed away, waiting for Cilla to join him. When she did, she linked her arm through his.

"Did you just tell the president of the Royal Academy of Arts that you would think about his offer?" she asked.

He shrugged. "I find being an independent artist quite nice these days. And anyway, I wouldn't want to make such an important decision without your input. I value your advice." He waggled his brows at her, leaning down and brushing the tip of her nose with his.

She laughed. "I never thought I would hear anyone say that to me. I don't think I will ever get tired of hearing it."

"I love you, Cilla Sinclair."

"And I won't tire of hearing that either." She shook her head. "Love is a wondrous thing, isn't it?"

"Aye, lass, wondrous indeed."

TELL THE WORLD THIS BOOK WAS

| GOOD | BAD | SO-SO |

CAROLYN MILLER LIVES in New South Wales, Australia, with her husband and four children. A longtime lover of Regency romance, Carolyn's novels have won a number of RWA and ACFW contests. She is a member of American Christian Fiction Writers and Australasian Christian Writers. Find her best-selling, award-winning fiction at www.carolynmillerauthor.com.

AMANDA BARRATT IS the ECPA best-selling author of several novels and novellas, including *My Dearest Dietrich*. She is a member of American Christian Fiction Writers and a two-time FHL Reader's Choice Award finalist. She and her family live in northern Michigan. Visit her at www.amandabarratt.net.

ERICA VETSCH IS a *New York Times* best-selling author and ACFW Carol Award winner, and has been a *Romantic Times* top pick for her previous books. She loves Jesus, history, romance, and watching sports. This transplanted Kansan now makes her home in Rochester, Minnesota. Learn more about Erica at www.ericavetsch.com.